Jack Barton lives with his girlfriend, now fiancé, Jamie and their cat, Baron Von Fluffington, in Chorleywood, Hertfordshire, where he is a long time Season Ticket Holder at Brentford Football Club and is almost always watching something nerdy, such as the influences for this book that is only the first of many.

For my wife-to-be, Jamie, to compete with the many stories she loves so much, maybe eventually climb the ranks to the top.

Jack Barton

Winter's Return

Austin Macauley Publishers
London • Cambridge • New York • Sharjah

Copyright © Jack Barton 2023

The right of Jack Barton to be identified as author of this work has been asserted by the author in accordance with sections 77 and 78 of the Copyright, Designs and Patents Act 1988.

All rights reserved. No part of this publication may be reproduced, stored in a retrieval system, or transmitted in any form or by any means, electronic, mechanical, photocopying, recording, or otherwise, without the prior permission of the publishers.

Any person who commits any unauthorised act in relation to this publication may be liable to criminal prosecution and civil claims for damages.

This is a work of fiction. Names, characters, businesses, places, events, locales, and incidents are either the products of the author's imagination or used in a fictitious manner. Any resemblance to actual persons, living or dead, or actual events is purely coincidental.

A CIP catalogue record for this title is available from the British Library.

ISBN 9781398441743 (Paperback)
ISBN 9781398455535 (ePub e-book)

www.austinmacauley.com

First Published 2023
Austin Macauley Publishers Ltd®
1 Canada Square
Canary Wharf
London
E14 5AA

Table of Contents

Prologue	9
Chapter 1	16
Chapter 2	32
Chapter 3	44
Chapter 4	50
Chapter 5	72
Chapter 6	87
Chapter 7	107
Chapter 8	121
Chapter 9	136
Chapter 10	161
Chapter 11	165
Chapter 12	183
Chapter 13	189
Chapter 14	206
Chapter 15	217
Chapter 16	228
Chapter 17	243
Chapter 18	255
Chapter 19	258

Chapter 20	275
Chapter 21	291
Chapter 22	310
Chapter 23	320
Chapter 24	342
Chapter 25	356
Chapter 26	369
Chapter 27	384
Chapter 28	397
Chapter 29	413
Epilogue	428

Prologue

The room was completely silent. This was once a classroom in a popular school at the heart of the Capital City, now though, it is little more than a dark, hollow shell where no happiness or learning could ever return to that could possibly bring back the light. But while it was silent, it was not still. For in the shadows of the long hallways and vacant classrooms still adorned with the cheery messages of hope for young minds and the joy of their imaginations, were the spectres of the once denizens of this city, and the mindless monsters that some of them had become.

Those that had been trapped in the Capital City when it had sealed shut that fateful day, those who were fortunate to have died, wandered the places that they had known so well as non-corporeal shades of those they had once been, colourless in their being, cast in a grey hue. They stalked their former homes and once regular places, silent as the grave in the literal sense. Here in this once house of learning, the spectres of the children that had attended this place still trudged through their halls or skipped merrily from one room to the other, while others stood mindless and expressionless in the peripherals. Those affected in a violently different way clung to the corners out of sight, scurrying across the dusty, degraded floors, scratching their way through the ceilings and walls. These were conscious-less beasts, they were degraded in their human form, some on all fours, some shambling on shattered limbs, their bodies inexplicably still standing, still moving.

The only thing these remnants of people feared were the roaming security bots, hovering on thrusters, despite their flaming appearance they produced merely a whisper as they left blackened streaks on the once red floors caked in dust and debris. These machines bore arms as a human but while one hand was reminiscent of life-like, albeit metal and menacing, the right consisted of an automatic gun giving sign of its hostile design. They were manufactured of a deep, dark black metal, hard and robust, with a head at the top of a chest piece that allowed the bots to see with luminescent blood-red eyes. The lifeless monstrosities had a strange profound fondness for the shades of their once neighbours and friends, fellow citizens of this ruin of a city, yet they avoided the bots with haste, tangling with them when no other choice was allowed, lest they be utterly obliterated.

The once grey walls were decorated with celebrations of the Crimson conglomerate that rules this region as the Board's representative, children's depictions of the workers of the companies, from humble farmers on distant worlds to the formidable soldiers portrayed as their valiant protectors. The tables and chairs where they would receive the limited knowledge and skills allowed to them were mostly still in place, only some overturned in the chaos that was the brief window of evacuation that signalled the start of the Capital Collapse.

Some of these seats were taken up by the ghosts of the little ones that had once come here so routinely for learning, that in death they followed the same pattern, never late for a lesson that would never come. They wore their uniform still, never able to change for the clothes they died in, a simple combination of black jacket and trousers, matched with what once would have been a red shirt that indicated the company that owned them. For these children, like all who had been born in the three settled systems under the Board's rule, had given a drop of blood at their birth to a contract they had never been given the chance to give consent to, a lifetime bond that sealed their purpose in life to the design of others.

A screen at the front of the classroom flickered on at the same time it always did, the signal for the lesson to begin, only there was no teacher to grant it as there hadn't been for nigh a decade. Prowling across the screen in a physically illuminating projection that gave true dimension to the image, was a ginger cat in a red trench coat bearing a black hat perched over one ear. He calmly strode to the centre of the screen and stood up on its hind legs, before giving a wink to the camera and lighting up a thick cigar that it then proceeded to smoke. The image blinked on and off as it struggled to maintain itself and when the recording spoke, the audio was distorted with a fuzz and the pitch warped occasionally so the hologram was rarely playing as it had in its hay-day.

"Boys and girls, welcome to school, I'm Crimson the Crime-Fighting Cat, and I'm here to get y'all prepped for the day ahead, a day chock full o' learnin' and graftin', the only way to be, to be a good and loyal employee of our generous Crimson Overseer Coalition. Today's lessons will be hard and some o' y'all will hesitate to fully commit your stunning young minds to this mighty fine essential teachin's but all o' you listen to me good and proper." The ginger cat said, speaking to the empty classroom in a calm yet hoarse voice, an authoritative tone.

"But I promise, should you leave the wisdom and guidance of our great Coalition, you will be tagged as WIDOWs, that's Workers In Deviation of Work-Orders, and me and my Obsidian folk and my brothers and sisters in the Stalwart inquisitor and enforcers will track you down and end your miserable lives. Break the contract and we all suffer, young ones. But maybe y'all don't believe your cunning friend, Crimson the Crime-Fighting Cat, so today's lesson is history, so let me fill y'all in on everything that built the system that protects and sustains ya, keeps the worlds on tickin'." The cat flicked off the burnt end of his cigar before snapping some furry fingers together and the image changed over to a video presentation with a different voice narrating:

"The year is 2304, and the Earth is gone. The rule of governance and the order of their law, the currency of their realm, the capitalism, socialism, communism, dictatorships, however they chose to rule, they all crumbled under the prelude to harvesting the world's natural resources too greedily. Even the institutions of religion collapsed as societies that had existed for hundreds of years crumbled, that which had been the bedrock of many people's moral compass, leaving anarchy and cold-blooded measure in its wake." The narrator was female, speaking over an image of a world of green and blue slowly turning red and ashen grey, steadily becoming covered in satellites and space stations.

"No world leader or government official was strong enough to stop the tide and the whole world suffered as a result. This was the sum of all failures that came from casting the veil of a great lie, granting the illusion of a vote and a choice, but instead those that were given power succumbed to its grand allure, gave into their selfish greed. But not our founders, not the first members of the Board. They looked to the stars with opportunity, with a future for all humankind, and they built the tri-systems for which all of you now work to contribute to the survival of us all." The voice beamed of a strong belief in what she was preaching to the empty stares of the spectres of the children that did not so much as register the appearance of the illuminated image before them.

"And so the terraforming of planets began, and it was fiercely competitive before the first Chairman was elected, and the Board given form, to maintain balance and control of the three settled regions of space, far away from the failures of the past. These systems are the Crimson, the Sapphire and Emerald regions. The lifetime contracts were installed so that every living person could have equal access to clean drinking water, to food and medical care, to a safe place to sleep and opportunity to provide for one's family." The woman said, over the crackling image of space where an animation of rockets flew to the points of a triangle that lit up in the colours of green, blue and red.

"And what did we find when we settled into our new homes? New friends and colleagues in the X-Human species, a species much like our human ancestors, except for the wonderful bejewelled eyes they bear of colours across the spectrum, and the exquisite shine of their skin. Male X-Humans exhibit a golden gleam, while their female counterparts are glistening with the silver glint on their skin. Yet we were not so friendly to begin with, and we found growing a relationship between our two humanoid kinds extremely difficult." The animation switched over to an image of a male and a female with the features the narrator described, the male had bright eyes in the colour of rubies, while the female had radiant, purple ones. The screen carried on playing into the vacant classroom as if there were a full roster of children to watch and hear its propaganda, no matter which species of human they belonged to.

"These new people, alien as they were, were never hostile, and showed no resistance when we sent down our colossal machines to change the planets to help us breathe our kind of air, to warp the atmosphere to our needs, even though we were unsure of their continued survival once we did. Yet we had no way of talking to them about it for they were silent, and a tight knit community, building a cross-species relationship was neither quick nor easy. But eventually our X-Human brothers and sisters relented to us and began to communicate. They began to learn English and so we settled on speaking that language, and they explained the truth of how they communicate with one another. Telepathy, the secret of their race. Speaking mind to mind in utter silence, the secret surrendered by the one they identified as their leader. Once we were able to confer, the Board labelled them as X-Human and welcomed them into the fold, as workers among us and to live with us as equals, and to have the same rights as those that arrived from the Old World." Next on the stuttering imager was the picture of a human woman and an X-Human man standing side by side, holding hands with smiles, and a child emerging between them, a blend of the species.

"We taught each other much. The X-Humans were without advancements, they lived in caves, harvested food from the land, and so were grateful when we welcomed them into the fold, put them to work and gave each of them a purpose to fulfil. And in return, they offered us an alternative to the faiths we had all left behind with the Old World. For our new family worship and study the sacred starways, the alignments of the stars that grant prophecy and wisdom to those skilled in the study of reading their meaning. But our society that we work so hard to maintain and build, is a fragile one, and is under threat every single day. WIDOWS, Workers in Deviation of Work-Orders, are everywhere, seeking to sow the seeds of chaos and ruin our fine region with destruction. And should they succeed?" An image of a group of silhouettes throwing fire bombs into buildings illuminated the screen, a violent depiction of what the COC wished to portray.

"'If we do not work, then we do not contribute to the Board. And then we will all pay', says our Section Chief, Roderic Thorne. These WIDOWS are selfish and they jeopardise everything we have been working toward. They could be your neighbour, your family or your friend, you could have passed them on the street this morning, they could be sitting right next to you, right now, waiting to grow up and betray you, to rain havoc across our glorious Coalition. The fact of the matter is this: do your job, do it well and we all reap the benefits of a fine and exquisite life, whether your future lies on the farms on Scarlet or on the golden roads of this Capital City, or we will all pay the price of disloyalty to the Board. So, where will you work?" Four names appeared, each turning larger as the narrator explained them.

"Will you stand up for others and police the Crimson? Are you willing to participate in protecting people? Maybe we won't give you a choice in the matter however, as we all need people to keep us safe. These are the best men and women from our region, head to toe in the most robust black armour ever known, visors of Crimson for being vigilant to any threats to you, armed to the teeth to maintain proper order. And if you show exceptional potential at a good and true young age, then you could be lucky enough to be inducted into the academy to become a member of our Elite guard, a most beneficial position under the command of our finest servant, Commander Winter. Welcome to Obsidian, if you are brave enough."

"Or maybe you are more suited to what comes after WIDOWs are caught, because there is a company for turning those degenerates into the core workforce for the region. We need people to seek out these WIDOWS, to investigate and track them down, to rein them in and put them to use. Stalwart Ironworks is the industrial backbone of the Crimson, forging the equipment for all of our workers and maintaining them so that we are as independent as can be to not be a burden on the Board. These fine men and women are the ones you see in the all grey armour and the green coats, they are the ones walking your streets and gauging your neighbours, they are the watchful eyes of the community. Welcome to Stalwart Ironworks, if you have the iron will to forge the future of our conglomerate."

"Stardust is our family and friends, they keep us informed of all we need to know and care about as well as managing our entertainment sector and education, they are the caring heart of our Crimson conglomerate, its beating centre. Welcome to Stardust, just be ready to heed our Section Chief's word to spread it to the people, it is he who dictates our past, present and future, after all."

"And of course, we must produce our contribution quota, we must meet profit projections and satisfy the Chairman, and for this we have two companies. If you're in a red jumpsuit and layered in the mud and dust of the land, then you are in the proud company of Crimson Sun, and you are one of the prestigious engineers of our artificial food that is sent to all corners of the Board settled tri-systems. If it is a black jumpsuit you find yourself in, then you are a smart one, for Ruby Consolidated Systems only takes on the best and brightest for the design and manufacture of our ingenious technological advancements."

"Although, while they do offer the best benefits in reward for the ideas that we can ten offer the Board, they do insist on one tiny small thing, a branding, just on the wrist, just to ensure those benefits go to the right person. Welcome to Crimson Sun, you are sowing seeds of our illustrious future. Or, welcome to Ruby Consolidated Systems, you bring about the advancements to herald a new era for the Crimson Company."

The presentation ended with an image of a flame burning proud and strong with the golden letters of the COC standing tall at the fore, before the ginger cat with the trench coat and hat re-appeared. He confidently swayed on all fours over to the tall, shining characters before standing up and leaning against them, taking a puff of his cigar before turning his hat so it showed his face in full. "So there it is, kiddos, work hard and all you'll see when looking at one of the fine men and women of Obsidian is a brave and noble protector, instead of death with an assault rifle." The cat produced a black pistol from the inside of his coat and gave the barrel a stroke with a grim, cunning smile. "Keep to your purpose, boys and girls, and whoever you so choose to be, because if we do, then we will all live long and glorious lives."

The words rang out into the vacant, perpetual shadow of the forgotten classroom, they rolled over the doodled-on desks, over the discarded toys and dented lunchboxes for the ghosts of the children to ignore or not have the senses to hear. One ghoul of a child sauntered forward; unlike the grey spectres behind her, this one still had her body, despite her uniform in tatters and rags, barely clinging onto her. And when she reached the imager, she picked it up and cast it across the room to an echoing bang, followed by her reaching down deep into her collapsed lungs and broken ribs and screaming at the top of her voice.

The scream pierced the loom of silence and ran through the labyrinth of corridors and lifeless rooms that formed the school until it passed out of the windows and doors and into the darkness of the streets beyond, and the city shouted its response, fuelled with tortured agony and hate.

Chapter 1

Unlike all the other settlements under the Crimson Overseer Coalition brand, the Forerunner was a space station rather than a terraformed world and it held no loyalty to a singular company within the conglomerate that owned this region of the settled tri-systems. Named for being the first non-terrestrial live-in/work-in space station constructed in the region, it had been designed as a launching point for the Coalition's product sent away for their contribution to the Board. However, there were unforeseen costs after its inception into the Crimson conglomerate's operations, the costs of having their freighters wait in line to be loaded with the goods that needed transporting first to this way station proved too high.

And it was the Section Chief twice before the current that saw the opportunity for a landmark facility where all the companies under the Board banner could merchandise and promote themselves, as a competitive marketplace. A unique spot where no particular brand dominated, instead they had to innovate their product, challenge themselves to convince workers to shift loyalties to them. On the whole, it was a success in its hidden intention, to create a battleground where these brands might compete, and right under their noses, people outside of the system could have access to trade routes, communications, damaging the Board's operations. For that, once Section Chief had had their fill of the brutal network of Board rule, and set the rest of their life to being a prickly thorn in their side, their legacy attracting, inspiring and protecting WIDOWs from all across the tri-systems.

The largest of the structures onboard in the main lobby area was that of the COC embassy, a foreboding building set all in a smooth black metal with red and golden trim, armed soldiers in the black armour and red helmet visors of Obsidian standing sentinel. With the docks at one end and the embassy at the other, in between was a vast variety of stalls selling all sorts of wares and trinkets, bars where workers from all of the worlds sought some rest and relaxation, stores bartering out-dated Obsidian and Stalwart Ironworks weapons and armour. Some advertised different walks of life, opportunities to move within the Crimson owned companies and those beyond in the Sapphire and Emerald systems. All except Obsidian, for when they recruited, it was for life, never to leave or transfer, and only on off occasion did they take on fresh recruits by their choice. A hospital was one side, run by the Stardust company where any and all could receive medical care, and aboard the Forerunner, where security was nowhere near as strict, this centre was known to look after WIDOWs as well.

Either side of the stairs leading down to the lower levels were holographic advertising boards, lighting up the entire central avenue, its voices and music ringing out into the crowds shuffling around the different stores and bars. All the different uniforms were present here. Farmers from the Crimson Sun planet of Scarlet where the red star of the Crimson system shone bright and burned the skin like acid, they bore red jumpsuits that took on more of a maroon shade from the constant mud and muck they had waded through. Men and women in tight black variants of the uniform walked this level as well, the burnt skin on the inside of their right wrist in the shape of RCS not wounding their pride as they strode with heads held high, knowing full well their lives were better than others.

At the COC embassy were the guards in black, workers of Obsidian bearing powerful rifles, staring down any who strolled by too close from behind the red visors on their black helmets, standing as resolute, intimidating figures. In the crowd were the ones in the light grey armour with green cotton jackets on top, the emblem of a hammer and the company name on their shoulders as they walked among the teeming masses, Stalwart Ironworks inquisitors, searching relentlessly for WIDOWs. Milling around them were people in grey over orange; operating the stalls as Stardust workers. Most prominently were the women in grey lingerie with orange trim enticing the visitors to the station to the private lobbies that could be reached with the stairs and elevators at either wall to access the top level. Bodies are cheap and easy to maintain but the rewards for allowing the customer to do as they wished with them were vast, both monetary and as a boost to the morale of the worker who pays who then produces much more for the company to which they are employed.

The currency of the tri-systems under the control of the Board was credit. Four different values, all cast in small metal bars used for the purchasing of goods and the payment of services. Platinum bars were rare and of the highest value, never seen outside the possession of the highest levels of management and the directorate that runs the COC. Gold bars were paid to RCS key workers as they produced the best goods for the conglomerate, while the silver and bronze bars were the most commonly seen use of the currency.

Not that the currency was always spent wisely. Workers from across the Crimson came to the Forerunner, not just for commerce where they could pick up food and supplies, upgrades for their armour and weaponry so they could better survive the more anarchic system than the conglomerate advertised. But for the gambling and drinking, the debauchery that raised their spirits from the sunken place that their work left them in.

"Oi, you. Yeah, you there pal, wake up. Yeah it's me, Crimson the Crime-Fighting Cat, big deal, yeah I know, best day of your pitiful life, right? Seeing this sexy piece of tail, but please, relax just for a second or this will get even more embarrassing than it already is," said the ginger cat in the red trench coat scampering across the handrail to the stairs down. The holographic image was life-like except for the colour being too strong on the red, and the light casting it shining down from the ceiling above. "Now, listen. Head over to your nearest Stardust stall and check out the new Mark 2 Obsidian Enforcer Pistol, now with .44 calibre round magazines! The best thing for keeping your family safe from WIDOWs, that is, if I don't catch 'em first!"

Along with the prowling cat in the coat and hat, other holographic hoardings shouted out into the crowds, trying to entice them into this business or that. A man in the attire of a Stalwart enforcer, clad in their armour, wearing the mask of their soldiers, light grey with white eyes, stood with his boot on the neck of a man wearing random bits of leather and furs, nothing like any uniform in the corporate owned regions. "You wanna be on top? Or would you rather be the one under the boot of civilised society? Join Stalwart Ironworks today!"

An image of a blonde-haired woman in stockings and a corset, all in grey except for the orange that ran along the crest of the cleavage, wove her way around the crowd, the latest in holographic technology as the artificial woman was able to stroke the shoulders of those she passed, feeling real for all the worlds. As she passed those who admired her exquisite look, she would whisper in their ear to tell them to look over in the direction of one of Stardust's girls who could take them to the upper level, or to usher them to one of their bars.

The floors, walls and ceiling were all aged and grey, lit up bright as the hordes of people crossed the station, taking in all the stalls and excitement on offer, making the most of their time away from the work rotations the best they could. Music played, almost deafening, a slow melody of instruments as a backdrop to a woman singing about the hope that brought the founders of the system here, to find shelter from the greed that had swallowed the Old World. Weaving through the crowd was a young woman, her head covered by a black hood from a cloak that she wore over the top of her jumpsuit of the same colour, making her anonymous as she passed through the lobby area to the bar next to the entrance to the docks where she had come from. This bar was the furthest establishment from the COC embassy, a fact that this woman was all too aware of as her aim was to not be noticed by the Obsidian police, or the Stalwart inquisitors observing the crowds.

With the wing of a once Obsidian fighter-craft acting as the bar-top, this woman took a seat on a stool there, at the edge of the Starcrest bar, waiting patiently for the bartender to notice her appearance as she knew he would. She was confident that now she was inside, no one would take particular interest in her, they would be too distracted by the drinking, by the roulette wheels, by the card games, and most of all by the girls on stage dancing to the music, entertaining the patrons. This place was darkly lit but for the wild spotlights of all the different colours touching random areas at a time, lighting up the girls, then the depressed lone drinkers at their tables then the ones too distracted by their games where they risked their wages to feel something more than the hardship of their work to notice the light on them.

Dazzling beams of red, blue, orange, green, purple, yellow, all the different colours, lighting up each spot in turn except for those they didn't that were left in the murk of shadow, which this woman knew all too well. Pulling back her hood, the woman revealed the brand on the inside her right wrist and she rested her elbows, propping herself up and crooking her head at the bartender in a sarcastic attempt to gain attention.

"Yeah, I see you there, Cait, give us a minute to wrap things up here," the bartender said as he finished serving his customers with a chuckle to himself.

Cait Jxinn was a 26-year-old X-Human, with brunette hair tied back in an especially long ponytail that dangled behind her cloak that was over the top of her RCS jumpsuit that clung to her body, perfectly sized, with leather shoes installed into the fit. Two piercing purple eyes shot out from a face that she had often been told was pretty, and her lips were a soft pink. She nodded when she was taken notice of then spun on her stool to take in the atmosphere of the bar and to peer over at the stage. On stage, she recognised the star attraction instantly as the one at the front of all the other dancers hoarded all of the attention from those present as she danced to the rhythm of the music with irresistible allure.

She had juicy, vibrant red hair that she flicked this way and that as she moved her body expertly in the grey corset she was wearing teamed with stockings and leather thigh-high, heeled boots. She strode across the edge of the stage, spinning on a heel, returning to the centre, raising her hands to her head, shaking her hips as she dropped near to the floor before rising back up. Then she went onto the tips of her toes before leaning all the back until she was on all fours backwards, before balancing onto her hands and flipping herself up to stand again, slowly with one leg rising at a time.

The crowd loved it, cheering every move the X-Human made, the lights reflecting off her shining silvery skin, her emerald eyes scanning over the crowd, flailing her arms out to the music but pointing here and there with hidden meaning. With a flick of her red hair over one shoulder, she stood side on, dropping into a crouch, she looked out over the crowd with a green eye surrounded by mascara and the masterful use of eye shadow. While she was down low, one of her dancers from behind her pranced from one side of the stage to the other, picking up an oversized red trench coat from the edge before she made her way to centre stage, wrapping it around the redhead while she remained down low.

Suddenly, seemingly without moving her hands that appeared to be holding up the coat as her back-drop dancer retreated, all of the lingerie she was wearing dropped to the floor. The corset, even the stockings and boots were left on the floor as she stood up and took a step back, holding the coat around her as the drunken crowd whistled and cheered. Male and female dancers stepped forward from behind a curtain, replacing the ones that had been on the stage, and these were in costumes in a homage to the kind of armour that Obsidian soldiers wear. They circled the red-haired woman dressed only in the crimson coat in a protective circle so that the crowd could no longer see her, and at the drop that marked the end of the song, the red coat fell as the Obsidian dancers faced their weapons out into the bar to the cheers and shouts from the people clapping their performance.

"She puts on quite the show, doesn't she?" Xin Zorkeefa exclaimed, placing a customary double shot of whiskey in front of Cait, his own X-Human eyes measuring her s. His were of a rare trait, Xin bore shining black jewelled eyes, standing out from the golden shine on his skin marking him for a male member of his species. This eye colour was seen as a beneficial trait to be born with, the stars decreeing for it to portend the bearer to have wise insight into matters and to be a natural leader, fearless in making decisions that could have dramatic, violent reactions. So he needed to be, in being a Stardust supervisor leaking information to known WIDOWs.

"No one owns the stage as much as she does, yet I gotta wonder if they'd be cheering as loud if they knew she was a WIDOW, and that she was using the stage to point out marks for Sam to steal from," Cait smirked.

"These guys have drunk enough that tits and legs are more than enough for them, and to be frank they've earned it. A lot of the workers here tonight have come fresh from Scarlet where they've increased output on the fake food they grow by one hundred and thirty percent, they must have gone through some kind of trauma to earn this time away." Xin replied, gazing over his patrons, catching hardly a glimpse of the thief Cait spoke of before he lost him in the crowds for where the thief was the master.

"Thorne wanting to increase the contribution or something?"

"No, my sources say he is trying to make the Crimson more self-sustained than ever before, there is tension between the Section Chief and the Chairman, they say," Xin scorned, as if the sentence had left a bad taste in the mouth. "Foul cunt doesn't care for the ones who have to sacrifice to build that grander form of empire he wishes to create."

While the middle-aged Xin Zorkeefa was among the management ranks of the Stardust Corporation, he had no love for the Crimson Overseer Coalition, and Section Chief Thorne, the one at the top of the hierarchy, in particular. He did his job and was most certainly a company man, but that didn't stop him using position to access information that he then passed onto a group of WIDOWs he had come into contact with to disrupt the Section Chief's operations. Yet he was a heavily private man, and while he took incredible risk in what he was doing, he never revealed his reasons why or anything about himself personally. It was in the value of the information he provided that allowed the hunted few to trust him and what he told them.

"Yeah, well, is what it is, right?" Cait dismissed, taking her whiskey in a single go, placing down the empty glass without too much care, letting it clank loudly. She wasn't fond of Thorne either so the subject didn't interest her, it would just be the two of them agreeing.

"Maybe not," Xin said, picking up a bottle from under his bar and refilling the glass as his eyes caught a familiar figure approaching, which made him wince involuntarily.

"Hey, Sam," Cait welcomed the thief who took up the stool at her left side. Sam Cal was human with brown hair that was immaculately combed to a fine peak, a perfectly trimmed beard of the same shade and sharp eyes to match. He was wearing the red jumpsuit of a Crimson Sun farmer but the emblem of the company, a sun setting over a field with a solitary worker tending it, was missing from his chest. He also bore a Stardust jacket over the top, grey with an orange fringe at the zip that went up from right hip to left shoulder, the emblem here also missing, where there ought to be a five-pointed-star in front of a male and female silhouette holding hands.

While it was a risk to wear multiple uniforms as it was common for WIDOWs to clash company colours as they didn't identify to a brand, Sam knew he wouldn't simply be arrested on sight for doing it, after all the vendors sold the items for a reason, to advertise, but he simply liked the style of his lucky coat. Although it did attract the interest of Stalwart Inquisitors who had picked up on the trend.

"Didn't think you were leaving the ship tonight, Cait. What brings you out?" Sam asked, shuffling the weight in the pockets of his jacket to make himself more comfortable with his takings from the evening. His voice was only this soft when speaking to Cait to which he had become an adopted older brother, despite his conscious reluctance, his usual self-serving nature dormant where she was concerned. He was 34 and had taken the young roguish woman under his wing, trying his best to teach her the lessons he had taught himself, the caution of mistrust that had helped him survive his years.

"Xin messaged me to come, he has something for us," Cait replied, looking at the bartender who was glaring at Sam.

"Cait is a pleasure to have here, while you, Sam, are a stain on my establishment," Xin retreated from his position leaning on the bar and stood with his arms folded, not taking his eyes off from the other man.

"Xin, charming as ever my dear friend, and a worthless bartender, to boot, for here I am sitting at your bar, without a drink," Sam grinned sarcastically, spreading his arms wide to display the empty section of the bar before him.

"And I'd happily serve you, if you stop stealing from my customers."

"You invited me to steal from the management that visit your bar," Sam shrugged exaggeratingly.

"I could see where Lena was pointing, and you strayed a little, don't lie to me boy, but as you're with this darling girl, you get one, and you'll drink what you're given." Xin grabbed a glass and poured vodka into it unceremoniously, sliding it over to the other man.

"Guilty," Sam winced with a mocking smile. "But I saw some scores I just couldn't ignore. So what's this about calling Cait here, why not Tomen if you have something for us to go on?"

If there was a leader to their band of WIDOWs, Tomen Malshux was it. A 35-year-old human, former Stalwart Ironworks enforcer turned rogue against the Crimson conglomerate who brought all of them together in the first place. Usually when Xin had something to tell them, Tomen would be the one to hear it.

"Because I'm not entirely sure I could be the one to convince him to look into this particular piece of information that I acquired. It's big. Far larger than anything else I've given to you to look into. But look, before I get ahead of myself, I have to ask something, I have a need to be cautious here." Xin looked around, he made note of the Obsidian guards at the entrance and exit, he clocked the Stalwart Inquisitors taking interest in a rowdy group of RCS workers crowded around a game of roulette, and settled on being out of ear shot.

Never before had Xin admitted to being cautious. It was such an obvious fact that they all had to be cautious in these treacherous times that it never needed saying aloud, so for Xin to do so, it meant to Cait that this was unlike any other time they had interacted, and this was something to be heeded carefully. "What's got you so rattled, mate?" She downed her next lot of whiskey, thinking she would need its courage.

"There's been a lot of chatter on the Obsidian channels coming out of the listening post orbiting that fortress of theirs on Carmine. Chief Thorne sent a team to try to breach the Capital, and they succeeded, why, I don't know, but they got inside. However, only one survived. She made it out and sent out a distress call that the listening post somehow found amid the signal buffer the sealed off city casts out, and they brought her back there, to the listening post. Now, I've heard the message that she sent. She spoke of the horrors that wiped out her team but she made a point of saying that she had found what they had been sent in to find, that she had located what she referred to as the vault, and that it was intact." Xin spoke quietly so that Cait and Sam had to lean in to hear properly, all the while the bartender would cast his gaze over their shoulders to make sure the Obsidian guards didn't strike up an interest at anything they may have heard.

"What vault?"

"That's just it, I have no idea. I've been in management level for some time, from just before the Collapse and I never heard about some vault in the Capital City. I have no idea what's inside it, but I have a feeling what could be."

"You think there could be some kind of proof there? About what really caused the Capital Collapse, don't you?" Cait's interest had peaked. "I mean, come on, they said it was a group of WIDOWs operating out of Dunnfink that poisoned the water supply and that's what set off the general evacuation alarm that triggered the sealing off the city, but there was never any evidence, they killed anyone that could have given testament otherwise."

"Exactly, we've never had a sure reason for what caused Rose City to fall," Xin continued. "But if some evidence does exist, then surely it has to be in a facility that is under some kind of secrecy or never been considered before. I think it's an Obsidian facility, maybe a cross-venture with RCS to design it, but whatever it is, the fact that it's new, means it has to be worth finding out everything to do with it."

"Yes but the city is sealed, Xin, under a dome of solid metal, it's impenetrable. What do you expect us to do, waltz up to the front door, give it a ratta, tap, tap and when they ask who's there, just explain our intentions calmly and whoever remains will simply let us in and kindly provide us with a map to tell us where to go, and have a description for what exactly it is that we would be looking for?" Sam put in, swigging his vodka and laughing. "Stick to pouring drinks, pal, leave the conspiracy theories to the drunks at your tables. The Collapse happened eight years ago, fella, get over it."

"People died there, Sam. Families were torn apart, don't you think if we have a shot for learning why, that we should take it?" Cait argued, turning to face Sam.

"And we will die there too, the second we step foot in that accursed city if half the rumours about what lives in that city are real. I've heard stories about ghosts, the bodies of those who once lived there still walking, tearing anything living apart, not to mention that the city's security is still online, they would obliterate us in a heartbeat. Good intentions keep you warm and snug at night I'm sure, but they don't stop a bullet, Cait."

"I wouldn't have said anything if I didn't think there was a chance that the truth of the Collapse was in there," Xin carried on. "If you and your team can reach this vault, then I'm sure you'll find something. I mean, look around you, consider what that truth could do for these people." He raised a hand, indicating over to the ones drinking at the tables, those lost in gambling away the means that they would pay for food and water, to those mindlessly enjoying the entertainment on stage, enjoying the bliss of the moment before the agony of their lives was to resume. "People in the Crimson are at breaking point, and Elias Thorne has been pushing them there ever since he took over as Section Chief five years ago. I've even heard that there are splinter groups within Obsidian itself doubting the man, doubting his father too, who was Section Chief at the time, now their Director, as they think something more happened. Who's to say how they'd react when handed the truth of it all?"

"What are we talking about?" The dancer from the stage approached the three and sat at Cait's right side, seemingly bearing only the red trench coat to cover herself up with, and she pulled her hair so that it all rested in front of her right breast. She was barefoot as she stepped up to sit on the stool, her smooth leg rubbing up against Cait as she budged the stool closer to the group to better hear the conversation. Two emerald green eyes peering across the group before settling on the bartender. "Couldn't get a cocktail, eh Xin? Anything fruity would satisfy."

"Hey Lena, looks like we could have a big job on the horizon," Cait answered her friend who was just a little younger than herself, turning to her and smiling at the joy in those fields of green in the orbs of her eyes. "By the stars, look at you, you're a little sweaty there, mate, get a little carried away up there?"

"Mmm maybe," Lena replied, running the fingers of her right hand through the ends of her hair, grinning to herself as she closed her eyes for a moment, letting in the feelings she enjoyed so much before meeting Cait's gaze. "But can you really blame me? Over a decade as Stardust's finest product, now I'm finally free, my body is completely mine to do with as I wish, and baby, I love the stage, the music, the clothes I get to wear to show all this off, the body I own."

"Looks to me that under that jacket, you're not wearing any," Cait smirked, jokingly eyeing her friend up and down, "and what a fine body you have," she winked.

"Easy there sugar, any more 'an lookin' and you'll need be payin', sweetie," Lena smiled large, her teeth showing as she then chuckled when Xin placed a drink in front of her with a luminescent yellow drink inside.

"We done with the foreplay, you two?" Xin raised an eyebrow, almost disapprovingly. "I'm trying to run a respectable establishment here, there's a level of depression here that I demand that all my patrons meet and you two are dangerously above the line. So maybe we should get back to the matter at hand?"

"Yeah, sorry Xin, so saying we go after this vault, how do we even get inside the Old City to begin with? The whole city is locked under an armoured shell, the evacuation alarm that cleared the city in the Collapse also sealed it up tight. The shell was meant to preserve the assets within, they didn't give two shits about any life caught up inside. I mean, even Obsidian can't penetrate it, well I guess, now they have but how do we? How did they do it?" Cait turned back to the bartender across from her, she was excited about the prospect of learning what really caused the Collapse but she needed more details to let herself feel any more exhilarated for the plan forming in her head.

"Obsidian got inside using the river that flows from the lake outside into the city. The shell covers the entrance and exit of the river but it seems like they found a way under it, but I wouldn't recommend that way."

"Why not?"

"Because in between the screams and howls of pain coming from the sole survivor from that team, the woman grumbled out mumbles of what they found there. Seems as though there were creatures in the water that ambushed them as soon as they got inside, so I think taking that route would be suicide."

"So how do we do it? Is there a secret knock? Or do we just ask them nicely to let us pass?" Sam put in with a mocking grin. "This idea is ridiculous, it can't be done."

"What's wrong, Sam? Lost your balls for the biggest score of your life? Nothing is more valuable than information." Xin teased the thief, knowing which buttons to press to frustrate him while at the same time enticing him into the task he wished to set before them.

"Life probably is," Sam shrugged disinterested and with a sideways glance to Cait but all he got in return was a disapproving glare that shut him down.

"You get in, with a landing key, only thing that will allow access for the docks to open," Xin said.

"Where do we get one?" Cait asked, somewhat disappointed that Sam couldn't see the value of what they were being given the chance to do.

"There's only three in existence, by way I hear it. One is in the executive office of Elias Thorne, aboard that station of his, Arcadia. Another is in the Embassy, here on the Forerunner, at the end of the strip, but it's locked up tight under the protection of about a dozen Obsidian Elites and RCS drones. And the last one was stolen, during the chaos unfolding immediately after the city fell, the Obsidian Police Captain took it, I suspect, as a bargaining chip for his life given his colossal failure that day. This Tobias Willis keeps the key to their secret buried, and they leave him alone, is how I would wager that being."

"And where do we find this Captain?"

"Well, I took the liberty of looking into that for you before I presented this information, and my sources found him. He's hiding out on Scarlet, in a colony away from the more built up corporate areas, he's got his own farm out that way."

"I know Scarlet like the back of my hand, not that I'm overly keen on going back there," Sam added.

"Should be sufficient motivation for you, though, for this job," Cait crossed her arms and leaned against the bar, staring at her friend.

"I'm not like those pathetic fools that are stuck on that burning hot planet, hands in the muck, degrading lives, all roads leading to leaving no mark on the starways more than simply shifting a small mound of dirt that it takes to bury them. But there's a lot of smaller farms away from the industrial fields where the majority of the synthesised crop is planted, you got a name for the one he's hold up in?" Sam scorned, shoving down the memories of his upbringing, taking a long drink of vodka to stomach remembering what he had learned in order to survive.

"Fifty-one dash F, you know of it?" Xin replied, surprised that he was finally hearing something resembling intellect from someone he had long since deemed to be lacking it.

"Southern hemisphere, fantastic, that's the side most exposed to the red star. I don't know it exactly but I can guess the nearest dock and town we can head to and seek directions from there. But say we find this guy, am I safe assuming the plan is for me to nick it?"

"Could do, or you might use the other component you'll need in order to get the key." Xin took a step back so he could lean against the cupboards behind him and drew a long breath, folding his arms.

"What other component?" Cait asked.

"Well, it's not like once you have the landing key that you can simply stroll through the city and the vault doors will be open to you. You'll need a guide for one thing, I don't know where the vault is within the city. And this guide ought to be a solid fighter too, as not all of your crew are built for a fight. Lastly, they will need an Obsidian employee passcode sanctioned enough in the hierarchy to access a facility at the highest level, which your Captain will also have, and two are needed if the usual protocols apply here, for locking up a COC location."

"And why do I sense that you already have someone in mind?" Cait mused, used to the way that Xin always prepared his own research before giving away any aspect of information for her and her team to work with.

"I do," Xin raised his eyebrows in a flash of considering whether he should really relent this grand idea that could so easily blow up in his face. "I found him. Truth is I've been searching for him for years but only now have I been successful, the stars must have aligned on cue for the timing is perfect. I have the location for Commander Nathan Winter, the once leader of the Obsidian Elite Division, before he turned his back on the company in the immediate aftermath of the Capital Collapse."

"And why would the Commander of the Obsidian Elites help us and not kill us where we stand?"

"You guys are insane," Lena laughed. "Talking about entering the Capital is mad enough, but seekin' an Elite? That's completely whacko." She took a long drink from the straw of her cocktail, her lips were a sparkling red that formed into a ridiculing smile. "Com'on guys, if this is a real gig, then it is way beyond our humble abilities."

"That's why you need Winter. He's not like the other Elites you may have seen, they've changed a lot since the Collapse. Now they are little more than posing grunts, made to dress in armour they haven't earned and grasp weapons they have no skill with, when they used to be so much more. This guy. If you see him with a sword in hand, you sprint in the other direction as fast as you possibly can, you even throw people in the way if you have to. Word is that he's helping locals as a sort of guardian protector, a detective looking into murders, break-ins, even roughing up supervisors on a whim. But there are mysterious deaths in the Coalition hierarchy all over Vermilion, especially in the city people are calling the new Capital city. I would wager my finest bottle of whiskey that either Winter is responsible or he is somehow aware and accomplice to whatever is causing those deaths."

"And how do you presume we gain the aid of this protector, as you put it?" Sam gazed at the emptiness of his glass before locking the bartender with a bizarre amusing grin. "And I always knew you had something extra special locked away, you're peaking my curiosity there, Xin, got any more goodies out of sight?"

"We don't take from our friends and those less fortunate than supervisor levels, speaking of which, anything you did take from anyone other than the marks Lena pointed out, you're leaving on the bar here for Xin to return in the lost and found. Now, Sam," Cait pointed out, sharply.

While the thief reluctantly emptied his pockets of the metallic tabs that served as currency and the other items he had taken from those he had pleased outside of Lena's marks, Xin fixed him with a glare of utter disdain, before looking back to Cait. "You can try paying him but I predict that you won't have the need to bring up money, I reckon you can persuade him simply by the point of the venture. He was the Commander of the Elites and yet he stepped away from the company straight after the Collapse, and I find that curious. He must be wanting to know the real reason why the city fell so pitch it to him, use that passion of yours, Cait, the fire in your belly that you've been fanning all these years, that hate against the conglomerate."

"So we'll need him as a guide and protector through the city, and he will then use his code, along with the one we'll get from the Captain when he nab his landing key, to open this vault, and that's it? Say, we find out the real cause of the Collapse? What do we do then?" Cait asked, her mind already set.

"You make it sound so simple, but that is the brass tacks of it. As to what comes after, if my suspicions are right, then we depose Elias Thorne and reset the Crimson how it ought to be, we bring justice back to this system."

"But that is the true and simple matter of it all right there, this is all just your suspicions. Who's to say for sure that there even is a vault or bunker or whatever facility this thing is? That Obsidian team that was sent inside there could have been misled or wrong. And how can we possibly know that the great and majestic reason for the Capital Collapse is in there? Not to mention, what is inside the Old City? You mentioned creatures ambushed the Obsidian team, what creatures? And what else might be there? This is all hypotheticals, man!" Sam punched the jet black starfighter wing that was the bar that stood between him and the bartender across from him.

"Name one job where we knew all of the exact details ahead of time," Cait snapped. "Plus you take a risk every time you pick a pocket, that doesn't stop you, does it? Plus, come on, really! You would be one of those poor souls tending the fields on Scarlet too if you didn't take the risk of forging transfer papers and creating a management position for yourself on Vermilion. So you don't have all the answers and the facts, when have you ever? Now, nut up and shut up, the adults are talking."

"You know I'm older than you, right?"

"Then start acting like it, and I told you to shut it, so not another word unless it's useful." Cait struck Sam with a stare while Lena laughed at her friend's outburst.

"Are you two done? I mean we keep tailing off here, I'm losing track," Xin shook his head as he returned to the bar, leaning on one elbow.

"Yeah, OK, we're in," Cait said. "Obviously I have to run it by Tomen first but I think he will agree. So what's the first step? Getting this Winter guy onboard?"

"Yes, then get the landing key. Come here before going to the Capital though, you'll be needing some supplies before making the journey."

"One thing," Lena placed a hand on the bar between Cait and Xin to make her point at wanting to add something impossible to ignore. "What if Obsidian sends more teams in? Or sends an army even? We've tangled with the authorities before, but nothing like this."

"Believe me, if half the things that I've heard about this Commander Winter are true, then he will be more than a match for them all."

"Alright, well, get that finest bottle of whiskey out and waiting for us to return, Xin. Where we'll be heading, we'll be earning it," Cait smiled, giving a pat on the shoulder each to Sam and Lena, ushering them to leave before sprinkling a couple of silver bars down as payment for the drinks.

Chapter 2

Cait led the way, Sam and Lena following behind as they left the Starcrest bar and back out into the strip of stores and other bars, just as drunk patrons were flagging down the Obsidian guards. They were shouting about being robbed, cursing at the men and women in the black armour, yelling at them to do something or they would face consequences. The three paid no mind to the small commotion building behind them and did not look back, ignoring the loud and bright advertising holograms that tried to stop their way to get them to spend more time spending money in this vast commercial lobby. They approached the security checkpoint for leaving the concourse and getting into the docks area and flashed some forged identification, lanyards from an artform of Sam's. The Stalwart Inquisitors that Cait had seen before as she had approached the Starcrest were standing behind the Obsidian officer who allowed them to pass, and the three breathed easier once the pair in the grey armour with the green jackets looked on past them, paying them no mind. The checkpoint was a small room between two sets of doors, cut into two halves by an energy shield that was deactivated by the Obsidian controller who sat at a desk in the middle of the room, their back to the shield. He was a bored and disinterested young man who may not have even glanced at the identification cards shown to him before waving the small group on their way, lazily pressing the button on his desk to allow them through.

Once the slowly sliding doors were finally open, begrudgingly scraping along their runners as if reluctant to let them leave, the group emerged onto the circular platform that served as the collective end to a multitude of catwalks and steps that led to a collective of docked ships. The floor was a pure white, a stark contrast to the deep, dark of space beyond the platform visible through the energised shielding of the space station. While Cait and Sam had boots implemented at the heels of their jumpsuits, Lena was barefoot, not that she cared at all, she was taking in the wondrous sight of all the different types of ships parked in this massive extension to what once was a giant ship itself.

"You'd think that guy saw practically naked women stroll through his checkpoint every day, he didn't so much as glance up at you," Cait laughed to Lena, confused how calm she was in only a trench coat.

"That's why I adore this place, it's a haven for WIDOWs like us, we just blend in to all the weirdness here. No company, no uniform, yet this is where they sell their wares, everyone is dressed differently, the county Inquisitors don't know where to look or what to look for, it's great, like nowhere else in the system." Lena beamed, securing the jacket around her body, stretching her toes on the smooth platform beneath them.

"Sure is, I mean it's a shithole really, but it's a shithole that we can call home so we love it," Sam shrugged, beckoning the others on with a nod in the direction of their ship. The three crossed the platform and ascended a set of steps at the far end before making their way down a long stretch of white metallic walkway to a large bulk of a cargo ship at the end. Here the spotlights dangling from chains above their heads were either dimly lit or not at all casting a convenient shadow over this area at the top of the docks.

Next to the platform where some large metal crates were being offloaded from the ship's rear ramp, was the cargo ship the group called their home, secured in place by being attached to a crane stemming down from the roof. It was not a pretty ship. It was coated in a lazy grey paint that had parts of the blackened casing of its frame showing from underneath, and the wings at either side were painted green, a dark shade that was fading and showed signs of scarring from regular wear and tear. The ship's hull stretched forward and under the cockpit like an armoured insect's eyes peering out from its shell and it showed no signs of having any armed defences. At the rear of the vessel were two men using a magnetically hovering trolley to bring down crates of a variety of large sizes. They were being received by an overweight woman wearing a suit of grey with an orange zip spanning from hip to opposite shoulder. She seemed pleased but concentrated on the matter at hand, keeping a log of the goods being transferred into her possession, she didn't notice the three approaching from the catwalk. Her security did, two men in the uniform of Stalwart enforcers, bulky grey armour beneath waist length green jackets, bearing laser pistols at holsters on their right thighs. These two guards produced their weapons in unison, aiming down the way at the small group approaching, but stood down as the woman took note.

"I trust you three had a good time aboard our Forerunner," the woman said by way of greeting.

"Xin was hospitable as always, but like always, I'm keen to get back to open space," Sam said in response, giving a wave over to the two men who seemed to have brought down their last crates as they removed their empty floating trollies to the hangar of their ship before coming back down. One was human, bald and with a black beard, over six foot tall and bulky built, he was dark skinned and wearing the same armour as the woman's guards. The other bore the same armour yet he was younger and X-Human, nearer to Cait's age, with eyes aflame in raging orbs of bejewelled, shining infernos contained with a face bearing a charming smile. He had the gold sheen of the male sex of his species, and he had glistening brown hair, combed to a point at the front, well-tended to.

The two men approached the other half of their group, the boots of their armour making thudding sounds and they stepped across the breadth of the platform, and the human spoke first. "Guys, this job's finished and I'm figuring we're straight onto the next, what did Xin have for us that was so urgent?"

"It's something you'll want to hear, Tomen, but we should head inside first," Cait replied.

"You not cold, Lena?" The X-Human at Tomen's side smirked, bemused by the appearance his friend had chosen.

"No, why? If you're feeling a little chilly, I have this coat, could lend it to you but it'll cost you, Miles," Lena chuckled, flicking the collar of her jacket up to cover her neck.

"Cost me what? My dignity at not being a total perv? No, thanks Lena, I'm good being the witty member of the group, you're the pervy one, keep the coat," the male X-Human retorted.

"Alright, I assume everything is in order, that we're good to go?" Tomen asked the woman in the grey and orange suit who was nodding at her clipboard, only looking up when realising she was the one the question was posed to.

"Yeah, we have everything we need. You really came through this time, Tomen, do you have any idea what's in these crates?" Her voice was hoarse yet excited, she pointed the tip of her pen in the direction of the metal boxes.

"They were the job, that's as far as I cared to consider them," Tomen shrugged.

"Inside each of those crates is one of security bots that the RCS love to throw among our communities to raise a little mayhem, the latest models with all the bells and whistles. And it just so happens that their core processors are perfectly compatible with the auto-surgical equipment that we use in the clinic here. So these machines of death will be broken down into tools to aid the living, kind of poetic, wouldn't you agree?"

"Usually I don't care about what comes after we pull a job, but got to admit that's a pretty good end result, I think we will sleep well tonight with that in mind after a job well done," Tomen nodded. "Until next time," he shook her hand and turned back to his team. "Alright, let's get on the ship and back into open space, and then you can pass on whatever message he had for us."

Tomen led the way as they all made their way across the platform and boarded their ship before raising the ramp, he pressed a button on a console at the side of the entrance to his vessel that activated the intercom. "Azuri, we're all onboard, take us out and meet us in the common area, I have a feeling that there is a discussion to come that we must all partake in."

"Cool, give us a few," a female voice replied through a speaker on the console.

The ramp brought the team into the hangar of this cargo freighter, a wide open space that had once housed the crates that the team had been tasked with attaining and dropping off, now it was just empty, ready for the next lot of stock. A rickety staircase was set into the framing of the ship on either side that led to the second level and cockpit, and it was the one on the left that the team used to reach the common area that served as host to the dining table and kitchen. The top of the stairs led into a large space that had a long wooden table next to the banister of the steps and it reached almost to the double automatic doors that led into the cockpit. It was a simple solid piece of pale wood, a dim beige colour with five seats either side composed of the same basic material. From the view at the top of the stairs, on the right side was the kitchen with a green wall and base cabinets, a worktop of the same colour as the dining table, and opposite was a window showing the view of the docks beyond. It was as the three men sat down at the table, with the two X-Human women milling around the kettle and cupboards in the kitchen area, making themselves cups of coffee, that they felt the violent jerk of the entire ship. The crane was detached from the ship's hull so the vessel was now supported by the propulsion of the engines before it set off out of the dock area via the colossal gates parting for their passing. The view out of the window shifted from parked vessels to the enormous infrastructure of the inside of the Forerunner docks to the stars and worlds of outer space. It was a marvellous view as the light from the red star from which the system took its name shone into the room, lighting it up, bathing it in an ocean of blood coloured light, twinned with the yellow light from the sister-sun.

"Quit the suspense, Cait. What did Xin say?" Miles took a seat on the window side of the table, taking a black bar out from a pocket on the inside of his jacket and pressing a button on its side, activating a holographic image illuminating out of it. Out of the image was a news broadcast from Stardust, documenting how a shipment of robo-sentries from Ruby Consolidated Systems bound for Vermilion had gone missing.

Cait and Lena had finished brewing their coffees, having added sugar and milk to the plain green mugs they used, and brought them over to the table, Cait sitting at the front of the table on the stairs end, while her friend chose to sit at her right side. Tomen strolled by them to sit at the far end, on the kitchen side, just as the double doors through to the cockpit opened and the pilot in the group entered, while Sam chose to lean up against the kitchen cupboards.

Azuri Prime was an X-Human with a complex variety of different shades of blue in her eyes matching the natural shades of a sea, she had black hair tied up in a twisted knot at the top of her head that relented a tail down that reached to the base of her spine. Her dark skin sparkled with the silver layer that marked her as a female and she wore a similar jumpsuit to Cait, having previously aligned with RCS, however she had a silver wing attached on either shoulder marking her out as a company pilot. "OK, I've put us on an auto-pilot drift, did I miss anything, people?" She asked as she took the seat at the opposite head of the table to Cait, sitting at Tomen's side.

"So Xin has something big for us. He says Thorne sent an Obsidian team to infiltrate the Old Capital on Ruby, and he says that they succeeded. Well, they were successful in getting inside but then they were attacked, they were caught in a massacre, there was only one survivor that the listening post picked up. She reported back that her mission was to locate a vault within the city."

"What's inside it?" Tomen asked, leaning on his elbow so that he was close to Azuri who was leaning forward with her arms crossed and resting on the table.

"Well, Xin didn't know anything for certain…" Cait began.

"…But we are working on the power of optimism and wishful thinking," Sam interrupted with a grin.

"Shut the fuck up, mate, and not another word unless it's something with some genuine value, eh? Let us with intelligence think, that's the one thing you'll never get your hands on," Miles quipped, turning his attention to Cait as he glanced over his tablet screen while Sam set a scornful stare on him. "Carry on, Cait."

"Xin doesn't know what's inside for certain but he's theorised that there has to be some evidence in there for the real cause for the Capital Collapse."

"Honey, even if WIDOWs such as ourselves didn't cause the Collapse, who's to say there's any evidence of what did happen? This was eight years ago now, surely Thorne or his dad would have got rid of it after all this time." Azuri's words spoke of being unconvinced but her tone suggested that she was open to it, but she had to be honest about her thoughts.

"But I've been thinking that is exactly why they went in search of this vault! If they caused the Collapse somehow, either by some project gone wrong or a cruel wave of change, then there has to be a history recorded of the exploits of it. Some kind of logs from those who worked on it because that's how they do everything, every detail recorded so that no investment goes wasted with no explanation. And what if it's unfinished? What if that is why they went back in? To recover what they lost and see if they can salvage something from it? I think it's extremely likely."

"And, not to cut you off but it has to be explored, why would we care? Why would we care if the truth is in there?" Tomen asked, sitting back in his chair, kicking one leg over the other and folding his arms.

"Why would we care? How can you say that?" Cait slammed her left fist down on the table and pointed at Tomen with his right. "If we can share the truth of what happened, it can give people hope, it could unite them, imagine that! What if people actually united, they would be too strong for not just the Coalition, but the Board too! We could dismantle the tyranny of the tri-systems!"

"And that's what people want, is it? Because, hmm," Tomen hesitated, forgetting the word that had slipped out of his mind as soon as it appeared, before he waved out a hand as he remembered. "Apathy, that's what I'm getting at. People don't need the truth of things, they just want things to be simple and easy. They want food on their table, water in their cups, a bed with a roof over their heads, a purpose in life, they sure as the stars are bright aren't seeking any conflict that could turn all of that to ash under the boot and inferno of the Coalition's vengeance."

"Too right, friend, that's the honest truth of it," Sam agreed.

"A bit troubling that you agree with me to be honest but yes, the Capital Collapse was eight years ago now, people have surely moved on and just want to get on with their lives. We'd only be bringing them misery and death if we were to succeed," Tomen finished, a cold expression on his face, not wishing to let his personal feelings of hating upsetting Cait undermine his genuine thoughts on the matter.

"That's not true, and I think you're being a coward," Lena put in, having taken a long draught of her coffee, slamming the mug down as Tomen finished. "We'd be bringing them hope, if we were to succeed, just like Cait says. Yeah people will die because they will choose to fight, don't you see?" The red-haired X-Human stared down the man but she wasn't finished. "And just what the fuck do you mean that they have moved on? What living under the crushing weight of a contract that they never gave consent to is peaceful?"

"You're forgetting that the contracts entitle the people to the basic means to survive, it binds them to work that provides food, water, shelter, a place in the worlds," Tomen argued back.

"Then why did you betray yours?" Lena raised an accusing eyebrow.

"You know why," Tomen coldly replied as the room fell silent.

"Yeah, and you disobeyed your work contract, Tomen. According to its terms, you failed to meet your end of the deal, by Board law, you ought to put that gun in your mouth and pull the trigger, or we should be doing it for you, had we not come to the same necessary betrayal by different roads. Besides, your contract entitled you to a fairly decent life, you were an enforcer in Stalwart Ironworks, you just made sure people carried on working, you kept them safe, I was a whore! My body was subject to such an abundance of horrors and uses that your mind would fracture to hear even the first few years of my experiences which all started when I was nine because my family sold me, and then my supervisor couldn't wait until I was eighteen and of legal age! My contract doomed me to having my body be an asset, something they used for their own designs and needs, so don't you dare even for a second justify them!"

"He didn't mean to—" Azuri began.

"He can fight his own battles, Azuri. I'm sorry but I want to hear him speak for himself. Go on then, enforcer, enforce your opinion, you dick," Lena challenged.

"Easy, Lena," Cait put a hand on her friend's, meaning to be a calming gesture.

"No, Cait, it's alright." Tomen put up a hand before starting again. "All I meant is that nothing is ever truly evil, you have to consider things by all their aspects. Especially with a job such as this. The consequences could be enormous. We are talking about invoking a war with Obsidian. We are talking about possibly having people downing their tools in revolution but think about that for a moment. If people do not work, then they are deemed unprofitable, and I have seen the outcome of such a determination. The conglomerate does not flinch in the face of an action they deem necessary, especially when it comes down to their contribution to the Board being harmed. And that's if they even choose to rise to it at all. I personally think they would choose to carry on their little lives because it's what's safest. Life isn't meant to be easy."

"Really, you're saying those words?" Sam shot up, his shouting close to laughter. "I said those exact words to you, back when we first met." He walked round to join Miles' side of the table, grasping the top of a chair and leaning over it. "I was young when I started on this path. I remember sitting at the family table on Scarlet, with my mum and dad, just a kid, and I remember the look in their eyes, and it was haunting to me, it was acceptance. They had given up, they used to say that, that life isn't meant to be easy, they told themselves things like that every single day. But I just couldn't stomach it. I couldn't let myself be dragged down the same path they had! So I learned, I stayed behind in school every day to learn my writing and reading. I observed everything, picking how to talk to people, what they would expect and what they could be told to get them to do things. A school friend of mine got a transfer as his grades were good enough for RCS recognition but he showed it to me before he left, and so I was able to forge one of my own. And I made a life for myself, better than anything my parents could have ever imagined, so limited, so pathetic. But yeah, I got caught, they threw me into the prison on Carmine, mining the metal for their armour out of the volcanic earth, I ended every day in pain, exhausted so much my bones and muscles could barely keep me standing. Life wasn't easy, but I refused to just accept that! So I got myself out of there as well, befriending the guards, letting them whisper gossip into my ear before they got too close just one time and I was able to nab myself a company card that I used as my ticket to freedom."

"I remember all this, Sam," Tomen said, his voice giving an easy suggestion that he didn't see where Sam was going with what he was saying.

"And my freedom brought me to the Starcrest where I met you. I told you my story, as I just did now, how I had to claw my way to any resemblance of comfort and a decent life only for it to be snatched away from me and leave me on the run for the rest of my life as a WIDOW. And I almost gave up, I won't lie, and I said those exact words: life isn't meant to be easy. And what did you say?"

"I said, that's the conglomerate speaking, not you," Tomen relented.

"What does that mean?" Miles asked, it being the first time he had heard how the two had met.

"He said that I was doing the conglomerate's work for them," Sam continued. "That they introduced and promoted sayings like that to plant the suggestions into people's minds, to introduce self-fulfilling prophecies, I think you called them."

Tomen nodded, recollecting.

"To give up, to just resign yourself to work and make your hands busy with no thoughts about anything else. To not think for yourself, to not unite," Sam fixed Tomen with a meaningful glare. "Maybe, Cait is right."

"Life isn't meant to be easy, what a load of shit," Azuri agreed, looking at the man at her side. "Come on, Tomen, you don't believe that. You just don't believe in people, and I kinda get that you're saying they're sick with apathy. But maybe the truth inside that vault will spark them into life, and I gotta say, I reckon that's a risk worth taking."

"I'm not hearing any guarantees that the truth of the Collapse is in fact in that vault. I'm feeling swayed, I'll be honest, but I need more," Tomen said and he opened his arms, leaning forward on the table's edge.

"It has to be, doesn't it? Why else would they send an Obsidian team in there? There has got to be something valuable in there, we ought to find out what it is," Sam added.

"Course your mind would go to whatever's valuable," Miles mocked but not cruelly, a friendly joke.

"Up yours mate, force of habit," the thief replied with a smile.

"Say we do this, how do we get inside the city?" Azuri asked, directing the question at Cait.

"Xin says the Captain of the Police from the Old City is hiding on Scarlet, running a farm or something, but he says he has a landing key, I think it unlocks the city docks."

"OK, cool, then what? How do we know where this vault is?"

"He doesn't know. We've only just learned about this now so we have no idea what it is or what it looks like. We don't even have any idea what we'll find in the city along the way, but Xin offered a solution to both those things."

"What's that?" Tomen asked, trying to be more open minded.

"He said we'll face threats in the city so he said we'll need a protector. Also, we will need two Obsidian high level employee passcodes to enter the vault. The Captain will have one. And the protector he suggests will have one, too." Cait chewed on the last sentence, knowing the next words she had to say will certainly trigger a reaction. "He said we'll find the Elite Commander on Vermilion, he said we should go to him for help."

"Are you fucking mad?" Azuri slammed both fists down on the table.

"Sorry, what?" Miles blinked, not believing what he heard.

"An Elite?" Tomen's eyes went huge, a swell of confusion building inside him.

"Apparently he left Obsidian, I guess he's a WIDOW just like us." Cait closed her eyes, she knew this reaction was justified.

"No one leaves Obsidian, you fucking idiot!" Azuri screamed, "Tomen, we can't go through with this plan, he'd kill us all."

"Why would Xin send us to meet the Elite Commander, Cait? That doesn't make any sense," Tomen asked.

"Are we really considering this?" Miles asked, laughing. "I mean if you're feeling suicidal, might I suggest we take this conversation outside?"

"Shut up, Miles!" Lena shouted at her fellow X-Human. "Xin said this guy is separate from Obsidian, he even thinks that he is murdering them on Vermilion."

"What did you say?" Tomen asked, a cool calmness in his voice.

"Xin mentioned that high-ranking members of the Coalition are dying on Vermilion, he thinks this Winter guy could be involved somehow," Lena explained, a little confused by the way Tomen sounded.

"There is a serial killer on Vermilion, it's why we've avoided the planet for so long," Miles added, flipping his tablet around which showed a news broadcast describing how Obsidian forces on the planet had found yet another body of a manager in the COC, hanging upside down, a bullet in his skull, and an eye missing.

"Cait, this plan of yours keeps getting more dangerous by the minute. So I want you to take a deep breath, and really consider for a moment what you want to do, and then tell us what you really think we should do," Tomen said, sitting back again and folding his arms.

The debating in the common room ceased as Tomen's instruction stamped down a blanket of silence, allowing Cait to think. She looked at each of them in turn, going around the room from Lena, and finally stopping on Miles once she had gone through them all. Looking at the X-Human with the amber eyes gave her pause. Cait had known Miles for a few years now and she knew him well, she knew this was a man who smiled in the face of extreme danger, would laugh at a gun pointed at him, but would rival a robo-sentry's systematic killing should his friends be in danger. If she could convince this sceptical yet honourable one, then she could convince them all. But that's when the weight of what she could say hit her, as she sensed Tomen had meant it to. She considered for a moment if she was wrong. How they would wade through dangers that she may not even be capable of expecting, let alone fighting, only for anything less than she had described. The best case scenario would be that she would lose their trust and faith, the worst case would be that they would all lose much more than that. But then her mind thought of the larger picture than one man could fill. She pictured all the lives in the Crimson, and flipped the thought on its head. What if she was right, and she didn't even try, the idea ran a chill down her spine and spoiled her stomach. All those lives, discarded to a doomed fate of never being given a chance at experiencing more, more than what the conglomerate had set before them. And so her mind was made up.

"United we stand, divided we fall," Cait said, leaning forward on her elbows with her hands clenched together, her stare fixed on a spot on the table a small measure away from her.

"Then I'm on your side," Lena put in and her friend looked up to meet her gaze, and she gave her a nod.

"I've tried for so long to not reach for anything that is beyond my grasp, but if you are certain that this score is worth sticking our necks out for, that this is for all or nothing, then you can count me with you," Sam added.

"I'm with you too, Cait. Not exactly thrilled about meeting an Elite face-to-face but hey-ho, nothing ever worth doing was easy or free from risk, so fuck it," Miles smiled, tossing his tablet on the table and leaning back, joining his arms behind his head.

"I've never been good at reading the pathways of the stars but I do honestly hope they have lined up for you to see this true, Cait. But you have never lied to us, and you are a delightful friend," Azuri said, seeking it was her turn to speak. "I'm sorry I doubted you and I really hope you know it wasn't personal. It's a terrifying thing that you've laid out for us today, but it's one that I will see through with you. We've been friends for years now and been through some seriously fucked situations, but we survived them because all of us are together. And I never want that to change."

Tomen sat as still as stone and his face gave nothing away to what he was thinking. Eventually, he said, "OK, so where do we start, Cait? This is your gig." He smiled, as a proud father might do to a child that stood up to them for what they believed in.

"First thing's first, I want that Elite."

"Actually," Lena smirked. "I think the first thing is that I should put on some clothes, this was a very serious conversation to have naked." And Miles eyebrows shot up involuntarily.

Chapter 3

After the Capital Collapse, the fall of Rose City on Ruby, Elias Thorne dictated that there be a super-station constructed to house not only his father, Section Chief at the time, but also the Directors of the companies that form the Coalition, which included himself. As well as these prestigious few were nearly two hundred colleagues of the Stardust Corporation that served the every will and whim of the Directors, maintaining their homestead in the cold, dark of space. A web of gigantic, thick support beams cast a net as the roof of this enormous station, there was glass between those immense battens of solid metal that rose up and bent in an elbow to then all meet at a central column that ran the entire length of the structure. Where a facility like this would allow for a view of the sky if placed on a world, here in the infinity of space, it allowed for an unparalleled view of the cosmos. The stars and worlds surrounding the station allowed for the most exquisite spectacle as a daily wonder for these premier members of the Crimson conglomerate.

With a segregated section just off the main structure serving as a docking hangar that opens at a craft's intention to land, this area led into a boulevard that had quarters for the Stardust workers on either side leading to a variety of restaurants, offices, brothels doubling as bars, and other services for these wealthy and powerful people. This all led up to the Obsidian fortress at the far end, in a similar design to the Forerunner, where their COC embassy was replaced here by the housing for the Section Chief. The impenetrable building with the most security in the Crimson system was designed to be the home of Roderic Thorne, but he relinquished this to his son when his ten year term as the COC's leader had ended. In typical fashion, he transcended his power and authority to his son, nepotism being as commonplace as to be disregarded at any and all incidence. Elias, as the Director of Ruby Consolidated Systems before he made the step up, used the wealth of knowledge and technological achievements of his company to design and construct this marvel of high society living partnered with extreme security measures.

The trees here were a lush green and made of a composite plastic, dotted down the central reservation that ran from the docks right up to the forbidding, dark as midnight metal building at the opposite end. Breaking up into the air, almost touching the framework at the roof, the fortress was an extremely tall and intimidating structure, of a near box shape with an outer wall protecting the entrance with an energy shield serving as a form of gateway. The path leading to the entrance consisted of small stones of pure white marked either side with rocks of obsidian, brought up from the Obsidian homeworld of Carmine. Either side of this stony path were patches of a naturally occurring black grass that seemed to gleam under the light of the stars beyond the glass roof, and off the street lamps that line the boulevard and light up the fort. A staircase cast in obsidian stone led up to the automatic doors that led inside, with an Elite guard standing resolute and sentinel either side of the entrance.

Several storeys up was the office of the Section Chief which covered the entire floor of the building, including the office area, the living area, private bathroom and a waiting room for the Chief's appointments to wait their turn to be summoned. One wall of the office area was entirely made of glass, enabling a stunning view of the planet of Vermilion beyond the station's framework. It was here where the Section Chief stood now, set in the uniform of his station, a maroon suit of trousers teamed with a jacket that had black trim and a zip running from left hip up to right shoulder, a golden emblem adorning his left breast. The emblem took the form of the letters COC embossed on top of an etched flame set behind a soldier silhouette protecting a field where a farmer was tending a field. This figure stood straight and strong, his posture as perfect as his hair was trimmed, designed into a forward facing arrow at the top with short cut sides. The style suited the expression on the man's face, one of focus and drive, as he glared at the planet beyond the confines of his Arcadia homestead with contempt, the world cloaked in a shroud of industrial smoke, so much so that this man could not see the surface beyond it.

In contrast, his office was the peak of prestigious living with all white walls and shining golden floor tiles, with a sofa of the smoothest white leather opposite a desk carved from a tree sourced from a forest privately owned by Elias Thorne on the world of Sanguine. This desk was of a snowy white with beautiful golden veins running throughout and across its breadth, and on top of this expert piece of craftsmanship lay a tablet with an illuminated holographic image. This was of a man in Obsidian armour suspended upside down, helmet lying on the ground with a pool of its bearer's blood welling inside from the eye removed from his socket. The image was cast in an energised purple hue which discoloured the image of the blood, whereas the crimson liquid steadily growing on the floor was of an undeniable dark, red shade.

"Thank you for bringing me this update, you did well, most would be too shy to bring me such grim tidings," Elias Thorne said to the corpse of a blonde, young woman in the garb of a Stardust worker, lying at his feet, a scorch mark on her forehead from a laser bolt. He turned slowly and stepped over her, with a disinterested glance down to make sure his shoes didn't run the risk of becoming stained by the blood on his floor. "Your service is appreciated," his voice was calm and slow, it brimmed with a sadistic intelligence, and the will to use it, and the nonchalance he bore for the ramifications of his actions. Elias strode over to his desk and pressed the button on the intercom unit mounted at the desk's corner, coolly waiting for the response.

"Sir?" A male voice came over the radio.

"I've made a mess, please attend with haste, I don't want the grout to stain," Elias instructed, smiling as he heard the bell of the lift across from the window beep as it was called by those who were rushing to see his command fulfilled. He picked up the tablet with delicate fingers, laying down his laser pistol with his other hand, and slipped back over to the window, observing the view again before his attendees arrived so that their only view of him was of his back.

Two men arrived in the same attire as the woman lying dead on the floor, each holding a plastic container seemingly holding their supplies for the task. They didn't dare to take a moment to take in the scene for if their emotions got the better of them, an unspoken rule to follow when around the boss. One was a blond haired stocky build of a man while the other was younger, just out of adolescence, a head of ginger hair atop a face doing his best to remain as cool as can be. But then the younger of the two spotted the gun sitting on the desk, the one that did the deed of murdering the woman they were hastily wrapping in a plastic sheet, and he froze, eyes wide. The laser pistol was made from a black metal, shining from the glow of the red star flowing in from the window, the only light in the room that was otherwise cast in a deep gloom. It looked much like a ballistic pistol, yet this energised weapon held its glowing purple cartridge at the top of the chamber giving it a menacing look. As soon as he realised his partner had stopped helping him, the older colleague grabbed him by the shoulder, shaking him violently, eyes wide and panic-stricken, desperate to break his trance at glaring at the gun.

"Is there a problem?" Elias asked, impatient to be alone again and taking a small measure of joy from teasing these underlings with his wrath.

"No, sir. This won't take but a minute," the younger of the two replied, getting back to his work, and they finished wrapping the body in the plastic sheet. Next, they sprayed a chemical over all of the blood, the pools and spills, and once it hardened into a crystalline form, they placed it into a refuse bag. The older one pulled out a box from his plastic holdall and produced a wipe that he used in between the tiles to ensure the final remains of the blood were removed, leaving absolutely no trace that anyone had died here at all, not that she had been the first. After squaring away their cleaning supplies, the two colleagues hoisted the body up and onto a stretcher that they folded out and retreated over to the lift.

"Did I say you could go?" Elias said, speaking quietly and calmly on purpose so that the other two men had to strain to hear him, and halt suddenly to obey. Turning on a heel, the Section Chief strode over to the two colleagues who were doing their best impressions of statues, still bearing the weight of the body between them. Elias could see the fear in their eyes, the hesitation at not knowing what manner of instruction they might receive next, their eyes could barely meet his own. In being 36 himself, Elias was between the two ages of the men standing before him and now up close, he could see that their uniforms were far dirtier than his, he assumed with a sneer that they were cleaning some room of his home. He laid a hand on the shoulder of the younger of the two on his right side, and looked the elder dead in the eye before turning his gaze on the one at his right. "Thank you, that'll be all." He said, noting the younger one's arms beginning to tremble.

By the time the two attendees had summoned the lift and left his office, Elias was back at his window. The only other space station in the region, the Forerunner, was slowly moving in front of his view of Vermilion, and beyond them, Elias could see the ashen wasteland of the planet of Carmine. When he took over as Section Chief, his father took up the position as Director of

Obsidian, and refused the residence on Arcadia, preferring to make housing for himself nearer his office on the homeworld of the security firm. It drove a wedge between the former and present leaders of the region, the father and the son who even after five years couldn't understand why they could not live and lead the conglomerate together. The world failed to be terraformed properly, the giant machines pelting the nutrients into the air to support human life malfunctioned. They cleansed the air but only by catastrophically fracturing the crust of the planet to produce rivers of lava, great volcanoes reaching up to catch a glimpse of the upper atmosphere. On the island with the largest of these mountains was the fortress and home office of Obsidian, where Roderic Thorne maintained the safety and security of the Crimson region, by decree of his son. The listening post was in the foreground of the planet, rings of metal surrounding a central spire, acting as the eyes and ears for Obsidian, the weapon that kept them far ahead of any potential threat, within and without the borders of the region.

Elias fixed his stare on the Forerunner, he always hated the vessel. For him, to have it not be devoted to one of his companies was an insult. Made worse that the hospital aboard it was staffed and facilitated for by a company from the Sapphire conglomerate, though he suspected with some level of assistance from within his borders. The Section Chief enjoyed his time with the girls brought to his home from the Stardust Corporation yet when he looked upon this space station, all he saw was a whore. An all-welcoming, free-to-use facility that bore him no loyalty. He would wipe it off the face of his window with his colossal Obsidian fleet yet he knew the Board would never stand for it, the trade between the different conglomerates posing a template for peaceful co-existence, to break that would be testament to starting a war. Not that he wasn't tempted.

The hologram illuminated out from the tablet, the image of the man suspended upside down, the void where one of his eyes ought to have been was the detail that Elias honed in on. There had been thirty deaths with this signature before the matter had been brought to his attention, and another fifty-two since, not to mention the other bodies that were left in the wake of whatever it was getting to the one they sought. Elias didn't recognise the man in the picture, only the uniform, and the manner of the display left for his authorities to find, a grand gesture to belittle, ridicule and horrify. So many of his management hierarchy stemming throughout his conglomerate had been targeted and murdered, all of them having an eye stolen, leaving Elias accepting a small iota of fear and vulnerability. Every time he replaced a manager or supervisor that was killed, their replacement fell victim to dangling upside down as well, losing an eye and he would be right back where he started, Elias could feel the fury of frustration building up inside.

"It's you, isn't it? Can't leave well enough alone, can you?" He cursed the open space. "I will find you, I will cast your life onto the pyre and see it ablaze," Elias promised to the one in the Crimson in which his threat was intended for, the one he would give all his power away, if it meant seeing that one man broken and decapitated before him.

Chapter 4

To walk the streets of Vermilion was to walk beneath the constant plume of industry, the sky and stars beyond it blocked from view, a dirty smog drowning the many roads and highways. Great chasms and canyons dot the landscape, some bottomless pits, others with lakes below so deep and dark the conglomerate could not presume to claim them as their own. Spanning the globe of this planet, from hemisphere to hemisphere and across the breadth of the world's equator, casting a web so vast every town and city was connected, were train tracks. The once completely natural world, not bearing a single construction, was the homeworld of the X-Human species, who preferred the caverns in the recesses of the canyons that ran like scars across their world to the metal and timber that craft human structures. Yet now it lacked even a single spec of untouched, natural landscape, it was now entirely conquered, having begun from the monumental terraforming machine that now sat dormant in the centre of the largest cityscape.

The docks for the city of Renn sat upon a hill overlooking the enormity of what was the largest city on Vermilion, not that it seemed to end as the towns and city blended together, intertwined by the network for which the conglomerate moved its workers and products. The only way to tell where one settlement ended and the next began were the great walls that segregated the areas that formed up as districts. Stalwart Ironworks insisted upon the defences as they built up the Crimson conglomerate's facilities, wary of the X-Human locals that might have chosen to interrupt their interests, slaughter their workforce. The docks were the largest section of this city, surrounded by tall street lamps, lighting up the entire area and all the ships calling it home at this moment. Some bore the colours of the Obsidian police forces, others were huge freighters in the deep red of Crimson Sun and some were Stalwart vessels. These brought in fresh workers from the prison on Carmine, reformed through the torture of gruelling labour, yet one of these had paintwork that had not been updated for some time.

"Try the bars first then the Obsidian stations but only if you have no other choice, we don't want to get made here, there's too many of them to evade," Tomen advised Cait as he lent against the framework of the doorway at the top of the rear ramp of his ship. He stared over the view of the city, his eyes drawn to the train station directly below them, a colossal box of a structure that housed the great metal snakes. From this vantage point, they could see the whole operation.

"Don't worry, we'll keep a low profile. It's getting late, hopefully the streets will be quiet tonight," Cait replied, following Tomen's gaze down to the train station.

"How can you tell? It's always dark here," Tomen muttered, turning his eyes to the sky, not that he could see it for the sea of smoke flowing up in rivers from the stacks that surrounded the factory below them, the main production base for Ruby Consolidated Systems, after the Capital fell.

"Look at them down there, Tomen. I can just about make out their faces from this distance but their pain is obvious," Cait said, descending the ramp, stepping across the smooth concrete surface that served as the docks grounds, over to the edge of the hill. "Look at that car!" She pointed at a huge car on the train being loaded at the periphery of the station, getting ready to depart, looking back at Tomen to join her.

He obliged, bowing his head, still apprehensive about what they were doing on this planet, walking across to join Cait, but his mind began to change once he saw what she meant.

"Tomen, just look at them all, they're wearing the same suit as Sam, all those farmers for Crimson Sun, they're crammed into that car like crops!" Cait gestured towards the horde of red shapes being forced into a cargo car by menacing troops in black. "And then look at that car, that's why we're doing this." She then waved a hand to the front of the train, to where men and women in Stalwart colours were loading up crates of stock with great care, moving them steadily and affording them more space than the ones who produced them. "They care more about their contribution to the Board than the poor people whose backs break to create it."

"It's the way it's always been," Tomen sighed, taking in the sight of the mass of people pushed inside the train, and he knew the reason why. He had seen so much of the conglomerate and learned the stark truth of their power. It was clear and present for all to see, hidden in plain sight. "People are the key resource of the coalition, of the Board, really," he continued. "The tri-systems run on brutality like this, using fear to blind the workforce from the very simple truth of things."

"What's that?" Cait asked, not taking her eyes off a group of workers in the same jumpsuit as her s, the black of RCS, being ushered into a freight car, a pair of Stalwart enforcers brandishing rifles keeping the crowd flowing.

"That there's more of them than there is of those in power. Right now they're divided, the conglomerate's clever, they've figured their play and they're executing it perfectly. But if we were to give them something, something to unite them…" Tomen smiled down at Cait who turned to him, interested in what he was hinting at. "Then united they would stand, divided they fall. Give them the truth of the Collapse, Cait, and there is a chance that they'll rise to topple the powers that be. What have they got to lose?"

"You know, that's what I want, it's what I've always wanted. But how do we get from obtaining the big secret to winning a revolution?" Cait's head dropped as if the thought was too heavy to bear, too difficult to manage, she contemplated with a screaming match in her head, could it all really be done.

"You start," Tomen started, lifting the young woman's head with a finger under her chin, forcing her to meet his eyes. "With the first step. Now go find us an Elite Commander, and take Miles with you."

"I can do this on my own, I don't need my hand held," Cait took Tomen's right hand with her own and gave it a gentle squeeze while tilting her head to the side sarcastically, gesturing she wasn't pleased with his instruction. Yet she stopped in her tracks when she saw Miles standing just a few steps from her.

"Come on, darling, we'll take a walk into town," Miles grinned, holding out his left hand, his right resting on the energised weapon in its holster on his right thigh, a ribbon of black gripping onto his dark grey armour.

"Dick," was all Cait replied, pulling up the hood of her black cloak that she wore over the top of her RCS jumpsuit, it reached down and covered only her back, stopping at the waist. It was made from the same fibres used to make the clothing Obsidian officers wear under their armour, resilient and sturdy yet light enough that it was comfortable, and she had put a shard of metal into the tip of the hood so it drooped down slightly to obscure her face. A gift from Tomen, when he first brought her to the Forerunner half a dozen years before.

The trains that ran all over the surface of the planet followed tracks that were raised high above the ground, and ran so hard and fast that the energy that propelled them shot off powerful bolts of brilliant pale blue lightning, striking out in all directions. For the most part, these energy spikes were contained within a funnel surrounding the railroad tracks, great pylons suffocating them and dispersing the power away in waves of bright light. When these pylons, the colossal metal towers, missed the bolts of energy, they struck at the buildings that followed the course of the tracks, scorching them with radioactive burn marks. It was deafening to pass through the roads directly beneath the tracks, the boom of the train passing by, the way it shook the foundations of the tracks, Cait and Miles walked through the city in silence, not wasting the effort to try to talk, knowing they would never be able to hear each other.

They tried every bar, Obsidian outpost, even the RCS refinery at the centre of the city, but no one could point them in the direction of the Elite Commander they were told to find. The city was immensely grey, from its buildings to its roads to its people, even the smog that lingered in the air had a dirty shroud to it, it left a metallic taste in the mouth. Cait and Miles passed by men and women in all the different uniforms of the conglomerate, without the small deviations that they would normally see on the Forerunner where people were given some small measure of personal choice. Here these people bore their uniform like shackles, trudging their way to work or from, heading in groups to this bar or this office, all of them seemingly lacking any form of happiness, not one of them even content. They hardly registered the peculiar sight of a Stalwart enforcer walking among them with an RCS colleague with a hood over her face, they simply did not care.

"These people must go through the worst kinds of agony, and for what?" Cait asked, more the open air than to the man at her side who was itching to take out his weapon, wary of the Obsidian soldiers patrolling the streets. However, there were no inquisitors here, this was firmly coalition territory, this planet given over to the RCS.

"I don't know, I've no idea what they're even making there," Miles mused, taking a glance at the enormous smokestacks stretching up above their heads, looming over the tops of the buildings.

"Robo-sentries," Cait said coldly. "The conglomerate demands a heavy shipment every day from this facility, thrice the number my old place back on Sanguine was tasked with."

"And where do they all go?"

"I don't know, I only remember that the ones I used to make were part of a constant stream of them to the Obsidian fleet that patrols the outlying borders of the region."

"Why?" Miles asked as he took in the sight of a pack of Crimson Sun workers leaving an office at his right side.

"Like I'd know," Cait shrugged off, noticing Miles staring at the group in red. "RCS regularly brings in groups of Crimson Sun colleagues to teach them how to maintain the crops properly. Can't have the contribution tainted by bad harvesting, that bio-engineered food is the backbone of the Crimson's survival." She scorned as they carried on through the many streets, a labyrinth of industry until they reached the final bar they wished to check, near the wall that marked the end of this city.

It was a rundown little building standing alone at the end of a long road under the shadow of the stone border, its windows old and ridden with cracks that had been taped over, its front door an old piece of wood long in need of a fresh bit of orange paint as it barely stood out from the grey exterior. It was hardly a single level high, the ceiling coming down low as Cait and Miles entered, hearing the familiar Stardust music of singing the praises of the other companies under the COC banner, the reward of dedication, the honour of a job well done. The entrance opened up to a series of tables and chairs made from a grey shade of wood on a worn down carpet that may have once been a red colour but it was so dirty with the tracks of its patrons it hardly resembled the shade. Beyond this sitting area was the bar made from the same material as the seating, and booths of orange leather lined the walls on either side, and more tables were behind the bar. It was lit up well in this main area before the bar but in the area behind it there was no light so no one sat there, only a single solitary figure could be made out by the embers of a cigar burning in the abyss of shadow, right at the back.

Cait and Miles approached the bar, ignoring the drunken workers at their tables, some silent and forlorn, others hurling jeers and laughing loudly, enjoying the end of their shift, but they took note of the Obsidian group in the booth in the centre of the right side. There was only a single bartender, a human woman, seemingly bored and disinterested by her surroundings. Middle-aged and brown-haired, pale and cleaning the draught taps out some muscle-memorised routine, rather than out of genuine care, she didn't even bother to glance up when the two X-Humans approached. She was wearing the grey suit of her company with an orange shirt beneath that was overtly visible as she didn't zip up her jacket all the way, revealing a large cleavage that Miles chuckled at, knowing she did it for the tips. It wasn't that she wasn't a good looking woman that Miles found the effort funny, it was that he knew that these people had worked so hard to earn their tiny stipend of pay, and they wouldn't give it away for some small amount of titillation, especially for someone not interested to even try for it.

"Two double shots of whiskey, and a single of information, ta, love," Miles said, tossing a single golden ingot on the bar between them.

The woman didn't look up at her two customers, her eyes only went from her cleaning rag to the money and that is where her stare lingered. "Must be some pretty expensive info y'all guys are after," she murmured, finally looking at the two.

"We're looking for someone, he would have been Elite Commander during the times before the Collapse," Cait said, using the index finger on her left hand to flick the rectangular ingot onto its short edge and spun it with her thumb.

"Oh, him," the bartender closed her eyes for a moment as the thought of the Commander was as a whip to her back. "Don't speak so loudly of him."

"Alright, so where do we find him?" Cait asked, glancing over to Miles at her left side who nodded in the direction of the group of four Obsidian officers in the booth over her shoulder, assuming that was who the bartender was referring to.

"He's behind me, the one at the table but go slow if you wanna talk to him, he ain't the most welcomin' o' blokes, if ya catch me meaning," the bartender replied, "and only one o' you go, I be doubt'n he'll 'preciate being outnumbered."

"Go ahead, I want to gain some local insight," Miles nodded in the direction of the only sign of someone taking up a table in the dark recess of the building, the small embers as the only sign of light, gesturing for Cait to go.

"Yeah, ok," Cait replied, her mind elsewhere as she found herself overcoming a wave of anxiety as she stepped away and around the bar, and she looked down to see her feet taking her over to the table where her goal was seated.

Even closer up, Cait couldn't make out the figure in the shadows, she could barely see the table and spare chair next to the silhouette, but a random impulse told her to ask before taking the seat.

"May I sit with you?" She asked, pulling back her hood and straightening her ponytail with her right hand as she saw the embers of the lit cigar lower, tapped against the edge of the Stalwart brand ashtray on the table.

"If you have something worth hearing," was the only response from the darkness, in a deep, low voice, brimming with confidence and a calm aggression, but completely lacking in interest.

"Guess I'll have to try," Cait said, taking the vacant seat and once in among the mob of shadows, her eyes adjusted somewhat and she was able to make out the man next to her. He was human, Caucasian, and all in armour below the chin. This was no common black armour of an Obsidian trooper. This had a plate covering the neck, a ballistic pistol holstered in the centre of the chest plate with armour stemming out to completely encase the shoulders and arms, his hands were in some metallic gloves perfectly formed to size, and his legs were armoured, ending in solid boots. He was neck to toe in blackened metal yet it was conformed to his size, clearly moulded to his body so well that it seemed as though he himself was made out of metal. A knife was holstered on the outside of his left forearm, the handle of it pointing out towards his hand that was holding a glass of whiskey, and he had a second pistol holstered on his left side at his belt where he had a number of containers and grenades. At the front of his right thigh was holstered some kind of blade but Cait could only see the hilt, two prongs of metal horizontally protruding from the grip borne from a dark leather. On his back was some kind of pack, but Cait couldn't make out what it was for. As for the man himself, his brown hair was shaved at the sides and long through the middle gelled all the way back, his eyes were brown as well, sharp and focused on something out in the bar, and his jaw was broad, covered in a cropped beard.

"So how does this work? Do I introduce myself? Do you introduce yourself? But I already know your name, but you don't know mine!" Cait rambled, her nerves shot as her eyes went to the helmet on the table next to the man where an armoured helmet cast all in black to cover the entire head lay which had ovals of dark grey marking where his eyes would be. And those ovals were staring directly at her.

"Just breathe…" He interrupted.

"Thanks," Cait murmured, stopping herself from carrying on and she stared down at her hands in her lap, her fingers rampantly fidgeting.

"…While I still allow it." The man raised his glass with his left gloved hand and finished his drink, and with his right he brought his cigar, taking in a long draw.

Cait looked over at him, stunned into silence, and could see his eyes properly now with the help of the cigar embers. He was glaring over in the direction where the four Obsidian officers were sitting, and while his face was cast in an orange glow, she could see his eyes roll over to her, just for a moment, and when the cigar was lowered from his face, among the exhale of smoke, she could make out his eyes slowly peel off from her.

"I'm assuming its help you need, I can't offer it unless you say what it is," he said, cold and disinterested.

Cait contemplated for a moment how much she should say, whether to reveal the entire scope of the plan, or just the part that she needed him for, to extract the landing key from the Obsidian Captain and guide them to whatever this vault was within the Capital City. She figured maybe leaving out the parts about what it could possibly lead to, lest he be put off by all the attention it could bring down on him. "I want to get into Rose City, my team and me."

"Easier ways to die," was all he said.

"What is worth doing is rarely easy, and believe me, this is worth doing. We got word that an Obsidian team breached the Old City. That they were searching for some kind of vault, and we think there could be evidence in there for what really happened to cause the Capital Collapse."

"You're incredibly naive."

"Why?" Cait asked, not understanding the insult.

"Everyone knows the Collapse didn't happen the way they say it did, worst kept secret in the system, but they've had eight years, any possible evidence of the real cause will be long since swept away."

"Then why would they send an Obsidian team to find this vault?"

"What vault? I lived in the Capital, there was no vault," the man replied, sternly.

"I don't know if it is a vault per say, it could be some kind of underground facility or a bunker of some kind, maybe it's not literal, that's just what they called it," Cait replied, not to be deterred. "My point is, Obsidian seemed certain there was something to be found there, and I want to know what it is. If it's valuable enough for them to invest the effort in breaching the city, then it's valuable to us."

"You keep saying we and now you've said us, I'm assuming you're a part of a team? WIDOWs, obviously."

"Yeah, I'm with the guy at the bar, and four others," Cait replied.

"A lot of graves to dig if your mind is set on this course."

"Not if you're there to back us up, to protect us as we make our way through the city to this…place, and get what we need, and then get out again. You were Elite Commander."

"I haven't been called that in a long time, you don't even know what it means."

"So what are you now?" Cait asked, hoping the change in subject was good for her, so that he could mull over the task she set before him.

"I do as I will, whatever satisfies my need to act, whatever helps hone my skills and my mind. I do enough in this community to buy their loyalty so they do not point people in my direction that are not deserving of my time. So far, you are killing the lady behind the bar." The man's voice remained deep-pitched and coolly angry but now it let on his sadistic excitement.

"And what kinds of things satisfy an Elite?"

"I play the role of detective for this planet, my skills and experience being far beyond any common Obsidian guard, it settles the locals to lay eyes on my armour and blade."

"So, you're a WIDOW, like us, but you're here in your armour, not even trying to hide it from that Obsidian lot over there," Cait nodded in the direction of the four officers getting louder by the minute, enjoying themselves, taunting the locals, insulting the staff.

"They pay me no mind because there is nothing they can do to oppose me, WIDOW or not," the man grinned, glancing at Cait with a certain cruelty. "Besides, they benefit from leaving me in peace. Just last night I put down the Tarot Killer."

"The what?"

"Tarot cards were used by people on the Old World, some kind of fortune telling act, using cards with images of great meaning to determine a person's fate. This twisted whore's son would murder random people from the street, displaying their bodies in a macabre nod to a particular card, leaving it on their corpse as a sort of signature. He hunted at night so I watched from the rooftops and eventually caught a glimpse of him, and that's all the window I needed, now his body lies in the city morgue, a hole in his skull. The Obsidian garrison failed to stop him, but I have far superior training, and he wasn't the first serial killer I'd tracked, so I was able to put an end to him."

"Obsidian would never accept the help of a WIDOW," Cait remarked, doubting the man's story.

"You're X-Human, couldn't you just read my mind to see I'm telling you the truth? I don't think acceptance is accurate, it seems to suggest some level of choice," the man grunted. "But enough about me. Your objective, breaking into the Old City, it can't be done, you may as well be asking me to break into Arcadia without a ship, it's impossible."

"And here I thought an Elite would define what's possible and what isn't. And you know as well as I do my people have devolved over the years, we've merged with humanity completely, that skill is all but a myth now."

"Well, this isn't possible. What's your interest in this, anyway? Why learn the deep, forbidden secret of the Collapse, what's it to you?"

"Because it would explain everything the conglomerate has done," Cait sighed, sitting back in her chair, hearing a creak from one of the rear legs that gave her pause. "I grew up on Sanguine, in the RCS factory there, not even half the size of the one in this city."

"I know, I can see that," the man said, nodding at Cait's right wrist, where on the inside was her brand, the initials of the company within a box, burned onto the skin to serve as a reminder of her obligation.

"Yeah," Cait said, nonchalantly stroking the scorched skin. "I was eighteen when the Collapse happened, it seemed so far away, a world away literally, but even on my backwoods installation, we felt its shockwaves. People started to question what they were doing, what they were working towards and eventually they had enough, they dropped their tools and came together in the square at the centre of the factory, to sit down, refusing to work until they could talk about getting some basic improvements. The sheer amount of people that died or were locked away forever when Rose City closed itself off, it just seemed to frustrate people that they didn't know why. Sure, the conglomerate said it was some group of WIDOWs out of the nearby town—"

"Bullshit," the man grumbled, crossing his arms and leaning back, but looking at Cait, patiently listening.

"Yeah, no one believed the lie, it just didn't make sense. Some sabotage to the nuclear reactor in the city was I think the company line, but anyway, people couldn't take it that they were expected to carry on as normal so a whole group of them came together in this square, and not just a few, there was a fair amount, maybe thirty? Forty? I don't know. But they all sat down and refused to work until some kind of conversation could happen, and all they wanted was to know what happened, and to improve their housing which was little more than a shanty town, to increase their access to clean drinking water, safer conditions, you know, pretty reasonable requests." Cait shrugged and then her eyes fell to the floor as she realised the next part of the story she was telling. "Well, my dad was one of this group, he was one of the main organisers."

"I can see where this is going," the man sighed, taking a draw from his cigar, Cait seeing the reflection of the embers of it in the pupils of his eyes.

"I mean they didn't use any kind of violence, they just sat down and wanted a chat, but the RCS management wouldn't have it. There were closed doors discussions straight away right as I saw my dad and the others sit out their work. I was finishing off a robo-sentry's torso plating, connecting it to the chassis when I saw them. I went to join them but my mum stopped me. My dad was X-Human, same as many of the workers that sat out their shift, but my mum was human, along with the majority that just watched. And that bothered me, I remember seeing the signs of what was to come, but powerless to do anything about it. I remember people talking all around me, the panic about production halting, how their quota couldn't be met now, how the contribution to the Board was being hurt by the second. And that's when it happened. Turns out there has to be a certain number of people to qualify as a peaceful protest, otherwise, if they refuse to work, then they are deviating from orders, they are WIDOWs and subject to immediate disciplinary action."

"Yeah," the man knew what she was going to say next, but his voice was flat, difficult to read to see if he cared or not.

"They brought in a squad of Stalwart Ironworks enforcers to back-up the Obsidian guards, and surrounded the people in the square, and shot them, killed them all."

"Standard procedure, cold bastards," the man said in response.

"Yep, I asked my mum about it afterwards, why she didn't let me join my dad, and she said that she knew what was coming, she stopped loads of workers from joining, what would have been enough to qualify, because she said it was essential. She said that the Collapse meant more than the initial loss of life that happened, she said it could lead to something far worse, that if we didn't keep up our contribution to the Board then we would be deemed as unprofitable."

"To be unprofitable is to be a cost, and costs must be eliminated," the man recited.

"Exactly. People might say that she was so afraid of everyone dying that she was willing to sacrifice a smaller group but I don't believe that. She always followed the company line, and I don't think she liked that my dad was questioning the word of the Section Chief, showing disloyalty. She basically killed him herself. All because of the Capital Collapse. She changed because of it, everyone did. And I want to know why. I need to know what caused my whole life to change. What tore apart my family."

"How'd you end up where you are now?"

"I ran away from home, away from the factory, my feet bringing me to a docks town, where they brought in new workers and transferred others to the other worlds, and I bumped into who I thought was a Stalwart enforcer. But this man had left his company, the way I'd left mine and he took me under his wing, he taught me to survive, he gave me a home, he gave me a second chance at a family."

"And now you want to risk it all for this vault, that doesn't even exist?" The mocking tone was obvious.

"Yeah I do, I believe it does exist, and I think you're the one who's incredibly naive if you think you knew of every facility in the Old City."

"Fair," the man shrugged.

"And I'm not a coward."

"Hmm?" The grunt was a mix of confusion and aggression.

"You speak of honing your skills, you boast of your experience, and yet what you actually doing with them? You needlessly threaten the innocent woman behind the bar as a playful attempt to try to intimidate me, when you should be realising what's right in front of you."

"And what's that?"

"I'm unarmed, unaware, and I don't care. I will get the landing key off the Old City's Captain myself, if I have to punch every soul between me and him to do it. I will wade through any threat in the city to find this thing, whatever it is and I am willing to take on anybody that tries to stop me. I will use what I find to spark a resistance, to inspire people to take up arms against the conglomerate, to kill those who keep us under their boot, I just don't care! I'm willing to do whatever it takes to build something better than simply surviving. And yet here you are, armed to the teeth, incredibly impressed with yourself, and you're not even willing to try. You're a coward."

"Who said I haven't been taking the fight to the conglomerate already?" The man said coolly.

"Well, whatever you're doing, clearly it isn't enough. It's small-time, it's safe. Yeah I've heard about the management deaths on this planet, you're saying that's you? OK, but who cares. Maybe you pick off one at a time, and maybe you cause some small disruption, but what does it really achieve? Seriously? Other than satisfying your ego."

"Careful, girl," the man casually reached back and Cait saw him pull out a rifle that he then lent against the edge of the table. It was a long black shape, with a brown leather pouch bound about the stock with huge bullets slotted into it.

"Girl? What? Another flaccid attempt to intimidate me? You'll have to do better than that, I've been hunted for half a decade now, demeaning me doesn't even register, dickhead." Cait leaned forward, shifting her right leg closer to the man, invading his personal space on purpose. "Now I came here expecting a real tough fella. I thought you'd be this super-imposing spectre of a man, one to strike fear as soon as you look at him, but you're just another WIDOW, skulking in the dark, doing whatever it takes to survive, and usual it's whatever means keeping your head down and safe. Such a disappointment."

"You don't know a thing about me," the man leaned forward in kind, their faces close together now, but his eyes glanced over to the Obsidian group in between meeting her gaze.

"Then impress me," Cait said with a wink. She could see his face properly now and could tell that he was only a couple of years older than herself, where she had expected to be meeting someone older than Tomen, someone of real experience. She stood up from her seat and stroked the other man's beard with her right hand, seeing Lena do this to trap a man's attention, before giving him a playful light slap. The look of bewilderment on the man's face almost made her laugh but she did her best to keep up the image of a strong, idealistic figure. She went to walk away before spinning on the spot. "The name's Cait Jxinn and my ship is docked up the hill. Figure yourself for something more than the shadow of your ego, come up and look for the Stalwart freighter, you'll know which one, soon as you lay eyes on it. I really do hope you'll rise to the occasion Mr Winter, or keep picking them off one by one, whatever suits your leisure, but just remember something for me."

"What?"

"There's always more where they came from, and there are so many of them, you'll never make a dent going through them one at a time," Cait ignored the thought of caution slipping into her mind, that she might be teasing a serial killer. "Come with us though, and you'll really cause some damage."

"I'll think about it, but consider me intrigued," the man grunted, looking past Cait at the Obsidian party that was rising out of their seats, even more rowdy, grabbing at a waitress.

Cait left it at that, she was surprised at herself, stealing some of Lena's moves but her instincts told her that they would work, and as she walked away towards the bar, she somehow knew that the man was watching her, rather than the group he was so interested in. Miles' look made her confidence shake as his face was fuelled by fear and he looked ready to run.

"What's wrong?" Cait asked and noticed that the bartender was gone.

"We're leaving now, we're in danger here, we don't want to get caught in a crossfire," was all Miles said as he grabbed Cait's arm, hard and almost pulled her towards the door.

"Miles, take it easy, those Obsidian officers are staring at us, you're drawing too much attention," Cait hastily whispered into her friend's ear as she peered over his shoulder, seeing the four in the black and red suits take notice of their speedy exit.

"It won't matter, they're already dead," Miles replied, hitting the exit button and the doors opened for them to leave. Cait shot a last glance over her shoulder and noticed the man she had been speaking to had stood up and stepped out of the gloom, his helmet on, and he held his sword hilt in hand but before she could see what happened next, the doors closed.

"What you on about? You're lucky I finished in there, why are you dragging me out there for?" Cait beat off her friend's grip but carried on walking at his side, having to nearly jog to keep up.

"Your new friend is not all he seems, the bartender told me. He's playing the part of some kind of detective, to cover up what he's really doing, he's hunting management," Miles said, hardly keeping his head still, checking the various alleys and windows that looked out on the main street they were walking down. Then he pulled out his laser pistol. A gun with a long dark grey barrel and a brown leather grip, with a glowing green cartridge at the top of the chamber, standard Stalwart issue.

"You can't take that out openly, Miles, you know that! If any Obsidian patrols see us, they'll kill us! Besides, I know he is, he pretty much admitted it, why do we care?" Cait didn't understand her friend's fretting, and was wary of him carrying a readied gun out in the open.

"Because he isn't some low life shanking people in the night, he is a serial killer. He hangs his victims upside down and takes an eye, and they're the ones he lets off easy and allows their bodies to be found! There's officially been over fifty deaths attributed to this killer but the lady back there told me true, he's killed far more, disposing of their bodies into the canyons. He's slaughtered entire brigades with his officer's sword!"

"That's impossible! He may be a good fighter but you're talking about this one man wiping out small armies, that's taking it a little far, don't you think?"

"No, I don't. I'm getting us out of here, he's too dangerous!" Miles carried on going in the same direction they had come from to get to the bar but turned around and aimed his weapon back at the establishment, just as the screams began to erupt.

"What is that?" Cait stopped in her tracks, staring back at the bar where the loud howl of excruciating pain had come from. "It didn't sound human," she muttered to herself.

"Welcome to what real agony sounds like," Miles replied grimly, his usual wit and charm faded away.

"They must have heard the shouts, look," Cait said, pointing back in the bar's direction as a squad of Obsidian troopers descended on the building, kicking the door open, swarming inside, automatic gunfire echoing up the street to where the two X-Humans stood frozen, watching. And then more screams drowned out the loud bangs and shockwaves made by the ballistic and energised weapons used against their adversary.

One thunderous howl of pain rolled the length of the road to where Cait and Miles stood and they felt their legs lose all strength, all they could do was stare as the flashes of gunfire stopped abruptly.

"We need to go," Cait muttered, her right hand reaching out instinctively for her friend, clutching his green jacket but before she could turn to go, the ground beneath them shook, resonating from the bar they seemed to have left just in time. They struggled to maintain their balance with wide-eyed stares to one another before finally sprinting with all of their energy towards the docks. The lights that washed the hill in a white light shone above the rooftops of the city, only just about visible through the veil of the smog. "No! Please, no!" Was a shout so loud as to be clearly heard from the distance they were at, but it was swiftly cut out by a sound like lightning crashing down with a fury of a deity? The two X-Humans doing their best to create as much distance between them and that sound as possible.

The run was hard as they struggled relentlessly to remember the way back to their ship, shouting to each other if one went the wrong way, yelling encouragement to one another to speed up, for fear of being caught in the carnage left in their wake. They did eventually find the road at the base of the hill, dodging the enormous trucks bearing goods from this city to the next, tyres as tall as them, all the while deafened by the blast of the train over their heads. Bolts of electricity cast off from the tracks as the two X-Humans found themselves clambering up the face of the mound, sweat streaming down their faces from the humidity. The dirt of the track gave way to the solid concrete of the shipyard and they pressed on until they reached the rear ramp of their ship, taking a last look out on the city of Renn, just as one last scream erupted from within the sprawling cityscape.

Nathan had watched the woman leave, finding himself completely bewildered by her, never before had he been so openly insulted by someone who he found immensely interesting, and he came to the conclusion that her proposition was worthy of further thought. But he had something he wanted to do first, and with his prey about to leave, the time was now. He squashed his cigar in the ashtray before standing up, grasping his helmet with both hands and placing it on his head for which it was perfectly suited, taking a deep breath in relief at being his full self again. His right hand went to his blade automatically, knowing it was what he intended, and he pulled out the hilt. Nathan observed the metal plates condensed together that sat at the top of the hilt within his grasp before using a swift flick of the wrist to have them slide apart into a full length sword. A simple use of his thumb and index finger of his right hand in reaching above the prongs of metal acting as the blade guard, he pulled them down, unleashing the weapon's power. Rotations of immense white energy shot up the length of the blade, pure, bright lightning dancing across the weapon's edge; it had a deep drone to it as it resonated with power.

This caught the attention of the four Obsidian officers, all dressed in the black suits of their station, red zips from the hip to the cross shoulder all open in the drunken, clumsy state, all except the eldest of the group. They were standing beside the booth they had used all night, one of them wrestling with a waitress in a grey top and short skirt which the man was trying to put his hand up. Her long blonde hair flicked into the man's face so that he was the last to see the one brandishing the terrifying weapon approach his group. She was young, could not have been out of her teenage years and she fought fiercely to wrestle out of the Obsidian's man's hold over her. This one had shabby dirty blonde hair and a smile that showed his missing teeth and may have been related to the one that had sat on the same side of the booth as him, only this one was younger and his hair reached down to his shoulders, but otherwise their faces were very similar. Across from them was a man with fluffy black hair and stern X-Human eyes of a shade of yellow, mouth agape with the menacing figure standing before him, paying no mind to the squabbling between the girl and one of his peers. While the one behind him was older than the other three, seeming far more sober than the rest for the caution in his eyes, recognising the weapon wielded against him.

"That's enough, Herving," the eldest of them said, to the one entertaining himself with the waitress, who was then alerted to the armoured figure standing before them, and gripped the waitress in a far different fashion, posing her as a shield.

"Stand down Elite, or I'll ring her bloody neck!" The drunken fool shouted.

"Shut up, don't you realise who this is?" The X-Human of the group said shoving the other man but the waitress was still held in a firm grip between the officer and Nathan.

"I'm not sure that you do," Nathan grunted, plunging his sword through the heart of the waitress, puncturing the chest of the man behind her, at the same time as smashing left fist into the X-Human's head, dragging it down on the table of the booth. The woman screamed in pain, as did the man behind her, until Nathan pulled out his blade, bringing it around back-handedly to decapitate them both. In the same motion, he brought his weapon crashing down, the X-Human with his head pinned to the table, seeing the executing swing coming, let out a booming wail before the sword met wood and his head rolled away. Then Nathan took a step back, savouring the moment, relishing in the look of terror on the faces of his remaining two victims, as the door to the bar came crashing open.

If the Obsidian patrol hoped to annihilate him with the element of surprise, it didn't work. Nathan reacted immediately, putting his left side forward, raising a clenched fist with a purple crystal embedded in the back of the glove illuminating an energy shield that covered his whole body. It absorbed the barrage of bullets and lasers from the troopers in the black armour and helmets with the red visors, leaving its bearer completely unharmed. And once they were all inside the bar, Nathan struck back. The jetpack attached to his back cast him forward, controlled by his helmet picking up the instructions from his brain waves, and he cut down two soldiers immediately with his sword, their cries of pain breaching the confines of the building. They rallied rifles, shotguns, pistols against him but none could make a dent in his armour, let alone punch through so did their best, but were ultimately slaughtered by the superior force.

Nathan carved through them with ease, slicing off limbs, using his shield to deflect heavier shots, letting loose an ocean of screams and shrieks of agony until he saw a second Obsidian team enter from behind the bar. He slashed at one guard far to his right, connecting with a powerful slice as he swung down low, spinning to avoid a shotgun that was aimed at him not a metre away from his face, and he grabbed the man by his leg. With his left arm, Nathan picked up the soldier, tossing him up into the air and catching him again, gripping his chest plate before leaning his fist into him and igniting the shield with a thought. Splinters of bone, a tidal wave of blood, shoots of intestine sprayed out at the onrushing second Obsidian force, blinding them and forcing them to seek cover. This gave Nathan the split-second he needed to flick up the cover of the screen mounted to the right forearm of armour and with a wink he targeted the cluster of guards, and a simple tap of the screen fired off a volley of small rockets from a mounted launcher behind his left shoulder. The ground quaked under the force of the arsenal arrayed against the Obsidian soldiers that were utterly blown apart, the shrapnel of the barrage tearing apart with a crimson mist dispersed into air, spatters of blood on every surface in the bar.

The only two Obsidian left standing were the older officer and his younger attending, both paralysed by fear in doing their best to hide under the booth table for cover. Nathan stood over them, his black armour caked in blood which he dripped all over the table surface when he snatched a grip of the younger of the two, dragging him out into the open space. The grey wooden tables and chairs that had once made up the seating area of this bar were splintered and rendered into pieces, cast to the far sides of the room, and the strained carpet was recovering the red colour it once had from the flooding of blood. The Elite stood in the middle of the floor, a head of blonde hair in the grasp of his left hand, his blade in his right, and the pitiless dark grey eyes of his helmet were fixed on the older officer.

"Did I spoil your evening's entertainment?" Nathan said, his deep and saturated in a cruel sadism, with a spark of violent glee.

"You've got me, Commander. Please, he's just a boy, let him go," the older man cried while doing his best to keep his composure. He had short, greying hair and glasses over his human blue eyes overflowing with dread. "Let him go, I'm begging you."

Nathan stamped down on the leg of the young officer, so hard that the bone splintered and a shard burst out of the other side as he crumpled to the floor, his head held up by his hair still in a vice-like grip. The Elite paid no mind to the whimpering of his prey, and brought his blade across so that it was held just a breath away from the young man's throat, the energy from it being so hot that it produced a burn after merely a moment. Then he sliced the neck open, producing a flowing river of blood falling to the floor, and the older man scrambled over, tripping over the body of his X-Human assistant, to slump at Nathan's feet. "No! Please, no!" He wailed and the Elite flung the young man's body forward so it fell onto his superior officer.

Nathan turned at the same time. Enjoying himself, he deactivated the energy flow of his sword before retracting the length, and holstering the hilt. "As if I would just let him go," he teased, beginning to pull out a cord from his belt as he eyed the ceiling light, assessing the weight it could handle.

"He was so young though," the officer wept.

"Then you should never have included him in your sick hobby. Those schools only house those children because they have no families to live with, most of them because the parents died following the instructions of corrupt management like you." Nathan judged the chains holding the main light fixture over the centre of the seating area to be the most secure so he extended out a length long enough of his cord and flung the end over it, catching it and laying it on the bar.

"They're worthless, though, we…we are officers, you just killed a young man with a promising future!" The old man spat, still cradling the carcass of his colleague.

"They are children, and you raped them. Ones with no families to console them, and you abused them. The most alone people in the system, and you somehow made them even more alone," Nathan scorned, taking the extension of the cord out to a length he deemed right and removing the knife on his arm, cutting the end. This loose end he tied around the old man's left ankle, he didn't resist at all, accepting that he was overpowered. With their heads so close that Nathan could smell the spirits on the old man's breath, he gripped the officer's throat tight, "you make me sick." Then he walked over to the other end of the cord that he left on the bar and yanked it hard, dragging the old man through the puddles of blood on the carpet which seemed to wake him from his grief and he began trying to untangle the end tied to his ankle. But he couldn't even loosen it before he was dangling upside down, his grip on the cord lost having hit his head when his body was pulled up above him.

"Is this it?" The old man grumbled, his head level with Nathan's chest once he had tied the loose end to the railing at the foot of the bar, securing the old man in hanging upside down.

"No." Was all Nathan said, taking out his knife again, admiring the shine on the blade. This was a combat knife, a basic grip of black leather on a silver handle with a serrated blade that he then slowly drew the tip of to the corner of the old man's left eye with his right hand. With his left, Nathan gripped the officer's head so the next part came easier. Carefully he drove the tip in and cut around the eyeball, all the while the officer screamed and attempted to thrash about but with his body upside down, he was powerless against the stronger man. It didn't take long for Nathan to pop the eye out and he caught it with his left hand, severing the optic nerve that kept it attached to the other man's head with his knife. Once the eye was removed, the old man stopped screaming and Nathan left him suspended for a moment, turning around and retrieving a shot glass from atop the bar, unscathed in the battle as he sheathed his knife. He placed the eye on the opening, sitting on the rim, as he retrieved a clear, composite cube from a pouch at his belt along with a tube with a form of crystalline gel. Nathan poured the gel into the cube that filled it to just below the brim before dropping the eyeball inside, pushing it into the centre with a thumb then closing the cube by flicking up the roof that had been pressed against one of the sides, attached at one of the corners and clicked it in to lock it.

"Now, we are done," Nathan announced, placing the cube in his belt at the same time as drawing the pistol from the holster at his chest. He pulled back the chamber, loading a round into it, and flicked off the safety before placing the end of the barrel to the old man's head that was lazily swaying in a circle. This was a ballistic weapon, black from handle to barrel, the chamber with a rounded roof running along the edge and the letters N.W. etched on the side.

"Why me? There are so many others like me!" The old man cried, his tears flowing over his forehead and onto the floor where his glasses fell to. The Elite Commander didn't care for the pleas and he pulled the trigger of his weapon, a loud, echoing bang leaving a gaping hole in the other man's skull. The shot rang out through the bar and beyond and Nathan lowered his gun, reengaging the safety before holstering it again, all he did while distracted, his mind dwelling on his victim's final words.

This kill did not feel like the others. No rush of euphoria, no sense of satisfaction. It was not enough anymore, this didn't feel like an accomplishment. He had been reminded of the grander region than his small world, of the larger enemy that stood against him rather than the singular victims he dispatched with ease. Nathan prodded the head of his latest victim, watching him sway, bored by him. He wasn't challenging himself here, he wasn't making an iota of difference and he wasn't being brave. Nathan found himself nodding and smiling to himself then shaking his head as he took out another cigar with left hand at the same time as removing his knife with his right. He sliced off the end, sheathed the blade then took out a lighter from the same container, lighting the thick cigar as he bit it between his teeth, taking a long draw as he stowed the lighter. He patted his victim's head with his left hand, taking the cigar out of his mouth with his right, then Nathan pushed so the body swayed even more but he found the whole thing simply tiring, his interest elsewhere. "She has a point," he admitted to the silent room.

Chapter 5

"Woah, hold it right there, friend," Tomen shouted, aiming his gun at the man walking up the ramp of his ship. "Make a move and we'll fill your armour so full of holes that when we're done with you, we'll string you up and use you for a cheese grater. Now, stop!"

"Tasty threat, now I'm hungry," Nathan quipped from behind his helmet, not hesitating as he travelled up the ramp to slap a hand on the other man at the top as he passed. "Besides, stringing people up is more my thing." The one in Elite armour carried on walking and entered the cargo area, looking all around, taking in the interior of the ship that he was correctly told would be easy to find. His rifle was strapped onto his back, his hands free of bearing any of his vast arsenal on his person, as unthreatening as he could make himself appear to be.

"I'm guessing you're the Elite Commander, though it don't give you the right to just step foot on my ship without my say-so," Tomen kept his energised pistol, the same as Miles', aimed steady at Nathan's helmet who didn't seem to be bothered by it.

"I was invited," was all Nathan said in response, and after having taken in the view of the empty vessel, fixed his stare on the man dressed as a Stalwart enforcer, aiming a weapon at him. "The woman, Cait, had a friend dressed like you at the bar, I surely do hope this isn't some WIDOW trap that I've wandered into, it wouldn't end well for you."

Tomen's confidence was shaken by how calm this man was, completely ignoring the gun trained on him so far as to make threats. "It's no trap, but one can't be too careful these days," he lowered his gun, but remained ready to rear it up at the first inclination of danger.

"True, but that little thing wouldn't even scar this metal, you'd be better off using it as a club—not that it would be more effective, it would just be more amusing," Nathan casually rested his hand on the hilt of his blade so as to not attract attention to it. "Now, where's Cait?"

"Knew you'd be a dangerous sort, knew that's why we came here lookin' for you. But Miles described to me what he saw out there, and perhaps you're too dangerous to be near those under my protection." Tomen put all his effort into sounding as confident in his abilities as his words suggested he was, knowing that if this was to turn into a fight, that it could very well be his last. He kept his gun lowered, however, giving the other man a chance to state his case.

"I don't answer to you, I came here to follow up a conversation with someone, and you are not that person. You're slowing me down, time of my life that I'm never getting back. So what's it to be?" The Elite tightened his grip on his sword hilt and slightly bent his knees after turning side on to the other man. He remained steady with thoughts, careful to not set off his jetpack too soon, knowing it would not do to kill a member of a group he was opening the door to befriending, unless the choice was made for him.

"The fuck are you?" Lena asked, passing through the middle of the two men as if completely immune to the tension between them. She had her red hair tied back dead straight and wore a red trench coat over a tight black low-crop top matched with a short skirt of the same colour, and long socks drawn up over the knee, black as well, and red high heel leather shoes. She looked at the stranger, clad all in a dark metal and stopped once she had passed him, "you Cait's new toy?"

"Never refer to me as that again," Nathan replied sternly in a cold, steady voice and only realised after that taking that tone was the cause of the smile growing on the woman's face.

"Sure thing, ya adorable little beastie. Well, I'm Lena. Come along, she's upstairs," Lena beckoned with a lazy hand ushering the armed to the teeth Elite Commander to follow her.

Nathan shot a glance over at the other man, and Tomen, sensing the confusion hidden behind that intimidating helmet, just rolled his eyes and nodded in the direction of the stairs that Lena was already halfway up. "I'm Nathan, by the way," the Elite introduced himself.

"Yeah I gathered, the name's Tomen, I'd normally say I'm Captain of this rig, nothing happens here without my word, but that one just does as she pleases," the one in Stalwart armour resigned himself to following with a sigh, holstering his weapon.

"Getting that impression," Nathan remarked as the two men ascended the steps to the common area.

Miles was standing by the kitchen cupboards, taking in a shot of vodka to settle his nerves when he saw Lena step up to the dining area, and he gave a nod, but then he saw the armoured man behind her, and almost dropped his drink.

"Steady, Miles," Tomen said, coming up the stairs and shaking his head when his partner gestured with a tilt of the head whether he should be reaching for his weapon.

"How you doing?" The fiery-eyed X-Human nodded at Nathan as he passed, then poured himself more vodka as the only response he got was a silent stare.

"So here I am, Cait," Nathan announced, waving a hand at the vacant seat at the head of the table on the stairs end.

"Go ahead," the X-Human with the amethyst eyes was sitting at the opposite seat, accepting that the man may take the one he indicated. At her left, on the kitchen side, Lena took up a chair, and opposite and one chair down, Sam sat, with Miles next to him. Tomen chose to lean up against the kitchen cupboards, Azuri coming in from the cockpit to stand at his side. "I'm glad you came, what swayed you in the end?" Cait asked, wary that this man before them had just slaughtered an entire Obsidian patrol, most likely on impulse in actually targeting the four officers she and Miles had seen.

"I'm considering that I need to up my game, up the stakes, and I have my own reasons for being curious about the true cause of the Collapse," Nathan replied, settling his rifle to lean up against the table. He removed his helmet and placed it down on the table, facing away from him, before running his hand through his hair to straighten it.

"Well, whatever those reasons are, glad to have you aboard, I'm assuming the next step is to discuss your payment?" Cait asked with a sideways glance at Tomen. She had been comfortable back in the bar, confident even at being the one to pitch this venture, but now she was in a negotiating position, she wanted the de facto leader to assume his position. Yet her instincts told to refrain from asking, sensing that Nathan was the type to want to speak only with the one who had invited him.

"Not just yet, I'm getting the sense that you lot are the seizing what's directly in front of you types," Nathan said, analysing each of the people before him in turn. "So what's your plan for after you achieve your objective?"

"First we have to get the landing key, then get inside the city, then get to this vault, then get inside it—there's a lot to do before we get to that point," Tomen put in, his arms crossed as he studied the other man carefully.

"Yes but it is a rather important thing to consider. Once that secret is snatched up, all of Obsidian will be on us, so what is your plan for that?" Nathan pressed, sensing that he already knew the answer.

A short silence descended on the room and Nathan was beginning to doubt the credibility of those he was to throw in with, until the loud X-Human with the cherry red hair spoke up again, "well, what do you propose? Mr…I don't remember your name," Lena asked.

"Nathan Winter, and I am impressed that you thought to ask, you lot had me worried, glad there is some sense in one of you at least," he said, meaning the insult. "Diving in armed only with good intentions and wishful thinking will simply get us all killed. I can send word to a friend I have in the Sapphire conglomerate, there's a chance she will help us. Also, I'd suggest broadcasting the data before we leave any facility it might be housed in."

"Why broadcast it? We'll be attracting attention enough opening the docks of the Old City, we don't want any more, surely," Sam added, confused. "I'm Sam, by the way."

"OK Sam, we send out the data because that way we won't be the only ones knowing the secret, it'll be out and our job will be finished, no matter if we extract the full data stream on a hardcopy or not," Nathan replied more diplomatically than he had been in years.

"And this friend of yours in the Sapphire, who is she?" Cait asked, impressed with how things were going.

"Molly Monroe, she commands the Guardian Guild, their version of the Elites from their version of Obsidian, Azurite. She was my wife's sister," Nathan replied.

"Was your wife?" Tomen asked, picking up on the other man's words.

"I said I had my reasons," Nathan replied, not impolitely, but stern to waver any attempt to probe the question any further.

"Why would she help us? I don't want to stave off one corrupt conglomerate only to be beaten down by the next," Cait flopped back in her chair, realising how high the stakes were in the game she had sat all of her friends at.

"For the same reason as I am sat at this table," his tone was dismissive. He answered the question but clearly had no desire to discuss the matter further. "So we get into the city, seek out and attain the prize, broadcast a form of it so the whole system knows, OK, what's next?" Nathan moved on with the conversation.

"Once we have it, we were told that Obsidian could splinter, that it could rupture their strength, what do you think?" Miles asked, with an inkling that the man before them would have a more accurate sense of things.

"Impossible to say, but it may only be a flash conflict, not something we can rely on as a sure next step, more as a confident distraction for seeing us get off Ruby with our prize," Nathan nodded, considering the prospect. "Obsidian is not some evil, faceless army, it's made up of real men and women, each with their minds but taught to conform with a brutality like nothing any of you could ever imagine. There will be some questioning the Collapse, doubting the hierarchy but we'll just have to wait and see what their reaction is."

"And what about your payment, Winter?" Cait asked, impatient for the subject, curious.

"While I'll be protecting all of you in the Capital, I'm assuming you'll be watching my back too. I'm a solid fighter but no matter how good one is, they can always be overwhelmed, so once we're inside the Capital, I'm going to need your help. I settled on it for lost, but this is an opportunity to get it back I won't pass up," Nathan said, looking directly at Cait.

"What do you want?"

"You know I was the Elite Commander, stationed in Rose City. I held an office in the Directorate's District of the city where I left a holo-diary, not your concern what's on it, but I couldn't get to it during the Collapse, and seeing as we are heading into the city, that is my payment. No money needed, nor a debt owed, only this."

"Alright, seems a little light, I was expecting money or something, but if that's what you want, consider it a deal," Cait nodded.

"So what we're saying is that once we have this secret, whatever it may be, a data-pack we're just assuming, that we have no idea for what comes next? That we're just going to have to take it as it comes? Wait and see? That's not a plan, guys," Azuri summarised, doubt clouding her voice.

"Whatever succeeded with a full and thorough plan, carried out completely to spec?" Tomen asked the group. "Nothing we ever did, surely. We done our fair bit, causing our little, minor nuisances but this here is our opportunity to do something really damaging, something worthwhile, we may never get a shot like this again."

"Then let's take it," Nathan agreed, looking over at Cait, the woman who had strung him along so well that he was now stepping out of the shadows he had called home for nigh a decade.

"So glad to have you with us!" Sam exclaimed sarcastically in a cheer, standing up and walking over to Nathan's chair, shaking the man's hand with a mocking grin.

"So our first stop? Scarlet, was it?" Azuri asked, looking to Tomen.

"We need the landing key, and the Captain's employee passcode, we get neither and we're finished before we've even started," the ship's leader announced as Sam strolled away from Nathan, over to pour himself a drink, a bottle of whiskey pulled out from a top cupboard.

"You meant to be some kind of thief?" Nathan asked, giving Sam a sideways glance.

"Alright, Scarlet's a short hop, skip and a jump from here, I'll set the gates," Azuri replied to Tomen at the same time.

"I'm a check for a nice hat, keep the glow of that damned star off my face, you coming sweetie? Think this meeting has adjourned," Lena took Cait's hand in hers as she stood up, making to leave while the others had their own private conversations.

"Yeah I've been known to have a talent for picking a pocket, a lock, lifting an item, getting into places I'm not meant to be, why?" Sam laughed confidently, lifting a small metal device in one hand for Nathan to see.

"Your technique is sloppy," Nathan replied with cold disinterest.

"What is this thing anyway?" Sam asked, turning the shape over in his hands.

"Restraint grenade," the Elite said, tapping a button on the screen at his right forearm and the small metal tab in Sam's hands came alive and tasered the man where he stood, electrocuting him into fits on the floor, before it shot out and clasped his wrists in handcuffs. Nathan got up and strode over to the man knocked out on the floor, his group either shocked by the display, or laughing, and he gave the thief a tap with his toe. "What? You didn't think I saw punks like you in the Capital?"

"You ready to leave, Winter?" Tomen asked him, smiling at the Elite's handiwork, enjoying the trick.

"I'm good to go but this ship isn't. It's quaint, it's nice, but useless should we get Obsidian or Stalwart interfering in our affairs, so we'll take mine."

"Yours?" Azuri asked.

"Elite starfighter, and don't worry there's enough room for all of your team."

Tomen agreed, not wishing to risk the only place he could call home for his tight knit group, and organised for his team to pack up any essentials to move across the shipyard to where Nathan said his own craft was parked. A crate of food and bottled water, some spare clothes, the team packed only what they could carry between them, being sure to take any weapons and armour with them for the task ahead. The two Stalwart enforcers strapped their rifles to their backs, kin to the pistols at their holsters, these held glowing green ammunition atop wooden stocks with telescopic sights. They also donned their helmets, light grey helms that covered their entire heads with white ovals for the eyes, as they carried boxes over to the Elite starfighter.

Nathan walked with Tomen and Miles, taking them to his ship, passing by the wide variety of docked freighters and ships, to his own craft at the far end. The lamps that ran a ring around the docks fought off the gloom of the night and fog, while they also dotted out paths between the landing pads so that the group could see where they were going. And the two former Stalwart men stopped when they laid eyes on the craft they would be using.

It was completely jet black and of a modest size, with a wing either side of a main hull where a cockpit was at the front with red-tinted glass stretching high, wide and low, giving the pilot an immense view of their surroundings. A great engine hung off either wing beside colossal cannons that were identical to the ones protruding from the nose of the craft, attached to the frame that supported the cockpit screens. Beneath the ship, attached to the belly, was a thinner cannon with rings of glowing red energy along its length. A giant gun was mounted either side of the fuselage behind the cockpit, eleven small barrels banded together that seemed to have its own section of framing so that they could be manoeuvred around. There was a ramp at the rear that lowered down at Nathan's command by use of the screen attached at his right arm, and led to the ship's interior. It was a small entry space that welcomed the three first with two automatic doors opposite the entrance, exit of the ship, with a ladder up to the next level in the middle of them.

"Put those down anywhere you like, here," Nathan waved a hand so that Tomen and Miles could put down the greyish metal boxes they were carrying. "The door on the left here leads to my bedroom, via the armoury, and the right houses the medico-table, shower and bog, it doubles up as a storage area. The ladder leads to the transport tunnel, seats lining either side of the ship's hull where the central path leads through to a set of double doors that open up to the cockpit. The equipment either side of those doors operates the turrets on the outside of the ship, screens will illuminate once the mounts are activated, they project the view the barrels have of the area outside the ship. I haven't had anyone aboard for probably half a decade now, feels strange to be giving out a tour. You two want to see the cockpit before the others arrive with the rest of your gear?" Nathan offered, and he was honest about how he felt, he was truly out of practice talking to people that he had no real desire to kill.

"Yeah go on, the girls will be almost finished, we're more waiting on Sam to wake up I suspect," Miles laughed, looking over to his friend.

"Lead the way, mate, we've got time to kill," Tomen nodded, and the three headed up the ladder making their way through the line of red cushioned leather seats through the doors at the end to arrive in the cockpit.

The floor they had travelled on to get to this room was simple black metal plating but here it ran for only a few metres more until it was met by the base of the cockpit screen that also acted as the walls at either side stretching back from the foreground to the doors they had just entered from, and as the roof over their heads. To their right was a console mounted to the wall with four screens detailing the ship's status for fuel, armour integrity, ammunition levels, oxygen quality, and everything else to monitor its condition. Opposite was another just like it, this one with a description and mapping of Vermilion, with controls for setting a course to other worlds. Chairs of the same red material as those in the transport tunnel were mounted to the cockpit floor in front of these consoles, the same as two that acted as the pilot's seat on the right side of the entrance, and the co-pilot's next to it. In front of the pilot position was the console bearing the controls for flying the ship, a break in between as this chair was elevated and with handles and pedals for manoeuvring the craft in all directions. This console stretched across the ship's front so the co-pilot had control of the weapons systems. In between the two chairs, this panel carried on in a T-shape, allowing both pilots access to the communications systems that operated the screen standing up between them, facing inward from the front of the cockpit. In the room's centre was a circular instrument standing on a platform that brought it up to waist level, the controls for this at the side.

"So this is where the magic happens. The artificial gravity for this ship is still state-of-the-art, ten years after its installation, and the weapons systems hold up as well," Nathan spun round and took the pilot's seat for himself, waving a hand to the two seats either side of the circular console for his two guests to sit. He removed his helmet and placed his rifle down, leaning it up against the console beside him.

"Quite the set-up you have here," Miles said with a grin, taking in the view of the screens on his side, the navigation maps and details of the planet they found themselves on.

"The idea was that an Elite's equipment must be able to keep up with its user, this was all the peak that RCS had to offer, back in the day. Suppose it still could be, plus I've made some modifications," Nathan stroked the panel that ran between the two pilot chairs.

"Seen a lot of action in this rig?" Tomen asked, noticing how the other man seemed to be reminiscing.

"Could say that," Nathan replied, returning to the present. "Guessing you two have seen your fair share of violence. How did you come to leave Stalwart Ironworks?"

Tomen removed his helmet first, placing it on the side, and Miles, seeing this, copied in kind and took his off. "We were on Sanguine together, in a small town away from the main metropolis on the planet, on the other hemisphere to the RCS factory, the central interest for the conglomerate in the world. No, our tiny settlement was where the workers for a Crimson Sun farmstead lived, Miles and I being a part of the Stalwart protection and enforcement that kept those colleagues producing for the conglomerate. They grew the food, we stopped them getting shot or abducted by the wild, psycho freaks that holed up in the caves deep in the forests, and for a while, yeah, things were calm and smooth. But, well, you ever make your way over to Sanguine?"

"Once or twice during my Obsidian days, not that it stands out in the memory," Nathan admitted.

"It's cold, snowy most of the time, which makes it difficult for the crops to grow, so production was…inconsistent, at best, and that made the conglomerate impatient with the workers we were assigned to," Tomen explained.

"These were good people," Miles took up, seeing his friend struggle for a moment. "Tomen and I didn't actually know each other back then, which is funny because the town we grew up in was so close, everyone knew each other. To these people, it didn't matter that we were Stalwart that we were there to keep them in line, they didn't care. They did their shift and around it, they were the friendliest people you ever like to meet. They baked bread with some leftover crop that I swear, if that's the fake version, I would die to know the real, it was that good, seriously. Where they tended to the cows, cloning them for milk, cheese and meat, they let the kids pet them, and taught them about why it was important to be kind to these creatures. They said how they gave their lives to give them meat and other food so it was their duty to treat them with respect, it didn't matter to them that they were made for that purpose the same way one makes a chair or a table. They were really kinda gentle people," Miles's eyes of a powerful, glowing orange reflected the fire that was building up inside him. "But they were deemed unprofitable."

"I see," Nathan said, seeing where this was going.

"The town had grown too big, people were living their lives, making families but the farm wasn't producing enough, the weather didn't allow it, even the crop is designed to grow in anything," Tomen explained. "The Crimson Sun senior manager who ran the site didn't even put up a fight when the instruction came down, nor did our supervisor. They were just told to cull the town, and so they made a list. These people were to be rounded up, brought to the centre of town and executed, just because they were seen as the least valuable of all the workers. And, we did. We kicked down doors, we dragged them through the streets, we took fathers away from families, ripped daughters out of their mothers' arms, beat down sons in front of their folks, and we completed the list. In under an hour, we had a group of people, all in those red jumpsuits of the farmer's company, all on their knees, hands bound, in the town centre."

"I still see it in my dreams," Miles added, shaking his head. "Why we ever let it get that far, I…I just have no idea. We just followed the instructions, speaking for myself anyway, I'm ashamed, I didn't even think about what I was doing, I just did it. I mean, these were people we had known our whole lives, from school age where we chose to become a part of Stalwart, from being inducted into becoming enforcers, to seeing them on the streets as we did our patrols. We knew them, yet we rounded them up all the same."

"That's the conglomerate's strength, they inspire so much fear in failure, that you become too afraid to see the means by which you succeed," Nathan offered.

"Yeah, guess it was something like that," Miles nodded.

"Well, we didn't go through with it," Tomen continued. "When the supervisor said to open fire, I made a split-second decision and I chose my enemy. I opened fire on my Stalwart brothers and sisters, I barely even hesitated. In that moment, I don't really know, but they just didn't seem to register to me anymore. To be able to turn their backs on the very same people they were laughing and joking with only the day before? I couldn't justify that, I couldn't explain it. It was wrong, so I did something about it," Tomen stifled a laugh which seemed to terrify himself that he had to. "They were so surprised when I turned my rifle on them," he said as he ran his hand along his weapon's edge, having first removed it from being slung over his shoulder. "I opened fire when they did, it was a thunderstorm of green energy blasts flying in every direction."

"It was snowing, I mean it was so cloudy that even though it was the middle of the day, it looked almost like night," Miles said, "something that stands out in my memory is a stone statue in the centre of it all. It was of a Stalwart enforcer from a hundred or so years before. He had killed some giant monster, some kind of predator native to the world, and made the farm safe again, they even used the corpse to supply nutrients to the soil."

"Was odd, wasn't it? This figure of a protector among a scene where the present day versions of him were slaughtering the innocent," Tomen agreed, remembering.

"So how did you two meet, then?" Nathan asked.

"In the fighting," Miles answered, his mind fixated on the traumatic memory so that his voice sounded completely void of expression. "They were so desperate to see through their instruction, I don't think it entered their wildest imagination that two of their own would turn against them. We didn't even say anything to each other, did we?"

"Nah," Tomen replied, shaking his head.

"We just went street by street, building by building, killing any Stalwart we could find. We found the supervisor, hiding in his office, put him down, and the Crimson Sun manager, too."

"Justice," Tomen nodded. "Then we took a freighter and made our own way, eventually bumping into a bartender on the Forerunner, called Xin, and he gave us snippets of info to go on, to disrupt the Coalition's activities, to do some good in the system, and make a little money to live on."

"Now, we make our own purpose," Miles added.

"Purpose," Nathan chewed on the word.

Back at the Stalwart freighter, Azuri used the control panel on the outside rear of the ship to lock the ramp and seal it up shut, putting the ship into its long-term dormant setting, adjusting it for a long stay. Sam, Lena and Cait were behind her, each carrying a bag of what they considered essential for the journey ahead and together they made their way to the far side of the shipyard, to regroup with their friends. They set off, Lena and Azuri walking together while Sam and Cait walked on ahead. They navigated through the twisting turns of the path through the docks, following the white glow given off by the street lamps, struggling to keep back the spectre of the smog looking to clog all the space in its sickly, tangy grey haze.

"You sure you're up for this?" Lena asked Azuri walking by her side as she tied the cord of her trench coat tighter around her waist to keep off the cold breath of the smog.

"I'm feeling fine, thanks Lena. Tomen wants me to stay on the ship at all times and I'm happy to do that, gives me a chance to rest," Azuri replied, sounding calm but for the apprehension in her chest that the ship she would be staying on was not her own.

"Good, let me know if you need anything at all, doll," Lena said, giving her friend a playful barge with her shoulder.

"And how you doing? What you think of this Winter guy?"

"Yeah I'm happy," Lena said, smiling as she took in the sight of the enormous lightning bolt shooting out from a cloud above her head followed by a clap of thunder so loud she almost grimaced.

"Happy? Really?" Azuri was confused, flicking her hair over her shoulder after a gust of wind blew it in front of her face.

"Yeah, I know, I ain't a fighter, an' what business do I have strollin' through the Old City, right? But way I see it is this. I wanted out of Stardust when I was a kid, and eventually I was able to claw myself out. I gained control of my body and my life, I was able to help myself, and I've done that now. But there are bigger things in play, others locked in those contracts o' theirs, and they need some help getting control of their lives. What kinda person would I be if I settled for helping myself and not liftin' so much as a finger to help others?"

"You'd be a survivor," Azuri replied, coldly on purpose, trying to shock her friend.

"That's just it, Azuri, it wouldn't feel much like surviving if I didn't do something with it, and besides, I like this guy. He's dangerous and maybe that's exactly what we need, the bloody, violent type—I got a good feelin' 'bout this guy." Lena's beaming green eyes shone out from her rose coloured cheeks and sparkling red hair, she was dazzling with life and energy.

"You really think we can trust this guy?" Sam asked Cait as they trundled through the docks, she had her hood up against the moisture of the fog so it was down to him to keep an eye on the officers maintaining the area, Stalwart enforcers patrolling the place.

"I don't need him to be trustworthy, I need him to be lethal, to protect us," Cait replied, giving the man walking beside her a strong, pointed stare. "If he does his part, and we get what we want, then we have a real and genuine shot at improving the lives of everybody. And I mean, everybody!"

"It's a massive risk, Caity. And this venture is plenty risky enough already. Having him along doesn't just complicate things, it times the risk by ten at least. What can I say, I don't think we need him," Sam sighed.

"Since when do you shy away from a risk?? You taught me that the only way to live is taking one risk at a time," Cait shot back.

"Yeah I remember but this ain't no usual risk, ya know that full well. We are talking about a guy you said cleared out a full Obsidian patrol solo, that ain't someone I be particularly thrilled to be havin' around us. I mean, what if we be just telling him what he needs to know to be grabbin' this himself, and then he wipes us out," Sam shrugged.

"Shut up Sam, you feel itchy, you deal with that yourself. Nathan is a means to an end, an end we can't reach on our own. So get your shit together and bolster yourself up, because this is just the beginning."

"And if he kills us all? He might choose to and it would only be a whim to a guy like this," Sam argued, getting emotional.

"Eyes on the prize, Bro. Just think of it, we get our hands on the secret then it opens all sorts of doors of opportunities, get you trinkets beyond even your wildest dreams," Cait suggested, trying to find a positive take on things for him.

"Well, I still don't like him being around, I don't think we're safe with him around, and I will do whatever it takes to keep us all safe, even if you and Tomen won't," Sam grunted but Cait had no interest in carrying on the conversation any further, she had got her Elite, now it was onto the next step.

"Feels just like any other ship, right? But be mindful, she flies fast and she flies agile, she'll respond as soon as you can think it," Nathan said, sitting in the co-pilot's seat, walking Azuri through the controls of his ship.

"She's a rowdy one, she doesn't like these low speeds, I can feel the engines urging me on, she wants to soar," the ocean-eyed X-Human replied with a wide grin, her hands comfortably gripping the controls. "I think she likes me," she said, eager as a child to see what the ship could do, and stretched out a hand to the man sitting next to her. "Azuri Prime."

"Nathan Winter," he said, turning slightly in his chair to face Lena and Tomen in the other two chairs in the room. "Lena, how you getting on with that console?"

Lena was seated in front of the navigation terminal, exploring the controls and pressing each of them in turn, bemused by them seemingly. "So this panel controls the coordinates the transit gates will take us to, it's very condensed compared to the one I'm used to aboard our freighter."

"It follows the same principles, input where you want us to go, and that'll do the rest for us," Nathan explained.

"And what does this do?" Lena asked, pointing at a large red button under a clear plastic casing.

"Switches the activating of the transit gates to manual, to the pilot's control."

"That's a thing?"

"It is on this craft," Nathan smirked as he stood up. "You're quiet, Tomen."

"Just settling the mind, nothing to worry about," was all he said.

"Well, we're hitting the early hours now, sleep where you drop, we'll make for Scarlet in the morning," and Nathan left them to it, leaving to the transport tunnel where Sam was tinkering with some identification cards while Miles sat opposite, cleaning his rifle, disassembling it on the seats either side of him.

Nathan slid down the ladder at the end, entering through the door at this right, heading into the armoury. The room was dim and dark but for the light dangling from a wire at its centre. It was cramped, barely enough room for the old armchair in the corner left of the entrance, the workbench next to it along that wall, the doors opposite the entrance and a metal cabinet attached to the wall on the right. With black walls, it was even darker and Nathan could barely see Cait sitting in the pock-marked, red leather chair, her hood up, covering her face. She didn't seem to notice him entering, so when he lifted her hood up and off, it startled her and she bolted her gaze up to meet his.

"I had hoped for a little space, but not seeing you anywhere else, I suppose I ought to have known that you'd be here," Nathan said, his voice was hoarse, as if talking to people socially had exhausted him.

"Sorry, I just wanted to be alone for a bit, it's been a long night you know," Cait rubbed her eyes, she was very tired, ready to sleep in truth, things had happened so quickly that she was certain that her friends had forgotten about the need to call it a night.

"Go in the next room, take the bed, I'll catch a few hours here."

"Alright, thanks Nate," Cait replied, getting up and moving across the tiny room to the double doors, activating with a touch of a button on the panel next to them.

"Nate?" Nathan turned, giving the woman an awkward wince. He had left his helmet and rifle in the cockpit, he felt naked with his face exposed.

"Yeah, Nate, I'm not calling you Commander or Winter all the time, that'd be exhausting, so get used to it," the X-Human called back as she stepped into the next room. The bedroom was small as well, needing to be in order to conform to the ship's size, with a simple double-bed up to the right side wall, cupboards lined above it and a dresser opposite. All the furniture in this compact room was of the same black metal as the walls, floor and everything else on the ship giving hint to its simplistic, functional design. Cait pulled apart the red sheets and flopped, her head hitting the pillow and she fell asleep in an instant.

"That's just it," Nathan breathed out heavily, tapping a button on the screen of his arm, opening the cabinet doors so that they slid into the walls, revealing see through glass shelves all covered in clear cubes with eyeballs inside. He pulled out one just like them and added it to his collection. "I was already used to it."

Chapter 6

"Coordinates set for Scarlet, Tomen," Lena proudly announced, having figured out the console the night before, and sleeping in the chair she found herself in.

"Good, activate the gates. Azuri, take us through," the man had put his Stalwart helm back on, his rifle strapped tight to his back, with Miles looking identical at his side.

The cannon below the ship blew out the transit gate, a net of vibrant blue electricity shocking shells of a dark metal spun out into the void, spreading wide so a web of lightning was cast between the dozen egg-shaped instruments conducting the energy. There were different star constellations in the abyss forming into a window inside the net of the lightning field, and the shells that marked the outer edge of the gateway rotated and dissolved halfway. They became fixed in place as Azuri piloted the starfighter through, and they emerged from the gate's kin orbiting Scarlet, the twin red and yellow stars so close that the light from them was almost blinding. Behind the ship, the shells oscillated again, recovering their other half from the other slither of space they had come from and the net of lightning drew them in, before it dissolved into atoms.

Scarlet below was a blend of light brilliant blue and golden sands, ceaselessly scorched by the rays of the twin stars. Azuri brought the ship down through the levels of atmosphere, piercing through radiant blue skies, dancing over a landscape of a rampant sea crashing against a long sandy beach. Great trees reached up to just below the ship's height, thick trunks leading up to canopies of green, as they travelled over the boundaries marking the seemingly infinite acres of crops, reaching up to the horizon. The black of the starfighter reflected the warm rays of red from the star beyond the sky as it soared over the fields of lush green flora nurturing the composite seed into growing into the artificial food that Crimson Sun produced. Buildings began to appear as they flew more inland but these were nothing like the metal teamed with glass structures from Vermilion where they had just left. These were made from the wood and sand of the terrain, a shantytown where the farmers called home, a contrast of fortunes for the Obsidian outpost for this area came into view, of concrete and boasting of grander expense.

The docks for this area were also a poor copy for the planet they had just left, trading the smooth constructed base of a cosmopolitan shipyard to a dry muddy stretch beaten into submission from the years of engine blasts and the sheer weights of the vehicles parked there. Azuri gave a short burst from the vertical propulsors so that the ship could be placed down more smoothly, an updraft of grit washed over the ship and its wings, a miniature tornado blooming from the power of the craft descending. Nathan felt the legs of his ship extend from the base under his feet as he finished putting his handgun back together, tossing the dirty white-turned-brownish rag back in one of the drawers under the stone workbench, along with the supplies he used to clean his weapon. He rubbed a gloved thumb on the stencilling over his initials, marked onto the side of the barrel, remembering the promise he made to this chunk of metal. The light bulb above his head swayed as the ship rocked just slightly, easing itself onto the hydraulic parking legs. This was the only mere light in the room, other than the glow from the cabinet at Nathan's back. From beyond the doors leading to his bedroom, he could hear the sound of the one he had left there beginning to rouse, he considered closing off his collection, but settled for wanting to see the look on her face.

Cait opened the doors and entered the armoury, straightening out her cloak that she had forgotten about when she slumped in the bed. Her eyes felt nearly glued together with crusts of sleep and she almost didn't realise her surroundings, nearly forgetting where she was. "Hey," she said mindlessly as she saw a pair of eyes looking her way from her left side and she stumbled over to the armchair in the corner, flopping into it, yanking her hood down over her face.

"You got six hours sleep, that wasn't enough for you?" A deep voice near her said and she realised Nathan was nearer than a metre from her.

"No, it was not. Give me coffee or there will be consequences, Nate," Cait mumbled, drawing back her hood and instantly wishing she hadn't. Near to a hundred unique eyes stared back at her, the petrifying presence they must have seen as their final view seemingly haunting them, the fear frozen in those eyes that lid lessly peered out into the room. That's when she realised Nathan would have been to her right as she entered the room. "What the fuck?"

"This is my collection, my shining pride and glory," Nathan presented with a dark smile, waving his empty left hand at the cabinet as he holstered away his pistol back at his chest with his right. "Each eye is unique," he explained, taking a random one in his hand, "and while I do try to remember their former owners," he shook his head, "some I just have to settle for enhancing the collection anonymously, they must have made for boring deaths."

"Nate, what the fuck?" Cait murmured again.

"You said that already," Nathan replied, placing the eye back on the shelf. "This is actually the first time I've shown someone else, this is very personal to me," he said, closing the cabinet with the screen mounted to his forearm.

"Yeah I bet, you called it a collection?"

"My accumulated accomplishments, each one a conquered foe," Nathan turned around to face her, leaning back against the closed cabinet doors.

"You've killed that many people?" Cait asked, stunned, not knowing what to think.

"No," the Elite answered calmly. "I've killed so many more than this, these are just the noteworthy ones," he said pointing over his shoulder with his right thumb.

"You're insane," Cait muttered.

"Quite possibly," Nathan replied, turning his pointing into giving the X-Human opposite him a thumbs up, with a wide grin showing his teeth.

"Why?"

"Ignorant question, Cait. The only language the conglomerate understands is violence and bloodshed. They deal it out across the region, and I deal it right back in kind. It's naive to think that anything less than the violence they inflict can be used against them to defeat them. We must surpass their brutality to overthrow them."

"Violence I get, this is something else," Cait said, seeing the man before her in a new light. Back in the bar, she had only taken note of the obvious details of his appearance but now that she knew he was a psychotic killer, she eyed him more carefully. His armour wasn't the clean and spotless of the standard Obsidian trooper, there were clear signs of use, scratch marks and repaired bullet strikes. The screen on his right wrist seemed to have come off at some point as it was now bound to his wrist with a strap of brown leather, a coiled black wire tucked inside, and the same material had been used to holster the pistol at his chest. At his left arm, the knife was holstered on the outside of his forearm and he had a watch and compass strapped there too in the same leather facing inward. His gloves had been torn and patched together in random scraps of brown and black leather, and the holster at his leg bearing the hilt of his sword looked the same. Magazines of ammunition were inserted into his belt at his right side and in a holster strapped to his left thigh. She could see better now that he had been in an enormous amount of skirmishes and firefights, and clearly had won them all.

"They deserve it," Nathan replied, offering her a hand up. "Come on, we've landed, let's meet the others in the cockpit."

The team gathered in the cockpit at the front of the ship, taking in the sight of all the activity of the Crimson Sun distribution chain as countless figures, all in the sweltering red jumpsuits of their company, shifting their enormous shipments of crates aboard various freighters. They could feel the heat of the planet through the red glass of the cockpit, beads of sweat appearing on their necks as they fathered around the centre, circular console. Nathan pressed a series of buttons on the side of this device, bringing a hologram of the area to life with a purple glow.

"So we're here," Sam pointed at the icon of a ship among a throng of buildings, squares indicating farmlands and circles representing settlements further afield. "These docks serve Klein, third largest establishment on this planet. If Xin's information is accurate, then we need to find fifty-one dash F, it'll be a small farm, most likely somewhere the Obsidian patrols visit only on the off-occasion. We can ask the locals, maybe join the workforce shipping out to it on one of the worker shuttles that serve the outlying areas, what do you think, Tomen?"

"Solid thinking, Sam. We'll try here first," the former Stalwart man pointed at a medium size dwelling near the centre of the settlement. "Looks like a worker barracks."

"You're overlooking the security checkpoints we'll have to pass to get there, guys," Lena pointed out, sitting in front of the transit gates terminal.

"Not a problem," Sam smirked. "You don't bring me along just for my sparkling personality, I stayed up a little longer, making use of my haul from the Starcrest, made these." He reached into the pocket at his side and pulled out six plastic cards. "Holo-tags, each imprinted with your name and image, these will get us past—they'll think we're an inspection team from the directorate. Sorry, Winter, I didn't have your image so couldn't whip one up for ya," he said with a sneer.

"Don't need one, no one turns away an Elite," Nathan didn't shake his gaze off from the console to give the thief the satisfaction of his full attention. "I don't think all of us should go, crowds attract attention," he added.

"True, Azuri, stay on the ship with Miles, monitor the Stardust broadcasts, see if you can patch into local Obsidian and Stalwart feeds, we'll need to know if they pay any particular attention to this ship," Tomen instructed. "Alright, let's do this," he announced and led the small team out.

Nathan adjusted his helmet, ensuring it was secure, then checked the strap of his rifle, glancing over his right shoulder to see the stock upright against the side of his jetpack, keeping it tight so it wouldn't interfere with his arm on that side. Meanwhile, keeping the sun off from her face, Cait drew her hood up, the black of it in matching with her jumpsuit made her feel hot but she was glad for the protection from the red sun's sizzling rays. It was tight against her skin which didn't help with her breathing as she started to sweat in the heat. Lena had gone out with the sleeves of her red trench coat rolled up, but immediately undone them as the crimson star set to burning her exposed skin, while a wide, grey, lightweight hat kept the rays from her face. She had done up her coat to cover her chest and relented to change her outfit for the burning sun, doing away with the skirt and long socks, changing into a thin pair of black leggings, matched with leather boots of the same grey as her hat stretching up above her knees. Tomen was in his full Stalwart armour, the light grey helm with the white eyes, the green threaded jacket over his darker shade of grey armour that covered his torso, arms and legs, boots of the same material. And Sam simply wore his Crimson Sun jumpsuit, discarding his Stardust grey jacket for this trip, knowing it would draw curious eyes.

While the yellow sun provided immense, clear blue skies, cloudless in saturating the world in light, the red sister-star tainted the air, turning it a shade of orange, and carried a burn like acid for any bare patch of skin left exposed to it. The group did their best to manage the oppressing heat as they followed the footpath of beaten down beige mud up to the Obsidian checkpoint standing at the edge of the shipyard. An electrified wire fence encircled the area meeting the black metal framing with the ambient red light acting as the security checkpoint for the docks. Tomen led so he was the first to be challenged, Sam next to him to add proof to the deception, the two women in behind, and Nathan at the back.

"Identification, from all of you," the bored, bald, middle-aged Obsidian officer asked, dressed in an Obsidian shirt and trousers, of the same fibres as Cait's cloak, and only wearing half the armour he was required to, to easier deal with the heat.

"Here," Tomen handed over the plastic card Sam had given him.

"So what's a Stalwart enforcer doing with a farmer, an RCS technician, I'm assuming a Stardust entertainer and a…" the Obsidian officer stopped short as his eyes caught the one in Elite armour glaring at him with silent threat from behind his helmet. "Pardon, sir, my apologies, I'll keep to my task," he said in Nathan's direction as he activated the hologram projector on Tomen's card, seeing it light up with a likeness of the man, and moving onto Sam. He moved through the group, checking their identification cards as efficiently as he could, his fingers clumsy with sweat and anticipation as he finally reached Nathan. "And your ID, please, sir?" He stammered, looking up at the Elite that easily towered above him.

Nathan placed his right hand on the hilt of his sword, in the holster attached to the front of his thigh on that side and leaned forward so his helm was mere inches away from the other man's face. "For your sake, I won't consider that you are asking seriously," his voice was deeply pitched and full of aggression.

"No, sir, of course not," the other man cried, doing his best to smile and laugh off the threatening tone. "Just a joke, sir, please," he whimpered, his eyes going to the blade hilt.

"And I will take it as such. Now, keep your eyes down and keep them there, do not dare meet my gaze again or it will be the last time that you have eyes," Nathan said in a steady, calm voice, his fingers gripping the hilt tighter, considering it, but instead moving on to join the rest of the group.

"That was fun," Lena remarked, biting her bottom lip. "Never seen someone threaten an Obsidian before."

"Wait until you see me kill them," Nathan replied back to her, and she could tell by the way he said it that he was smiling, and flirting.

"Come on, you two, the barracks in this way," Tomen ushered, nodding in the direction of the larger building out of the row of identical, sandy structures.

The road was little more than a dirt track formed by the passing shuttles that were large metal vehicles with rugged tyres that dropped off hordes of red jumpsuits only to pick up a similar sized group at the next corner to take them to this farm or another. Tomen led Sam, Cait, Lena and Nathan passed these rushing vehicles to the large building at the end of the street. They ignored the neon signage advertising the refreshment offered at the Stardust establishments further into town, and the old recordings of Crimson the Crime-Fighting Cat, talking about the honour of a hard day's work.

They pushed aside the wooden sheet that acted as the door and found row upon row of simple metal benches where near to fifty dirty, rundown people, all in the red jumpsuits of Crimson Sun, were scattered about, reeling from the agonising shift they just survived. Fatigue was strewn across each of their faces, blood and mud shrouding their true appearance, here and there they were marked with terrible bruising, one or two had missing limbs. Sam passed through them without hesitating, seemingly searching for someone in particular, while the rest mulled near the entrance, Nathan putting the sheet acting as a door back where they had found it. The farmers took particular interest in the one in the Obsidian Elite armour and the other in the Stalwart Ironworks armour, some of them wincing almost instantly, expecting some harsh introduction.

"We mean you no harm, I promise," Cait projected throughout the building, seeing how some of those in the red jumpsuits were turning to rage at the idea of the authorities in their shanty home. "We pose no threat to you."

"They are always a threat," an old lady struggled to pull herself up from the floor to sit on a rickety section of a bench, pointing at Nathan.

"That is true," Nathan said in reply, going over to the woman and kneeling in front of her. "But killing people like you is of little interest to me," and he placed his right arm over an outstretched knee, leaning on the hilt of his blade. "I seek more satisfying prey, and for this purpose I seek farm Fifty-One dash F. Tell me where it is."

"Nathan, don't threaten the locals," Cait placed a hand on his shoulder, giving him a look that suggested she didn't believe intimidating these people would get them what they want. She pulled back her hood and looked around the room, taking in the sight of these down-trodden souls, making sure she looked at each and every one of them. "We need the location of this farm as we believe that the man running it used to be the Obsidian Captain for Rose City."

"And why are you looking for him?" A male voice asked from amongst the crowd.

"Because we've been told that he is in possession of a landing key that unlocks the docks for the Capital City. But not just this, his employee passcode, along with the one belonging to my friend here," Cait waved a hand at Nathan who had risen back up to stand by her side, "unlocks a vault in the city."

"What's so special about this vault?" A woman asked, standing up from a bench, her blonde hair dusty and the ends of it wildly split in among the ponytail it was tied in. "And what is so special about the lot of you? You're WIDOWs, aren't you? Workers In Deviation Of Work-orders. Just by being in here, you have sentenced us all to death if they come through that door! You know they won't discriminate between the ones they want and the ones who might be helping them. You should just leave."

"If we leave without what we came for, then that threat of violence? It will never go away. Help us though? And we might be able to do something about it," Tomen put in from behind Nathan and Cait, taking out a canteen from inside his jacket and giving it to a young girl near his feet. "It's water, kid, take it and pass it around, sorry to not have brought more."

"What d'you mean do something about it?" The woman asked, taking a step back as Nathan got up, moving a pace forward to stand between her and Cait.

"We believe the secret of the Capital Collapse is in this vault, the true cause, and we intend to use it, to spark up a resistance or just cause them a world o' hurt," Cait replied. "But we can't do anything without your help. First, we gotta find farm number Fifty-One dash F."

"And what will you do to him when you find him?" An elderly man whispered through his pain, his joints in obvious agony as he sat crooked on a bench, his eyes a foggy kind of white giving sign to why he didn't look at any of the group in particular, just in their general direction.

"Once we have what we need? I'll string him upside down, claim one of his eyes and leave him for scarecrow for the conglomerate to find and it will herald their time has come," Nathan answered, confidently and striding the breadth of the deep yet narrow building.

"This sort of person hoards information for their own gain and are like to keep it to preserve themselves, so say this one sticks to type, what will you do?" The old man pressed, straightening himself as best he could manage.

"Then I will inflict pain, I am no stranger to doing whatever it takes," Nathan replied honestly.

"Good, break him," the old man grinned, yellow teeth showing in between the gaps and others began nodding and agreeing.

"So where is this farm?" Lena asked.

"I'll take you to the shuttle that goes there, there'll be one soon, just follow me," an X-human woman announced, standing up, her hands bloody from recent work.

"You said about resisting, how?" A young boy asked, kneeling among a crowd taking up a bench against the side wall.

"Once we find the secret of the Collapse," Cait announced, looking the boy dead in the eye before looking to the rest of the building. "We will all come together. The Collapse was used as the excuse to raise their abuse of us all, and we intend to pay them back for that in full. They use their might to divide us, to keep us apart, to keep us down and scared. I say, fuck that. With the truth, we can finally unite, with this secret we can stand against them. United we stand, divided we fall."

"United we stand, divided we fall," the farmers collectively mumbled, getting progressively louder.

"Time to go," Nathan turned back to his group as the Crimson Sun colleague who had volunteered to show them the way joined them, as well as Sam who returned from the far corners, seemingly satisfied with what he had been searching for.

"What were you doing?" Tomen asked him.

"Sometimes Stalwart Inquisitors put on the farmers' uniform, blend with the crowds to catch out WIDOWs, but we're ok," Sam replied, flicking his gaze quickly among the group.

"You were gone for a while," Lena pointed out lazily, more interested in straightening her hat.

"Just wanted to be sure," the thief replied with a deep breath.

"I don't care," Nathan interrupted. "Tomen, Sam, these people stuck their necks out to give us what we need but they may play the same risk in turning us in for some reward. Get some food and fresh water from the ship, bring it here. I'll take Cait and Lena with me to the farm." He gave no room for argument, his tone confident and the outcome already assured.

Cait and Lena left the barracks with Nathan and the farmer, following her down the road and around the corner while Tomen and Sam left for the ship, seeing the sense in what they were tasked with doing. The rumbling, deafening shuttle arrived shortly after they did at the stop which was nothing more than a small metal sign dug into the ground, marked simply with a red cross against its plain state. "Take this to the end, the farm you're after is as far from Obsidian presence as it gets, good luck," the farmer said as a form of goodbye, and she watched as the three WIDOWS boarded the shuttle.

They rode over colossal stretches of land where every so often a small number of their fellow travellers was offloaded to tend to their assigned section, so they had some time to sit and observe the farmers who eyed them with a curious, anxious stare. "Wish I'd brought something to read," Lena mused, pulling her boots up and looking at Cait, and Nathan past her on the same side of the shuttle where seats were lined up either side.

Eventually they arrived at the final stop, beyond the rises of hills and through a valley where a river ran parallel the full way, past countless, identical farmsteads, here they found themselves in a settlement not too different from the one they had left, only smaller. Instead of homes however, the formations of dried mud and sand were for shelters from the incessant heat and rays, hollow alcoves of structures, or sheds bearing the tools of their work. The workers here made the ones they had seen seem privileged, for these were on their knees in the muck tending to the sprouts of green, to the filth that turned their red jumpsuits a dark, wet brown. Supervisors stalked their steps, figures in pristine red jumpsuits, with black gloves to protect their hands from the muck and the flaring red star, kicked the workers back into the crop should they reel their heads up for air. As Nathan, Cait and Lena approached the centre of the farm from the stop at the base of the shallow hill, they followed a track through the crop, lined either side by wooden fencing, and they saw the brutality of the overseers in plain view. A man punching a woman down for some unknown reason, his black fist taking to red as he carried on connecting blow after blow. The group kept their focus, stepping along the path to approach the large building made of a pale, white wood that stood in the epicentre of the farmstead, at the height of the hill.

"You two go on ahead," Nathan said, looking around him and catching a scene where a male overseer was dragging a female worker over to a small, shadowed structure, away from the working populace. "I'm seeing a need to observe our surroundings."

"What'd you mean? We need you in there," Cait didn't understand and stopped where they found themselves, at the bottom of a small trail made from wood that led up to the building's door.

"Nah, it's OK, Caity, I think I know what he means to do, let him do his thing, and we'll do ours," Lena nodded to Nathan before leading her friend up the trail, leaving the Elite outside alone.

Cait and Lena approached the door, a bright red thing up against the pale, bland wood that formed the structure rising up before them, and it was Cait who knocked. A young man answered it, dressed in a simple version of a Stardust garb, a plain grey jumpsuit of the fashion of the Crimson Sun red variant, and Cait's own RCS one. He had a shoot of brown hair and a vacant expression, he looked at the two awkwardly, as if he struggled to register their presence.

"Hello?" He said, his voice was a whisper, something disturbingly lost about it.

"We need to see the man who owns this farm," Cait said, embarrassingly not remembering the Captain's name.

"You want to see Mr Willis?" The young man asked, confused.

"That's his name," Cait smiled, looking at her friend. "Yeah, we need to speak with him."

"OK, my sir is through here," the young man didn't ask who the visitors were, instead just standing aside so that they could pass him and then he could close the door.

"What can you tell us about the Captain?" Lena asked, giving the young man a puzzled look as she passed him.

"He won't like you, he doesn't like X-Humans," was all the reply she got. Cait and Lena followed their host through this bottom level of the building, walking along a strip of red carpet on a bare, wooden floor through to the rear, where an elderly man sat in a chair, looking out of the window. "Mr Willis, there are two freaks here to see you, sir," the young man introduced then spun swiftly and exited the room.

"The fuck he say?" Lena spat but he was gone too quick for her to get any kind of response. They found themselves in a room unembellished with any kind of decoration but for the black leather chair that the old man sat in, staring out of the window that was opposite the door to the room, along with a bookshelf lining the wall at the right side where two men in Obsidian armour stood, utterly silent. "Shit," she said, seeing these two armed figures standing there.

"Captain Willis?" Cait asked, doing her best to ignore the Obsidian soldiers.

"I really must invest some time into evaluating my attending team, for them to think letting in two of your kind into my home is acceptable," the old man turned around slowly in his chair, the glow of the red star outlining the frame of his wrinkled face. He was wearing his Obsidian officer uniform, a black suit, zipped to conform to the body of its wearer with a red streak running from shoulder to opposite hip, and his face showed all of his age, deep lines from eyes, covering his forehead, and his hair had long since turned to white. His skin was pale and he seemed to have very little to his body, to fall should he stand.

"You have something against X-Humans, Captain?" Lena demanded, her eyes of emeralds beaming with challenge.

"Quite frankly, yes I do. You and your ilk are an affront to the Lord, and just by looking at you I can tell you are not pure of your blood, so you are both hybrid abominations, the filth of you, you revolt me," the old man glanced at his two security guards, but something stopped him short of asking for them.

"What lord?" Cait's own amethyst eyes burned with a steady rage, not willing to stand there and be insulted simply for being born.

"The Lord! Heathen cunts! You don't even recognise the benevolent, forgiving Lord who put breath in your breast for you to be standing here in this moment. Ignorant savages. The Lord is what made man in his own image. Human man," the old man twisted the words, pronouncing them carefully. "The fact that you are women is bad enough, to come here so presumptuously as well, but to be demons, a stark betrayal of His mighty, perfect design! A shame the terraforming did not extinct your species with the majority of the indigenousness beasts that we cleared to pave the way for the survival of His benevolent race, the white man!"

"You're insane! I'd heard about the religions of the Old World, but nothing like this," Cait remarked, not knowing what to do.

"Look, whatever you think of us, we don't give a shit," Lena shrugged and stepped forward. "We came because we know you have something, a landing key, that opens the docks of Rose City."

"And I'm meant to just hand this over to you? Please! Get out of my house before I have these two spray your brains all over these walls!"

"Where the fuck is Nathan? This guy has been breathing long enough!" Lena shouted and waved a hand in dismissing the old man in the chair as she turned away from him.

"Nathan Winter? You brought that man here?" The old man's tone changed, the venom lost from it completely and he sunk into the chair.

"I'm here, Tobias," the voice from behind made Cait jump while it produced a dark grin on Lena. Nathan stepped into the room and immediately the atmosphere changed, his very being altering the state of play to his advantage without mention of threat or intention. "It's been a long time, Captain."

"Evidently, not long enough," the older man squirmed in his chair, looking over to his guards. "Weapons up!" The two Obsidian guards raised the rifles they brandished, black metal with a magazine underneath holding the luminescent red laser rounds, and they aimed them at Nathan's head, slowly.

"What's wrong with your staff?" Cait asked, thinking back to the one who had let them into the house, and seeing the same sort of slowness from these two guards.

"RCS and Crimson Sun came together some years ago to try synthesise biological means for subduing a workforce to the will of the one who manages them, it didn't work at every attempt but I have access to an early prototype, keeps these people more agreeable and less inclined to betray the location of my home," the old man waved away, disinterested.

"So you are hiding," Lena smiled darkly.

"Yes. The Collapse, however it may have happened raised several security risks to the directorate and the Section Chief themself, and as the Captain of the Police for the city, I was blamed for these lapses. So I took stock and took up residence here, sneaking away anyone useful to make my life more comfortable."

"So you admit it wasn't a group of WIDOWs that caused it?" Cait stepped forward, despite the guns from the guards still trained in her direction, albeit at Nathan who was fully armoured.

"Obviously! You brought the ultimate WIDOW hunter with you after all," the old man smirked. "No, whatever caused it, it was something else."

"And you took a landing key, as what?" Lena probed.

"Insurance. Whatever caused the Collapse, it is still there, and that key unlocks it, so should Thorne or his new boy leader come for me, I can dispatch men to use that key and reveal their dark secret."

"That's what we intend to do," Cait said, taking a glance at Lena.

"What? And that makes us allies? Just talking to you is making me physically sick in my mouth, I can taste the vomit. No. I haven't used the key because they have not come for me, and they have not come for me because I have laid no plan to use the key. They probably know I am here, and what I possess, and what I am doing here, but right now I am probably of no real consideration for them. This place is a farm like any other, we work under the Crimson Sun banner, we meet our quota, and that is as far as my communication with the Coalition goes. It is a steady, uncomplicated pill to swallow. You three are just a dangerous ingredient to my otherwise perfect concoction, so I do not think I need talk any longer, you have sated my curiosity at your presence, goodbye."

The old man lifted his left hand quickly then brought it down in a violent wave and his two guards fired powerful red bolts of energy soaring straight at Nathan's head but both missed as he leant back. He raised his right fist, activating the energy shield to repel the following blasts as he took out the pistol at his left hip, raised it up and as the barrel met his shield, it lowered a section to allow it and he fired a single shot through the red visors of their helmets. Nathan deactivated his shield as the bodies landed in twin heaps on the floor, and then his attention returned to the old man, taking a step forward.

"You've had your time to talk, and there's been plenty of it. I want the landing key. I want your employee passcode. Now." His demands boomed, rivalling the loudness of the gunshots he had just fired and near as deadly.

"Commander Winter, there is naught in your power to rally against me, I will not give you the key or anything else. Kill two of my guards and I will simply summon more, I have a whole facility here, full of employees to give their lives to ensure my safety!" The old man sprayed back, looking over Nathan's shoulder expectantly.

"No one is coming, Tobias," Nathan said coldly with a mocking tone. "Seeing one of your supervisors go to rape one of your workers was more than enough motivation."

"What did you do?" Cait asked him.

"I killed them all, the Obsidian guards, the supervisors, they're all dead. The workers are fine," he said, not turning back to her though.

"Monster," the old man cursed.

"Hardly, that comes now," Nathan slid out his knife at his left forearm slowly, intentionally building the anticipation in his victim before striking in the blink of an eye, bringing the tip of the blade down deep in behind the right kneecap of the old man. He screamed and wreathed in agony, crying and flailing weak, pathetic arms at Nathan who steadied himself into a crouch at the foot of the chair so he could apply pressure, bending the knife downwards before twisting it. "The landing key, the passcode."

"No!" Blood flowed from the knee and soaked the chair, dripping onto the floor, Cait watched in a measured sense of purpose, while Lena let herself enjoy the moment more than she meant to.

"The landing key, the passcode," Nathan reiterated, removing the knife slowly before inserting it under the left knee of the older man then striking it down fiercely, cutting through the bone, severing the shin in half.

"Bookshelf! The book on..." The old man was near slipping out of consciousness so Nathan stood up, removing his knife with a twisting motion from where it was embedded in front of the ankle and pulled the other man's head back violently with his left hand, balancing the tip of the blade on the inside of the left eye.

"The landing key, the passcode."

"Book on the shelf, blue cover, called the Bible, the key is tucked behind it, my code is on a bit of tape attached to it, now stop, please, stop, no more, I, I can't take more," the Captain slumped to Nathan's will, he wept, wetting the tip of the blade now digging into the flesh at the corner of the eye.

Cait walked over to the bookcase, stepping over the bodies of the Obsidian guards and taking out the blue book with the right name, and after she reached into the plain wooden shelving, she drew out a small rectangular shaped golden cartridge. She turned it over in her hands, seeing a section of opaque tape attached to it, the numbers 5572 scrawled on it. "This is it."

"That's it," Nathan nodded, looking over. "Now you and Lena wait for me at the shuttle. You may have stomached seeing this much, but you won't want to see what happens next."

The two X-Humans left the room without question and the breath was stolen from their chests as they had to step over constant bodies as soon as they did, as Nathan left a trail all the way to the old man. Bodies of Stardust attending staff, Obsidian soldiers, Crimson Sun supervisors littered the ground, from the interior of the housing through to everywhere around the farmstead. They took a moment to steady themselves as they saw the workers of Crimson Sun calmly burying the bodies into the soil, seemingly unaffected by whatever violence had been used to slaughter the ones who were abusing them. Both Cait and Lena wondered how Nathan must have killed so many yet they hadn't heard a single gunshot or shout of pain or for help, they never suspected this was happening in the slightest. One farmer looked up at them as they passed and there was a look of contentment on her face as she nestled a body under the surface of the ground with a toe, "the bodies are good for the soil, they're very nutritious. About the only useful thing they've done for this place."

The shuttle was there waiting for them at the same spot they had left it, the driver was being told to stop by the workers, and the two X-Humans assumed Nathan played a part in that. It was in this moment that they realised they were the only two of their species here, and that the workers were predominantly female, the Captain having stuck to his beliefs. They clambered onboard, the shuttle empty but for them two and they sat in utter silence for a moment, contemplating what they had just seen.

"For me, Cait," Lena said, "that's justified, what Nathan did in there. Yes it was fucking violent and unnecessary, but look, it got the job done," she shook the golden card shaped object in Cait's hand, feeling the cold in her friend's fingers as she did.

"I know, it's just, I've never seen anything anywhere close to that kind of violence before," Cait stared at the landing key, her eyes fixed on it.

"Caity, listen to me," Lena peeled off her friend's fingers from the landing key, taking it and putting in a pocket of her red trench coat, "and look at me, too."

Cait turned to her friend, her eyes stuck wide open, processing what they had seen.

"That in there, is why we need him," Lena started. "The conglomerate has the power, we are outgunned, outwitted and hilariously outmanned. But we have the Elite Commander on our side and look at what he can do. He is the unknown variable in all this. Even we don't know what he'll do next, how could they? With that level of violence and skill? That is someone that I am very glad to have on our side, wouldn't ya agree?"

"Guess he's just a means to an end, right? We hired him for this purpose," Cait nodded, her mind scrambling to rationalise anyway it could.

"Finally we have someone capable of really dealing out some hurt to these fuckers, I see that as an absolute win, Caity, I'm sorry, I am really happy with this guy. I'm not afraid to do what it takes here."

"Nor am I, Lena," Cait replied, finding her strength again, balancing her mind. "Another scumbag repaid for his crimes against us, the ones who built the Crimson. An eye for an eye," she smiled.

The air was thick with heat inside the shuttle, the doors left open to allow the two X-Humans in the rear of the transport some relief of a draft, this ended once the one in the Elite armour boarded, slamming the button on the inside, next to the doors to close them, signalling to the driver that it was time to leave. He put his back to the opposite wall and slid himself down to sit on the bench, his jetpack scrapping, metal on metal, until he was finally seated, taking off his helmet with a deep sigh, unstrapping and removing his rifle next, placing it at his side. Nathan's hair was glistening with sweat, his brow noticeably wet and he wiped it with his right glove, using his left to straighten the loose strands of hair dangling over his forehead back into the slick-back style with a single smoothening stroke. The two X-Humans watched his every move, staring, suddenly reminded that this lethal weapon that back in the house they had left was a faceless, unstoppable force, was just a man, a living being.

"You get another trophy for your collection?" Cait shuffled where she sat, the bench not allowing for much comfort, being nothing more than a length of metal.

"One I'd wanted for some time," Nathan replied, nodding, oblivious to the savagery he had just deployed, somehow ignorant of the horror of what he had done in claiming his memento, his tone sounding genuinely innocent.

They followed the road back to Klein, the town where their ship was docked, ready for the next phase, but this journey felt longer, the lack of apprehension for what lay ahead which was present on the trip to the farm meant the passage of time felt stretched out. Cait gave up trying to get herself comfortable sitting on the bench and had settled for being on the floor, leaning her back on it instead. She hadn't got her coffee, Nathan not having a fully stocked kitchen and she knew not to ask about it once in the town as it was obvious that it was simply a worker slum, and that she wouldn't find any. So she collapsed into sleep, worn down by the obscene heat, by the stress of the occasion, witnessing Nathan's brutality, and now she leant up against Lena's leg, her head resting on her friend's lap. With the bumpy tracks, the lack of proper construction of the roads, Lena got uncomfortable, sliding herself down gently so as to not wake her friend, sitting next to her and resting her head carefully down on her at the centre of her crossed legs.

"She ok?" Nathan asked Lena, giving an upwards nod at the sleeping woman between them.

"Yeah, just knackered, I reckon," Lena tucked Cait's loose strands of hair behind her ear and softly brushed her cheek with the back of her hand.

"She sleeps soundly for someone provoking a war."

"What?" Her emerald eyes locked onto Nathan as Lena reeled Cait back to her lap as she began to roll off.

"Lena, you seem more realistic than most. Think about it, how exactly do you think all this is going to go? Very soon what you saw back there won't just be the new norm, it will pale in comparison to what will have to be done to succeed here. Murder? Torture? This is only the beginning, and bear in mind, we haven't seen them throw any punches our way yet," Nathan warned, staring down at the sleeping woman, clutching the rim of her cloak with delicate fingers.

"Yeah I know," Lena relented. "But she isn't to blame for that, this revolution has to happen, and I will back her until the very end."

"I never said anything about blame, in fact I think the opposite. Soon, when things never known before will come to light, and she being the one to present it? The people in their droves will look to her for what happens next, after that. The system cannot come crashing down overnight, too many people rely on it, millions, so once the power vacuum is created, someone will need to fill it."

"You think people will want her to lead? Be Section Chief?" Lena looked down at her friend, sleeping peacefully, blissfully unaware of the consequential conversation centred about her happening right above her. Cait had been facing

Nathan but rolled over, near headbutting Lena in her groin but it didn't hurt, just mustered a chuckle. "This idiot? Really?"

"Revolution has been considered before, by countless others and back in my days as an Obsidian soldier, I did my fair share in eliminating those people, those dreamers. Here is one dreaming in the waking light of day, someone willing to make real and tangible change, so what I'm saying is that eventually someone will consider it for her. They will look at her and see hope," Nathan looked at her now, surprised at himself, at seeking genuine connection.

"She is special, seen that ever since we met." Lena adjusted her coat so that she could be more comfortable in having her friend invade her space, settling for having Cait's head rest on her inside right leg, and she lifted her left leg to bend in front of her to keep herself upright. Her coat crumpled behind her back so she yanked out, drawing it over her left side, covering Cait's head in the process.

"You like that trench coat?" Nathan grunted, watching the X-Human adjust herself.

"Yeah, why?"

"You look like that cat, especially with the red hair," Nathan, remembering the smoking cat mascot of the COC, pulled out a cigar, clipped it with his knife and started to smoke.

"Yeah, it's something I like to do, I don't know, take the piss really. I'm a WIDOW and I look like their favourite lil kitty cat, I think I look cute," Lena beamed, her juicy red lips forming into a smile, a picture of red, as they matched her hair and jacket.

"And guess where they got the idea from," the Elite sighed, tilting his eyebrows to the cigar in his hand as a hint.

"No!" Lena chuckled, then grimaced as she thought she woke Cait.

"I used to wear a red trench coat on top of this armour when I was Elite Commander in Rose City, similar to yours but a bit darker and a bit longer, until Elias thought it was a good joke to make a mascot out of it, my cigar smoking and what I did for a living."

"That is fucking amazing, you were the inspiration for that fucking cat! That's made my day," Lena laughed.

Nathan grunted and took an overly long draw from his cigar, allowing himself to relax and settle his mind and body, remove himself from the moment for a short bit, and he closed his eyes, rocked his head back to lean against the shuttle.

"Meow for me, bitch," Lena teased and her words upset the other man's rest as his eyes slowly opened and locked onto her. "Just this one time, go on, for me."

"No," Nathan's voice went deep with regret for sharing that piece of information.

"I didn't think so," Lena bit her bottom lip, "so what do we do next?"

"We resupply. We'll head over to the Forerunner and grab a drink before we head to the Old City, too," Nathan replied, shifting his gaze to where Cait's head was hidden under Lena's coat above her lap. "Get this one some coffee."

Chapter 7

The boardwalk spanning the length of the space station was teeming with people, all comers welcome here from the furthest stretches of the tri-systems, beyond the borders of the Crimson region. For the Forerunner was unique. In refusing to be owned by a single company identity, it opened itself up to everyone, the various brands and services from each of the conglomerates set up shop and catered to all. While this did put off the more prestigious members of this corporate monitored society, that was seen as some measure of relief for the throng of lower level workers seeking a place to relax away from their shift, away from their supervisors' prying eyes. The break in wealth was visible even here however, the tell-tale signs of success and backing. In among the recesses of the hull, between the larger outlets and amenities, were smaller stalls as the less powerful companies brokered their goods, such as local farms owned by the Crimson Sun brand, selling wares outside of the product they produced that went to the contribution.

Nathan led Cait, Lena and Miles over to the lesser of the two Stalwart Ironworks stores, near the shadow of the COC embassy, over at the far end of the Forerunner. The look of the people in the crowd changed as they approached the house of the authority for this region. The colour and personal touches to their appearance fading into those who bore their uniform in the standard decree. This store bore the Stalwart colours, an overtone of grey with dark green awnings but the man behind the counter wore these mockingly, dressed in a grey Stardust suit under his jacket, instead of the armour that would mark him out as a true colleague. He was human, possibly around Nathan's age and was talking to a rifle on his store counter as he cleaned the length of the barrel with a well-used cloth. Two scrupulous brown eyes flicked up at the small group's entry, and his upper lip flickered as he recognised the one in full Elite armour.

"Winter, back so soon? I was hoping for a longer summer," the man dismissed, putting his eyes back to his work, loading in a clip of glowing green bullets into the top of the rifle. He fetched a tin of polish from one side, washing some onto a cloth and applying it to the wood that acted as the frame and stock for the weapon.

"Spare the wit for someone who cares, Siobhan," Nathan scorned, walking up to the counter, crossing the store that was cast in a dim light, clearly not too well invested in for their interest must be in the flagship Stalwart outlet across the way. He passed by display cases enclosing all manner of different craftsmanship; weapons, armours, machinery outside of luxurious technologies, such as parts for a ship.

"You know it's Siob-han," the man took no interest to raise his eyes to the customer at his counter, preferring to keep to his work.

"Sure, like you work for Stalwart Iron works," Lena laughed, not caring that they hadn't met before. "I've seen the name written down before and I've had girlfriends with the name so I know how's it said, honey, and that there is a name peculiar for a bloke, Siobhan." The red haired X-Human grinned, applying her curiosity to a pair of pistols on the counter next to the man who took a disliking to her pronouncing his name as Sha-vonne.

"Yeah, it's a weird existence we live in, but my name ain't the epitome of it, it's Siob-han, if you want my business," he rounded up the two chunks of black metal under the palm of a single hand and stashed away the weapons under the peering eyes of her emerald, shining gaze.

"Funny," Miles added, "it said Stalwart above the door so I figured we were giving them business," he said, folding his arms, dressed all in his Enforcer armour and garb.

"Funny, you're dressed as one of them, am I to assume I'm talking to one of their lackeys? Or can we get down to whatever it is you want? I figure it is a safer assumption that it's something beyond your usual wants and whims, huh, Winter?"

"Bit rude, isn't he?" Cait said quietly to Lena.

Nathan paid her no mind, leaning on the counter so that the other man knew who to direct his attention to. "Just a bit. This lot and a couple others are with me, I need quality kit and materials to outfit them, and not any of this, I need these to be styled to their attributes."

"And I apparently need a sign telling people how to say my name right! Let's see if the stars are aligned, could this be a magical day?" The man who preferred his name to be Siob-han, spun dramatically, leaning one side back on the bar and raised a hand up to the empty space on the wall above his head. He paused there silently and still for some time, the other man across from him with his party behind him, wondering if he had truly lost his mind. "What the fuck? I thought the stars worked for me, I wanted something and it didn't magically happen? This is outrageous, I must register my complaint with the Section Chief immediately!"

"Quit the attitude," Nathan took out five bars of a shining platinum and cast them on the counter space between them.

"Now, if you had just started with the money instead of your charming personality, we could have moved this along all the sooner, mate," Siobhan pressed a button hidden on his side of the counter and a panel on the side wall opened up, revealing an extension to this room.

"Here's a list of materials, and the rest they can choose for themselves," Nathan handed over a small piece of paper to Siobhan as he ushered the others forward with a nod in the direction of the new area open to them.

"You not coming?" Cait let the other two approach first, looking to Nathan before she went herself.

"No, I'll join Tomen and the others at the Starcrest, I could use a drink. Stick with these two and pick out a weapon that feels natural to you, do you have any experience with a particular firearm?"

"I'm a good shot at close range, like I've practised with Tomen and Miles' rifles, but I don't really know, plus I've no idea what armour I'd need, I've never thought about it."

"I've already arranged something for you on that list, you just concentrate on selecting a weapon, take a look at the shotguns, don't let the size intimidate you," Nathan put a hand on the X-Human's shoulder as a way of saying goodbye and left them to their shopping.

His fully armoured presence parted the crowds for him, Nathan found, as the general sprawl were too busy to care but once they laid eyes on his Elite armour, they hastily got out of his way as he passed through the sea of people to the bar near the docks. Looking out of the dark grey ovals of his helmet, Nathan could see the fear and tension struck on their faces, but here and there were stark contrasts to those emotions as a rare few seemed genuinely pleased to see him. On his snaking path through the horde of people, Nathan brushed past a few people who recognised his armour, and a peculiar strain of surprise hit them, not pleasant but also not terrifying. It was as if they saw the embodiment of a chance. One who was capable and because he was so skilled, so experienced, so known to them, there were the embers of a dwindled hope coming to life in their eyes, albeit a shy one that they couldn't express into words as if the air would poison it. Instead they were silent, but their expressions gave Nathan just a moment's pause, it was something he had hardly expected to see.

The Starcrest bar was alive, music blaring out and rolling over the drinking, joyful flock who cheered on the dancers on stage or played away their wages in the gambling games on offer or sat in groups, complaining of a supervisor or an experience they had shared on their rotation. Obsidian guards were posted at various points throughout the establishment, the black of their armour lost to the shadows but for the glaring red visors of their helms. Spotlights of any and all colours struck out from the stage end into the dim bar that was otherwise a dreary place to be, the walls undecorated so were simply the dirty grey of the Forerunner's hull. The stage on one side lent to the entertainment for the bar at the far end, under the balcony of the manager's office, where discreet conversations could be had, for the other end providing sufficient distraction. It was here that Tomen, Azuri and Sam were talking to their usual bartender, discussing how their trips to Vermilion then Scarlet went, as well as why they had arrived here on a different ship. Nathan mapped a route from the entrance that looked onto the long stretch of the establishment with the bar on the right and the stage on the left, through to the rest of his budding group that avoided the larger clusters of Obsidian guards.

"All I know is they still don't have any idea what caused her injuries, and until she wakes up, we still won't know what really lies in the ruins of the Old City," Xin was saying, his pure black eyes flicking up to Nathan as he approached the bar, before turning his gaze back to Tomen. "I am sorry, my friend. I hate to send you in there blind, but I have nothing to give you."

"I know, you've never let us down before, and this is far from the typical gig, I'd just hoped for at least some minor detail," Tomen finished his beer and wiped the foam from his trimmed goatee, taking a glance at Azuri to his right. "This is far beyond the usual risk."

"For far beyond the usual gain," the woman with the glowing, blue bejewelled eyes, all in a skin-tight black RCS jumpsuit, the spotlights reflecting off the silver wings at either shoulder.

"It better be, no risk is worth it without just reward," Sam put in, past Azuri, eyes only for his drink in solemn thought.

"It doesn't matter, we plan for the worst, take it as it comes," Nathan took off his helmet, placing it down carefully on the surface of the bar, taking in its appearance as he did, seemingly not recognising the craft the wing had come from to make it. He spun it slightly, mindlessly, so that the smoky ovals of the eyes were pointed at the bartender who was watching his every move.

"Mr Winter, name's Xin Zorkeefa, and this is my bar. My Stardust contacts were the ones who found you on Vermilion and I passed that onto my friends here in the hope that we bring you back into the fold, the Crimson needs you."

"I was perfectly content on Vermilion, what you did was disturb my peace and intrude on my activities. Not a wise thing to do, to interfere and seed yourself in my affairs," Nathan shot back, resting his left elbow on the bar.

"And this is what an Elite Commander is? A grumpy git with a bad attitude?" The bartender poured a double shot of whiskey into a glass and passed over Nathan's way, who took it in hand with a slightly raised eyebrow. "I'd hoped for more."

"Lay off, Xin. He's delivered so far, he got us the landing key and the Captain's employee passcode. To hear Cait and Lena tell it, you wiped out a lot of people to do it, too." Tomen said, turning his gaze over to Nathan at his left side, nodding. "I'm not usually so agreeable when my family is put in harm's way, but seems like harm's way doesn't leave so much as a scratch on you."

"Captain Willis was supposed to be surrounded by Obsidian guards turned to farming supervisors, how did you manage to obtain his key?" Xin asked, leaning away from the bar, cleaning a glass with a stainless, white cloth.

"They didn't fight like Obsidian trained, I didn't even have to ignite my blade," Nathan downed his drink then peered at the remaining droplets at the bottom of his glass.

"Why are you so comfortable with killing?" Azuri asked him, drinking the last of her juice made from a synthesised apple flavouring.

"Because they deserve it," was all Nathan offered.

"Because they murdered his wife and son," Xin interjected, his eyes unwavering in staring at the other man, even when Nathan placed his glass don't gently and fixed him with a glare.

The essence of emotion in those sharp brown eyes was of a calm aggression, and Nathan said nothing when he stepped off his stool, nodding in the direction of the door over Xin's shoulder. "That your office, through there?"

"Yes," Xin replied, not understanding.

"A word," was all Nathan said, inviting himself behind the bar and to the office beyond, calmly lifting the cut off section of the starfighter wing to access the back area, leaving his helmet with the others who were sharing nervous, silent glances.

"Of course, my friend," Xin waved a hand in the direction of his office door as a gesture saying that he would follow but was forced into the position of leading the way as Nathan nodded in the same direction, but with his left hand resting on the gun at his holster on that side.

He opened the plain white door that led to the metal stairs leading up to his office, Xin doing his absolute best to not look behind him at the one whose steps rang out so loud, that even shook the structure of the steps with each one that he took. They ascended in utter silence, neither one speaking until they finally reached the top and took the door to head into Xin's office. For a manager's office, this was a strangely basic room, the only light coming from a dangling fixture before the centre, leading to a simple wooden desk that sat in front of a wall of tinted glass that led to the balcony overlooking the bar. Xin pushed open the door and stepped inside, immediately being picked up by his grey suit at his back and smashed against the ceiling light, then just as fast his leg was gripped and he was slammed down again into the unforgiving floor, his ribs collapsing and crushing his chest from the impact. Before he could think, he found himself launched head first into his desk, destroying it under his weight and, reeling from the pain, he turned to see the towering figure of the Elite bearing down on him. The impact with the light unhooked it from one of its two chains that held it up while breaking the bulb so the room suddenly dropped into shadow, the light blinking into nothingness as the figure approached, unsheathing and setting loose a fearsome sword. As the room plunged into an opaque darkness, Xin's eyes could only see the last of the light reflecting off from the edge of that blade, only for it to come hurtling towards him from a downwards strike. He couldn't see it for the lack of light but he could hear and feel it cutting through the material of his desk a mere breath away from his head. Then it came to life, a lightning storm breaking at the hilt rushing down the length of the sword to Xin's eyes at the tip, a tidal wave of white electrified flame, an inferno of rotating energy rushing towards him. The flames were pure and bright while the lightning that infused it was of a striking gold, completely encasing the shining grey of the metal at its core.

"That is not your story to tell," a growl pierced the veil of shadow, coming from the figure beyond the haze given off by the colossal energy resonating from the weapon.

Xin couldn't reply, the sword and its power were little more than a couple of inches from his brow, ready to be struck down on a whim, he could feel the heat from it, the oppressing force come to bear in the weapon of limitless destruction balanced directly above him.

"Look at me," Nathan demanded, making sure his blade was balanced just perfectly that it didn't burn the man under his power, but was also close enough that he could see the individual waves of power emanating from his blade's hilt in those jet black, shimmering eyes of the X-Human. "You found me on Vermilion?"

"Yes," the man whimpered.

"Do you know what I was doing there?"

"You were helping people, some kind of detective?"

"Don't play with me, feeble attempt at hiding your intelligence."

"You're killing members of the management hierarchy."

"No."

"What?"

"No," Nathan said, "it's much more than that, that would simply make me some kind of hunter. No, I don't just kill any member of management that I see or I would be drowning in blood. I only kill those who abuse their power, take advantage of their position. I know them as soon as I see them. They seem to glow, to stand out from the background like no one else, and that's how I know who to kill."

"Ok."

"You seem to glow as well, Xin. Peculiar thing, seeing as my new companions claim you to be an information broker, a wrench in the conglomerate's plans. Care to explain why you give off the same aura as my other victims?" Nathan lent in and brought his blade down just a bit, easily carving through the remnants of the desk in splinters on the floor, intensifying his threat.

"I'm a manager, got to be it, right? I am your ally, Winter. Do you think I got people to discover you as a threat? No, it was because I had hope that you would return, because you are exactly what we need!"

"Explain, carefully."

"Cait has the naive will to spark the revolution but not the strength to win the conflict it will provoke. She has the perfect character to lead the people into a better, brighter future but she will need you at her side, a powerful protector that the people know and will recognise! The Elite Commander, still alive after the chaos of the Collapse, and willing to right the wrongs of the Coalition, just as you did in the city's heyday! The people need you! Thorne has to pay for what he's done, and you're strong enough to do it!"

"What makes you think I have any interest in that?"

"Because you accepted Cait's invitation, why else would you be here?"

"My reasons are my own," Nathan stood up and removed his blade, keeping it ignited as both a threat and a source of light.

"I'm sorry about your wife and son, Winter."

"Don't ever mention them, again."

"If their brief mention is enough to warrant this kind of response, then you are exactly what we need."

"I'm not the same man as I was, Xin. I'm not interested in being anyone's protector, I made a deal and I'm getting what I want out of it that is as far as my interest goes."

"Hmm, may I stand?" Xin asked, still lying in the wreckage of his desk, wood splinters caking his suit, his head bleeding, his chest aching as if hit by a colossal hammer.

"Slowly," was all Nathan said.

"How else? Can't exactly spring up," Xin coughed as he laughed, using the corner of his ruined desk to lever himself up. "Let's talk out on the balcony, can't see you in the dark. I have a switch, you know, it was next to the door, if you just wanted the light off, didn't have to use my head."

Nathan reeled in his blade and followed, he did consider for a moment keeping the other man in this room but knew the music of the bar would drown out their conversation so no one would be able to eavesdrop. Besides, he was still in complete control, the other man would hardly be able to overpower him, even if he were to call down to the guards in his establishment below. The balcony was a shallow thing, giving a view of the stage over the stretch of seats and gambling tables, and a narrow slither of the bar beneath their feet. Cait, Lena and Miles were just turning up to the bar when Nathan stepped out to join Xin who was straightening his suit, and leaning up against the metal railing around the frame of the balcony.

"You know I still have my suspicions, bartender," Nathan grunted, his left forearm resting on the balcony railing while his right was settled on the hilt of his blade resting at his leg.

"Intelligence always poses a threat, it hints at intentions not yet spoken," was all that was said as a reply.

"And what are your intentions?"

"You play chess, Winter?"

"I used to, back in the Old City, your point being?"

"I love the game. I love the strategy of it, the out-thinking and out-manoeuvring of an opponent, I use the same methods every day in my life," Xin explained. "It can seem cold and calculating but I expect you know it for what it is, and to agree with it. I give information to Tomen because I know his group can handle what I give them. I need to be cautious doing that, or these same Obsidian guards will arrest me and drag me down to that volcanic cesspit of a world they call home, chuck me in a cell and cut into me until I squeal about all I've done." He waved a hand at the floor of his bar and all the Obsidian guards posted around its perimeter. "So I need to out-manoeuvre my opponent, the Crimson Overseer Coalition and their vast network of operators, if I am to do any good in this system."

"And what is your goal?"

"Honestly? The Coalition is a failed system. And the ones who pay the price? Are these people," Xin nodded at his patrons down below him. "I can either serve them drinks, serving my purpose or I can do something about it. I decided the latter, and my moves and calculations have brought you into my path."

"You may not be so glad that you did."

"My head certainly isn't glad but I can take a hit, although you are far stronger than anyone I've ever met. My goal is to make real and beneficial change to this region, that's the brass tacks of it. If I were a piece on a chessboard, I'd be the King, not to brag or anything, but I'm best suited to operating behind the scenes, making things happen by bringing others into play, using their strengths to outwit and weaken my opponent."

"And sacrifice the pawns?" Nathan caught Xin's gaze then cast it down to his group below them at the bar.

"It's not like that, I'm not a fighter. As you said, I'm a broker, I facilitate actions from here, that's where I'm best suited."

"Where it's safe."

"And you want me to apologise for that? Because some wield a gun the same way I wield information? Don't judge me, Winter, you have no right."

"What kind of a system are we living in when a bartender tells a serial killer not to judge him?" Nathan laughed darkly.

"Don't undermine your own importance in this grand game of ours, Winter."

"I'm not here to play."

"I thought the same as you, once. I wonder what piece best suits you? A Queen perhaps? Powerful and able to attack at will? Or a Bishop maybe? One of faith, in this case in your own strength and beliefs, self-aware and confident. No," he paused. "I think a Knight is best suited to you."

"What is it about hanging people upside down after you've killed them that inspires people to think you're some kind of protector? Do I need to start hanging them here before you see that I am not the same man that I once was? Protecting people? Building a revolution? Fighting for them? You have the wrong man. I don't care."

"Really? Well, what I was actually going to say was that you can spring over the pawns to strike in a way no other can and hit the ones really with the power, but if that's what you took away from it, that's your affairs," Xin shrugged.

"Don't be coy with me," Nathan took his hand off from his sword hilt, leaning on the railing on his elbows, bringing his hands together, seeing the faint stains of blood on the leather of his gloves.

"Fine, then don't be meek with me. I'm not the only one who remembers the Elite Commander in Rose City. You were an inspiration. Young and aggressive. And not interested in the politics of your position. You killed corrupt members of Obsidian, intimidated abusive managers, safeguarded the common worker."

"There were no common people living in Rose City."

"Yes, you're right but they were still people, Winter. Still deserving of the lives that the Capital Collapse, that Elias Thorne robbed them off, no matter that they were managers, supervisors living in luxury."

"On the backs of others," Nathan pointed out.

"I thought you didn't care?"

"And I thought you said your head hurt? Perhaps it would hurt less if I removed it from your neck."

"One of the doctors in the Sapphire hospital might say that you use threats and intimidation to keep people at a distance so that you don't open yourself up to the possibility of another loss in your life. Whereas I say you're just a dick. But a useful one," Xin conceded. "So where do we go from here?"

"I'm still committed to this. My contact will deliver my list of requirements and the gear this lot will have picked out to my ship in a few hours, after that, we get some rest then head to the Capital," Nathan peered down at the bar, where Cait was discussing something with Lena.

"Good."

"I'm still not convinced by you."

"My feelings are reeling in pain," Xin said in a flat tone.

"You'll get over it."

"You know, same man or not, you're in the grips of a loss you felt near a decade ago, and I think we both know why."

"Careful, bartender," Nathan growled.

"This is probably one of the longest conversations that you've had for some time, or maybe you've had something like this today or yesterday, but you catch my meaning. You haven't talked to anyone about them, have you?"

"No."

"Then maybe you need to, it'll be good for you. Before you arrived, Tomen was telling me that you've been spending time with Cait, maybe that's who you could talk to about it."

"What good would it do?" Nathan sounded his usual, low and deep toned, but inside he felt something he hadn't felt for nearly a decade and it gave him a moment's chilling surprise. He felt a desire to make a genuine connection. The feeling almost made him be sick.

"Because maybe you're not the same man, but maybe you could be better," Xin looked over at the man at his side, analysing everything he could find on the face glaring back at him.

"Don't hold your breath," Nathan was growing bored and besides, he needed something from this man. "On a more pressing topic, I need your help."

"Yes, deep psychological help, but I'm afraid all I have on tap is beer, whiskey and other alcoholic delights, want me to get you debilitatingly drunk?"

"No. I need your Stardust communications access, I need you to get a message over to the Sapphire region, to someone specifically, is that something you can accomplish?"

"Depends," Xin looked out over the length of his bar, disinterested.

"I need word to reach Molly Monroe, she leads the SCAR version of the Obsidian Elites, we'll need her help after we've recovered whatever contents of this vault."

"And what makes you think a SCAR would ever help a soul in the Crimson? They would be undertaking an extraordinary risk coming here looking for trouble."

"Because she was my wife's sister, and she will be as keen at the prospect of revenge as I am. She's a formidable character, and would be a coup to name among the paltry list of allies we can call upon," Nathan lit up a cigar, measuring the risk of what he was asking against its benefit.

"What you're asking, which I don't think you've factored into your consideration, is that you are telling me to stick my neck out, really gamble on a risk that whatever message I send even gets through, and that it doesn't get picked up by the Obsidian listening station."

"Everyone's hands must get even some small measure of dirt on them for this venture to succeed. We must stick our hands into the muck to make something of it, to shape the future. Anyone left with their hands still clean, has no place in the new worlds we will be making," Nathan struck an eye over at Xin, seeing if the other man would take up the request.

"What do you want me to tell her?"

"Tell her to return to the Crimson, that there is no justice in the tri-systems but for the vengeance we seek for ourselves. Beyond that, doubt she'll need much motivation."

"Consider it done, Winter. Now then, if you're not going to dangle me from my ceiling, I suggest we re-join the others down stairs," Xin went to leave but stopped short, giving Nathan the opportunity to object, or to stop short of signing off on his own death sentence.

"Just never mention my wife and son again, Xin. I don't have a reputation for granting second chances for a reason," Nathan warned and led the way off the balcony and back into the pitch black office.

"I'm aware, Winter, as it's exactly the reputation you do have that you are here."

Only Sam seem to notice the two return from the office space above, his eyes moving to the cloth Xin was using to dab at a wound at his forehead as they returned to the rest of the group. Nathan returned to Tomen's side to retrieve his helmet, moving in between him and two excited X-Humans who had joined the group, discussing the new equipment they were eager to try out. Miles meanwhile was separate from the rest, chatting up a young bartender as she served him a pint of beer in an ice cool glass, he took her fingers in his to warm them as she placed the glass down which produced a playful giggle.

"What happened to you?" The man in the Crimson Sun jumpsuit asked the X-Human bartender as he resumed his place opposite the team.

"Tripped up in my own office of all places," Xin lied.

"So I'm assuming that was the loud bang we heard from up there?" Sam pressed.

"What else would it have been?" The bartender grinned, an expression that said clearer than he could with words that he wasn't going to say any more than that.

"So what's our next move? Bunk in the hostel over the way?" Sam offered the group.

"No, Stalwart Inquisitors have that whole complex bugged for audio and they have full camera surveillance of the area," Nathan dismissed.

"Since when?" Tomen asked.

"Since always. The Embassy uses it to gather information on WIDOWs and disgruntled workers staying there, makes them for easy targets."

"So what? Head straight down to the city?" Lena asked.

"No, we'll rest up on the ship again, out adrift, then head down to the city in the morning," Nathan stated, and as Tomen gave a nod, it seemed as though they had their plan.

"Any news we should be aware of?" Tomen asked Xin.

"Well, I wanted to wait until you were all here," the black-eyed X-Human began. "Obsidian have been quiet lately, real quiet. They know about what you did on Scarlet, they've acknowledged what you took, but they haven't put out a response, I have no idea what they intend to do."

"Why? What did you expect them to do?" Nathan asked, with a slight chuckle.

"What you mean?" Cait asked him.

"Well, why risk Obsidian lives when they can have us do the dirty work of retrieving whatever it is they originally wanted from the Capital, and kill us when we're done. Elias always considered himself a tactician, he wouldn't make a move if doing nothing suited his interests, he was never one to panic, calm in a storm, that one." Nathan scooped his helmet up so that it rested up against his body on the bar, tucked inside one elbow. "It doesn't change anything."

"Glad you're so calm, I think I actually would have preferred a race to the city or something. Something to show the threat to us, not just have them lying in wait," Lena scorned, adjusting her coat to wrap around herself.

"Well, we're all in this together, to whatever end," Cait said, and Xin brought along a tray filled with shot drinks and handed them out, keeping one for himself. She raised one up, "united we stand, divided we fall."

They all raised their drinks in unison but no one echoed the sentiment. A feeling of grave anxiety taking most of them, only Nathan was steady, and Cait was cautiously optimistic. The next step was ahead of her, on the road to a greater Crimson region for all.

Chapter 8

"Give us today's summary, Grey, anything interesting going on out there?" George MacArthur asked his senior most technician as he reclined back slightly in his chair, taking in the view of the nearabouts fifty desks slightly below his elevated platform. Like all Obsidian facilities, all of the furniture from the desks to the chairs to the doors at the sides and the floor, walls and ceiling, even the desktops, were all of the same black shining metal. One wall was not of this material however as it was pure glass, giving a spectacular view of the twin suns and their flock of planets making up the Crimson region. A technician in a black suit and red trim sat at each of these desks, scouring through various streams of data, the broadcasts the planets put out about their contributions, the communications from the wide network of Stalwart Inquisitors in their pursuit of WIDOWs, and whatever they could pick up from the two neighbouring systems. The light for the command centre of the Obsidian listening post came from the crimson star beyond the giant window giving an ambient red glow to the room, matching the colour of the floor lights lining the maze between the desks.

The best in this field was arguably the man standing before his manager, giving the end of day report. He was an older man, past fifty and was grey haired, he wore glasses that covered his tired blue eyes, and his suit was so well used the inside of his pockets had holes in, the red of the trim losing its brightness. Here, on his manager's platform, Alex Grey could see out to where his desk, and the others identical to his own, were laid out in a pattern bearing no significance all surrounding a circular holographic imager on a platform of its own. That would be where the Section Chief, or the Obsidian Director, or one of the management team would project themselves to speak to the team based here. While his colleagues' desks were up to code, bearing no personal decoration beyond a family photo and a simple memento, Grey preferred his to be empty, filled only with his work, not wishing for any distraction from the duties he felt strong belief in. He scratched his beard with his left hand as he balanced his clipboard with his right, an electronic pad where he had jotted down everything his team had gathered that day to bring to his manager's attention. The platform they were on was on the opposite end to the window wall, with the two entrances either side below. It had a small set of steps leading up to it from the centre of this control room that led to the only desk at this height, the same as the others but for being just slightly wider, and the one sitting at it responsible for all the others.

"There's a few things today, actually, Mack," Grey started, scanning his eyes down his list, flipping it over to the pieces of paper he attached to the back that provided the details he needed to accompany each point he had to present.

"Such as?" MacArthur, known as Mack to the colleagues he had a fondness for, a certain favouritism, was a stocky man, over six and a half feet tall, and was bald, boasting a thick, bushy beard instead. He had dark skin and his beard was a black thatch that framed the base of his face that was usually sporting a smile, not a man burdened by the seriousness of his work.

"There was a report of a bar scuffle on the Forerunner, our guys were called to the scene, arrested two women. Farming town on Sanguine was found empty after failing to report any contribution for two days, reports as to why seem to suggest that it was wiped out by the weather, not enough people to sustain it against the conditions. There was also a farm owner on Scarlet found dead, looks to be another victim of the serial killer plaguing Vermilion, the man's eye was missing, all hands reassigned to other areas as the overseer team there was also killed."

"That one's a real menace," Mack sighed. "You've really got more?"

" 'fraid so," Grey went on. "We had an Inquisitor contact us. He claims that he was told this attack would happen, on Scarlet, I mean. But he didn't report anything as it came from an unreliable source."

"Well, if this source was right about this incident then he may know of other things to come," Mack mulled over. "And if he has information that might be anything vaguely close to the serial killer then we want to know about it. Get one of your techs to make contact with the Inquisitor to set up gaining more from this source, no matter how unreliable they may be. I'm assuming by unreliable, he means a WIDOW?"

"Yes the report stated such."

"Interesting, but not unusual." MacArthur clasped his hands in front of his groin and he lent back in his chair, nodding to himself, "go ahead and tell whatever tech you assign this to that they will need to get the Inquisitor to bring this WIDOW in. Further information could be paramount here. Is there something else?"

"One more thing. We tracked a signal emanating from the Forerunner that was broadcast to somewhere in the Sapphire but we weren't able to decode it before we lost the trail. However, the border guard with that region has reported increasing signs of Azurite vessels passing along the boundary."

"Well, that's definitely troubling, I would certainly like to know what that message said. Get your relief to form a team, I want the trail of this broadcast re-acquired and analysed as a priority task. Roderic Thorne will be incredibly disappointed with our performance if we can't provide an explanation for our neighbours' rowdy behaviour."

"I can stay, organise this team and set the objective, if you need, sir," Grey offered, tucking the clipboard against his body, and putting his other hand in his pocket, trying to seem as casual as he could.

"No, not at all actually, I'll set the relief senior tech up myself, I almost forgot, I've got some news for you," Mack brought himself forward and smiled at his long-time friend and colleague.

"What's that?"

"Your survivor finally woke up."

Alex Grey was the technician that discovered the sole survivor's request for help among the louder frequencies surrounding the thriving town of Dunnfink, nearest settlement to the Old City. He heard her cry for help and honed in on her signal, relaying it to the team of Elites that were sent to go rescue the only member of the team sent into the Capital to make it back out, albeit not in one piece. Grey did his work and he did it well, using his station to contact the Obsidian forces in the region to clear a path so that the Elite team could bring their patient up to the listening post with as clear a path as possible, getting her into the trauma clinic as fast as could be managed. Usually a technician that had gained some renown for their work would celebrate, joining their colleagues in the mess hall, getting ridiculously drunk and having a wild time, but Alex Grey didn't consider his work that way. He saw it as his duty, his purpose, and nothing more. "OK, that's good," was all he said.

"Grey, let yourself have this one, consider it an instruction if that breaks a smile on your face. What's wrong with you? You saved a life. And you did it using your skills, your experience—you're a role model to the others with a performance like that."

"There were nine members of that team, I only helped one. And it was the Elites who did the saving, you know that, Mack."

"Don't bullshit me, Grey. They would never have known where to go to find her without you finding her transmission, and they would never have made it in time to get her into the clinic without you clearing the way. It was excellent work! Take the win! And if that doesn't convince you. Go see the woman with that stupid, depressed look on your tired, old face and tell her that saving just her life wasn't enough for you. That it was all or nothing, and that her being alive just doesn't cut it for you."

"You know it ain't like that," Grey grimaced.

"Then what is it like? Wanna be a big hero and save everyone? Be more realistic, Grey! Alex, for all the starways, you did an amazing thing, and you should be proud. Although maybe it's a feeling you can only allow yourself once you actually see her breathing and awake, so go, your shift finished twenty minutes ago, anyway."

"Maybe," Grey closed his eyes, took a deep breath and went to leave.

"Oh, one more thing." Mack interrupted and his technician turned to receive further instructions. "On the back of that excellent work, I wanted to reward you. And before you start protesting, one: I know you don't want to move out of your current position, and two: you don't get a say in the matter, you're getting rewarded."

"Fine, what did you have in mind, boss?"

"You know, I used to think like you did. Being a technician here is something rather special, you have an immense impact on the lives of each and every soul in the Crimson, affecting their lives for the better. We interpret everything because the digital state of the region is a complex labyrinth of communication and conspiracy which makes our work here so important, we do what we do to keep all the people safe. It wasn't until nearly a decade ago that I saw a different purpose for myself, a different way that I could serve the people of the Crimson."

"A different way you could serve the company? You mean becoming management, because I don't want that, Mack," Grey protested.

"The company gets by perfectly fine on its own, Grey, you needn't worry about it. I'm talking about helping people, being the change that you want to see, or at least helping it along the way and not standing in the way of those more proactive in those beliefs. You're a good tech, Grey. Certainly the best I've worked with, and for that reason I spoke with Director Thorne himself to hash out a significant pay rise for yourself. You'll actually be nearly my level, and I'm telling you Grey, start using that uplift to buy natural food. You haven't lived until you've tasted real, untampered food, like steak! By the stars, give that a go as soon as you can! Really enjoy this pay increase, Grey, you earned it."

"Thank you, boss. I'll be sure to celebrate it somehow."

"You mean sit in your bunk all on your lonesome and eat the kind of plastic crap the rest of these fools suffer through, kinda pathetic, mate," MacArthur raised an eyebrow in the other man's direction, confident that what he was saying was true.

"What I do with my time is my own business, boss," Grey pointed out, not politely.

"Yeah, just your business, where's the fun in that? Listen to me, go see this survivor, see the real reward of your good work. Talk to her, hear the life in her, the life you saved. Then consider whether your actions were heroic or not, and let yourself have the win."

"Maybe, sir," Grey relented, only so the conversation would end and he could leave. It was getting uncomfortable now, the purpose for them talking having become heavily diluted by idle chit-chat.

"OK, well, if that isn't much of an interest to you, I hear she got a replacement arm for the one she lost, a state-of-the-art, pneumatic one. Get her to give you a hand job for saving her life, with that thing you'll be spraying all over her in under a dozen seconds, I bet," MacArthur laughed, amused at his own suggestion.

"She'll be like to rip the thing off, more like," Grey allowed himself a grin and a chuckle.

"Well, sounds like an adventure, can you finish before she tears your fella off? Interesting exercise," the manager shrugged. "You're dismissed, Grey. Your relief ought to have arrived by now, send them up on your way out."

"But what about—"

"Dismissed, Grey! Damn it, man, there's more to life than this, go celebrate your good work and see the poor woman lying in the hospital bed, she would probably appreciate a visitor, but leave that pathetic, doe-eyed look here, she doesn't need to see your self-inflicted depression."

Alex Grey discarded his clipboard back on his desk as he saw his relief, a very capable woman stepped up to the platform he just left. He considered setting up an itinerary for himself for the next day but shook his head with a smile, he figured he should probably follow the advice given to him, he was turning into a serious workaholic. Grey firmly believed in Obsidian, in the policing of the system and the way they did it, and in the purpose of the listening post and the part it plays in the function Obsidian serves. He felt no hesitation about staying late to lend a hand usually, but today, after the light-hearted instruction he was handed along with the fact that he was tired, having completed his thirteen hour shift, he decided to call it a day.

He left by the door on the platform's right side, passing through the two guards that were posted at either side, into the small lobby area containing the lifts. The listening post consisted of half a dozen rings surrounding a central spire with the command centre at the outpost's second-top most level, the hangar above it, and the other levels descending the column and its rings. Under the command centre was the mess hall and living quarters for the management team and medical staff aboard the station. Next, was the hospital level, the trauma clinic and gym. Below that were the technicians' barracks, and the living quarters for the other staff, such as the cooks, cleaners, maintenance workers, while at the bottom of the station was the base for the guards posted here. All the walls to this small area that only served to grant access to the lifts were pure white, as with all the walls and floors outside of the command centre. It made for dreary decoration of his home, but Grey didn't care, he paid it no mind, he was content with his purpose in the system and didn't invest a thought if it didn't lend itself to that sense of being.

The lift arrived after a short wait and by that time a small contingent of his colleagues had joined him so Grey felt a little bit crowded in the lift down to the mess hall. He did intend to join them in stepping off at this level, to grab a bite to eat, maybe something natural as Mack had suggested, but he impulsively decided to follow his manager's other suggestion. He pressed the button for the level below, heading for the onboard hospital.

He hadn't stepped foot here since they first brought the survivor here. Alex remembered that day well as he passed through the same hallways as he had that day, only back then they were swarming with bodies. The Elite soldiers in their fearsome armour, the doctors in their polycotton, black coats, the nurses in their red scrubs, all circling around the gurney being rushed from the lift to the trauma clinic at the centre of the level. And the screaming. The woman on the bed being wheeled with all haste would not stop screaming at the top of her voice, finding air in every crevice of her lungs to fuel the echoing cries that were like nothing Grey had ever heard, or could have ever imagined. A slick trail of blood followed, and Grey had followed that day, curious if his work had been helpful, if he had served his company and purpose well, and he was shocked to find that he had. An arm flung up from the wreathing body being held down onto the white sheets of the gurney for just a moment long enough for the technician to see, and he couldn't describe how he felt at the sight. It was partnered with the terrified shrieks that rolled down the hallway, horrific wails of the things she had seen, what had done all this damage to her. Not that he could hold onto those feelings rising in him for long as the bed was pushed through the double doors of the operating room. And suddenly he couldn't see the hand anymore, or, more as a relief, hear the screams.

Now, though, there was hardly a soul to be seen. It was late, not that night showed itself in the deep, dark of space, it always looked like night out of the windows around the top and sides of the rings that ran around the centre area. And this ring, on this level, was occupied by the resting patients' area on the far side of the exercise zone. It was here that Alex walked round to, passing patients asleep in their beds, the medical staff at their work before he finally found the bed he was looking for. The woman lying in the bed caught Grey by surprise. She wasn't crying in agony or howling how she had been about the things she had seen down in the Old City. Instead, she was rather peacefully stroking and gazing at her new arm that started at her left elbow and spanned into a metallic hand, all cast in a shining chrome layer of plated skin. She was younger than Grey expected, of an age where she could have easily been his daughter, if he had ever found someone willing to be his wife, she could have only been 26 or 27. Short brunette hair was slick back and glistening above tanned skin, with curious brown eyes absent of pain or trauma, and pink coloured lips. She was pretty, her face beaming of a kind of innocent, scrutinising nature as her fingers delicately danced across the plating and cables of her new limb, clearly not concerned by it. Grey almost forgot that this woman was a soldier, and had to be a good one to have been assigned to a team with such a special purpose as to be sent into the Old Capital, as she had such a petite frame, not the bulk of a usual trooper.

"Oh, hi there, guessing you're not one of the doctors," she said as she noticed the man staring at her, flicking her eyebrows up as a way of saying that she was referring to the uniform he was wearing.

"No, no," Grey stammered and he realised out of the blue how unpractised he was in talking to people outside of work. "Name's Alex Grey, I'm a Senior Tech here," he said, replying with a sterner voice than he meant, in an attempt to cover up his blunder. Unlike his colleagues who often roamed in groups outside of their shifts, Grey preferred to be alone, seeking solace in exercising alone, eating alone and going to bed alone. He didn't mind, it was his chosen way of being after all, but it did mean that outside of the conversations he would sparingly have with his manager, he was lost in how to talk to people casually, without an agenda.

"Would you be the Mr Grey that heard me call for help? The doctors only told me that much, I guess I haven't been awake too long to learn anymore," she smiled, a young person's smile, showing her teeth and vibrance of life, in spite of her recent experience.

"That's me," Grey put a hand through his hair and looked around where he found himself. The bed was directly ahead of him, a basic thing of white metal, the same colour as the floor tiles beneath his feet, and walls above the head of the woman he was talking to. To the left of the bed from his view was a cabinet with a tray on top of some kind of medical instruments, next to the IV bag that was hooked up into the woman. While on the other side, there was a simple wooden chair, and a series of screens monitoring her health: her heartbeat, her breathing rate, the purity of her blood from radiation, among other measures. "Mind if a seat, just for a bit," he said, indicating at the chair with a hand.

"Yeah, course, you saved my life, least I can do is let you sit your arse down, right?" She laughed and Grey was amazed by her bravery.

"Well, I played my part I suppose, I contributed some small bit to the effort that brought you here. I'm glad to see you up and awake," he said, raising his glasses back up his face by lifting their corner up with his thumb and the end knuckle on his index finger.

"Well, we both know that if you didn't hear me call out, I wouldn't be here to talk to you, now would I?"

"S'pose not."

"Fuck! I'm being rude, I haven't told you my name! I'm Elle Black, pleased to meet you," Elle reached out her new left hand and Grey took it, giving it a shake.

"Alex Grey," he replied instinctively, and instantly regretting it.

"Yeah I know," she laughed. "You already said. So how long have you been a senior tech here, Alex?"

"Six years as a senior and thirty-three as a standard tech, straight out of school, I'm actually from Rose City."

"No way! That's mad, you were living there before the Collapse! Sorry to be the one to tell you this but your home city has changed a little since you grew up," Elle said sarcastically, causing herself to chuckle.

"Yeah, I don't doubt it," Grey smiled, looking away from the woman and taking in the view she had from her bed, and it wasn't all that interesting. Other than a simple table with a plastic plant beside a nurse's clipboard that sat opposite her bed, all she could see was the white tiling of the wall of the ring they were in.

"Yeah I know, not much of a view, huh? As soon as I woke up I asked for a transfer to Ruby, somewhere with a view of the lakes, maybe a beach, something nicer than this shithole of function over comfort," Elle laughed, "you call this hunk of metal, home?"

"I know it isn't a pretty sight but you get used to it and besides, a job's a job, it serves." Grey fixed the woman with a curious stare, there was something about her that didn't fit this setting, something he couldn't quite figure out. She was genuinely cheerful, despite resting in a hospital bed after an induced coma to let her body heal from the surgery of introducing a replacement limb, it was the last thing Grey expected her to be after that kind of ordeal. Yet here she was, talking about an upgrade to her current settings and making light-hearted conversation. The gown she was wearing was a thin piece of cotton, only meant to suffice in covering up the more private areas of the body but this was a small thing, it left little to the imagination. Her smooth, sandy skin peered out from behind the white gown but was covered in fresh scaring, glued shut wounds and skin grafts, a shadow of the elegant beauty it once had. Grey found himself tracing these scars, trying to map what might have caused a particularly horrific slash that ran down the length of her left leg, starting at the top of her thigh and rotating around at the knee to strike down just shy of the ankle, when Elle caught him looking.

"See something you like?" Elle teased with a giggle, enjoying the sight as the other man coughed into his hand to cover up his curiosity.

"Relax, I'm near double your age, was just trying to figure out what in all the starways did that to your leg?" Grey nodded in the direction of her leg, flicking his glasses back up with the knuckle of right thumb.

"If I told you, I doubt you'd actually believe it."

"Well, I'll do my best to avoid seeing my old place, I suppose," Grey shrugged with a smile.

"Yeah put off the trip down memory lane for now, why don'tcha?" Elle replied with a wink and a laugh, straightening out her gown down over her left side more, covering her body up.

"You don't sound anything like a standard trooper, what were you doing on a mission like this?" Grey couldn't put it off any longer, he simply couldn't picture this woman wielding a gun, let alone hardened to use it, she simply seemed too joyful and sweet.

"My job," she said straight. "Maybe I don't sound like a standard squaddie but that's because I'm not one, I'm in the Elites," she grinned and shrugged, blinking slowly.

"Been a long time since I've seen one of you, probably back before the Collapse, really."

That made Elle prop herself up and turn slightly to face her visitor more openly, she gripped the edge of her bed on that side and pushed herself forward, forgetting that the front of her gown was now drooping slightly. "Did you ever see the Commander?"

"Winter? Yeah once or twice but it wasn't a good thing to catch a glimpse of him." Grey grimaced as he recalled his former home, leaning back in his chair, he drifted his gaze over to the table opposite Elle's bed. "He was young when he was named Elite Commander, even younger than you are now. And it was big news, it caught a lot of attention, Thorne senior giving a position that important to someone so inexperienced and unknown. But he came from a high up Obsidian family that threw him into the Elite academy when he was six. People in the right places started to learn his name and I guess that opened the door."

"What was he like? Really. Why wouldn't it be a good thing to see him? If I was around back, then I would beg for a position by his side, they say he was the best fighter in Obsidian!"

"He was aggressive in his purpose. The way he ran rule over the Elites was so new, so innovative, but it was bloody too, he organised assassinations within the conglomerate, bet you didn't you know that!" Grey intended that to serve as a warning but it seemed to excite the woman even more. "If a manager, or even a director, stepped out of line in a big way, he'd end them. And he built up quite the reputation for it too. Rather famously, the Director of Stardust, a right, scummy pervert, was shot in the centre of Rose. His head was blown off as he did his usual thing, parading himself among his dancers on the stage during a celebration of the anniversary of the city's birth. The crowd didn't even gasp, they knew the guy was no good, and they knew from where the shot had come from, and why. Winter was a leader in the Obsidian hierarchy that had the will to make big, dramatic choices, but with the sense to do things close to being the right thing. That's why people still idolise the man eight years after he disappeared," Grey cast his gaze back to Elle, expecting to see her somewhat disappointed, deflated by her hero being dragged through the mud to some extent, but instead her eyes were wide, she seemed eager to learn more.

"Yeah but no one really knows why he disappeared, and we never had another Commander since, we get our orders straight from the Director or Section Chief, now," Elle grabbed her pillow and rested it against the railing that was the edge of her bed so that she could more comfortable listening to the man speak.

"Do you know why? Why there's not been a new Commander?"

"No," Elle's eyes were brimming with curiosity, questions long living in her mind, finally being answered.

"Well, then you're talking to the right man. Being a senior tech for so long, you find things out that the company probably isn't too keen you knowing," Grey folded his arms, flicking one leg over the other, oblivious how comfortable he was talking to this woman who had been a mere stranger only moments ago. "Positions high up in the conglomerate, such as your senior managers, like the Elite Commander, and the directorate, and the Section Chief, all of them have a special bond with their contracts. The drop of blood they gave to their contracts at birth, like all of us did too, was used to match with their unique DNA, and the authority of their stations. Meaning, only they can have access to whatever it is they do. The Head of RCS wants to cut his workforce in a factory? Only they can do it. The Section Chief wants to name their successor? Only they can do it. A new Elite Commander is needed? They would need the old one to transfer his power."

"What's the point in that?" Elle scrunched her nose, she didn't get it.

"Well, it's actually the system that all the companies under the Board have to conform to. And to be blunt, it's a slightly corrupt system to be truthfully honest. It means the positions of power stay within the tight knit group at the top of the pyramid. They get to hoard all the best jobs and give them only to their friends and family members, under the guise of security, of course. And who argues where security is concerned? They're doing what they're doing because it keeps us safe and because of that so-called kindness, we're not meant to look too closely at it." Grey had to exaggerate his sarcasm as he actually believed in it. But because his colleagues would usually tease him about how solid his belief in his job was, he decided to play it safe and seem far more relaxed than he actually was.

"So because of security they can't just promote someone to Elite Commander? Seems stupid," Elle still didn't get it.

"Well, yes, because in their minds, their positions are everything to them, power is everything. And the fear of losing that power? Considerable," Grey nodded with a smile. "So they locked the power in. Because they consider the worst scenarios. Like say, if one of them in power were to be murdered as a ploy by one of their underlings to make their position vacant, and assume it for themselves. Wouldn't work with the system in play, as the power would simply go back to the Board and they deliberate over why it wasn't handed over, which would trigger an investigation, and the murderer would be discovered. So, you see, it's simply impossible for them to just name a new one as they wouldn't have the power of the position that still remains with Winter. A new one wouldn't have the power within the Obsidian mainframe, they wouldn't be able to issue any instructions, or schedule any work orders, and most importantly be the source of their pay. They'd just be shouting random things, no one would have any reason to listen to them."

"Yeah but I'm still paid."

"Only because the Director has probably needed to do it manually every time, it takes someone in the right positions to authorise their own actions. But that's where there's a chink in the chain of command, because now, what if something happens to the Director? The Elites, and now the whole of Obsidian, wouldn't receive their pay because they wouldn't have transferred their power. Then imagine what would happen if someone killed the Section Chief."

"No one gets their pay?"

"Absolutely right, the entire system would grind to a halt," Grey nodded. "Whether he meant to or not, Commander Winter exposed the true, fragile nature of not just the hierarchy within our own Coalition, but of the Board as well, as the same system is deployed all the way to the top, to include the Chairman themself. The fact remains, however, will he take advantage of it?"

"It's Grey, isn't it?" A strong, firm voice broke the conversation, coming from behind the technician who had to almost fully swing around in his chair to see the small group of officers' approach. "Be mindful how you speak, those words are dangerously close to misconduct, Mr Grey."

"I'm sorry, sir. What I was saying does not reflect my true feelings towards Obsidian, I give you my word," Grey stood up as soon as he recognised the obvious high rank of the man leading the pack of newcomers.

"And what would they be, Senior Technician Grey?" The man chuckled out the words which somehow made them more intimidating to the shorter technician. This officer stood tall with his muscular build, bearing a serious expression on a dark skinned face, under a head of black hair cropped to a well-defined point at the front. He was clean shaven which matched how he maintained his pristine uniform of the standard Obsidian Elite armour but with a black leather long-coat over the top, bearing a red cape over his right shoulder and halfway down his back on that side. Two stern brown eyes shot out from a protruding jaw, they locked onto the other man who bore the same uniform as his own party, as they too wore the black suit with the red trim of an Obsidian officer.

"I'm sorry, sir, I don't recognise you," Grey regretted mumbling out. He knew every officer and manager on the listening post, his surprise showing at meeting someone of such a high position that he didn't recognise.

"Alex, this is Vice-Admiral Constantin Reiku, he has temporary stewardship of the Elites, under the direct supervision and approval of Chief Thorne," Elle introduced, doing her best to make herself presentable, sitting up and ignoring the pain of doing so.

"Yes, Miss Black, but I was asking technician Grey about his feelings towards our company," Reiku's glare beamed an angry authority, the weight of those eyes similar to the force of being hit by a hammer.

"I believe in the system and I believe in what we do in Obsidian to protect it. Millions of lives depend on the system, families, people fulfilling their purpose, putting their hands to honest work and it is our duty to ensure they are free and safe to carry on that contribution so that we might all benefit. If the system should be attacked and thrown into chaos, forced to fail, all would suffer, so the importance of our work cannot be understated," Grey held eye-contact with the Vice-Admiral, thinking that he would most respect that rather than looking anywhere else.

Reiku was silent, his arms clasped behind his back as he stepped forward slowly, his steps echoing off the floor, louder as he got closer to Grey. "I respect your sentiments, Grey." The Vice-Admiral's voice was quiet and near to a whisper, fully knowing that the others present would have to strain to hear him. "But now it's time for you to leave us, the conversation I must have with Miss Black is highly confidential."

Grey took one final glance over at the woman by his side who gave him a nod so he felt polite in leaving and he took the route furthest around the Vice-Admiral to make his exit. And once away from the woman in the hospital bed, he suddenly realised just how comfortable he had been in that fairly long conversation. It was the most relaxed he had been with someone in a long time, even though he hardly knew anything about his new friend other than her name and that she was an Elite. And yet the look on her face when she saw the officer, Reiku, gave him pause. So once he was out of their view, his curiosity got the better of him and he tucked himself into a crevice behind the bend of the ring. From this distance though, he could only just about make out what they were saying.

"…did you see in the city? What happened to your team?" Grey recognised Reiku's voice.

"Sir, we were set upon right after we infiltrated the city's shell. They were all over us, we lost half the team on entry," he could hear Elle reply, her voice sounded different to before, far more serious and professional.

"What set upon you?"

"They were dead people but they were even stronger than us, they wrestled a man double my size to the ground and tore out his throat. And they were dead, definitely dead, but they were still attackin' us, even after we put bullets in 'em. But I have a feeling they were the ones less affected by whatever happened to 'em as some were way bigger, like way, way bigger, more like ferocious beasts, they tore my team into pieces, one of them ripped half my arm off when I put my knife in his eye! And the robo-sentries wiped out the rest of my squad as we tried to circle back to our entry point. We thought we were zoned in contending with the carnivorous beasts, that we were slaughtered when the automated security descended. Only reason I got out was that they were so busy killing my team, I got pushed over under the weight of one o' them. One of their bodies fell on me and we fell back together into the river, I almost drowned. I eventually managed to swim out through the small gap we used to enter the city and called through my location."

"You mean to say your team abandoned their objective? Did you not investigate the facility?" The Vice-Admiral's voice was cold and emotionless.

"Sir, we were overrun and overwhelmed in minutes, straight after we breached the city perimeter. We made our way into the city and found the bunker but they set upon us again, we had to bail or die. The mission was a bust barely after it began."

"And you can confirm that all of your team died?"

"Well, no, I mean I saw most of them die but some went out of sight and then I got pushed into the water and I couldn't get my head up for a bit so I guess one or two of them could have lived a little longer, but how should I know if they're still alive?"

"True, you wouldn't know. So we will simply have to go and find out."

Grey's eyes went wide and he craned his neck around the bend to see the Vice-Admiral and his officers crowding around the bed where on it was the woman he had been talking to who was bolted upright, and she looked utterly petrified.

"You're not serious," Grey could just about hear her mutter.

"Section Chief Thorne has already given the order, we're sending a second team into the Old City."

Chapter 9

It felt as though the memories of the rifle came to life as Nathan reassembled it after cleaning it, examining each knock and painted over scratch as one might reminisce with an old friend. The simple workbench, a lump of wood nailed over a set of drawers with a backboard holding up various tools, and a vice attached to the front so he could mix and match his ammunition, served to prop up the weapon. For the most part, the rifle was black. From its stock, to the frame, the barrel and the trigger handle, the scope at the top and the grip under the end. The only thing of a different colour was the pouch bound around the stock, made of a brown leather that housed bullets of a higher calibre than those in the box at the weapon's base. He had taken his gloves off so Nathan could feel every blemish in the gun's framing, tracing them with his fingers as he placed the parts together.

As he screwed his scope back into place, his fingertips found a scratch that he hadn't yet covered over, and he remembered how he had run out of ammo when defending himself on impulse when searching a house on Sanguine. He was only a teenager at the time, a fresh member of the Elite guard, sent to accompany an Obsidian squad going through the worker towns on the planet looking for a kidnapped small boy. The family at the house were a little rough looking but were courteous enough in letting the team in, they didn't interfere in the search of the house either. But they became agitated when Nathan asked why they had children sized clothes in their bedroom, yet no children of that age were living in the house. That's when he noticed there was a basement hatch under the dining room table, an area his team hadn't searched yet. Nathan pushed the table aside to the kitchen cupboards and opened the hatch wide but there was no light down there so he hopped straight in. Using his lighter in his left hand and holding his rifle in his right, he gazed about the improvised addition to the house, where a small child was being held in a makeshift cage comprised of wooden stakes and rope. As he held the lighter up to the cage, the light encouraging the young boy to crawl towards him, Nathan heard a second body drop into the basement but his instincts told him to spin round. He did and saw a knife coming rushing down at him, deflecting it on impulse by lifting his rifle up to get in the way, dropping the lighter on the floor as he grasped his weapon with both hands against the weight of his attacker. It was easy for him, he shrugged the man of the house off, throwing him to one side and putting two bullets in his midriff, and another in his head to be sure. When he hoisted himself up out of the basement, he found that his team had secured the wife and the two teenage sons, none of them surprised by the discovery under where they presumably ate as a family. Nathan would occasionally wonder if the kid was meant to have been one of those meals. But it wasn't a thought that plagued his mind as it had occurred to him at the time and he had decided to deal with it, permanently. It was one of his first times having an Obsidian policing team backing him up, but if he was at all nervous by their presence, it didn't show. He calmly read out the concern of the family's behaviour, and carried out summary action against them, a bullet for each of their heads as they knelt under the control of a trooper. Nathan coolly brought his rifle up and dispatched them, doing his job with an inspired, measured composure.

Once the scope was reattached, Nathan raised it up, using the dials on the sides to adjust the reticle at the centre of the glass so that it was accurately lined up for his use, hardly noticing the X-Human enter behind him. Cait entered the armoury, wearing her RCS jumpsuit and her hooded half-cloak, but between them she bore an armoured section on her torso, a plated corset, perfectly conformed to her body, the same black as the rest of her outfit. "Is this how you're meant to wear this?"

Nathan placed the rifle down, turning and leaning back against the workbench, scrutinising the woman standing before him and turning his head slightly as he saw the magnetic catches were a small bit skewered. "Looks good to me, just a few finishing touches, you don't want it coming undone while we're out there," Nathan remarked, using his fingers intricately to undo each of the three magnetic catches on Cait's side, clasping them shut and locking them by pinching the plates together. "That's better," he judged his work and looked up at the two beaming bejewelled eyes of purple staring straight at him. "Something wrong?"

"Nah," Cait turned away from him and retrieved her weapon from the bedroom where she had slept, while Nathan again took the armchair. "So you really think this is a good fit for me?" It was a simple pump-action shotgun, cast in the black framing of an Obsidian weapon with housing on the side for additional shells, and a grip handle under the barrel for easier control.

"If you're not a practised shot, shoot more," Nathan shrugged, turning to his own weapon as Cait tried out putting the stock of the shotgun into her shoulder, running her eye down the length of the weapon. "If the kick bothers you, click the stock in and you can have it recoil into the air, won't be an issue. Use the strap though, you don't want to lose that thing, you'll be surprised how easily you forget things when you're running for your life."

Nathan was screwing a suppressor onto the end of his rifle as Cait removed her cloak before flinging the strap of her shotgun over her shoulder and around her neck, adjusting her hood over the top so that she was comfortable, and then she cast her gaze over to the man at her side. "Wait, I have the loud gun, you're making yours quieter—am I just a distraction so you can get away?"

"Thought had crossed my mind," Nathan replied with a dry sarcasm. "No, no, you won't be using that weapon until you have no other choice, I'll be doing the main bulk of the fighting and I don't want to be announcing where we are with every shot." He eyed the attachment carefully, considering it, and, after finding a slightly shorter one in his assortment of parts on the upright board behind his workbench, he swapped it. The weapon was made longer for the introduced part and Nathan strapped it carefully onto his back, saddling it against the side of his jetpack, casting his eye down to make sure it wouldn't interfere with his legs, but it only just about reached further than the back of his thigh. Next, he placed his gloves back on and checked his equipment stowed in the belt at his waist. Magazines of ammunition for his rifle and pistols, some spare bullets of the larger calibre, his lighter and cigars, a canteen of water, a flask of whiskey, some food bars and grenades. Satisfied, he picked up the sleeping roll, a basic looking thing made from a blue, thermal material, and went to sling it on the opposite side of the jetpack to his rifle but stopped when a thought occurred to him.

Cait, seeing the other man freeze, cast a curious look over to him, "something wrong?"

"No," Nathan replied, more bluntly than he meant to. "Maybe, I had a conversation with your bartender, that Xin, on the Forerunner."

"His words get stuck in your head? I swear the man could be doing so much more, he has a real talent for laying his ideas into people's minds," Cait laughed and leaned against the closed metal cabinet, flicking her eyebrows up to herself in remembering what was on the other side of those thick, bulky doors.

"I don't remember what he said exactly, it's more the feeling in my gut that they caused that won't seem to go away." Nathan grasped either side of the workbench and leaned against it, before turning his eyes to his helmet that lay at the corner of it, the shadowy grey ovals watching him. "I'm considering that it might be a good idea for at least someone on this venture of ours to know my reasons for getting involved in all this." He didn't turn around, the idea of opening up didn't seem wise to him, it didn't sit well, but something about giving it all up to Cait, something about that felt like something he would be OK with.

"OK, well, it's your business. So I didn't want to pry but if you're feeling like sharing, least I can do is listen," Cait took the armchair and worked out the clips so that she was able to detach her shotgun from its strap and lean it up against the table next to her.

"I guess I start from the beginning? Never really done this before," Nathan smiled to himself, not quite believing how hard this was.

"But didn't you have a wife?" Cait figured probing might actually be helpful.

"Monique Monroe, before she took my name."

"How did you two meet?"

"I was assigned to Rose City as an Elite guard maybe fourteen years ago now, when I was eighteen, freshly graduated from the academy. She was working in the Ruby Consolidated Head Office in the city and I was called there for a task, some kind of data leak and she was helping me uncover who it was selling the secrets to the competition in the other systems. She was only a bit older than me and we just, I don't know, clicked, I guess." Nathan turned around and lent against the workbench, folding his arms and looking over at Cait. "I asked her out to coffee after we found who it was, and that was that."

"You asked someone out for coffee? Hard to imagine you relaxed," Cait held a strange smirk on her face, her imagination contorting into all sorts of shapes. "Nah, can't picture you without the gun," she laughed.

"Well, believe it or not, I was actually quite social, once upon a time," Nathan allowed himself a chuckle. "But you know," he said in knocking himself out of blissfully getting lost in fonder times, "things changed," and so did his tone.

"So what happened?"

"We got to dating. Dating turned to spending all of our free time together, and eventually we got married. It made sense to combine our colleague profiles so that we could afford a home, somewhere we could start a family. And we both worked in the city, but both agreed that we didn't want to live there, being so close to our managers. So we took up some advice we were given and bought a place in the nearby town, a short trip down the main highway, a little place back then called Dunnfink."

Cait adjusted herself in the chair and flicked an eye over at the metal cabinet on the far wall, knowing the end of the story she was being told.

"And we did just that, started a family I mean. I was maybe twenty-one? Yeah it was three years after we met," Nathan nodded to himself. "We had a boy, Harkness. And let me tell you, this was one good looking kid."

The smile on Nathan's face disarmed Cait completely, it was the first time that she had seen him looking remotely happy, somewhat human. She felt bad for not seeing him as anything other than the weapon he was so good at being, the infamous Elite Commander, a fearsome warrior, maybe with no equal. But the man standing possibly only a metre or so away from her seemed someone different entirely, like she was having a glimpse of a ghost. A bittersweet feeling came over her, she knew this temporary feeling of comfort for Nathan wouldn't last.

"He had my looks but his mum's attitude, he was a genuinely good lad, nothing like me really, none of my aggression, but then we were able to give him a far better upbringing than what I got. My parents are Obsidian officers, they work in the policing progression department, they come up with new ways for the enforcement of Board law. They're loyal friends of Roderic Thorne since his Section Chief days, he helped them get me a place in the Elite academy and then probably played a hand in my promotion to Commander. I was only six when I started my training, I didn't want that life for Harkness. But thing is, he might be alive if I had sent him off to Carmine."

"What happened to him? I'm guessing it has something to do with the Capital Collapse?"

"If there were warning signs of what was to happen, I either wasn't made aware of them or just didn't see them, because it really did happen as quick as they say it did. The day was completely normal until the alarm went off. And you have to understand, this was an alarm from the first days of the city, they weren't sure about the reliability of the terraforming process back then, so this was basically a last ditch measure, it was outdated and forgotten about. And there were two, the initial alarm set the sequence for evacuating the city, the second one went off to confirm it."

"But what actually caused it?"

"No idea," Nathan replied. "It wasn't sabotage by a group of WIDOWs or whatever the company line about it was, that's for sure. No, we'll just have to find out what caused it, but it was that general evacuation alarm that signalled the start of it. And let me tell you, I have never seen panic or fear or confusion anything like what I saw that day, it was completely insane. And the hierarchy didn't do anything to help things, they prioritised their own safety. We were given the order to gun down anyone who got in the path of evacuating the leadership, to assume they were WIDOWs out to assassinate them. That order turned the streets to chaos, into a warzone, a bloody race to flee the city. And while all this carnage was going on, the armoured shell was rising up from the city walls, sealing the city up as it thought that there was a terraforming failure on the planet and that it needed to seal itself off to protect its citizens. Which just made the fucking idiots panic even more, scrambling over warm corpses to get ahead, to get out."

"And where were you in all that?"

"I commanded the Elite guards from my place at the Section Chief's side, my own job being to protect him and the directorate. I ordered my people to clear the way but with the least loss of life, we needed to keep the panic down to make it much easier. But people didn't want to listen when they were seeing the shell rise up above their heads, blocking out the yellow sun. They panicked and gunned down the civilians. I can't tell you how many died, and this was just on the streets of the city. The alarm lasted for thirty minutes so you can imagine, it was utter bedlam. And not everyone made it out, maybe a few thousand were left trapped inside."

"You think any of them are still alive?"

"Maybe. Plenty of food in there. Whether there's clean water, that's the thing, the shell covered the river, it bore straight into the ground as well up and over the rooftops, so if the reservoir under the city is undamaged, then maybe."

"So the city sealed itself off, and you had this huge herd of people?"

"Essentially yes, everyone who made it out was now homeless and scared, they travelled down the main highway, small fights broke out, we had to step half a dozen times, to keep everyone in check. But halfway to Dunnfink, the directorate called an emergency meeting. But this one was different. Usually I'd be there, to protect them. Yet this time they used robo-sentries from RCS as security. And the next thing I knew my own Elites and a large contingent of the Obsidian forces were given the order to invade the small town and subdue the locals, by any means necessary. You remember that Captain Willis? The one with the landing key?"

"Yeah, gotta assume he was there?"

"Well, I caught up with one of my Elites last year, one still loyal to Thorne, but once I carved into him enough, he gave up a small detail. You see, Elias liked this Captain. Kept him at his side as his confidant within Obsidian. This Captain Willis was present in this impromptu meeting of theirs, and it was him that gave the order to move into Dunnfink with all force."

"You think he got that order from Elias Thorne?"

"I do but what I don't know is why. Elias was Director of RCS at that time, he had nothing to do with Obsidian or keeping the peace, but if he wanted to interfere without his father's knowledge, having a friend in the company would be the way to do it. Maybe he came up with the order on his own, or maybe he twisted one that came from the Section Chief, either one would've been easy."

"So they stormed a peaceful town? But that's murder! How is this the first time I'm hearing about this?" Cait sat forward, perching on the edge of the armchair, keen to hear more.

"They did, and covered it up under the guise of security. According to the history books, they wiped out a cell of WIDOWs that caused the Collapse, having used the town as a base. And sure, people died in the crossfire but the formidable heroes of Obsidian did their job, and they did it well. Any and all sacrifices in this skirmish could not blemish the record that the Obsidian troops were the courageous protectors of the Capital citizens."

"Is that what happened to your family?"

"I didn't know anything about the order to invade the town until it was already too late. I was up on the highway, looking down a pair of binos at a break of land that would be good to let people have a rest on, when I heard the gunfire. Dunnfink was on fire in under a minute. They subdued or killed every person they came across, most of them X-Human as the housing was poorer. I used my pack to fly over the chaos to reach our house on the far side. I actually thought I would beat them by flying, but they got there first. I kicked in the door and two Obsidian officers were at my side, and across the room, my wife was still cradling my son's body. She tried to shield him. She had a single bullet in her head, and he was shot through his eye, it was just a bloody gash, completely gone."

"Obsidian troops killed your family?"

"Yeah," Nathan blew out and held his head in his right hand, covering his mouth first then his eyes, hating recalling that dreadful day.

"But why? What threat could an unarmed woman and a child pose?"

"You have to understand," he considered his words for a moment, before crossing his arms in front of him. "Obsidian soldiers are so compliant because they are so tightly wound to follow instructions from the first day of training. They are basically built up to be absolutely terrified of defying or failing in their purpose. And I don't mean they're anxious about it or somewhat apprehensive, I mean real, literal fear of failure. And they attach that fear to their superiors, they see them as avenging forces, there to kill them should they disobey. The Elite I worked over last year said that they killed my family because not only did they not recognise them, but because they were so afraid of me especially that they dare not fail. My wife and son died because the two Obsidian in my house were too afraid of what I would do to them if they didn't shoot at everything in sight, to protect the Directorate whatever it cost."

"And you think that Captain pointed out your house? Or?"

"No, I doubt he or anyone else would be brave enough. I think they invaded the town in the hope that no one would look too closely at one house being hit, maybe they got a little encouragement but nothing that would've stood out."

"And you think Elias did the encouraging to the Captain?"

"Just a theory," Nathan grunted.

"And why would the now Section Chief have made a move against you like that?"

"That's what I want to find out. Back on Vermilion, I could feel it, I was starting to settle."

"Settle?"

"I'm not the same anymore, Cait, I don't feel anything like who I used to be," Nathan looked over at Cait and she could see what he was saying could have been true, the ghost she had seen was gone. "On Vermilion, I was building another life, another purpose for myself but it's more than that."

"What'd you mean?"

"I don't even eat the same food, I never sleep a full night, and I see things differently now. When I see some of the management of the Coalition, it's like they glow, I just can't ignore them and I get such an energised feeling, like I'm starving. It starts in my chest, like a hit of adrenaline but it's like fire, it spreads to my arms and legs and infects my brain. I can think of nothing else, but to hang them upside down, take an eye and put a bullet into their skull. There's a desire in me now, to keep adding to the collection in that cabinet."

"So why is Elias still alive?"

"The new home of the Section Chief after Rose City fell is that Arcadia station of his, his small, little armoured town for his directorate friends with servants to see to them. They're far too dug in to attack, it'd be suicide." Nathan bowed his head, his eyes lost in the shadow, the dim bulb in the room unable to reach them. "It does cross my mind but back on Vermilion it just didn't seem worth trying, he's too well defended, why try with no chance to succeed."

"And now?"

"Now, it seems like I can do more by living, like I might actually be worth something again, hence this olive branch," Nathan turned to the X-Human sitting by his side and if he considered himself capable of forging a connection again, then he would consider what he felt to be the embers to start a fire.

"But that's why I kinda wanted a chat along these kinds of lines, too. I wanted to ask you something," Cait considered her thoughts, wanting to be accurate in giving them breath.

"Go on," Nathan's voice sounded like a challenge but he hadn't meant it that way, it was just the way he talked.

"Say we get to this vault place, or whatever, and say we actually make it out of there and away with whatever we can find to prove how the Collapse actually happened, what will you be wanting to do next? What would you want to do with this proof?" Cait's purple eyes scanned the man as deep as she could, trying to breach his defences to see past the seemingly vacant expression on his face.

"With this, we can pick up a following, put an army together, work with Molly from the Sapphire and produce a force to take on Elias, and then we burn the Coalition down, we get ourselves a true victory," Nathan replied confidently, nodding.

"But what of the lives that depend on the system to live? I'll be the first to say the work contracts need to go, they're wrong and tie people down to the ground and let the waves wash over them, drowning them slowly, but the system otherwise works! It's just the people who run it who need to be overthrown, and with the proof, we'll remove Elias Thorne and install a new Chief, one to look out for the people of the Crimson," Cait stood up, crossing her arms as she walked over to stare blankly at the metal cabinet on the wall.

"That's a half measure, Cait, you know that. There are no guarantees other than those we make for ourselves. With what they've done, there can be only one action to take. They all have to die."

"And you think I don't agree? This is the fight I've wanted my entire life, ever since I saw what this system does to good people who only want a bit of fair treatment but instead got shot where they sat! My dad dreamed of a better future for people and looked at what happened to him when he tried playing their game! They cannot be reasoned with, Nate! They kill us if we step out of line, so we need to kill 'em right back for the same fucking thing!" Cait spun round so she was standing directly in front of him, her toes right up against his, her face mere inches away from the deep frown glaring down at her. "But that's just it. You have to have the strength to say no, to say enough is enough. Open war? The Board would never sit idly by as we knock off a third of their members. The full weight of the Sapphire and Emeralds conglomerates would descend on us and we'd all be killed."

"Then they die as well," Nathan replied, his voice like ice, confident and hard.

"So what? Conquer the Crimson then just keep going? To what end? Take the Crimson, take the Sapphire, take the Emerald, take the fucking Chairman too, but then what? Thousands, maybe millions dead and for what?"

"Justice," Nathan grunted through his teeth and his eyes were aflame with rage, ready for a fight.

"What we're doing here," Cait started and rested a hand on the man's chest to try to ease him down. "It can't be about destruction. We have to give people a chance at better lives or else what's the point?"

"The point is retribution. Yes it means avenging for the past, but we have to be the heralds of the future or it will have no place for us. The past is gone, bearing sentiment for it is death. Leave the system behind, we have to kill the ones who stand in the way of progress."

"And what progress is that? A future built on blood and bone?" Cait winced and couldn't meet Nathan's eyes, his honest aggression being incredibly intimidating to look at.

"Of those deserving of death, yes." Nathan raised Cait's chin with the knuckle of his right hand index finger to have her meet his gaze, "war is the only way."

"No, it isn't, people would die, Nate," Cait replied, stronger than she meant and she waved his hand off, turned and stepped away from him. "I'm prepared to take on the leadership of a conglomerate, I can sure as the stars take on you." She brought herself back around to face Nathan, her right hand clenched in a fist to help her keep her focus, she didn't want to back down at all.

"People will always die, Cait. I only mean to determine which ones," Nathan replied, too content with his words to seem completely sane.

"Then you are my enemy," the X-Human with the purple eyes announced, holding her resolve against the figure clad all in armour and an arsenal about his person. "If you really believe that war is the way ahead, then you are the enemy. At least, Elias doesn't seem to want to start a war with everybody."

"As far as you know," Nathan grinned and spread his hands wide, extending his presence in the room.

"You know what I do think I know?" Cait gambled with a smirk, fully aware of the risk she was about to take.

"What's that?"

"I don't think you're fully committed to that," she stepped up to Nathan steadily, placing a hand on his cheek, inspiring a confused expression on his face. "I think there are remnants of your old self still alive inside you, I don't think they'll let you. I don't believe that you'll wage a war to kill thousands because I don't believe your humanity is completely burned away."

"And what makes you so sure of that?" Nathan peered down at Cait, his gaze was ruthless and piercing, aggression a blazing inferno in his bold, brown eyes.

"Because someone who is just a serial killer wouldn't feel a need to open up to anybody," she said with a soft smile, "or weigh caution and not attack a fortress in favour of giving himself a chance at a better, meaningful life."

"Am I interrupting something?" Lena appeared at the door linking the armoury with the rest of the ship, leaning up against the frame with a cheeky grin. She was already dressed in the armour she had chosen from Siobhan's shop, yet still wore her red trench coat over the top. She wore a Stardust branded grey leotard under a black armoured vest that only covered the top half of her chest, this was connected to long tights of the same colour by buckles that travelled across her stomach to the where they met the material at the top of the thighs. These tights met black leather high heeled boots just above her knees. Across her vest, Lena had strapped a holster bearing huge calibre rounds, each with a red tip, and she had a pistol in a holster at her right side, attached to a belt. On her back, she had a brown backpack with a sleeping roll tied to its top, and next to it, she had her rifle, a colossal instrument that almost reached the floor from being clasped over her shoulder.

"No, we were just finished," Cait smiled, and went to leave but halted when she saw the pack on her friend's back. "Shit, I fucking forgot it," she said, dashing back into the bedroom behind her.

"What? She left the condom on the side?" Lena winked at Nathan but he simply grunted and turned around, picking up his helmet, prepared to go.

"Alright, now I'm set," Cait reappeared with her own matching bag on her back, and she took a glance at Nathan. "Here, give me your sleeping roll, it's in the way of those rockets you got attached to your jetpack," she held out a hand.

Nathan knew he had covered up the launcher behind his left shoulder so was grateful to free it up and handed the roll over, where Cait slung it behind her own left side before giving Cait an upwards nod to leave the armoury.

"So what were you guys talking about?" Lena mused with her juicy red lips forming a sly grin.

"Well, where do you stand on this? War?" Cait asked her friend as they entered the small section of the ship linking the two lower areas to the upper floor by the ladder separating the two doorways. "Or revolution?"

"I don't know, where do you stand?" Lena asked, looking her friend in the eye.

"Well, I'd prefer a revolution that sticks to building a resistance within our own borders, against just our conglomerate. We remove the bastards who keep us under their boot and we make the necessary changes before setting the system to tick over again," Cait explained, hoping her friend would agree with her, after her chat with Nathan she was nervous that she was being unrealistic.

"Then that's what we'll do," Lena shrugged. "Trusted you this far, will trust you to whatever end," she gave Cait a playful couple of slaps on her cheek, a strange way of showing affection. "What, this one wants war?"

Cait smiled and shrugged back at her, she respected Nathan's opinion and saw the merits of it, but she firmly believed it was wrong.

"Nah, he'll do as he's told," Lena winked at Nathan and he glanced away from her eye contact. "Come on, they're waiting for us on the bridge." She didn't waste time, Lena turned and grasped the ladder, bounding up it with swift agility, Cait watched her go before following with Nathan in behind.

Miles was sitting calmly in the transport tunnel, his new rifle across from him as he adjusted his helmet and pulled on his gloves of the same light grey colour, and straightened his olive green jacket. The weapon he had chosen was a later model of the rifle he had taken with him when he left his hometown, back on Sanguine. Whereas his old, familiar weapon was of a wooden structure with the cartridge at the top, and was single-shot, needing to be cocked after each energy round fired, this was an updated version. This one was Stalwart issue as well but the framing was black metal with the magazine behind the trigger, the energy rounds within the casing glowing a radiant green. He glanced over as the three approached at his left side but looked past them when he counted one fewer than he was expecting. "Where's Sam?"

"He's not in the cockpit, I just came from there," Lena offered, turning her head towards Cait who just widened her eyes in a confused look.

"He's probably down in the storage section, one in his own company that one," Miles figured, rising and making his way to pass the incoming group as they headed past him to the bridge. "I'll get him."

"Hurry up, Tomen wants to brief," Lena passed on.

Miles reached the ladder at the end and slid down, a hand and foot either side, slipping down the length of the metal until he reached the floor, and activated the switch at the side of the door leading through to the storage area.

When the door opened, the X-Human with the ember beaming eyes entered and passed by the medico-table which was simply a more comfortable gurney with a terminal attached that served as the onboard doctor, finding the man sitting on a chair next to the shower cubicle, opposite the tiniest kitchen Miles had ever seen. The room was constructed from basic grey metal plating on all the surfaces, from the floor to the walls and on the ceiling where a single bar light was attached, giving the room just a slight tinge of light. Sam was sitting on a basic white chair, made of leather and set on wheels, he was up against the wall so that the medico-table blocked the view from the door so he didn't see Miles come in. He was in his red Crimson Sun jumpsuit with his Stardust jacket over the top, the Stalwart helmet Miles had got for him was resting by his feet, alongside the shotgun Cait had got him, a twin to her own. He was hastily putting away his tablet, already switched off so was just a small black bar that he placed in an inside pocket of his jacket as he struck a look up at Miles. "Everyone up and about?" Sam asked, picking up his helmet and weapon, resting the gun on the bed of the medico-table while he placed his helm on his head.

"Yeah we're assembling on the bridge for Tomen to brief," Miles looked at his friend curiously. "If you've been up, why you still here? It's cramped as fuck in here."

"Nothing wrong in a bit of alone time," Sam replied. "If you must know, it's something of a ritual of mine, before a job, it settles the mind." He shrugged as he flung the strap of his weapon over his head, having it dangle under his arm before tightening it to his side.

"Huh?"

Sam's only reply was to roll his eyes behind his helmet and clench a loose fist in his right hand and follow a jerking motion, swaying his hand from side-to-side with a shrug of the shoulders, a signal Miles understood with a chuckle.

"Whatever, come on, they're waiting on us," Miles ushered his friend through the exit and up to the upper level, to join the rest on the bridge, the X-Human picking up his new rifle as they passed through the transport tunnel.

Once all inside the cockpit, the team gathered around the circular console in the room's centre behind the two pilot chairs, taken up by Azuri in the pilot's and Cait beside her. Tomen stood in the gap between Azuri and the terminal that controls the ship's status where Miles took up a seat. Lena took the seat at the transit-gates terminal with Sam standing next to her, between her and Cait.

Nathan crouched beside the circular console, his armour connecting to it from a cable stemming out from under the screen on his right arm. He used the controls on his touch screen to bring up a holographic image of a map of the Capital City, the purple illumination of the city lighting up the room from the unwilling darkness of space beyond the cockpit windows. The only other lights in the room were small bulbs planted at the top of the terminals at either side, and one above the doorway so there was a dark gloom to the cockpit as Tomen began his brief.

"While we do have this map, we are essentially going in blind, I won't lie to you," Tomen began, the white ovals of his eyes on his helmet moving around the room. "We don't know where the vault is exactly, nor do we have any idea what threats we'll face. But we've all agreed that the prize is worth the risk. So here it is. I believe the best place to look for this vault is here," he pointed at one of the districts, "in the Directorate District."

The city was perfectly round, hence how it had become completely enveloped in an armoured shell, and was divided into six sections. At the centre was a circle, and from there branched out broad walls that divided the different sections of the city, reaching from the border around this centre circle out to the outer rim of the Capital. Inside one of these sections was a small alcove cut out of it with a wall separating it from the rest of that district. The different areas of Rose City were the Obsidian Head Office at the city centre and the Directorate, Residential, Commerce, Leisure, and Common districts, with the alcove sitting in this final area.

"I've discussed this with Xin and we believe this is our best bet," Tomen explained. "They would want to keep it safe and close by."

"I agree," Nathan put in, having stepped back after setting up the console and now leaned against the doorway of the cockpit. "But it's not as though we can head straight there. We have to land in the shipyards, there in that small bit bolted onto the Common district and go all the way through the city to reach the Directorate District."

"If that's what we have to do, then that's what we're in for," Tomen nodded. "We'll go in a straight line, going through the city centre—"

"No, we should go around," Nathan interrupted.

"If you know something we ought to, best to share it now," Tomen leant forward on the circular console in the centre of the room so that purple hue from the holo-imager lit up the face of his helmet.

"When the city sealed itself off, an entire battalion's worth of Obsidian soldiers were trapped inside, along with their General, a man named Ardamus. If he is still alive, then we have to take every precaution to avoid him."

"Makes sense, ideally we'll go completely unnoticed through the city," Tomen replied.

"Yes, so we should go district by district, avoiding the Obsidian Head Office at the city centre, just in case. Ardamus was never a solid believer in Obsidian but he's a formidable character and after eight long years, if he's still alive, there's no saying about the state of his mental being. He could be unstable. And an unstable, incredible leader at the head of an army is something I would rather avoid," Nathan crossed his arms, gripping his helmet with his right hand.

"Fair enough," Tomen nodded, staring down at the map. "So we land here," he said, pointing at the alcove in the Common district. "And that presents us with a choice, either we go to the Leisure district or the Commerce. I say, Leisure. I'm sure the line about WIDOWs sabotaging the reactor at the RCS Central Office in the Commerce district is all bollocks but given the length of time it's been, I'd say it's worth avoiding all the same. So we take the Leisure route out of the Common, that'll take us to the Residential and from there we'll have moved around the city to be able to get to the Directorate district."

"That's an awful long way to go, mate," Miles put in, leaning forward in his chair so he could get a better look at the map. "Are there no shortcuts we can take if going through the centre is out? Didn't the city have a metro system underground? Can't we use those tunnels?"

"I'm not planning on it because we don't know what threats we'll face, it's safer to expect that they're not a safe route," Tomen replied.

"Hey Nathan, no safe assumptions you can make? Surely there was something before the day of the Collapse that might give us an idea, huh?" Azuri asked, her legs up on the spinning pilot's seat, her shining blue eyes beaming out into the room.

"There were hospital admissions through the roof with some kind of sickness but that was just the previous day and it wasn't my concern so I wasn't made aware of anything. The only thing I can say is that we need to be prepared for anything, we don't know what's in that city," Nathan warned.

"Or it could be nothing, right?" Sam asked, posing the question he felt needed airing.

"Then what wiped out that Obsidian team? Couldn't've been nothing," Tomen stood up and placed his hands at his hips. "No, there has to be something nasty in there. But this isn't the first job we've taken when we know for sure that we're walking straight into trouble. We just have to keep our heads."

"So what you're telling us is that we just have to go in and take things as they come?" Lena asked, nodding to herself.

"Yes," Tomen replied, keeping his answer brief, knowing everyone present was mulling over how insane this venture was.

"Well, no use getting our minds in a bind over something we ain't got no control over," Lena laughed and sat back into her chair. "So what are we waiting for?"

"No, I think we're all set," Tomen announced, "unless anyone has something to add?"

When no one spoke up, Tomen nodded and looked around the room.

"Alright then. We do what this man says," he said, pointing firmly at Nathan. "If he gives any one of us an instruction, then we follow it without question—I can't understate how important that is, got it? He's here because we need him to keep us all safe, so we do what he tells us to. Right then, Azuri, you're staying on the ship. I want you to monitor all transmissions in the area, I want to know if there's something we ought to know while we're out in the city. Now, everyone, check your radios while you're all here."

Nathan had added personal radios to the list he gave to Siobhan. Each were transmitters activated by a button on a mount attached to their chests that worked in tandem with ear pieces so that the team could talk to one another from afar. At Tomen's order, they each made sure they were hooked up correctly, and practised using them, much to Nathan's annoyance.

"Testing, testing."

"Hello?"

"Hello!"

"Hiya cunts!"

"Alright, by the stars, that's enough," Tomen shook his head. "Get your packs and get ready. Lena, set the transit-gate, and Azuri, prepare to take us in. Cait, be ready with the landing key."

Cait noticed Sam fiddled with his jacket so he could easily access an inside pocket, making sure the strap of his shotgun and his radio piece didn't get in the way. "You OK, Sam?"

"Yeah, fine, just getting focused," he replied stiffly, not meeting her eye contact.

Lena took up the transit-gate terminal at Tomen's instruction and programmed in the coordinates for Ruby, giving Azuri a thumbs up when they were locked in, received a nod in return then she fired out the gate, casting it out into the cold expanse of space. Azuri flew through it, the electricity of the gate catching on the surface of the Elite Starfighter as she guided it into the new section of space, granting a view of the planet now directly below them. In the warmth of the yellow sun, Ruby boasted vast green ranges of land along with enormous stretches of blue seas and lakes, the settlements of the Coalition barely black marks on this colossal world.

The black wings of the starfighter soared through the clouds and descended, travelling through the sky as Azuri piloted it over the vast stretches of open land and over the various highways and railroad tracks that link the far afield towns and cities, linking the world together. Great concrete and glass monsters reached up into the wealth of open sky as the ship glided among them, passing between them. Outposts were attached to the top of these buildings, bases where Obsidian police watched the skies, ready to engage anything they deemed unlawful. But Azuri paid them no mind, taking advantage of the sheer volume of Obsidian craft in the area, blending in as one of them.

The once small dwelling of Dunnfink, now a sprawling metropolis, turning once luscious green pastures into concrete as it grew akin to a living organism, came into view, and the team admired its grand size from staring past their feet through the red haze of the cockpit glass. Obsidian outposts aplenty as the ship wove a path least observed and Azuri kept to the busier lanes as much as possible as great serpents of private and Obsidian crafts busied themselves in the traffic among the heights of the city. Nathan stood behind the centre console that split the two pilot seats and his eyes caught the sight of where he had once called home. His house and the land it occupied were gone, replaced by a gigantic, escalating stretch of farmland under a tall banner of the name Crimson Sun. Even the simple grave markers he made for his family were gone, slabs of rocks inscribed with their names above where he had laid their bodies to rest alone, replaced by a patch of their synthesised seed. Despite it being only the smallest glance, it was able to light a spark in his chest that seemed to burn at Nathan's centre with a chilling, icy inferno, a raw raging aggression, numbing him to all other emotions so all that he could feel was cold.

Eventually, they left the city limits, leaving Dunnfink behind, and followed the long highway towards their destination. This stretch of road was an elevated concrete path, a great towering arrow that ran over the lengths of hills, grasslands and the enormous lake that sat beside their goal, the gargantuan shell that covered the once Capital City.

"I bet you didn't think you'd be coming up on this sight, coming back here, huh?" Lena asked Nathan, arriving behind him, placing a hand on his shoulder as she took in the view out of the cockpit window.

"Welcome home, Elite Commander," Sam mocked as he turned and left for the transport tunnel, and Nathan could hear him telling the others that they had arrived.

Cait was seated in the co-pilot's chair and was gripping the golden card of the landing key, clutching it as a mother grips and protects her new-born, the importance of it the same. When she looked up at Nathan, silently asking if now was the time, she received a nod but a feeling overwhelmed her and caused her to hesitate. This was it. This was the moment they entered the city, and the goal she had brought to them was to either lay ahead, or be nothing at all at the end of an incredibly long, dangerous road. She looked over at Azuri who was concentrating at balancing the ship over where there was a long black line breaking up from the shell's lower hem, reaching up almost to the top before arcing and returning to the base, forming a semicircle shape. The pilot then looked over, meeting her gaze. Cait's own amethyst eyes meeting the ocean blue, bejewelled eyes of her friend, and there was a moment where Cait could have sworn that she could hear her friend speaking in her own head.

"Please don't be wrong about this, Cait," Cait could swear she heard her friend think and that's when it struck her. If she was wrong, then she would lose the trust of her friends forever, the people she had come to consider as her family. Especially in putting them in this much danger, it were all for nothing, things would never go back to what they were, she would never be forgiven, she thought.

"Are you ready?" Was what Azuri actually said, and Cait nodded, placing the gold card into a slot on the console at her right, the one between the two pilot seats, turning a previously red light to green.

At the base of the shell, along the bottom of this semicircle shape, green lights blared into life just as a thunderous roar bellowed out from it, breaching the confines of the ship's hull, shaking it violently. The two X-Humans in the pilots' seats glanced at one another with the same thought, each realising someone was going to hear that ear-piercing sound, and come investigate, just as the next roar echoed out, as the shell began to open. The semicircle cut out from the shell, disconnected at the top with a gust of dust raining down then dropped steadily, all the while a screeching, painful scream of metal on metal rang out into the sky. A siren began to sound, a horrendously loud wail declaring that the docks were now open, the shell inviting the Elite Starfighter in through the small entrance that the landing key had produced.

"Hold us here, I'll scout ahead," Nathan announced, turning away from the cockpit screen and making for the rear of his ship, and passing the rest of the team seated in his transport tunnel as they waited for landing. Lena gave him a thumbs up as he passed but he didn't know how to respond so he just nodded her way, it produced a smile so he settled for having done something right.

Once at the base of the ladder, in the small section at the rear of his ship, Nathan hit the button lowering the ramp and as it did he put on his helmet, firmly pressing down until he heard a faint click, meaning the armour on his neck had magnetically connected to his helm. The ramp lowered with an alarm stapling the little section in a bathing orange light that turned to green when it was all the way down. Below the ship, the shell looked absolutely enormous. It covered the top view Nathan had, blocking all sight of the horizon, a great dome of rusted, aged grey, spanning as far as he could see up, right and to his left. And the shipyards were there, open to him now, and Nathan could see the vague shapes of things in the foreboding shadows that lay lurking there, waiting for their intruder. The wind rushed into the ship, flowing easily over his glove as he stretched out his hand, feeling the air of a place he had previously not dared to see foot in again. A home left behind, a family gone, a previous self-abandoned and forgotten. But Nathan put those things to one side and burned them in the corner of his mind, allowing nothing to distract him from his dreadful task ahead. And with a sigh, he jumped.

His jetpack purred, leaving a slight warm feeling on his lower back as Nathan glided smoothly over to be above the shipyards before lowering himself down, bringing his rifle about, looking down the scope to see if any threats were visible to him now. But all was still as he slowly lowered himself past the lip of the shell. The bright ray of sunlight behind him casting a large shadow of him on the objects caught in the light, subjugated to the natural light for the first time in just under a decade. A variety of ships, utterly caked in dust, forlorn crates of unknown goods, and skeletons, still in the tattered rags of the companies they once served littered the grounds of the shipyards as Nathan descended, making for the wide open space in the centre. Here was the platform for taking off, a rolling section of metal pulled along on great chains to glide over the concrete to move ships about without the need for taking off. Nathan hovered still for a moment, just inside the mouth of the docks, the perpetual silhouette that had once dominated the interior reared up the insides of the shell as if reaching out to grab the one invading their silent slumber. The low hum and roar of his jetpack was the only sound to be heard, the small electric flame underneath it being the only artificial light, the docks being nothing more than a graveyard beneath the one who had once served as its protector. Through the scope on his rifle, Nathan peered down at the area below, looking for some sign of life, anything as he didn't know what to expect, but once he saw nothing but stillness, he slowly allowed himself to drop. He controlled his descent, a steady, slow burn on his jetpack so that he could carry on looking through his scope without losing his balance, and eventually he touched the ground. A plume of dust washed up, granules from years of neglect flying up around the heels of his boots, and meeting knee high and Nathan crouched in place, shutting off his pack.

 The Elite Commander remained there, crouched in the middle of the landing pad, only moving to turn on the spot to analyse the entire area, clocking every shadow and nook, anywhere where something, anything could come rushing out to greet him. But nothing came. There was no sound, not even the light hum of machinery, or the low buzzing of insects, there was absolutely nothing. He stood up and looked all around him as Nathan lowered the barrel of his gun and prepared to call the team to land, but there was an instinct stopping him, something made the hairs on the back of his neck stand up, some unseen party, watching, lurking in the recesses. But Nathan shook his head and went to radio the others, turning where he stood but then he found himself in a mirrored world of his own, except cast in a purple smoke, a fog he couldn't see past, the docks around him mere decoration for this moment he felt caged within. He looked around, confused and not knowing what to make of it until he started to feel a presence all about him, an enemy drawing in. Nathan threw his rifle over his shoulder, securing it to his back and unsheathed his blade, extending and igniting the length, the white energised fire washing along the metal fighting against the purple gloom that engulfed its bearer. He drew up his blade, ready for a fight, holding his ground, but nothing came.

"You've committed to a road you can never leave, a road where your ending is already assured, your blade shattering before fate's unyielding chronology. All your strength is worthless against the might of those that will rally against your will. You will lead these worlds into death and ruin, your intentions laid to waste and struck onto the anthology of mankind's ceaseless conflicts as the selfish abandon that is your creed. Your aggression leads to only one destination, your doom," a pitiless, elder male voice whispered into the veil of this fractured, frozen moment in time.

Nathan held his blade firmly in his right hand, pointing the tip in all directions, ready for a fight that never came, challenging the shadows to strike. He rotated it around in his grasp, patient for an enemy to emerge yet nothing arrived, and then his weapon began to vibrate. Nathan stared at his sword, watching as the rotations of energy rising up the weapon's length began to stammer and struggle, the handle shaking in his hand. Then it shattered. It burst apart, shards of his sword crumbling to the ground as he was powerless to stop it, resigned to watching. This weapon had served him for his entire Elite career, protecting him for over a decade, being a conduit for his rage, the instrument for his savage symphony, now nothing more than a rod of metal. Nathan couldn't believe it, his chest tightened as he felt vulnerable for the first time in a lifetime, and his left hand instinctively went to feel the break, but the heat of the white fire made him shoot his hand back as the sword was alive and well, as he found himself hurtled back into the dusty murk of the Capital docks.

"How we looking, Winter?" Tomen's voice entered Nathan's ear as he looked all around him, seeking out whatever voice he had heard before, finding nothing and no one about him, he was entirely alone.

"All clear," he replied, looking up at his ship holding steady beyond the remit of the shipyards before turning his attention to the great metal doors that led through to the city. They were shut and Nathan knew they would be locked under the environmental sealing protocols so he didn't bother trying to push them open, instead heading straight for the panel at their right side.

"I can see the pad's clear, coming down," Azuri announced over the radio as Nathan unfurled the cable he kept tucked in a compartment behind the screen mounted on his right forearm, plugging it into the panel that he opened much like a cupboard. Inside were various lights and switches, nothing was labelled but he didn't need them to be, his suit would serve to meet his needs, his screen giving him access to the city's mainframe at this connection point.

The ship maintained its balance, its engines, one attached to either wing, rotating so the thrust turned upwards, steadying itself for the descent onto the landing pad, the upwash of dust and debris creating a screen all around the craft. Nathan meanwhile downloaded the mainframe to his screen, gaining himself access to the various systems maintaining control over the city, analysing each one as they popped up, with certain things catching his interest. It didn't take long for the transfer to complete, about the same time as it took for the ship to extend its landing legs and settle on the pad, so Nathan was able to disconnect and meet the team as the ramp lowered. With a couple touches of his screen, in waiting for the ramp to fully come down, the lights in this section fluttered on, forcing the shadows to retreat, granting more visibility over the desolation of the area. Nathan peered over his shoulders, seeing if he had missed anything in the dark but settled when all was still, just as the team began clambering down the ladder.

"Welcome to the Capital," Tomen announced, the first down, stepping down the ramp, only taking a moment's glance back to make sure his team were following suit. Cait was next to step out, followed closely by Lena with Sam, Miles and Azuri coming down after, with only the pilot not bearing a backpack and cradling some kind of weapon. The two former Stalwart enforcers wearing their helmets, while the others decided to leave any kind of protection for their heads onboard, favouring being able to see more clearly in this unknown place.

"The reactor at the RCS Head Office is showing a leak so the Commerce district is out, the air will be toxic, but the substations are still active so we still have some power in the city. I can control how we distribute it using my screen," Nathan explained to Tomen as he joined him on the ground.

"That leaves only one path open to us," Tomen nodded.

"The Common district is through those doors," Nathan pointed at the enormous doors, straight down a ways from the landing platform they were standing on. "Through that will be the Leisure then Residential, and finally the Directorate districts."

"Can you open the shell? Get us some more light?"

"It's possible but opening the shell, opens all the doors, and who's to say what we'd be letting loose? Dunnfink isn't far down the road and there are other towns and facilities within a day of here, it's a risk to them. Figured you'd have a moral problem with that," Nathan replied coldly, disinterested.

"Yeah, having something of a moral compass will do that to you," Tomen gave Nathan a hard stare but figured nothing would come of questioning his senses for things, settling instead for him at least understanding the need to be cautious for protecting innocent lives.

"Moral compass?" Cait asked, reaching the two men.

"Don't worry, it's nothing," Tomen shook his head and looked over at the doors then to a vacant hangar space behind them. "We'll get Azuri parked inside there, and then we make a move."

"Care to help with the platform? Or's there a switch for this thing?" Azuri asked Nathan, flicking her eyebrows up at his wrist.

"We need to move the team off the platform then I can," Nathan said, stepping away from the group without waiting for a response, heading over to the doorway through to the city.

Once the team had finished joining Nathan away from the platform, he activated it using his screen mounted onto his right forearm, bringing the metal plate to life. The chains jangled as they flowed to bring the platform over to the vacant hangar, one of the dozen or more sections built around the outside of the docks, a safe place to keep one's ship. Once inside, Nathan used a great crane mounted to the ceiling to pick up the ship, allowing for the platform to return to the centre, as he placed the ship down onto the concrete ground. The lurching and aching of the machinery was fairly loud, Sam and Lena especially, glancing around nervously, wondering what might be hearing them.

With the ship now stowed away, Tomen joined Azuri in walking her back to it, as the rest of the team listened to Nathan advice on their weapons. The hangar was a tall, metal structure, with a variety of machinery and tools at the sides for maintenance for the ships, a large fuel tank to top it up, and an enormous shutter, to close it off from the rest of the shipyards. "Keep the shutter down, we don't know if anyone'll be following us inside now that the way's open," Tomen instructed his pilot as they approached the rear ramp.

"Yeah I figured. I'll put her on emergency power too, that'll keep her off any energy readings or radar screens, just in case," Azuri agreed. "And while I'm waiting I'll see if I can make use of any of this old crap to tune this baby up some, wonder when she last saw a little TLC."

"If you leave the ship, arm the ship's weapons to automatic, they'll watch your back," Tomen said, looking around at the various wear and tear of the hangar.

"They won't operate on emergency power, my love, I'll just have to watch this fine hind myself," the blue-eyed X-Human smirked, slowly stroking her butt with her left hand, sticking her tongue out at the man at her side, knowing they were out of view of the others.

"You do that, keep it safe for me when I get back, and this," Tomen placed a gentle hand on Azuri's stomach, imagining the child forming inside.

"I will, I promise I won't take any stupid risks," Azuri smiled, planting a kiss on the man's helmet where his mouth would be behind it. "Can't I see your face before you go?"

Tomen obliged, throwing his rifle behind him, having it dangle from its sling, and lifted his helmet off with both hands before embracing the woman, bringing her in close and kissing her softly on the lips. He held for a moment longer, looking deep into her eyes. "I'll see you both soon," he said before breaking off the hug and placing his helmet back on.

"Just come back safe, don't lose your head," Azuri called over to him as he went off to re-join the others.

Tomen heard the rolling metal of the shutter dropping behind him as he stepped out from under the confines of the hangar, moving across the length of the shipyard to where the others were standing ready at the doorway, reaching it at the same time as the landing platform locked itself back in the dock's centre.

"Ready to begin?" Cait asked Tomen as he approached, the rest were standing waiting to go.

"Let's go, ready up, people," Tomen instructed and his team made sure their backpacks were secure, their weapons were good and ready, gripping them set for a fight, and Nathan sent power to the doors, opening the way to Rose City, the fallen Capital.

Chapter 10

Elias felt a swelling feeling of pride and accomplishment as he surveyed the planet below his office window, the once home of his station, of the Capital City, now serving as little more than a worker planet, lacking any asset of any real significance. An intentional ploy for as soon as he had taken up his role as Section Chief he established the new central offices for his companies away from the catastrophic failure that enormous metal dome represented, and the secret beneath it. It served his needs for any curious and intelligent eyes, those of his Directorate that he by no way trusted, to be kept far away from the former beacon of the Crimson conglomerate's wealth, in case they were to begin measuring the prizes kept inside. The largest prize of all, Elias jealously pondered, gauging its value, savouring the opportunity to be reunited with it, never mind to him that it caused the greatest calamity of the modern era.

With the light of the yellow sun touching the far side of the world, out of sight from his Arcadia space station, his office was lit with the warm, ocean of blood light coming in from the red sister-sun, giving his shadowy room a forbidding ambience. But Elias didn't pay this any mind, for his thoughts were honed in on the world below him, where, on the other side, he had heard of the Old City becoming open. An Obsidian trooper stood at Elias' side, presenting a holographic imager to him, maintaining a connection with his favoured officer, the Vice-Admiral Re iku where he was aboard the listening post station across the other side of the system.

"The city is open, Chief Thorne, our assets in Dunnfink have confirmed sightings of the Elite starfighter making its way to Rose City having arrived via transit-gate just above the upper atmosphere," the Vice-Admiral was saying.

"And we can confirm that this one matches the one leaving Scarlet on the day Captain Willis was murdered?" Thorne's voice was calm and controlled, his mind conjuring his next steps half a dozen ahead at a time.

"Yes, sir, the markings match those noted by the attendant at the Scarlet shipyard. I believe we can call it conclusively now, Commander Winter is the killer we've been looking for, the one who takes an eye for a trophy from each one of his victims. The skill required to eliminate so many of our security forces in taking down the senior members of the Coalition lends towards this as well as the evidence of this ship that we've tracked since it left Vermilion."

"I concur, Vice-Admiral, but I am satisfied with allowing matters to continue as they are for now."

"As you wish, sir, so to confirm, we are not to engage the Commander?"

"No, leave him and his team be, unless there is no other choice, he is doing our work for us," Thorne said with a sly smile. "That small band of WIDOWs were able to track down Willis and produce a landing key for the city, after all, so this proposes an interesting opportunity for us to not invest our resources so wastefully. I have your orders ready, Vice-Admiral."

"Proceed, sir," the Vice-Admiral was ever loyal to his Section Chief, his voice beaming of his solid belief in his leader as his tone was close to a grunt, sounding displeased but only impatient to carry out his instructions and impress his superior.

"Reiku, we will go ahead with the secondary survey team, brief your Elites. I want that facility accessed, and the research and all data and samples relating to it recovered in its entirety. Your team is to hold back however, to await the progress of the WIDOW team already inside the city, to see if they can pave a way to the bunker, saving the effort being on our part. Once they are able to clarify some determination on the status of the WIDOW team, they will report this to you. You are to remain on the listening station for this reason and to monitor this task. You will then report to me and I will advise the next steps. But to be clear, Vice-Admiral," Elias took his gaze away from the view out of his window to stare down the imager directly, "you are not to engage the WIDOWs without clearance from me."

"I understand, Chief Thorne, and if the WIDOW team are successful in breaching the bunker and attaining the data themselves?"

"Then I will be aware of it. I already have a plan in motion for that eventuality and have set up the necessary steps to manage it, to turn that potential loss into a triumphant victory."

"As you say, Chief Thorne, leave this to me," Reiku replied, his brow furrowing, itching to get on with things, never one to encourage lengthy conversations.

"Then return to your duties, Vice-Admiral, and perform admirably, for a promotion is on the cards. I'm in need of a Chief Admiral whose abilities and loyalties are as impressive as yours," Elias nodded at the Obsidian trooper holding the imager who turned off the transmission at this silent command.

"Is there anything else you require, Chief Thorne?" The trooper asked, his voice slightly muffled by the helmet he bore making him simply just another faceless, anonymous guard to this leader who was indifferent to their personal identities.

"Not from you. Bring me some entertainment, I feel like having a treat before these testing hours ahead," Elias turned away from his window, taking up the seat behind his desk, picking up his tablet as the trooper went away with a simple nod, leaving the office by the elevator opposite.

It didn't take long for his instructions to come into fruition, as Elias peered up from his tablet, where he was looking at the statistical data relating to the farming increase in output on Scarlet, he saw the Stardust girl enter. A young girl, only eighteen or nineteen, stepped up to stand in front of the desk, dressed in a tight grey shirt, barely leaving anything to the imagination about the large chest beneath, paired with a skirt of the same colour reaching barely halfway down her thigh. She wore grey tights too, with simple shoes to finish the look. Her smooth brunette hair was down to her shoulders while her eyes were large, brown and innocent as they locked onto the man who was admiring her from head to toe.

"You called for entertainment, sir? How may I pleasure you today?" The girl asked, reciting from her script, the Stardust company training kicking in as she saw her purpose as servicing crucial workers to improve their mood so that they in turn will increase their efficiency.

"I have some work to be getting on with," Elias called over her, his tone dry and lifeless. "But I would like some sight to enjoy while I busy myself."

"As you say, Chief Thorne," she replied, unbuttoning her shirt and pulling down her bra, revealing her breasts for the Section Chief to see before sliding a hand down the front of her skirt, "is this what you wanted, sir?" She asked, putting all of her effort into sounding like she was actually enjoying what she was doing, and not completely sick to her stomach and wanting to fall down the deepest, darkest hole.

"And what I want, I get," Elias grinned, one eye on the girl, the other on a datasheet displaying the correlation between the snowy weather on Sanguine and their decrease in manufactured food. He glanced from the girl back to his work, back to her again as she steadily walked up to the other side of the desk, back to his work, and then back to her as she sat on the edge, stopping her lip from quivering from the tears she held back by biting it, while maintaining intense eye contact with him. Elias then absent mindedly approved action to be taken by Stalwart Ironworks to rectify an unprofitable town on that planet, all too distracted by the girl not a metre from him. "And now I'm far too distracted to work, I want something different," he grasped the girl's leg, wrenching it violently towards him, dragging her across the breadth of the desk, having her almost crash on top of him. He was far stronger than her and as he stood up, knocking his chair spinning back, he forced her to stand just in front of him before bending her over his desk. It was all too easy for him to overpower her, putting his elbow into her back as he gripped her hair back with his right hand, using his left to tear down her tights showing the young, smooth flesh beneath. Elias wrestled with his suit just as a message popped up on his tablet that had been cast spinning across his desk, entirely dismissed as it illuminated a report from the Stalwart team he had been communicating with. It was confirmation that the orders were set, one hundred and forty seven lives set to be written off, not that the Section Chief noticed.

Chapter 11

The doors swayed open lazily and croaking with age and neglect, revealing the city beyond. Nathan used his screen to transfer power to the Common District and the street lamps illuminated the immediate entrance area and the wide web of streets connecting to it. The doors led through to an open space, with wild flowers growing on grassy patches surrounding a large stone water fountain at its centre, it cast a great flow of water up into the air before letting it swill around in a pool at its base. Beyond this space, three streets branched off, separated by buildings decorated in signage displaying that they cafes, restaurants, clothing stores, all businesses to prepare visitors to suit the grandeur of the Capital City. Advertising hoardings shone bright with neon at the tops of these structures, their radiant light reaching up the shell above them, blocking out the sky. The air was thick with a grey haze as a layer of dust was rattled loose by the opening of the shipyard, life reintroduced to these stale, forgotten avenues, grime and debris cast up from the roads, walls and buildings.

"I don't hear anything, I thought Xin said those Obsidian guys were attacked right as they got in this crypt," Sam pointed out, nuzzling a skull with his toe, moving it away from the rest of the skeleton as he noticed the sheer pile of them to the side of the doorway.

Nathan bore the other man no mind and walked steadily up towards the fountain, brushing a layer of dust off from its border with his left hand as he rested his right on his sword hilt on his leg. The rest of the team took a moment to themselves, looking all around them, taking in the sight of the dead city, curious about everything, while Cait stepped forward to join their guide. "He's right, Nate, I don't hear or see anything."

"That's because you're thinking too loudly," Nathan responded, coming past the fountain and gazing down the length of the street directly opposite the space they were standing in. "Hone in on your heartbeat, let all the thoughts pour out of your mind and listen just for the beat. Then reach out," he explained.

Cait didn't quite understand but she obliged and held her questions, letting them go as she tried to find her heartbeat, finding it beating quicker than she thought it would be and then winced as she failed to capture what Nathan had meant. But she tried all the same, listening to her heart beating in her chest and then closing her eyes, ignoring the incessant comments of her friends behind her. And that's when she heard it, a faint murmuring, a whispered groan. She let go of any questions about it and instead took a deep breath, reaching out with her mind to leave herself open to hearing whatever it was out there in the city. Then the city came alive to her ears. A sea of whispers and murmurs way off in the distance washed up to her and she looked over at the man who was waiting for her to notice.

"Do you hear them now?"

"What are they?"

"This city isn't as dead as we might have hoped," Nathan replied. He scanned the three options available for pressing on that opened up at the end of the open space, three roads with each their own unknown variety of risks and threats. He knew the one to the right would branch off into smaller roads but this main avenue would lead to the Commerce district, seemingly impassable now for the leak of the power plant attached to the Ruby Consolidated Systems Head Office. The centre boulevard spanning the length rolling out directly in front of them would undoubtedly lead to the Obsidian base at the city centre, a path Nathan was not keen to take, wary of what might be contained behind those high walls. So remained the left road, the one leading to the Leisure district, the ideal route, but that's when the dust started to vibrate all on its own accord.

"Nate, what's happening?" Cait asked as she watched the small particles skip and dance off the surface of the border of the fountain, the ground shaking minutely, causing not only this concert of dust, but also her muscles to tense.

Nathan meanwhile was staring dead ahead, unmoved and not necessarily bothered, while the rest of the team stepped up to join them, Sam rising from where he was inspecting the mountain of skeletons, a pile evident of those who had tried to escape the containment but failed. "Lena, use your scope, look down the long road dead ahead, tell me what you see," Nathan instructed as he glanced around the buildings, seemingly looking for something.

Lena pulled her huge rifle over from her back and reeled up the weight of it to get the stock comfortably cushioned in her shoulder, the scope brought up to her right eye as she peered down the scope, aiming down the long road. Either side of the narrow stream of concrete were trees, still standing tall and boasting lush green coats of leaves, and buildings lined each side, shops, parlours and eating establishments, all with loud, bright advertisements to entice travellers to the city inside. But Lena could not lend any attention to any of these for her eye was drawn the shambling shapes coming towards them, the breath stolen from her lungs as her mind struggled to comprehend what she was seeing. "Guys, there's people coming but err…"

"What?" Tomen asked, his own rifle already shouldered and he passed the fountain, trying to get a better look at whatever his companion was seeing.

"These guys are dead, I, I can see some of their guts hanging out, one's got so much missing I can see right through 'im. The fuck is going on?"

"Doesn't matter. Lena, take Cait and make for that building there, you'll have a perfect view of the entire street from there: take them out from height," Nathan pointed over to the tall Obsidian outpost that stood at the start of the road where the things were just coming into clearer view. "Miles, take the left flank, Tomen you have the right, Sam you're watching the other two roads to make sure they come at us those ways," he then pressed a couple of buttons on his screen and the doors through to the docks began to close.

"Do as he says, people, prepare for a fight," Tomen slapped Miles' shoulder and pointed to the left side of the centre road's opening, and began to almost skip past the fountain, glancing back to it, pointing at its base. "This'll be perfect, Sam you take up this position here, call out anything you see down those other two roads. Winter, where will you be?" He stopped just shy of the opening of the road before stepping slowly towards the right side, gazing through the windows of the buildings there, making sure nothing might spring out and surprise him.

"Advancing down the middle," Nathan replied coolly as he watched Cait lead the way for her and Lena to enter the Obsidian building, cautiously opening the entrance glass double doors and making for the stairs just on the inside. This structure was far taller than the rest, a tower of black metal and high glass windows, perfect for a vantage point for even a casual marksman like Lena, as Nathan had judged.

"You call the play, mate," Tomen replied to him, crouching down and peering down his weapon's scope at the swarm of people taking shape at the far end of the road, taking up the entire landscape, staggering towards them. "What in all the starways is going on here? These people are dead," he grunted.

"You never heard of zombies? Aim for the head, mate, they all say aim for the head," Miles mirrored his partner, taking in the sight of the things coming towards them as Nathan stood still between them.

"We're set, Nate, got a good view of the road from up here," Cait announced over the radio, causing Nathan to glance up their way.

"Good, watch Lena's back in case anything gets past us. Lena, aim for the stragglers and the ones at the back, Tomen and Miles will thin them out at the sides, and I've got the centre," the Elite Commander ordered, the dark grey ovals of his helmet's eyes shifting to the other end of the road, gauging the danger approaching.

They were in clearer view now, under the musky light of the streetlamps and neon signs, men, women, children too, all in shredded garbs of their company uniforms, the black of Obsidian, the grey and green of Stalwart Ironworks, the grey with orange from Stardust, red from Crimson Sun and the dark jumpsuits of RCS. Their bodies were shredded too. Most were missing limbs, an arm or a leg, it didn't matter, it didn't slow them down from the steady pace the horde was setting. Everything loose on a body was hanging off the majority of these humanoid shapes, from jaws dangling from one side, muscles as ribbons barely carrying the weight of the limbs they were attached to as frail string, the intestines, liver, stomach were slipping around under the broken skin torn asunder by savagery or time. As they drew closer, the whispers carried on the wind were more defined, a cold breath exhaled from the depths of the dead city towards the team, full of dust and decay and a metal tang from the machinery that recycled the air under the dome.

"Have you come to save us?" A young voice sighed but it came from a vertical corpse as it trudged down the crumbling concrete.

"The stars have led you to us, we're saved," a male voice murmured on the current of stale, cold air flowing down the road.

"Please help us, please, it's been so long," croaked a stumbling carcass that was at the head of the pack, pushing the walking body of a child out of its path with a mindless shove.

"Lena, I know it weighs the barrel down but keep the suppressor on. Tomen, Miles, keep those weapons on low energy bursts, I don't want to announce our presence here, this horde might have just come this way from the alarm when the dome opened," Nathan ordered, in a tone that invited no argument. "We go loud only on my signal."

"Mother went away, the day the sky disappeared, I just need someone to care about me," a corpse the size of a child whispered without having any lips, halfway up the street now.

"It's been so lonely here, won't you be my friend? I just want a friend!" An angrier voice, still barely a rasping mumbling, came from one near Tomen's side.

"Why are you out so late, boys? Boys!" A female carcass wheezed from its hollow lungs as it crawled, clawing at the loose concrete under its decomposed fingertips.

"Honey, why did you leave me? I was all alone, I've been so alone!" A husking cry came from a female shape that barely resembled a person anymore as she used the buildings to steady itself passing along.

None of them seemed to be mouthing the words, the whispers just seem to be emanating from a general crowd, a constant quiet groaning that was as a shroud blanketing over the dead things making their way up the road. The dim, white from the streetlamps joined the numerous cascade of colours from the neon signage to cast these ghastly shapes in an all variety of shades of vibrancy, the bones, intestines and strewn out muscles in full view cast across the spectrum. They came into full view as these things reached the halfway point of the road, passing by the restaurants that were once packed with people, the shops that excited them with goods from all over the tri-systems, possibly the same as those who were trundling by those shattered windows, echoes of their once selves.

"There're all human, there're no X-Humans," Lena pointed out startled over the radio as she cast her scope over the mass of disgusting bodies.

"Hold steady," Nathan said as a reply, crouching down in the middle of the road, taking a glance over his shoulder back at Sam, "any movement down the other roads?"

"Nothing, we're clear," Sam announced, he was crouching down by the fountain, placing it between him at the main road as best he could while being able to watch down the other two forks in the road.

Nathan brought his gaze back to the shapes coming up on his team, staring down the barrel of his rifle, flicking a switch on the side of it, near the trigger, changing it over to the sniper configuration. He then loaded a bullet from the brown leather holder attached to the weapon's stock into the slider on the right side of the scope, using the cocking mechanism to load it into the barrel. "Open fire," he said so calmly that the others nearly missed it, Tomen being the first to fire his weapon, casting powerful green energy blasts into the crowd, destroying the head of the first and catching the rest all over. He then took a deep breath and listened.

Tomen and Miles obliterated everything on the flanks, the bodies collapsing over on one another creating small mounds that the rest had to awkwardly clamber over to carry on down the street. While Lena picked off the ones at the back, the more built ones as she preferred the more solid targets to aim at, popping one skull at a time with her enormous bullets, destroying one head at a time as if her rounds were explosives. Meanwhile, Cait kept her shotgun trained at the top of the stairs, propping herself up against the wall where Lena had her rifle pointing out of the window above her. The X-Human with the red hair tied back in a ponytail, the same as Cait, so that it wouldn't affect her vision, rested on one knee, the other stretched out the other side as her friend as she controlled the rifle, balancing it on the ledge of the window. It was anti-materiel so it packed a punch but Siobhan was knowledgeable about making the weapon work for the user. He installed various compensators in the length of the weapon so Lena could take the brunt from each shot far easier. Cait looked up at her friend who was concentrating carefully, and she could see each breath she exhaled as she hastily focused on each new target she picked up with her scope. The purple-eyed X-Human had her hood down so that she could better hear if anything were to try to approach them up the staircase, but it was a sound from beyond the walls of their abandoned office that gave her fright.

Nathan kept his scope trained down the centre, brushing off the deafening roar coming from behind this horde of decrepit bodies coming towards him, keeping his eye on the shape that caught his interest. It pressed up far quicker the corpses in the foreground and burst through them, splintering bone and spraying congealed blood all over the road as it cast the carcasses aside in barrelling forward. This was a far larger creature yet still bore resemblance to the human form, it seemed to be comprised of bodies having merged together as it claimed broader arms and legs, connected by great joints of mashed bone. Having blasted its way through the pack of zombies, the beast screamed a high pitched wailing cry that projected spit from the two skulls hideously forged together. The foreheads were nearly one with the eyes all over the face, the mouths joined together in a sickening chasm with teeth. Its skin was rotten, a blend of green, brown and grey, as it planted itself on all fours, with the limbs from the two corpses fused together, bursting with power, the bone and muscles intermingled. Nathan fired his shot, knowing Lena would be too scared to take her eye away from her scope to see this beast bounding down from the far reaches of the road towards them, and the bullet met its mark. The beast had just pounced, using the power of its dual sets of legs to propel itself forward, its long disjointed arms raking up the concrete as it clawed itself towards its prey. All to be laid out flat when a bullet drove its way through the centre of the two heads, its leap making it crash into the ground, rolling and flailing as it landed, smashing into the corpses stumbling at its sides.

    He didn't move, remaining crouched, Nathan flicked the switch back to its regular setting and began firing his weapon using the bullets from the magazine beneath, each one hitting its mark, popping skulls with ease, cluttering the road with the remnants of this horde. Tomen and Miles kept up their fire, the left and right sides beginning to thin as the seemingly sentient herd trundled along the road in a central column, avoiding the green lights that struck them down. But here they met only the unstoppable carnage of the ballistic thunderstorm coming from the single soldier, crouching down, measuring up the next shot as the bullet from the last one met its target. The Elite Commander didn't miss one. With every shot fired, a staggering carcass collapsed to the ground, only to be trodden over by the next, that met the exact same fate. The whispers they sent ahead of them never stopped, murmuring delusions from the lives they no longer had. Some were confused, begging for the comfort of the loved ones they saw in the group of fighters desperately trying to stop their advance. Others cast out vile insults, words only those who had felt death's chilling embrace could utter, lipless and having lost their tongues long ago.

    "I can hear your heart beating, I can taste it on the wind, I smell the iron in your blood, your soul feels weak against my teeth, you don't taste like you want to stay alive!"

    "Your loved ones are here with us, they are saying to rip you limb from limb, they only want you to join us, join our family. They told us your fears, of your selfishness, they sang of it when we stripped them of their skin," a whisper rolled against the shattered windows, crashed at the corpses forming into walls, blocking the rest from pressing onward.

"Behind you! They're coming from both sides!" Sam called over, stepping out from behind the fountain, his hands shaking as he brought up his shotgun but he didn't have the chance to take a shot before Nathan appeared at his side. The Elite fired several shots at the horde stumbling down the road from the Commerce district side, before reloading in a blink of an eye, pulling a magazine up from his belt and hammering more rounds down the opposite road, the one he aimed to take. Then he brought his rifle back towards the other road, slowing down the steady charge with precise shots, thinning the herd, creating a dam with their twice-dead bodies. They kept coming, however. More and more degraded, scarcely standing corpses emerged from the three roads, bursting out of the buildings too, some coming from the rooftops, falling to the ground in twisted, revolting shapes with stomach-turning crashes.

Nathan didn't slow down, shooting down a sum of the lurching dead on one side before switching behind to steady the advance on that side, leaving the central avenue for the two former Stalwart men to halt the horde that never seemed to stop. "Go loud, there's too many to be precise," he calmly instructed and unscrewed his suppressor after slotting a bullet into the head of one corpse that collapsed onto the ground, tripping up the two at its right, and as its legs flung up into the air, it dragged down two more.

"I can see clear road behind the centre mass, Nathan, but there's a lot of them still, and a couple more o' them big o nes," Lena called out over the radio, over the sounds of Cait's shotgun firing as a handful of corpses ascended the outside of their tall building, smashing the windows to force an entry.

Nathan barely had the time to turn his head to follow Lena's direction before one of the lumbering beasts emerged from one of the side buildings with a burst of brick and mortar spraying in all directions as it bounded, blindingly quick, to tackle Nathan to the floor, scrapping him against the road as its weight carried on the momentum. Three heads fused together screamed, gnarled and salivated over Nathan as he took out his knife from its sheath on his left forearm, plunging it into one skull at a time. The thing didn't die straight away, picking the man up with its mutated giant hand made from a pulp of pasted bodily parts, smashing him into the road surface, again and again, and again until Nathan finally killed the thing. He stabbed at it violently but assuredly, not panicking, not delivering a blow too deep as to slow down the next strike, each one having power behind it until the giant freak of a decomposing mass crumbled on top of him. Nathan brushed it off, bringing himself up onto one knee, flicking on the safety of his rifle before tightly strapping it behind his right shoulder before standing up as he sheathed his blade, turning. Then he was absolutely taken out, his head colliding with the concrete as a beast flung itself at his midriff, and Nathan just about got himself standing again before another one took a hold of him as it charged.

Miles kept up his fire, reloading his clip as swift as his practised fingers could move, removing any wasted time between his barrages of green electricity zipping across the ever-shortening gap between him and the mass of undead descending on him. Until a cloud of debris smashed against his back as one of the beasts annihilated the wall just behind him, using Nathan as a battering ram. A lump of brick hit the back of his head, and while his helmet protected him from any sharp damage, Miles' head rang with the shock of the blow as he was sent rolling on the ground, his rifle slipping from his grip.

Tomen more saw the lack of fire on his left side rather than the explosion that caused it, and what had caused that, but after peering over, he stood up and side-stepped that way, keeping up his fire. He kicked Miles's rifle back over to him before chancing a look inside the building where the dust was still settling. "The fuck was that?" Tomen called out to Miles as he took up firing at one of the hordes coming down the neighbouring roads, joining Sam in keeping the undead back.

"Winter! Do you seem 'im in there? Is he alive??" Miles called out to his friend just as he brought his rifle up between two outstretched rotting arms reaching down to him stemming from a hideous corpse, somehow knowing where to attack without any eyes in its fully decayed skull.

"Winter!" Tomen sprinted up the opening in the wall that the creature had made, and immediately leapt aside as its body was thrown right back out of the hole it had made, near split in half with a scorched crevice in its torso. The interior of the building, seemingly a restaurant from its array of tables and chairs blown to either side by the fight, was completely lost in shadow, except for the bright singular light rushing forward.

Nathan burst through the gap with the force of his jetpack, decapitating the twisted, congregation of heads atop a beast of near a half dozen fused corpses with his ignited blade. The white flames frolicked across the length of the blade, entwined with golden lightning striking against its edge, and Nathan brought his sword up, ready for the next fight, the light of it reflected against his black helm. "Everyone, fall back to the fountain. Cait, Lena, come down," he said, his tone was calm and controlled, not a single breath too quick.

"They're all over the stairs!" Lena called down the radio, and Nathan looked up, seeing the rifle not firing from the window anymore, before he had to shift his attention as the pack from the Commerce district side reached the open space with the fountain. He carved through them with ease, his sword effortlessly gliding through putrid flesh and misshapen bones, and he soon made his way through the lot of them, forming a vile pile upon the ground.

"You're in an Obsidian outpost, look around. There should be handguns and grapples in a cupboard up there, or do you need me?" Nathan asked, turning his stance towards the pack staggering towards his group from the central avenue. He pressed a couple of buttons on the screen on his arm and set the targeting of his missiles to fire line-of-sight, aimed and fired with his helmet registering subtle, intentional winces and winks with his right eye. Nathan fired off five missiles into the crowd, obliterating it, the ground quaking from the immense force he unleashed. Sprays of blood and with bones as solid debris, the walking corpses themselves became the shrapnel that shredded the others at their sides, as Nathan's volley stalled their advance.

At the same time, the window at the top of the Obsidian outpost on the side facing the fountain smashed, and a cable shot out like a slash of lightning, striking the top of the fountain, latching itself there with a sturdy metal claw. Cait and Lena came riding down it, each grasping their weapons in their right hands as they used their left to hold onto the carabiners they used to attach themselves to the cable. Lena hit the fountain first, stopping herself by kicking out a leg against the fountain spire, with Cait crashing behind her, who unfastened her friend before getting herself down. "Need you? We got this handled," Lena remarked to Nathan with a grin and a wink. "Believe I'm actually enjoying myself?"

"Just focus," Nathan dismissed, sending off a barrage in the direction of the Leisure district, "we're advancing, this way." He jogged forward, down the left side road, leading the way with his sword, slicing through the remaining dead to clear a path. The debris caused by the explosions rained down a plume of dust and cement spraying out into the road, barely visible in the low light of the perpetual night under the dome. Cait, Lena and Sam, those without helmets to protect their eyes and mouths, coughed and sputtered as they followed the rest, each of them using their free arm to protect their eyes from the fragments of building and road swarming in the air. "Tomen, Miles, you have the flanks, we need to move faster," Nathan called back, sheathing his blade away and taking his rifle off from his back.

"Lead the way, Winter," Tomen called over the radio, not wanting to shout, trying to sound calm for his team's benefit.

Nathan shot precisely, aiming for the ones that when they fell, they blocked the ones in behind them, creating little buffers for the team around him to have more time lining up their own shots, as small mounds built up along the way. From the area with the fountain, they headed further down the road but they almost came straight into another large pack of the whispering dead marching their way. The barely dim light from the streetlamps illuminated an alley to their right and Nathan took it, leading the way, constantly shifting the barrel on his gun, aiming dead ahead, checking the tops of the walls either side, never remaining still and keeping up the fast pace he was setting.

All hope for a subtle entry into the Capital City was lost. The destruction of Nathan's rocket barrages were extremely effective in quelling the threat of the ceaseless army of the undead, but they shook the ground, the explosions ringing out, vibrating against the shell so the noise was carried across the breadth of the city. The booming shells from Cait and Sam's shotguns meant that the stragglers of the hordes of rotten, trudging corpses needn't be able to see them to follow, they were given a beading line of loud bangs to use as a trail. Lena was using a ballistic pistol she found back in the Obsidian outpost, her rifle strewn against her back. She brought up the middle of the pack with Nathan in front, the two Stalwart men either side, and Cait and Sam watching their backs. The alley they had taken was narrower now than where they had entered and soon enough they were bumping into each other, knocking one another against the walls as they desperately tried to get their weapons up. Soon enough the attacking, decaying dead began hurling themselves from the rooftops either side of the alley, falling down as literal dead weights, crashing into the team or the undead in pursuit.

One seemed to jump down at Lena, smashing her against Miles and the wall, coming down on top of her, incessantly biting at her neck. Its revolting jaws were merely an inch away from her pulsing neck before the former Stalwart man regained his balance, gripped the thing by its bare ribcage and threw it at the identical pack making its way up the path towards them. Nathan, hearing Lena's struggling under the weight of her attacker, turned and casually threw a grenade at it just as it re-joined its kind, thanks to Miles, and when the explosive went off, the force of it brought down six or seven, temporarily blocking that end. He fired his rifle ahead, taking out the nearest to him before flinging another grenade behind him and destroying the tops of the buildings above the dam of corpses, bringing chunks of concrete cascading down to firmly block off the zombies scrambling over their shattered kind. A gust of dust joined a spray of putrid, congealed blood landing on Cait and Sam who took no time to measure their relief at not becoming overwhelmed as they helped Lena and Miles on to keep up with Tomen and Nathan. If the explosion that blocked off one end of the alley was loud, then the roar of the beast clawing against both sides of the alley as it tore its way in from the other end was truly deafening. It rammed down the staggering skeletal figures in its path, pounding them into the floor and walls under its enormous, powerful limbs and body made from numerous bodies mashed together to make this horrifying monster. Nathan shoved Tomen back, flung his rifle over his shoulder, and drew out his blade, extending the reach of the edge at the same time as igniting it, bringing up in an upwards arc, catching the rampaging beast in its stomach as it reared up to attack. It flung its arms up, ready to wallop them down with all its might but Nathan gave it no chance, using the scorching burn on his sword to carve through the belly, slicing open the neck, and tearing off its fused face, having it slump at his feet. And then he instantly yanked his blade back and drove it through its head with an immense thrust, plunging it deep into the tangle of skulls up to the hilt.

With the beast having forged a path for them, they could now see the opening at the far end, and Nathan tightened his rifle's strap with his left, favouring his sword for now to slice through a path as the rest fired their weapons past him. "We're almost there, keep pushing," he announced calmly, still sounding as though his pulse had never left its resting rate.

"How far is the next district? I want those big fuck-off walls between us and these fucking things!" Tomen shouted back, stamping down on one skull and he used his rifle to obliterate another with a sizzling round of green energy.

"No guarantees they won't be on the other side, too, but it's not far, stay with me," Nathan barked back, wading through the sea of rotting, clawing corpses all lipless whispering to them.

"I used to teach a class near here," one was muttering, hardly more than a whimper of a breeze. "Now the young'uns fill my belly, they cried and cried and I'd no way to help them, but I could help me," it said, coming from a skull barely framed with strands of blood-soaked blonde hair, hardly the picture of the woman it once was.

Miles blew that face apart with a shot from his energised rifle, before smashing the butt of it into another that tried breaking through the armour at his leg with its teeth. Yet another one fell from the building above his head but it announced itself with a loud sigh so Miles was able to see it coming, he lifted his rifle to put it between them before throwing it to the ground and crushing its head beneath his boot.

Eventually they came out of the mouth of the alley into a wide street lined with empty shops either side, and it was completely vacant, not a living, or undead, thing in sight. The streetlamps took up vigilance, broadcasting their weak light into the street but losing the battle against the burden of the eternal night, its darkness claiming the road. These shops bore no bright advertising either so there was hardly a light to see by but this suited Nathan just fine, content that he could only hear their innumerable foe way off in the distance. "Cait, Sam, Lena, all of you hold your fire unless another horde descends. Tomen, Miles, switch back to stealth, let's see if we can lose them, and make our way to the next district." Nathan gave out his orders as he screwed his suppressor back onto his rifle, after having flicked the blood from his sword, placing it back in its sheath.

"The fuck is going on?" Sam grumbled to himself, his eyes wide with fear.

"Not now, focus on looking all round, we need to know if a pack comes near," Nathan said back to him but noticed he wasn't heeded so he grasped the other man's shoulder. "You hear me?"

"Yeah, yeah, gotta focus, got it," Sam reloaded shells mounted on the length of his weapon into its base before clicking on the safety, nodding to himself the whole time, a desperate rush to regain his balance.

"Nate, what do we do?" Cait asked, following Sam's lead, copying him.

"Fuck one'nother and wait for a gory, bloody death?" Lena shrugged, ejecting the clip of her pistol and replacing it from a pocket of her trench coat. "I call Cait as my fuck-die buddy," she declared, all too giddy.

"Shut it, we cling to the edges and make our way onward. We'll cross the river soon, using the bridge and then it's a short hike to the doors to the Leisure district, might be there could be a small place we can hold up and take a breather," Nathan instructed, placing a fresh magazine into this rifle and stashing the half-used one at his belt. Not waiting for any kind of reply, he stepped towards the building that had once been a library, rifle at his shoulder, moving carefully up the street.

"Fuck it," Miles sighed, following, as did the rest, with Tomen providing security at the rear of the team, keeping an eye at the far end of the road as well as the alley they had left behind.

Nathan led them forward, clinging tight to the side of the road, occasionally having to pick off a solitary carcass that stood in their path. Their heads popping being the only sound around as their bones clanged to the ground if the Elite couldn't get near enough to catch them to avoid the sound. A smell began to become evident as they progressed further into the city but it was like nothing any of them had ever experienced before, it was beyond foul.

"We've got a pack ahead. They're looking lost and vacant, reckon they've no idea we're down this way," Lena pointed out, looking ahead with the aid of the scope atop her rifle.

"We'll cut through the buildings," Nathan replied, carefully using the handle to open the door to the restaurant at his side with his left hand and led the way with the suppressor at the end of his gun. The lights inside flickered, barely bright enough to highlight the layout of the wooden tables and chairs but enough the team could tell they were alone inside. Nathan wasted no time however, crossing the length of the seating area, his boots making rustling sounds against the filthy carpet underfoot. He opened the double doors to the kitchen and ushered the team inside, the dark grey ovals marking his eyes on his helmet never leaving the direction of the door they had entered through.

"You reckon any of this stuff is good to eat?" Cait asked, to no one in particular.

"No, don't trust any of it, not even the water, we don't know how safe any of it is," Nathan instructed, making his way across the chrome surfaced kitchen through to the back exit. "The river's not far now, just on the other side of this building," he explained, stepping out into the small square that acted as a home for all of the bins and refuse for the parade of shops on this street. Nathan waved a hand so that he stepped out alone, he drew his rifle up, checking the tops of the buildings, analysing the windows, checking for any sort of movement before settling his weapon at the back door of the next building.

"Good to move up?" Tomen asked him, watching Nathan open the door and disappear inside.

"Come join me, it's just a tourist office," Nathan responded, his tone calm and measured, and the team rushed across the square to meet him.

The building they found themselves in was a showroom of some kind, an array of desks with electronic billboards behind them, advertising the worlds and companies within the Crimson region. Here screens twitched images and videos portraying exaggerated luxuries of the wide sandy beaches of Scarlet, the marvel of industry of the train network on Vermilion, the lush forests with trees reaching the clouds on Sanguine, plenty of retail therapy available on the Forerunner space station. They offered career tangents too, striking images of proud managers standing tall above a labouring workforce, the figure always a silhouette with the end message being "this could be you!"

"The fuck's this? Scarlet ain't anything like that!" Sam shouted at a screen displaying people sunbathing under the red star on a blanket of soft, near white sand as the waves softly washed against the shore with a calm breeze.

"This is the Capital, Sam," Tomen put a hand on his friend's shoulder. "These people got to choose their careers, not like us born into them. And they weren't like to dip their hands in their muck if mummy and daddy had anything to say 'bout it, nah, these were meant to be the supervisors, managers, the directors of the future. These people didn't know the real system, they didn't have a bloody clue."

"Then they deserve what happened to them, 'cause this is a fuckin' insult, Tomen," Sam snarled back, picking up a Crimson Sun branded ashtray and tossing it at the screen, cracking the screen, killing the video.

"We don't even know what happened to them, so don't be saying that crap," Tomen left Sam to wallow in his anger, moving over to Cait. "You holding up ok?"

The amethyst eyed X-Human was perched on the edge of one of the desks, she had pulled her hood up and as she bowed her head, her face was hidden from view. "Yeah, I'm fine," Cait replied, bringing her head back up, bringing her hands up from where they had rested against her legs, now covering her mouth. "Just settling my mind. This is all a lot to take in," she sighed.

Tomen stepped up to her and leant against the desk at her desk, pulling her hood down and pulling her close to him, "we'll make it through this, we will. We always have and we will again," he said, promising her. He took his helmet off for a moment, giving himself just a short bit of fresh air and his eyes met hers, "but we've got a long way to go."

"Don't worry about me, I'm fine. Wouldn't've pitched this whole thing if I didn't think us capable of pulling this off," she said with a hint of a smile.

"I'll always worry about you, kid. Never apologisin' for it neither," Tomen grinned back at her.

"I'll get you to one day," Cait elbowed the man side then nodded up at Nathan who had ejected the magazine of his rifle and was using his half-full one to top it up before reloading it back in. "Well, he seems to live up to the hype," she watched as the Elite then restrapped his rifle onto his back, produced his sword, extended its length then set to wiping it against the uniform of a body at his feet. "Even if he is a little weird."

"He got us out of that mess. Gotta admit when I saw that first horde of whatever the fucks, I thought we were dead," Tomen said, placing his helmet back on. "But he sure seems the real deal."

Lena stared at a Stardust desk, near to Nathan, reloading her rifle when the screen flickered on, playing its advert. It showed a human man stepping off from a freighter, arriving on the Forerunner. Lena, her attention captured by her former company's message, immediately recognised the age of what she was seeing, the docks of the space station she often frequented having changed in a multitude of ways since this was filmed. The man in the video seemed darkly stricken with a forlorn, depressed look as he slowly made his way up to the main avenue aboard the station.

"Miss out on that promotion of a lifetime?" A cute, female voice asked the audience.

The man could then be seen passing through a crowd, he was beset in dirt, in a near brown Crimson Sun jumpsuit while the others were in their brighter, cleaner, uniforms milling about far happier.

"Wife leave you for the new supervisor?" The voice came back with a playful tone, nearly laughing, "She take the children, too?"

He laboured up the stairs at the side of the main avenue of shops and bars, staying away from the crowd busying themselves with exuberant enthusiasm for the exaggerated bartenders and vendors.

"Did you also get diagnosed with Terraforming Sickness? Well, hey at least it's not contagious! So the only one who could die would be you," the woman feigned a concerned voice, still playing a sexy vibe.

The man could then be seen settling into a small lodging, on the top level of the Forerunner's main lobby, overlooking the hive of activity below by looking out over the balcony, as he fiddled with buttons on the holographic screen coming from the tab in his hands.

"Lose your home in payments for the medicine those Sapphire quacks swear will save your life?"

The man's expression then changed to one of relief, as the camera panned out to show a woman down by his crotch, her head bobbing in regular movement.

"Stardust: because everyone needs that one thing in life that never lets you down," the female voice

"Cunts," Lena remarked to herself, not noticing Nathan step up at her side.

"So you used to do that?" He asked, it was straight to the point, albeit about something personal but for Lena, that suited her far better than mocking or pity.

"Yeah, I met Cait on the Forerunner eventually who taught me to live for myself, gave me these friends but it was a little late, I'd already experienced so much," she recalled, running a hand over the scope of her rifle.

"To experience horrors as revolting as that and come out as this confident, determined person? That takes a special kind of strength, Lena, the kind few are so lucky to possess. I saw too many go a whole other way in the Capital," Nathan placed a hand on her rifle, cleaning off a bit of dried blood with the tip of his thumb through his glove.

"What way was that?"

"Drugs, and a lot of them. They hollowed themselves out until there was nothing left inside, nothing to feel the pain anymore, I assume."

"I can see how they woulda been tempted, I'd be lyin' if I said I never thought o' the same," her illuminating green eyes looking over at the man at her side. "You have that kind of strength too, you know."

"I'm not so sure. I used to be different, I used to be more," Nathan mindlessly ran a hand over the length of Lena's rifle at its barrel. "Sometimes I remember being the kind of man who cared, who fought for what he believed in but after my wife, my son, when they were gone, he died and I mourn for him, because I am not that person anymore. That's why I'm not so sure it is strength. Everyone is presented with the darkness at some point in their lives, and most have the strength to turn away from it, to be good and caring for people. But I embraced it. I let it fill me up, replacing whatever good what was inside so now I don't even recognise myself in a mirror anymore. I'm changed now, I'm driven to blood and addicted to my aggression. No, I don't think it is strength, or at least not the same kind."

"And what are you going to do? Mope about it? Look around you, if you're really this new and terrible thing, then why are you bothering to talk to any of us? Why tell me any of this? Wanna know your deepest, darkest secret, Winter?" Lena took Nathan's hand that was inspecting her rifle in her own, giving it a squeeze, causing him to meet her gaze. "You're not as cold and dead inside as you might think," she said with a smile, slightly sticking her tongue out, curling it as she looked him up and down before winking and hoisting her rifle up and over her shoulder, strapping it to her back. "Now, unless you're playing for time thinking you'll be getting the same service out of me as this bitch is giving that little, sick fella, then maybe we've lingered here long enough and need to get movin'?"

"Guys," Miles called over. He was at the far windows, peering through towards where a wall of concrete lined the bank of the river, with the bridge just up its length, where a man was staring right back at them. "We're being watched."

Chapter 12

His very presence was a distraction for all of the technicians in the control room as Alex Grey looked up at the management platform to see the Vice-Admiral standing there, surveying his new resource as the entire listening post control room had become his dedicated asset. Grey then looked past this menacing figure to the one sitting at his desk behind him, where MacArthur was the busiest Grey had ever seen him, frantically working on his terminal. And in following the Vice-Admiral's orders, MacArthur turned on the huge imager at the centre of the command centre, the image of Elias Thorne illuminating the far corners of the room. His unimpressed scowl seemed to find each colleague in turn, intelligent, assessing eyes reaching down into their souls.

"What is our status, Vice-Admiral?" The image of Elias Thorne demanded, standing tall over the desks of all the technicians working double shifts to learn the steps of the WIDOW team in the Capital before they took it.

"The secondary team is in orbit above Ruby, ready to be deployed, Chief Thorne. On your go, sir," Vice-Admiral Constantin Reiku's booming voice drowned out the general buzz of talking among the technicians.

"Very good, and how is Commander Winter faring in the Capital?"

"Our surveillance shows they've entered the city but the dome is creating a blackout of what's going on inside, we will land the secondary team inside for them to set up a communications relay for us to learn more."

"As expected," Thorne nodded, but before he could say anything more, his holographic image began to stutter and break, until it was gone completely, replaced by a high-pitched squeal.

"What's happened? Where is the Section Chief?" The Vice-Admiral shouted, banging his fist against the border railing of the managers' platform, pointing around the room. "Did you do this? Is this how you serve your company? Bring him back up, now!"

The technicians burst into life even more intense in their work than before, desperate to give this intimidating figure what he wanted, searching relentlessly for answers as the squeal that pierced the ears of everyone in the room got even louder. Then suddenly it stopped. Each small grouping looked to the next, gauging whether they had beaten them to it, but all of them were completely baffled.

"United we stand, divided we fall," an unknown voice, definitely female, echoed out over the expanse of the command centre.

"What was that?" Reiku turned round and slammed a fist down on MacArthur's desk, putting his face hardly an inch away from the other man's. "The best time to answer me was two seconds ago," he coldly spat.

"I'm working on it, Vice-Admiral," Grey saw his manager reply, the damp of sweat started to appear on his brow and the senior technician found a drive in him to protect his superior. Grey pulled up his chair and got to work. First he checked the station's own servers, checking for any breach, but found nothing.

Think, he told himself. So considered a worst case scenario, and a wave of anxiety came over him after he found the first signs that his hunch was correct. Grey double checked the Stardust broadcast wavelengths and, per his expectations, found them to be pumping out empty signal, jamming the airwaves from sending any other signals. Then he checked other communication types, tapping into Stalwart, Crimson Sun and RCS communicate but found them dead, he couldn't even find their channels on the spectrum. And now to confirm the worst case scenario. Grey searched for broadcasts coming into the Crimson from beyond its borders, scanning the void between the set channels and eventually soon enough, he heard something small, something tiny, something hidden under the ambient noise caused by the net of deafening silence Stardust's network was casting. It was a short burst transmission, using the Coalition's own communications network as cover so that it could be undetected. The message they just heard being used as a distraction, Grey found a faint signal surrounding the Forerunner meaning something was being broadcast from there, but he couldn't hone in any closer than that.

"United we stand, divided we fall," the voice said again.

"Who is that?" Reiku barked out over the command centre.

"Don't know, sir!" One voice called out.

"It's strange, Vice-Admiral Reiku, it's not like she's speaking directly, nothing like you'd expect in a broadcast. I think it's been extrapolated from a recording of someone's voice, so it could be anyone," a young technician offered, standing up from within a small ensemble of his colleagues that had gathered around his workstation.

"Inspired work, tech, you've told me a great deal without actually saying anything," Reiku snapped back, shaking his head.

"Sir!" Grey called out, using the other technicians blurting out the first things to enter their minds, gaging to impress the upper level manager in the room, as a distraction, biding his time to get his work exactly right. "I've got something that requires your attention," he called over, raising a hand in the air to be noticed by the management platform, the correct procedure.

"Setting an example for your lesser colleagues, well done Alex, beam what you have to my station and come join us up here," MacArthur called over, beckoning his trusted colleague over with a nod.

"United we stand, divided we fall," the voice said again, and the threat of it felt heavy on Alex Grey's shoulders as he stood up from his desk and took up the long winding path to the platform. He knew the severity of what he was about to present, he knew exactly what the words everyone was hearing was about, what it was designed to signify.

"So what is your conclusion, Senior Technician Alex Grey?" Vice-Admiral Reiku asked by way of greeting, staring down at the other man, his eyes flaming with rage, daring him to be right about what he intended to say.

"The Stardust network, the backbone of the majority of the Coalition's communications is being blocked by a complete blackout, that's how we lost the Section Chief. And what we're hearing? That voice is a signal, it's emanating from the Forerunner but whoever is responsible for it knows what they're doing, they're evading every means I have for honing in and identifying them."

"But why? What's their goal?" Reiku interrupted, folding his arms, standing intentionally close to the senior technician.

"Their goal was to create a diversion," Grey replied confidently, ignoring the attempt to intimidate him. "To make us focus solely on this message, which I think relates to a WIDOW's attempt at sparking a revolution. But underneath this message, under the blanket of muted transmission that is blocking the Stardust airwaves, there was a short burst message sent into the Crimson."

"What message?" Reiku backed off, turning away.

"I don't know, it was so short that it was practically undetectable to even know it happened. But I was looking for it, so I was able to find the vaguest hint of it."

"Well done, Grey," MacArthur nodded, sitting back in his chair, proud of his teammate. "So is there anything we can draw conclusions about regarding this message?"

"I do think there's one thing, Mack. You remember that outbound broadcast to the Sapphire region? I think this was them sending a response," Grey flicked his glasses back up his nose with the knuckle on his right thumb before scratching the back of his neck, glancing over at the other man.

"What outbound broadcast?" Reiku rounded, his anger turning to confusion clear on his face.

"A message got through to the Sapphire region that we weren't able to intercept, we have no idea what it was," MacArthur answered with a disinterested shrug.

"Wait, so our communications are down completely?" Reiku looked at the manager in the chair with alarm and the other man must have read his thoughts because MacArthur leant forward so quickly he almost tipped his chair.

"What is it?" Grey asked, forgetting he was in the company of his superiors.

"Hang on, I'm hacking into the Stardust network, we need to bring it down and reboot or nothing will come back up," MacArthur hastily typed away at his terminal but was visibly struggling to find his way around the systems.

"Move over, Mack, allow me," Grey offered and his manager didn't hesitate, leaping out of the seat and steadying it for his colleague to take over his efforts. Alex input his login to access the Stardust network and found himself rebuffed, as he anticipated whoever was responsible was trying to protect their work, but he piggybacked on the signal they sent telling him his attempt for entry had failed. That brought him into the inner workings of the Coalition servers, right at their point of access and this was where Alex thrived.

"United we stand, divided we fall," the voice echoed again but this time Alex Grey wasn't distracted in listening to it to discern its meaning, this time he was entirely fixated on his work.

"Alright, I've got them. I'm shutting it down then we just need to wait for it to reboot. But Stardust is our everything, it's the backbone for the entire network, all the others use it so we will lose all communication while it resets," Grey warned his superiors.

"We already have, Grey, just do what you need to do," MacArthur said over his shoulder, watching his colleague work.

Grey did as he was bid and pulled the plug on the communications network, annihilating the Stardust broadcast and killing the separate signal where the voice was coming from. An eerie silence descended over the entire command centre, the red sun bathing the room in a wash of crimson, the only real light in the room, with the air thick with apprehensive impatience. Every technician was weighing up different thoughts. But Grey figured he knew what the majority of them were thinking. What if the Senior Technician, their team leader, was wrong? What if by turning off the communications web, he had left all of Obsidian open to an attack? What if his position were to become available because of such a mistake? Yet Grey paid them no mind. He was confident, and he had the backing of his manager at his side and now even the Vice-Admiral himself looking to him for answers. He felt assured in his position, rewarded for his faith in Obsidian.

The system came back nytne with a fluttering static before all the broadcasts they had been missing came through all at once. There were too many to count from all sorts of places, and Grey found MacArthur's terminal was overwhelmed in trying to hone in one to put on the imager. But his eye was caught on one in particular and he put it up, illuminating the room with a holographic image of a panic stricken Obsidian officer.

"Listening post, come in! I repeat, we are under attack! We're being fucking massacred out here! We're the border guard with the Sapphire region, and they are attacking! Three Cosmics are already down! The fleet is on the brink of breaking, we need assistance, now! Right fucking now!" He screamed down the imager, his face spread wide across the command centre for everyone to see, the fear there infecting the technicians who could only stare on, powerless.

"Where is Admiral Thorne?" Reiku demanded of the giant holographic officer, his cold, stern temperament returning.

"The Admiral has turned against us, sir! His fleet has joined the fray on the Sapphire side, we're overrun! We won't last much longer, Vice-Admiral, sir! Request immediate assistance or the border will fa—" The broadcast went dead.

"Get him back," Reiku growled at Grey, still sitting at his manager's terminal and he did everything he could but the signal was gone.

"They're gone, sir," Grey replied, not daring to take his eyes away from the screen in front of him.

"Anything else we might have missed?" Reiku clasped his arms together behind his back, recovering his composure.

"The border's gone dark, sir, no transmissions at all, and no response to pings so they must be destroyed," Grey reported, reading the colossal, never-ending list of information appearing on the screen, reports coming in from all across the Obsidian infrastructure.

"Admiral Thorne attacked the border guard? That makes no sense," a technician called up to the platform, the team down among the desks all in hysterics.

"Quiet! The lot of you," Reiku boomed without shouting, imposing his authority. "Grey, what else?"

"I don't quite know what to make of what I'm seeing, sir. But the space above Carmine has gone dark, too. No response to pings. There's a riot on Scarlet. And another one on Sanguine, a Stalwart team was just found dead, they were sent to cleanse a town deemed unprofitable but looks like they never got there. The officer reporting seems to think Elites took them out? I don't understand that, I don't understand any of this."

"Grey, get back to your station, MacArthur, get us back in touch with the Section Chief, I wish to touch base with him before I head to the Forerunner for answers on this transmission. Gentlemen," the Vice-Admiral turned to face them, taking the time to look each of them in the eye. "We are at war."

Chapter 13

Nathan stepped out gingerly, scanning the left and the right with his rifle, only moving out cautiously once he established that the road that ran alongside the length of the river was clear of the undead and their larger companions, the monstrous abominations. On one side of this road were more of the same building he had come out from, various kinds of businesses enjoying the one time picturesque view of the water. Now though, the river was little more than a sludge, polluted with the decaying bodies that were at its bed and imbued with the split open organs and intestines that bobbed along its surface. It was entirely still, no wind or current to move the river along giving it a disgusting odour, almost visible to the eye in a small fog above the water line, scarcely seen from the street lights illuminating the way. Here, like the entrance way from the docks, the dome cast a constant shroud of night, making it difficult to see, but the sight of another living soul was clear to see.

With a thought, Nathan tilted the thrusters on his jetpack and burst forward, a quiet yet frighteningly swift attack that saw him boot over the other man, pinning him under the weight of his boot onto the low wall that acted as the barrier for the edge of the bridge. Tomen and Miles followed out from the building but missed Nathan's darting strike, he crossed the space in the blink of an eye, and suddenly they were seeing him stamping the barrel of his rifle into the stranger's forehead.

"Something capture your curiosity?" Nathan analysed the look of the man under his control, having not expected to find anyone alive in the city after the grisly sights of the hordes of undead.

"You just looked lost, sir, I was just a wonderin' if you needin' some help?" The man whimpered, he was dressed in a grey jumpsuit suggesting he was of Stardust, and he had fitted it with a hood that he wore up. He was covered in the kind of filth that builds up without regular washing and his hair was in greasy strands poking down under the hood, with a piece of cloth wrapped around his neck, pulled up in covering his mouth. He was X-Human, eyes of a luminescent yellow staring back at Nathan, infected with fear.

"You have some place safe?" Nathan bore the end of his suppressor attached to his rifle into the man's head firmer, digging in enough to near break the skin.

"Yes! Yes! I can show you, I can show you! It's safe, I swear," he wept, grasping Nathan's left arm that he was using to keep the rifle firmly against the man's forehead, while his right was ready to fire.

"Any tricks, and I drop you," Nathan leaned back and stepped off, replacing his rifle to his back and gripped the man by the hood, dragging to the floor at his feet, grasping the back of his neck, holding his head down. "Now, show us this safe place, before I change my mind and break you," Nathan growled into the man's ear, before hoisting him up and giving him a short shove to get him moving.

By the end of this short exchange, Tomen and Miles had come over, checking either side of the street they were on, and watching the crest of the bridge, not knowing from which direction the next attack may come. They each took glances at the stranger though, caught in the same confusion, the same disbelief. "What's going on?" Tomen asked, waving the others up from where they were watching at the doorway they had just left.

"I made a friend, he's going to show us his safe place," Nathan announced with a sadistic sense of enjoyment. "Come now, lead the way," he said, pulling out his pistol from his chest holster.

"This way, this way," the gold of his male X-Human skin was dull, dry seeming and nearer to the colour of the river than to Miles' own shade, something Nathan and the others took note of.

"And we're just trusting this guy? The fuck he come from?" Miles asked, watching as the stranger started to shuffle down the street, pulling his hood aside to peer over his shoulder, checking if they were following him.

"What's going on?" Cait asked, as she, Lena and Sam joined the others, glaring at the stranger in utter befuddlement.

"If this man survived this long, then he can tell us more about what's going on in this city, and he claims to have a safe space, we're checking it out. Now, follow," Nathan didn't wait for a response, just waved a lazy hand in the direction of the stranger now a ways up the street, on the same side of the river, and the team followed his direction. Tucking in behind the group, Nathan watched the rooftops, grasping his pistol firmly, expecting to be attacked.

They followed the river for a stretch, passing by the empty ruins of shops and parlours, bars and offices, until they reached an alley with a set of stairs set into one side, leading to the top of the building on the right, with a bridge crossing the waterway directly opposite the entrance. The stranger stopped here, waiting for the others to catch up before he pointed at the rickety, metal staircase, "we go up, friends, up to the stars, up is survive."

"Sure," Tomen replied, not lowering his rifle from being shouldered ready for a fight, as he ignored his instincts to leave the stranger, to keep away, sensing a danger to come. But the group followed, with Nathan at the rear of the pack, giving a nod when they looked to him to make sure he still meant to follow.

"This is not a good idea, just follow the random freak back to his pad, brilliant, really seeing the benefit in having the Elite Commander tag along," Sam whined, aiming it for Cait to hear but she paid him no attention.

"Well, why don't you stay out here and grab a snack with the zombies? You're a shit human being, maybe you'll make a better sandwich," Miles shrugged, laughing to himself.

The stairs shook and rang with every step they took heading up to the top level, entering through a doorway into an apartment overlooking the river. They stepped into the living room, an area with a worn out grey sofa with a holographic imager opposite which was a simple silver box on a sideboard covered in dust, with a kitchen opposite this entrance. There was blood spattered on all of the kitchen surfaces, all across the grey and orange cupboards, and the plain metal worktop, with spewed bodily fluids in a puddle leaking onto the floor. Lena almost threw up at the sight of the discarded ribcage cast on the floor by their feet as they entered, while Miles tripped over it, falling onto the arm of the sofa, finding grip from the mass of clothes piled there.

"Still think this was a good idea?" Cait asked, taking in the room, noticing the hanged pictures gone astray, the litter of clothing everywhere, and the tangy, revolting smell of something rotten hanging in the air, but there was another aroma competing with it. "Is something cooking in here?" She put the question out there and immediately regretted it.

"I'm good baker, I make pie with only the best ingredients, I make good smell, for good people?" The stranger's eyes were wider than they normally ought to be, whether out of surprise or something, it wasn't clear. "You really shouldn't be on streets at night, this is no longer nice neighbourhood. But they no come up this high, this is nice, safe place. Happy, safe place," the X-Human stranger gave a little clap to himself as he rushed over to his kitchen, checking the oven that was on.

"What's going on in the city? What's happened to everyone?" Tomen demanded, taking off his helmet and immediately scrunching his nose in having to tolerate the smell.

"Some have got real mean lately, happened yesterday, since then they attack people like you's, only leave alone peoples like me's," the stranger said, fixing Tomen with an intense stare. "No, people like you are their favourite."

"You mean humans?" Lena asked, recovering her composure, doing her best to avoid looking at the remains of people scattered about the apartment.

"I do, they no like human anymore, I think they not so bad, they have nice qualities," the stranger crouched down in front of his oven, the waft of heat washing out clouding what he said next.

"Sorry, what?" Cait asked him, thinking she had heard him say something more, but the stranger paid her no mind, taking out a pie, placing it on the worktop before shutting the oven door.

"Perfect," he murmured to himself, drawing back his hood, removing the rag from his mouth and taking in a big whiff of his creation. He then shifted over to one of his cupboards, and took a nervous glance past the group, past the sofa to the door at the far wall.

Nathan saw this and, having remained silent, simply observing up to now, moved across the room, putting the others between him and the stranger so he wasn't seen and positioned himself near the door, his pistol still in the grasp of his right hand. He pulled it behind his back, taking out his suppressor for it from his belt and attached it out of sight of the stranger.

A knock at the front door to the apartment drew all of the eyes from the group in alarm, a sound they had hardly expected to hear. Not a frantic banging as though some other random soul might have seen them and come here seeking help, instead this was a calm series of taps, something that didn't seem to worry their host. The door was on the same side of the apartment as the kitchen so their host, who had just finished getting out a large plate from his cupboard, only had to slip out of the alcove and take a short couple of steps to answer it. None of the team thought to stop him, it was so unexpected, they didn't know what to do. Nathan was just curious to allow things to unfold, but even he had to admit to being surprised at the one who had called the door.

Entering inside by the host stepping to one side was a woman in an elegant red dress, clearly ready for an evening where she intended to impress, the silver sheen of her female X-Human skin on clear view as a slit revealed a leg up to the inner thigh. Her hair was silver too, and her eyes were surrounded in a dark shadow. She looked beautiful but her blue bejewelled eyes were vacant, seemingly not registering her surroundings.

"I have your gift, just here," the host scurried over to the kitchen, picking up the pie with his bare hands, neglecting the sheer heat from it, and placing it on the plate he had retrieved.

As he moved the pie, the other side came into view where a section of bone and flesh was protruding out of the crust, swamped in congealed, thick blood but the two X-Humans exchanging the plate didn't seem to register this. The woman didn't so much as look the man in the eye or make a sound, she simply took hold of the plate she was given and stood perfectly still.

"Miss, are you ok?" Sam asked her, his mind clawing at a need to raise his gun.

"Love, that pie's a little worse for wear, can't you see?" Miles asked, causing the woman to snap her head round to face him, without moving the rest of her body even the slightest bit. Her eyes didn't meet his gaze though so Miles removed his helmet and placed it and his rifle down on the side table next to the sofa, before crossing the length of the furniture towards her. "Might want to take a closer look at it," Miles warned, pointing at it with his left hand as he steadily approached the woman, gently placing a hand on her arm with his right, all the while their host was staring emptily at him.

The scream that erupted out of the woman was piercing, deafening and Miles almost fell back in stumbling back to scramble along the back of the sofa to retrieve his gun. "What the fuck, lady !"

"Shut up, miss! Shut the fuck up!" Sam snapped, bringing his shotgun up and aiming it directly at the screaming woman who was now glaring at Miles, her eyes fixed on him, never blinking.

"Sam, take it easy!" Tomen barked at him, forcing the shotgun down for him and crossing the apartment to join the two strangers. "What in all the starways is going on?" He asked the male firmly as the other one stopped her screeching wail.

"I have company, darling, maybe we will talk more later?" The male X-Human said to the woman and she calmly made for the front door, pie in hand.

"What the fuck?" Lena swore to herself, watching the woman leave without sign that she ever fully recognised her surroundings.

Nathan, meanwhile, used the commotion as cover as he silently opened the pale, wooden door their host was so nervous about and slipped inside, no one noticing his disappearance for the strangeness of their host. Cait walked up to the man, her shotgun raised against him. "Why are there so many clothes chucked everywhere?"

"Is that really a priority, right now?" Sam laughed nervously, glancing over to her from where he stood nearer their entrance, while she was in the kitchen alcove now.

"Well, think about it, where do you think the meat came from for that pie?" Cait spat back at him, a panic building up in her chest.

Tomen realised the same thing immediately after Cait reached the man, pointing her weapon at his head. But the former Stalwart man didn't have time for any passive threats, he wanted answers, so he marched the length of the apartment and planted a kick at the X-Human's chest, blasting him back into the kitchen cupboards where he fell. It made a large bang as he hit the wood of the cupboards then became a heap on the floor but Tomen didn't care about the noise, stamping down hard on the man's hand, breaking it before placing his rifle against his head. "I asked you what was going on in this city, you've yet to give me an answer," he said before firing a warning shot next to the man's face, burning a dark mark on the wood behind him.

"You won't get anything out of him, Tomen," Nathan called over, returning to the main room. "He's lost his mind more than I thought. He's got an Obsidian soldier in there, tied to the bed."

"Winter, what is going on? Tomen looked down at the X-Human with disgust and confusion aplenty."

"Whatever caused the Collapse seems to have affected humans and X-Humans differently, that much is clear. We saw the effect it had on humans out there, and we're seeing the effects on an X-Human right here," he replied, crossing the room, gun in hand.

"He was covering his mouth, d'you think it could be airborne?" Lena put in, darting her gaze to Nathan as Cait went off to investigate the contents of the other room.

"No, my suit would have picked up any trace of an airborne toxin," Nathan replied from behind his black helmet, now standing over the X-Human pinned to the floor under Tomen's boot.

"Oh fuck, fucking, fucking, fuck!" Cait yelled from the other room, Sam rushing in to join her and together they gawked at the body tied to the bed. Barely breathing, tied down on her front, was a woman with black hair on the orange sheets, a bone sticking out from the skin of her right leg, and a section of her chest was caked in blood, seeping in the bedding. She still had her Obsidian armour over her torso, albeit slashed to pieces, such as where her main wound was, but her leg plating and boots had been removed, leaving her bare.

"He doesn't want you's in there! He don't like it, he don't like it! HE DON'T LIKE IT!" The man under Tomen's boot became enraged, thrashing his arms uselessly against the strong leg that kept him firmly locked in place. He fought relentlessly, pounding against the calves of the former Stalwart man, until Nathan shot him in the head.

"There was nothing he could tell us," Nathan sighed, removing his suppressor from his pistol, his body language obvious in saying that he was not happy for having his time wasted.

"It was worth a try," Tomen said, glancing over at the man at his side as he stepped off from the body of the X-Human. "What do we do about her? She alive?"

"Not in any condition to be moved," Nathan replied, making his way back to the bedroom.

"How many people do you think this guy killed and made into food?" Lena picked up a jacket from the back of the sofa, found a sticky patch of blood where there was a hole then chucked it on the ground.

"Going by the amount of sets of clothing, quite a lot," Tomen remarked, going over to collect his helmet and put it back on.

"Ah shit," Miles began. "Hey Tomen, tell our new friend to tidy this place up, we don't him to pay a penalty," he said, tapping a notice attached to the wall by the entrance door that read 'This is a Stardust owned domicile, you will maintain it and uncleanliness will result in penalties against your pay'.

Cait couldn't undo the power cables that the man had used as restraints on the woman, tying her to the four corners of the bed, but she did manage to cover her up with a sheet at least. She yanked at the strands of wires but they were tied so tight that they had broken skin and were embedded in the flesh. Short breaths proved that the woman was still alive, she left a small patch of saliva next to her mouth on the pillow, and her eyes were closed yet Cait couldn't tell if she was just asleep or unconscious. Sam wrestled with the bonds at the woman's ankle while trying to not focus on the shard of bone sticking out of the leg, with a layer of pus surrounding the exit wound. It was a sickening sight yet he kept his mind and hands focused on helping Cait to release the woman from her bonds. There was just about room for them both to be crouched down by the double bed, with only a simple wardrobe opposite the bed and a bedside table bearing a half drunk glass of water as the only other furniture.

"What are you doing?" Nathan sounded entirely disinterested, confused.

"We need to help her, maybe we can get her back to the ship, you have a medico-table onboard!" Cait shouted but not taking her eyes from the knot that her fingers couldn't break free.

"Look at her leg, Cait, look at all of her. She isn't going anywhere. Not to mention she would survive the journey to the ship, and nor would we if he had to lug her the whole way," Nathan said, walking around the bed to place a hand on Cait's shoulder. "Step away. Go in the other room, with the others, you don't want to see this."

"What? What you doing? She's still breathing!" Cait wailed, shrugging off the hand, devoting all of her strength to pulling on the cable, but all her attempts did was tighten the bond, sinking it further into the woman's wrist.

"Cait, Sam, out the room, leave Winter to do what has to be done," Tomen appeared at the door and gave no suggestion for answering back in his tone.

Cait began to cry, tears appearing in the corners of her eyes as Sam picked her up, near dragging her out of the room, made to watch as Nathan placed a gloved hand over the woman's nose and mouth, so casually, so easily. "No! We can help her! Stop it!" She kicked and fought but Sam was stronger and he brought her back into the living room and Tomen closed the door so she couldn't see.

"What are you doing?" Lena asked them, not having any idea what was going on, simply feeling afraid as she was powerless, made to watch her friends fighting among themselves.

Nathan then opened the door, stepped through and closed it gently behind him, and Cait caught a glimpse of the woman on the bed, left tied there, with the sheet now covering the whole of her body. "Why did you do that?" She launched herself from Sam's grasp and threw a punch, connecting with Nathan's helmet, which did nothing to him but left her reeling in more pain, her right hand throbbing.

"I did what had to be done, I just didn't hesitate, that is what freaks you out," Nathan growled back, the dark grey ovals for his eyes on his helmet giving nothing away but a cold indifference.

"We could'a helped her!" Cait instinctively grasped the trigger handle of her shotgun that she had been leaving to sway against her chest, a silent threat.

"I did. What you would have done would only have caused her even greater pain and longed out her death, is that what you wanted? Killing her quickly was a mercy and sooner it was done, the sooner she was out of her pain. Or were your feelings in need of attention before you could come around to that simple, basic truth. She was in pain and you hesitated, I didn't and she's out of it. Simple as that," Nathan explained roughly.

"Really? Simple as that? Murder is that easy for you?" Cait spat back at him, walking right up to him and pointing a firm finger into his chest plate.

"And so what if it is? How exactly was your hesitating any better? You may as well have been causing her the pain yourself," he tilted his gaze down to meet hers, refusing to back down.

"Because it's not right!"

"Right and wrong? There's no such thing. All that matters is your will, are you willing to do what has to be done? Or are you like the pitiful rest, who hesitate or shy away? Doomed to lives of no significance, but not because of some cruel act of fate, but because they simply weren't brave enough to lift a finger and have a real impact on the stars that be!"

"We could have done something, something to help her," Cait was losing her spirit for this fight, feeling her mind swayed, she was seeing the sense in what Nathan had done.

"I did, I killed her quicker than time would," Nathan softened his tone as well, knowing he had made his point. "Besides, we've been lingering here too long and something's bound to have heard that woman's scream. We need to move," he announced. Just as one of the powerful beasts pulverised the wall from the bedroom side, grasped Tomen and threw him out of the window, above the imager, out into the road.

It had just about enough time to produce a blood-curdling roar in Sam's face before Nathan had his sword drawn and sliced off the two heads sticking out of its deformed body, then ignited the blade, and drove it into its mid-region, hoping to hit a heart or vital organs. It was hard to tell if he hit anything crucial as the various torsos fused together were distinct and spread across a sizable joined belly so Nathan twisted the blade as he withdrew it, before giving it two strong hacks for good measure. A splash over his shoulder told Nathan where to look for Tomen and, wasting no time hesitating, he took off with his jetpack, hurtling out of the broken window, heading straight for the river.

The team sprinted for the fragile metal staircase bolted to the side of the building, making their way down using the way they came, but came under attack as two more of the beasts dropped down from the rooftops, as undead piled on top of each in crawling up the steps. In the alley, away from the vague light of the street, it was pitch black, near impossible to see as gigantic arms swung at their heads from the beasts too large to fit among the stairs, or the gnashing teeth of the corpses steadily ascending, taking up the whole way down. Miles' energised rifle shots were the most luminescent thing in the alley, sparks of green flying everywhere as he did his absolute best to protect the group with him. Sam and Cait blasted anything that moved with their shotguns, desperately trying to clear the way down but where the front line fell, more just crawled over them, making forging a path fruitless. One of the beasts leapt from the top of the stairs where it had no luck reaching through to snatch at the team, instead breaking the brick of the building opposite, making an outcrop for itself where it reached across and clawed at Lena's shoulder as she fired off her pistol. She screamed and in her pain, dropped her handgun, it sent clattering against the metal as it fell through the crack in the middle of the staircase, falling to the ground so far below. Lena tried to wrestle free from pure fear and terror but when she looked down at her right shoulder, she saw the fingers of three hands morphed together dug into her flesh, the fingertips like hooks, stuck in her.

"Miles!" Lena called up to her former Stalwart friend who was half a stairway up, shooting at the undead that had made their way to the roof above their head, slotting them each before they had the chance to jump down on top of them, instead crumbling and dropping to the ground harmlessly. He heard her cry however and sprinted down to her level, using his rifle at this close range to shoot her free, separating the hands from the rest of the abomination at its wrist. It was just in time as it leaned in to bite at his head, instead having it recoil violently in pain, lose its grip and scrape down the face of the building. The three fused hands were still hooked into Lena's shoulder and she collapsed in pain, giving Miles a clearer view of Cait and Sam below, struggling to keep back the tide of the dead things.

Nathan carried on his jetpack's thrust even after bursting through the surface of the river, reaching out instinctively for Tomen, the slimy consistency of the water too dirty for him to see through. But his hand felt something solid, something that moved against his grip and he arched his back, giving a strong burst. It tore them out from the clutches of the water, throwing them onto their backs on the bank of the river, a small clearing below the low border wall that ran across the top of their heads. A slick almost liquid covered the two men from head to toe and Nathan glanced over at Tomen, making sure he was still breathing. "You didn't swallow any, did you?"

"No, no. I just about saw the river coming," Tomen rested his head back, sucking in the air, despite the awful smell coming off the water. But a hand reaching up the length of his leg shocked him, dragging back down towards the river. He dragged himself back up the bank with his left elbow while unslinging his rifle with his right and began shooting at the shapes that were emerging from the water's edge, as more of the dead came crawling out. Even with Nathan's pistol firing at them joining the energy blasts from Tomen's rifle, the dead kept dragging what little remained of their hollow bodies up the river bank. The veil of whispers coming from them re-emerging but this time it was too unclear to leave anything distinct. Nathan arched his back and gave a short burst with his jetpack, enough to bring him onto the low wall and he rolled backwards to stand up behind it, ignoring the heat that caught the back of his legs from the thrust. He shot two more with his pistol, the ones nearest to Tomen before reaching down, lending his free hand to hoist him up, killing three more at the same time.

"How many fucking are there?" Tomen grunted, more to himself as he scrambled over the wall, regaining his balance before firing down at the creatures digging their grip in the space they had left, clawing their way up to them.

Nathan holstered his pistol and tossed a grenade down the short way to the river, gripping the man at his side, pulling down to take cover behind the wall. As the explosive went off, nulling the advance of their foe, the two men's attention was drawn to the metal staircase where the rest of their group were utterly surrounded, fighting back a wave of stalking corpses from all directions. At the top of this set of unstable stairs was a monster, larger than any of the other mingled, blends of bodies they had seen, glaring down its tree trunk sized legs at the firefight escalating below it. With arms as broad as the hull of Nathan's ship, it reached down and began to pull the structure of the stairs away from the wall, while bellowing a throaty, guttural roar from its mouth of a hundred jagged teeth, thick beads of blood mixed with saliva drooling down. Its silhouette against the shell beyond it made it seem even larger and with a strong pull, it tore out one corner of the stairs, sending a half-dozen undead tumbling out of the side from the jerking motion. The Elite Commander calmly strolled forward a step, then fired off a rocket barrage, it soared across the breadth of the road and alleyway to meet the monster directly at its engorged neck, exploding with a crack of thunder as its body went thundering down through the crack between the two buildings.

The heap of mangled flesh and scorched bones collided with the opposite building just above Miles' head, just close enough for him to flinch, cowering down, lifting his free arm up to protect his head. The crash sent up a flurry of brick and dust, creating a small screen that was hard to see through so he missed where the body of the ginormous abomination had a limb caught in the staircase a couple of floors below them and pulled at it with its stifling weight. The already shaking stairs wobbled on its bottom mounts to ground, reeling away from its remaining mounts to the wall and went smashing into the building opposite.

"Miles, lead them up, head to the rooftops," Nathan instructed over his radio then grasped Tomen without asking, gripping on his jacket before taking off from the ground. They ascended, fast, tearing past the chaos of the alley to hover for a moment on the rooftop of the building they had just left, Nathan releasing Tomen before dropping down himself.

"A little warning next time," the former Stalwart man commented before shaking himself off and joining Nathan at the edge of the roof, shooting down the remaining undead on their patch.

"Stay here," was all Nathan responded with after watching the staircase sway then leapt over it into the gap, catching the steps as it lent back his way as he gripped the side of the other building before turning his jetpack on full. The force and momentum pushed the staircase back against its mount and held it there, giving stable footing for Miles to lead the way with the rest of the pack up the steps to join Tomen who covered them with a hailstorm of accurate fire. Raindrops of fiery, green lasers cast down all around them as they clambered and climbed the steps as fast as their legs could carry them, Sam supporting Lena with her injured shoulder.

Once the team were off the staircase, leaving just the dead as they awkwardly made their own climb, Nathan shut off his jetpack, kicking away from it in a backflip, only reactivating it a breath away from landing on the ground. He hovered for a split second, killing the momentum of his drop then shut off the thrust and unsheathed his sword, slicing away the framing for the stairs with easy, lazy slices. With a grunt and the sound of metal scraping against metal, the set of stairs collapsed, falling down towards the street, reaching up to the river but Nathan opened up his jetpack to avoid it, bouncing off the opposite building to control his climb and join the others at the top.

"Anyone else hurt?" Tomen was asking the others as Nathan re-joined them, finding him carefully peeling out the mash of flesh caught in the workings of Lena's shoulder, using Sam's coat to put pressure on the bleeding while he worked to clear it. Nathan stepped over briskly, removing his helm, crouching down at their side, placing it beside his knee as he reached over to Lena's shoulder to help.

"Concentrate on applying pressure, I'll get it out," the Elite ordered and Tomen obeyed, not having a better suggestion, Lena didn't interject either. Nathan tugged at it gently, finding the tips of the fingers buried deep beneath the skin so he focused on each one at a time, applying the slightest pressure to Lena's skin to push the deformed hand up. That allowed him to gain a grip of that finger so he could extract it more carefully, ignoring Lena's cries, focusing on the task at hand.

Cait gripped her friend's left hand tight within her own while Sam chucked off his backpack, routed inside and found a revitaliser. This instrument, branded all over in RCS logos, was a breathing mask linked to a tank containing a chemical designed to help with the healing process as well as acting as a painkiller. He had to wrestle Lena to get it on her, fighting against her screams to secure It but it worked in calming her down, allowing Nathan a smoother time in working on the thing attached to her shoulder.

"Tomen, we've got silhouettes on the other rooftops," Miles pointed out, hunching down beside them, staring through the scope on his weapon. "We don't have long until they're here with us."

"Any come up, take 'em down, Lena's in no position to be moved," Tomen briskly replied before realising his tone. "Do what you can to hold them back, mate. You did real good back there but I need you to keep up the rate, can you do that? I can't take my hands away to help cover us," he said, with a more straight tone.

"Aye, I'll do that," Miles replied, moving off to check on the far end of the rooftop they were occupying.

"I'm gonna go help him, unless ya need me?" Sam asked, looking at both Nathan and Tomen, getting shaken heads in return.

"Take my rifle," was all Tomen said and awkwardly shifted his weight so Sam could unbuckle the weapon from its sling and run over to where Miles was crouching down, observing a group of shadows take up a far off rooftop.

Cait held onto Lena's hand and let her rest against her chest while Nathan carried on pulling out the gruesome hand, with Tomen stopping the bleeding best he could manage. "It's going to be OK, sweetie, don't you worry," she comforted her friend, stroking a loose strand of red hair away from the forehead up against her chest.

"I know you're probably used to it from your Stalwart days but you should really consider switching to a ballistic weapon," Nathan said to Tomen, giving him a small nudge with his elbow, seeing the other man on the periphery of slipping into a deep, dark hole of overthinking.

"What? Why?" Tomen asked, sounding as though he had been woken from a dream, and not a good one.

"Laser rounds are slower. Sure, they burn and that alone can kill when it's not an immediate kill shot, but face a skilled opponent with an energised weapon and it could get you killed," Nathan went on.

"Never let me down so far," the other man replied, sliding out a soaked section of coat, replacing it with a different bit then folding it over to keep the pressure on.

"As I said, a skilled opponent. When we get back to the Forerunner, we'll leave this lot to drinks with Xin and I'll get Siobhan to get you something more fitting," Nathan said, gingerly removing the second to last finger, having to break it to get it out.

"Your contact is called Siobhan?" Tomen scorned, bewildered and pronouncing the name Shavonne.

"Yeah, though he thinks it's Siob-han, strange name but a reliable outfitter," Nathan replied as he finished removing the last section of the ghastly, decrepit flesh, tossing it aside before reaching into the bag on Tomen's back.

"Almost forgot I was wearing this thing," the former Stalwart man remarked before seeing what Nathan had pulled out, it was a spray can and Tomen darted his hands and Sam's coat out of the way so Lena's wound could be completely saturated in it. "What is this stuff anyway? Got it from your stash under your medico-table," he murmured, watching Nathan work.

"It can't be found in the Crimson, it's a Sapphire product, stimulates repair like nothing I've ever seen," and once he finished explaining what it was, the product was clearly performing as designed, with Lena's shoulder and neck becoming enveloped in a golden foam. "She's lost a lot of blood," Nathan gauged as he removed the revitaliser, placing it in Tomen's backpack.

"She going to be ok?" Cait asked, giving her friend a small shake to keep her awake.

"Yeah, we just need to encourage her body to make more," Nathan replied, placing the aerosol can to one side and stroking his beard.

"Guys, they're getting closer!" Sam called over and once Nathan, Tomen and Cait looked over to him, it was clear that there wasn't reason for him to hush his voice as the dead were on the very next roof over.

"We have to move her," Cait exclaimed, chewing their end of tongue considering just how to do that.

"I can give her a small transfusion, that'll do it," Nathan seemed in a world of his own, not listening to the panic-driven comments of those around him. "Can't be doing it here though," he said, replacing the can he had used back into Tomen's backpack before standing up.

"So what's the plan?" Tomen asked him, watching the other man put his helmet back on.

"Cait, ditch anything we can live without from Lena's bag, including her ammo, we're leaving the rifle. I need her to carry my jetpack. Then you are going to stow your shotgun and use my rifle. I'm going to carry Lena," he instructed and without delay, the purple-eyed X-Human lifted her friend up a bit more into her lap, opening up her backpack. The dried spill of blood on the side of Lena's wound gave Cait some small skin-crawling sensation but she ignored it as Nathan unslung his rifle then took off his jetpack, unbuckling the X-shaped strap that went criss-cross against his chest.

Before long they were set to go, with Cait wielding Nathan's rifle, and him carrying Lena on his back, just as the dead began to hurl themselves across the chasm between the buildings over to their rooftop. Tomen led the way, following Nathan's direction who was tucked in just behind, in tearing off the door that led to the stairs into the building beneath their feet, finding more corpses staggering towards them as predicted, and used it as a bridge to get over to the next building. He was the first to cross, stepping over it quickly, aiming his rifle he retrieved from Sam dead ahead, ready for the next pack to come rising over the edge of this rooftop. The rest of the team followed in close behind, Miles the last to pass over, checking the depths below his feet, looking for movement in the windows below, finding none, then he kicked the door down to slow down their pursuers. With all the team on the same rooftop again, Nathan jogged Lena on his back, shifting her head to rest over his right shoulder, clearing the way for unleashing another rocket barrage. It wiped out the dead that had stalked their way to where they had treated their friend, caving in the roof with the sheer force of the blast.

To get back to ground level, Tomen kicked in the door leading inside, and they found themselves in a hotel, travelling through floor after floor until they finally reached the bottom, having avoided more of the undead. The lobby for this building was covered in an array of grey and orange, clearly a Stardust establishment and was the most lit area they had been inside since standing in the sun in the shipyards. All of the lights were working and on, none of the team was immune to having to wince their eyes, having gotten used to the constant dark, but the downside was that it made inspecting the way harder, the street beyond being nowhere near as lit.

They carefully stepped out, Miles leading this time, checking both sides of the road before finding the bridge they had seen before, the one where Nathan and Tomen had gone under the water, opposite the alley. He double-checked his surroundings before hitting his radio at his chest, "all clear," he signalled. The rest followed and they made their way to the bridge, crossing it slowly, not wanting to get tangled up in any fights here, over the water where the environment itself would be used against them. Yet they passed peacefully and the road was eerily quiet, granting an untrustworthy break.

"The doorway to the Leisure district is beyond the next square, it's just a communal area so no buildings, but keep your gun up," Nathan advised, unable to help out immediately if a fight did break out, having to use both hands to keep the groggy Lena on his back.

True to his direction, the team came to the end of the road they were on, finding it leading into a large open space, far larger than the one with the fountain at the city entrance from the docks. All around the perimeter were restaurants and other tourist offices like the one they had passed through earlier, surrounding the entrance to the metro system beneath the city, which was a dome of decorated golden arches over what looked like the mouth of a cave. The team moved across the space, deliberately slowly, not wishing to be caught out in the open, crossing to find a set of towering metal doors, the exact same as those they had passed through before.

Nathan gently placed Lena down at his feet and crouched down, bringing up the screen mounted on his arm, as the team hunched down around him, checking every angle for the next attack. He pressed a couple of buttons but let out a sigh when his screen blinked red, "fuck," he grunted.

"What is it?" Tomen asked him, switching the leg he was putting his weight onto to be able to hear the other man easier.

"The power can't connect to these doors, they're off the system," he said, his voice a deep drone of frustration.

"So what do we do now?"

"We go under," Nathan replied, glancing over his shoulder at the entrance to the tunnels beneath their feet, the metro system.

Chapter 14

It was when the Obsidian guards disappeared from their posts around the edges of his bar that Xin started to let himself feel that something was wrong, something was happening. His patrons carried on oblivious, entertaining themselves with drinking, gambling, enjoying the show of the guys and girls dancing to the rapturous music on the stage that lured most of the attention. A group of exuberant RCS workers laughed and cheered around a roulette table, chanting the ball to fall on their lucky numbers. A Stalwart man was drinking a beer alone at a table, his rifle propped up against it, silently musing to himself. While a gang of Stardust women came together at a table making the most of a round of cocktail jugs, passing around the straws, each sampling all of the flavours as they giggled and jeered with each other. The setting was normal, nothing out of place, except for that glaring detail that the bartender couldn't ignore about his bar, the guards had left them to it.

That's when he saw the man enter, this one immediately standing out for his full Stalwart Ironworks armour beneath a well-worn green jacket, the large pack he bore on his back, but mostly because of the gun in his hands. For in the grips of his light grey gloves was a bulky, heavy gun with a belt of luminescent green rounds wrapped around its length, not a weapon worn openly without a clear and obvious intention to use it. He bore the grey helm of his company but removed it once he approached the bar, placing it down and fixing Xin with a curious stare. "Yeah, you're the one, he said I'd know you to see you, I'm guessing 'cause of the eyes," the man said, looking round but not with a sense of urgency.

"Got a name, friend?" Xin asked, doing his best impression of someone not fazed by a man with a big gun coming in looking specifically for him.

"Name's Siob-han, Winter sent me to grab you if things went south. Obsidian has surrounded the station, we have to leave." The man in Stalwart attire gave no indication in his voice that he was giving the one across from him any choice in the matter, nodding upwards at him at a bottle of vodka behind Xin, on a shelf. "Although one to help the nerves would be a treat, pal."

"Yeah, OK, what'd you mean leave? This is my place. Siob-han, was it? Odd name in bringing odd, well, pretty much everything," Xin obliged a drink, pouring the vodka into a tumbler he had to hand, sliding it across the bar to the other man, if only to see if he could get something more substantial out of him.

"I reckon they know you sent that broadcast out. It was the woman that came to my store with Winter, right? X-Human like yourself, with purple eyes," Siobhan downed his drink, slamming the glass down, then used the same hand to point at his own, brown human eyes.

"Cait, her name's Cait," Xin replied.

"Cool, well, see, I don't think Obsidian took kindly to your little meddling in their network, they've sent cruisers to surround this station, they'll be boarding any minute. I need to get you out."

"And Winter said I was what? Valuable? He would've asked this of you right before he slammed me through my own desk up in my office," Xin pointed up above them with his thumb, "and threatened me with his sword. He doesn't trust me, so why send you?"

"I've just told you that we're basically surrounded by a small army, and that I've been sent to get you, safe assumption would be that this is a good thing, hence my big gun, or would you 've preferred I'd nabbed something even bigger?"

"I never settle for safe assumptions," Xin crossed his arms, leaning forward against the bar. "Because a smart play for Winter would be to have you turn me over to Obsidian, get them all distracted thinking they had quelled an uprising before it had taken oxygen to its flame."

"Little late for late, the uprising has already begun," Siobhan shrugged. "Those words, they kicked off a pretty severe riot on Scarlet, looks like the little group of WIDOWs must've made an impression down there. Not to mention the Chief Admiral turned his colours."

"Chief Admiral?"

"Titus Thorne, the old Section Chief's brother, Elias's uncle. He attacked the border guard from this side to allow the Sapphire conglomerate in, word is he's inspired quite a few to leave Obsidian, apparently the company's fractured," Siobhan looked around again then struck his eyes to roof, hearing something that Xin did not.

"Just from a few words?" Xin didn't believe it, he thought it was all madness.

"Not necessarily, the word has gotten round now, pretty much everyone knows now, someone aboard their listening post has a big mouth," Siobhan placed his helmet back on and glared over his shoulder at the entrance.

"And what's that?"

"That the Elite Commander has entered the Old City. That he intends to find out why it fell and that he will return with evidence. Seems like just him returning from the shadows was enough to inspire a cult following," Siobhan explained, shouldering his weapon. "The consensus is that the Admiral intends to aid Winter, and kick off a resistance. And that the Sapphire is here to reinforce them, but something tells me you'd know more about that than me."

"He asked me to send a message to a contact of his in the Sapphire, which I did, that's all," Xin replied, starting to hear a commotion outside his doors, even over the loud music blaring from the far side of his bar.

"Sure, yeah, you're just a Stardust bartender and I'm just a Stalwart lackey, what would either of us really know about what's going on? Alright, time's up. Either you come with me, or you stick around and wait for them to figure it was you who broadcasted that message, once they sifted through the bodies most likely. So what's it to be?"

Xin considered it for a moment, looking out over the length of his bar, weighing up what would be best for everyone who had come to his bar, who had come here with the promise of a safe place to get away from the ceaseless troubles of their shifts, the agony they were forced to endure to be given this small measure of peace. But if this man was right, and he had put them all in danger by helping Cait and her team with his ploy, then he was responsible for it, he figured with a sigh. And if he were to do anything to justify that, then it was to see things through, to not stop here and pretend to keep mixing drinks as though nothing else mattered, he had to put the other foot in. "Alright, I'll come with you," he said, removing the grey jacket of his Stardust uniform.

"What're you doing?"

"I keep this here, in case of trouble," Xin pulled an armoured vest out from a cupboard under the bar, along with a handgun, an Obsidian model laser pistol, red energy rounds encased in a sleek, black casing.

"Well, at least you can watch my back," Siobhan remarked, and ushered the other man to follow with a nod in the direction of the doors.

Xin rounded the bar, taking a moment to glance back at his other bartender, a young woman too distracted by talking to a small group of the Stardust entertainers who had just finished their piece on the stage.

"You try bringing along people and we'll be too large a party to ignore, we'll have more luck just the two of us," Siobhan said, tracking the other man's view.

"Yeah, s'pose you're right," Xin resigned, following the other man up to the doors, patiently waiting as Siobhan took the time to observe the outside before he nodded to indicate that all was well.

As soon as they stepped outside, they instantly knew they had left it too late. A solid line of Obsidian troops stood across the breadth of the main avenue of the Forerunner, blocking the way to the docking hanger, with an officer standing just behind them, taller than them, well-built and gazing upon the travellers to this station with clear loathing. The common workers were either shouting at this line, trying to get out or were carrying on as if nothing were out of place, watching the adverts or flirting with the Stardust men and women, or interacting with the stalls. Yet the tension in the air was rising, it was clear that the forces of Obsidian were not here to be subtle, and were growing impatient at being ignored by the vast majority.

"Silence!" The officer boomed, his command like an explosion, it was so fierce that people were stopping dead in their tracks to gawk at him, not having any idea what was going on. The ambient music obeyed his instruction too, a trooper hauling the Stardust colleague out of his cubicle on the top deck, shooting the console to shut off the songs that were helping with the feel of carrying on as normal.

"The fuck is that guy?" Siobhan exclaimed quietly, hastily grabbing Xin and hauling him out of sight, using the protruding frame of the Starcrest entrance for cover from the view of the docks entrance.

"Vice-Admiral Constantin Reiku. If he is here, then we are all in danger," Xin murmured, now grasping the heat of their situation. "This way, we can't take them all on," he nodded in the direction of a maintenance door at the side wall, past a vacant Obsidian recruitment stall.

The door was a hunk of solid metal, opened with a spinning wheel at its centre and was incredibly heavy, Siobhan and Xin having to work together to get it open, cursing as the hinges loudly creaked, but the general clamour of the crowd dying down was just enough to cover the sound. They entered a narrow corridor, a slim space between the main section of the station and the outer hull, used by the maintenance crews to access the systems tidily tucked out of sight. Now though it served as a means to slip by unnoticed, out of the sight of the Obsidian forces locking the space station down.

Through an air vent, in between slats of metal, Xin was able to peer inside his bar as they passed it heading for the docks. Evidently they had left just in time. A swarm of soldiers in black armour, bright red visors lighting up their helmets as they kicked down the door, hastily engulfing the entire area under their control. The patrons weren't given much of a chance to notice their sudden appearance before the Obsidian troops started hauling them out of their seats, dragging them to the ground, knocking over tables, casting drinks flying into the air. Screams and shouts formed a flood in the bar as some began to resist, only to be pummelled to within an inch of their life, or shot if the trooper was feeling like moving things along quicker. A wave of terror filled Xin up to his very brim, these were people he saw near daily or were fresh faces, ones he was curious to make acquaintance with, all getting beaten and dragged to join the others in the main section.

"There's nothing we can 'cept move forward, you got that, mate? Can't be doin' any heroics or we're never makin' it outta here alive, you 'stand?" Siobhan gripped Xin tightly at the top of his grey vest, pulling him in so he was a mere inch away from him, "there is nothing to be done for them."

"I know, I get it," Xin whispered back, holding back a coughing fit, the air was stifling in this confined space, it was hot and the dust was itchy in his throat.

"You'll likely not come back here, best come round to that idea quickly, the sentimental don't last long in the Crimson," Siobhan adjusted the belt of his ammunition, stopping it from dangling off the barrel of his weapon so loosely before pressing on.

They followed along the dusty trail, following the slight curve of the hull in the cramped metal funnel, a dim channel of grey with the off red coming from the rust where the moisture from the air recyclers overhead dripping their chemical mixture. It didn't take long until they passed the structure of the Starcrest bar, opening up to a length that led up to the panelling that separated this commerce area from the shipyards in the next section. Siobhan led the way but stopped when he encountered their path being blocked by a locked door of the same type they had used to enter, the wheel not budging so he had to dip into his bag to bring out a blowtorch. "Stand in the way, between me and that vent, we can't have 'em see the torch," the Stalwart nodded over his shoulder, telling Xin where to stand.

"Got it," he replied, the X-Human standing awkwardly next to and somewhat above the other man, the air vent in question square at Xin's chest, just high enough for him to see out from. They were at the small rise to docks, to the side of the checkpoint, behind the line of Obsidian troops who had stepped forward some several paces. "They've moved forward, what are they doing?" He whispered, just loud enough over the sound of the torch burning through the locking mechanism at the door's left side.

"The embassy has a standing army at the far end, they're creating a trap. The force from this side is the unstoppable force pushing the crowd into their immovable object at the other end. They really want to find out who sent that broadcast," Siobhan didn't allow himself to become distracted, carefully dismantling the lock to get them away from the chaos he was expecting to erupt at any moment.

"A message was sent from this installation," Xin could see the Vice-Admiral address the crowd who were stumbling back, fearful of the array of rifles being pointed in their faces by the bulky units clad full in armour. "Identify this Worker In Deviation Of Work-Orders immediately! They have committed gross misconduct relating to their contract with the Crimson Overseer Coalition, and as such are subject to serious disciplinary action. Bring this individual or individuals forward, or the entire populace of this installation will be subject to the same action in the assumption that the required outcome will have been dispensed to those responsible for this blatant disregard of their employment commitment!"

"You can't do this!" Someone in the crowd shouted.

"I'm reporting this to my supervisor!"

"We didn't do anything!"

"Chief Thorne will never allow this!"

"Where is the Board in all of this? Where is the Chairman?"

"How do they think the Board won't respond to this? Reiku's lost his mind," Xin mumbled as Siobhan finished removing the locking mechanism, easily turning the wheel release to open the door onwards.

"Something tells me he hasn't, that he's just following directions from the big boss. And shut the fuck up about the Board," Siobhan replied, closing up his bag, hoisting it onto his back and picking his weapon. "When have they ever lifted a finger to help us? And the Chairman? Forget about that cunt. No one outside the directorate has even seen what they look like, just goes to show they want no accountability for any of our grief. Whoever they are, they're getting fat on the back of our contribution and leaving it to monsters like this to keep it on coming."

"That's not true," Xin scorned back, giving a grave stare. "The Board just doesn't know, not the same as being complicit."

"Don't bullshit me, Xin," Siobhan snapped, squaring up to the other man. "I don't know what comforts blinded you as a Stardust manager but the rest of us can see it plain. Ignorance ain't the bliss they say it is, ignorance is the fuel of indifference that supplies the ones like this Reiku to do whatever the Coalition wants to do. The Board be damned, we're on our own. Now come on, my ship isn't close, we've got a trek on our hands and we don't want we're walking into."

"Let's just get out of here," Xin nodded just as the Vice-Admiral's patience had run out.

"Very well, I will then assume you are in agreement with the heinous act perpetrated here today. And as so, subject to its consequences. Section Chief Elias Thorne is grateful for your service, and releases you from it." The Vice-Admiral, with his red cloak flowing from his black on red suit, the uniform of his upper management prestige, gave a short, sharp cutting motion with his hand. "Open fire!"

"We need to move!" Siobhan thrusted open the bulkhead leading into the docks, throwing Xin through it as a blizzard of red laser fire lit up the crowd in the main concourse of the Forerunner, the two behind the safety of the vent just about seeing the fire starting before dashing through their exit.

Xin landed on his front, sprawled out on the snowy white platform with the various ships of the Obsidian fleet suspended in flight above the selection of stowed crafts taking up the landing bays of the hangar. A small gathering of Obsidian soldiers were at the far end, standing at the railing that surrounded this platform's edge, looking at a manifest of crates being offloaded a Stalwart freighter, with its captain lying at their feet with a bloodied eye socket, and turned their attention at the ruckus. Siobhan stepped out guns blazing, casting a shower of green lasers at the five soldiers caught unawares, smashing them in their midriff, the force of which throwing two over the railing to fall through the many levels of docking platforms, into a deep abyss of gloom. He wasted no time, yanking Xin up onto his feet, engaging the troop that was guarding this side of the entrance to main thoroughfare, them having witnessed their dramatic arrival. Xin brought up his own weapon, hitting a lone soldier square in the chest as he rushed down a catwalk towards them, rifle up and ready.

"It's this way," Siobhan shoved Xin in the direction of one of these pathways, a slim bead of white over a stem of metal, one of the many walkways sticking out from the main platform that acted as the gateway to the Forerunner's main section. Behind the two, coming not only from the maintenance hatch they had left but also from the checkpoint they had bypassed, were the echoes of screams and shouts over the buzz of energised fire.

"The Coalition prospers, watering the next seed of a bountiful harvest of our prized crop, with the blood of traitors! Though, our product is so intuitive to not need watering to grow so your deaths are little more than pest control!" Reiku's voice bellowed over the noise, the gunfire moving further away, progressing down the length of the station.

"Keep up, Xin! Move your arse!" Siobhan called back as the X-Human became embroiled in listening to the events of the concourse, fear gripping him, freezing him on the spot. His shining black eyes filled with despair, people had known, people had grown to enjoy the company of, speaking to them most days, gunned down because of what he had done. "Xin! There's no time!" The Stalwart man shouted in the other man's face, doing the trick in bringing him back to the present moment.

"Lead the way," he replied, and Xin followed his rescuer down the decline, running across the long length of metal as the enormous Obsidian vessels over their head lit up the recesses of the docks with spotlights, identifying the crafts at rest.

"They're going to start destroying the ships, they know we're escaping!" Siobhan called over his shoulder as they reached the next platform, lower down in the hangar, near to its middle level. "If those doors seal, we're done for!" He pointed up, beyond the upper levels and the Obsidian ships, to the two huge, broad doors, massive metal plates sat either side of a gap of outer space, an energy shield of luminescent purple keeping the atmosphere inside.

Just as they reached this next level, three Obsidian soldiers emerged from a separate catwalk in an attempt to cut them off, Siobhan gunning down the left and centre but the one on the right managed to hit the Stalwart man in the chest, having him lose balance and fall to the ground. This remaining soldier then turned his rifle to Xin but the X-Human kept his momentum, running into him, barrelling him over and wrestling with him on the cold, hard surface. The Obsidian trooper was stronger, forcing his way on top before delivering a series of punches to Xin's face. In the tussle, Xin had lost his grip on his pistol, he desperately tried to raise his arms to protect himself but the hits kept coming until the soldier got a red laser blast into his neck, below the helmet, an arterial spurt of blood drenching Xin immediately. The X-Human breathed a sigh of relief as the trooper slipped off from him, collapsing to one side, and he rolled his head back, seeing Siobhan resting his left hand against the front of his right collar bone where he had been hit, and in his right he had Xin's pistol. Siobhan struggled back onto his feet before clumsily crossing over to Xin to help him up, using his left to pull him up from the platform floor.

"You ok?" Xin asked him, sucking in air though his battered mouth and finding a need to spit out a gob of blood.

"Yeah but no way I'd take the kick on the rifle so I'm holding onto this," Siobhan replied, raising the gun between to show what he meant. "Besides you seem to prefer throwing yourself at them, odd tactic for an odd bloke I suppose," he chuckled from behind his light grey helmet, bowed over, grasping his thighs to support him. Then he took a deep breath and looked up just in time to see another Obsidian ship enter the hangar, this one far larger than the rest that it took up nearly all of the open space above the docking bays of the top level. "Shit, it's a Cosmic," Siobhan grunted and grasped Xin with his left hand, gripping the collar of the other man's armoured vest, leading him down further into the bowels of the docks, heading for the bottom most level.

Then the large ship, the vast black goliath kin to the armour of its troops with a red bar displaying its bridge like the visor on their helmets, began firing on the crafts below it. Raging infernos from these explosions reflected on the smooth, shiny armour of this monstrous vessel that fired an arsenal of lasers and rockets, to destroy everything not a part of the Obsidian force come to quell the spirit of resistance. Debris and fragments of the desolated ships rained down in fireballs on the lower levels, coming down either side of Xin and Siobhan as they crossed the final catwalk to the Stalwart man's craft, a simple grey fighter, room enough for only two people. The explosions within this closed, caged in area were deafening, as were the crashes of the ships torn and ripped asunder as they crumbled off from their high platforms, plummeting down to the base of the space station's hull.

Siobhan's ship was little more than a wing either side of a small hull, it had two seats, a nose and tail at the other end, that was it but it had an engine attached at the base of each wing which meant it could fly. He pulled out a remote from a pocket in his jacket and hit a button, causing two ladders to eject from the cockpit down to the floor, one for either seat. "Get in, quick!" Siobhan shouted to Xin who clambered into the rear seat, while he took the pilot seat for himself, slinging his bag into the small baggage compartment behind the X-Human as quickly as he could with his injured shoulder.

A screeching alarm began to sound, joined with the entire docking hangar becoming bathed in red light, and Siobhan knew exactly what that meant, hastily firing up the engines before he had even pulled down the cockpit hood. The thrusters purred into life just as the meteor-like hunks of debris landed ever close to them, Siobhan banking as soon as he took off in order to avoid being smashed out of flight just as they had begun. He aimed his ship up, preparing to climb but the air was hammered out of his lungs, a punch of terror. The Cosmic class vessel, the largest in the Obsidian fleet, was destroying all of the other ships, even a few that attempted to take off, stragglers that escaped one massacre only to run into another one. It was an enormous killing machine, saturated in the inferno of its victims, as it blocked the way through to the now closing gateway out of the Forerunner.

"If we're leaving, now is the time," Xin reminded, leaning forward from the rear seat where he had the same view but it was the view of the closing doors that he feared more than the monster blocking the way.

"Was just looking for our opening," Siobhan replied with a sigh, then spotted a Stalwart freighter fall off from a top platform, completely ablaze and coming down straight at them. He dodged it, flying up and having to rotate to pass around it in the space it vacated as it spun in flames, before coming up directly in front of the Cosmic's bridge.

The rockets and lasers that lit up every other ship now came for them, tracing them around the roof of the Forerunner docks before Siobhan was able to fly away to a far corner where he could flip them over, pointing them towards their exit, and opening up the engines. They soared at immense speed, heading straight at the Cosmic ship's bridge, flaming energy beams and devastating rockets rushing towards them but the Stalwart man spun this way then the next, dodging until finally rising just over the crest of the larger ship's hull, and breaking out in the expanse of space. The great doors that acted as the entrance to the space station ground shut just behind them, cutting off the smaller Obsidian craft that might have considered giving chase.

Both men took a moment to breathe, having expected to no longer enjoy the luxury, as their tiny, silver ship cruised above the space station, successfully having escaped the clutches of an overwhelming force. From here, they could see the vastness of the terrible destruction wrought on the place. The main concourse which was covered in a glass feature gave them visibility to the horrors within. Fires blazed, and while they were too far away to see anything in any kind of detail, they could at least see the lack of movement, where blobs of shapes were perfectly still.

"Where do we go from here?" Xin grumbled, his eyes glued to his former home, not having a single idea what would happen to it now.

"Winter said to wait on Sanguine, so that's what we'll do. We'll lay low, maybe see if Admiral Titus can shed any light on things," Siobhan replied, powering up the transit-gate cannon attached to his ship's belly, programming in the coordinates using a screen past his controls.

Xin took a final look at the Forerunner, and found his mind and feelings caught in the shadow of a great tsunami, standing beneath a giant wave of disbelief. This space station had been his home for years, he left behind friends there, people he could have warned or saved by not getting involved at all. He thought back to the young woman who was serving behind the bar with him not even half an hour ago, turning his mind to wondering what had happened to her. She was talking to the entertainers as she often did, Xin recalled, so full of life and joy. But a startling realisation took hold of him. She was not the first casualty in this resistance against the Coalition he had helped to start, and she wouldn't be the last.

Chapter 15

"You really couldn't have picked a better place, you know that," Miles put flatly, looking around the funeral parlour, he'd taken his helmet off and was wincing at every coffin his gaze landed on.

"It'll do, just watch the square, let me know if anything arrives," Nathan wasn't interested in the squeamishness of his teammates, he simply carried on past the former Stalwart man into the middle of the show room. He waited here, on the rich, purple carpet with the walls of red, with coffins of various sizes, materials and colours displayed all around him as he carried the dazed Lena in his arms.

"Back's clear, there's an office back there, I cleared the desk so you can put her down there," Tomen told him, keeping the red leather door open for Nathan, ushering him through with a nod. "How's she doing?"

"She'll be fine, she just needs a small amount of blood," Nathan entered the short corridor, following the red walls to the doorway at the far end, propped open with a chair, safe assumption leading to this being the office Tomen mentioned.

"She probably needs quite a bit of blood, right? I'm no doctor, but—"

"A small amount will do, she'll be fine, Tomen," Nathan rebuffed, leaving the Stalwart man at the door in a confused state.

"But what's so special about your blood?" He'd removed his helmet too, clutching in his left, rifle in the right, his mouth slightly open in bewilderment.

"Strength," was all Nathan said in calling back to him before disappearing inside the office.

"Give him a hand, Cait, though I have the feeling he'll be wanting some privacy if he's about to stick a needle in his arm," Tomen said to the X-Human as she joined him, giving him a pair of raised eyebrows as a reply and following down the hallway.

The office was a small room with no windows, the light coming from a lamp on a side table, with the bulky wooden desk that had been pushed up against the wall being the room's only main feature, with a chair sat next to it. It followed the same decorative pattern as the rest of the parlour, a lush lilac colour carpet with red for walls giving it a dark, contained feeling which suited Nathan just fine, he was sick of open space. "Where's her bag, again?" He called over to Cait as soon as she appeared in the doorway, "she has what we need in there."

"Sam's got it," Cait replied.

"Alright, come on, you can give me a hand bringing back what we need, Lena will be fine here for the moment," Nathan placed Lena down on the desk gently before wiping off the excess golden foam from her wounded shoulder where he had applied the aerosol treatment. "Looks good," he said to Cait, passing her back into the corridor.

"So what's the idea here?" Cait asked Nathan as they travelled through the short hallway but she dropped the topic at the same sight that had frozen the rest of the team.

The stranger next to the doorway captured the silent attention of everyone in the room, bemused not just by her being there but also because she had a clear stab wound in her stomach, and she had not a spec of colour about her image. From head to toe, this woman was cast in a greyish hue, her skin, her hair, even her RCS jumpsuit were lost of their colour, she appeared only in varying shades of the same dull tone. The woman was human, her hair dark for not being able to tell anymore what it might have been, and her face bore a warm smile, completely strange for the horrendous gash at her gut. "Well, you don't seem to fit the picture," she said, her voice was rasp, more like an echo of what it may have once been, similar to the wave of whispers that preceded a horde of the walking corpses.

"The fuck?" Miles laughed with his rifle half-raised, "I thought you were just another zombie, shame on me and call me a racist, you're a ghost instead."

"Oh come on, what's next? Seriously?" Sam murmured to himself, backing into a coffin, leaning against, blankly staring at the woman in grey.

"You got this far into the city and I'm what surprises you?" The woman looked at Miles with a cheekiness to her grin, raising an eyebrow.

"Sugar, at this point I ain't even having a surprised scale no more, it's just shit, shit, and more shit, different colour shit, and shit with teeth, I'm done,"

Miles laughed, raising his rifle at her, then dropping it before raising it again, not knowing what to do.

"Sounds reasonable," the ghost shrugged. "So whatcha doin' in these parts? Y'all hardly tempting the land o' the dead as I and my more hungry cousins are," she said, looking at each person in turn.

"Looking for why the city fell, looking for evidence," Cait stepped forward from where she and Nathan had stopped at the doorway to the corridor at their backs. "Can you help us with that? What's your name?" She tried to sound brave but she couldn't help cringing at her own awkwardness.

"Fuck if I know," the woman shrugged. "All's I know is X-Humans turned nutty and we humans got the raw deal. Most of us died on the day, bodies all over the street. Some became those zombies out there, and when they get too close, they splurge into those beastly fuckers. And then those like me, I got stabbed in the days after, when everyone turned on each other, not knowing who to trust, and now there are ghosts roaming the city, bored just to watch time go by." She stepped further into the centre of the room, Cait watched her move, a bit unsettled how her footsteps made no sound.

"Really? There was nothing in the build-up that…maybe stood out to you?" Cait pressed, moving closer to her, trying to seem friendly, spreading her hands out wide, ignoring the fact that she hadn't received a name.

"You're RCS, too, huh?" The ghost pointing to her own branding on the inside of her right wrist, indicating to Cait's with raised eyebrows.

"Yeah, I grew up on Sanguine, at the robo-sentry factory there, following Mum and Dad's footsteps you could say," Cait shrugged.

"Yeah I did that, too," the ghost chewed on the tip of her tongue, "look where that got me, and look where's it got you, eh? What would mummy and daddy say if they could see their little girl digging through the ruins of a bygone city? Battling zombies, communing with spectres?"

"Probably not much, they're dead," Cait cut off bluntly. "But I'm not what's important. Is there nothing you can tell us about why the city fell?"

"Well, why don't you ask him?" The ghost pointed over Cait's shoulder, to Nathan standing behind her. "Stop lurking behind little girls, Elite Commander, letting them do the talking are we?"

"You know me?" Nathan growled, passing by Cait and crossing the length of the room to Sam, "Lena's bag, where is it?"

Sam barely registered the question, blinking into the waking world from staring at the ghost, "this one," he said, kicking the nearest one on the floor to him.

"You won't even look at me, now, is that it? What've you forgotten your citizens already?"

"You're not familiar," Nathan replied, looking back over his shoulder before returning to rifling through Lena's bag for what he needed.

"You murdered my sister! She was innocent!"

"I don't remember you," Nathan grunted, ignoring the ghost and the looks he was receiving from the others in the room.

"Yeah I bet, so allow me to freshen your memory. The clinic in downtown Residential just opened but it was understaffed, only one or two doctors on shift at any time, maybe a nurse, and my sister on reception. A patient who was shot in the street, some kind of gambling disagreement or some such shit, but he was being attacked in his bed, right? The guy who shot him came back to finish the job. Well, two teens were visiting their mum at the same time. And this rough guy shot them in the process, killed them, didn't want witnesses, I guess?" The ghost stood above Nathan who was still taking items out of the bag, taking no notice of her. "Well, my sister was on her imager, with her earpods in. So she didn't hear the shots. True, if she hadn't had them in, if she were just sitting at her desk like some kind of fucking drone, then yeah, maybe she would've been able to do something after that first shot that killed the gambling guy. But she couldn't hear anything, and those two teens stepped out, wrong place, wrong time. They'd come in to visit their mum in the same ward as where that fuck had just shot that guy, so he shot them too, and that's my sister's fault? If she had heard the shots, who's to say she wouldn't of just died too? But what did that matter to the Elite Commander, huh? Captain Willis was busy over on the Directorate, probably running lackey, sucking dick of little Thorne junior. So you came. And you just decided that my sister was negligent, was that how you put it? That those two deaths were her fault? You shot in the fucking face!"

"I do remember now," Nathan rounded on her, spinning and standing, facing up to the ghost so fast that even in her non-corporeal state, she took a step back afraid. "And I'd do it again. Your sister did let those two boys die. She failed in her duty, she was charged with looking after people, what would have happened if it were one of her patients calling out in pain? Left to die by her ignoring her responsibility?"

"She was just the receptionist!"

"So that makes it OK to leave people to die? Not her job, not her problem?" Nathan probed, placing a hand on his sword hilt, a smile growing behind his mask when he saw the shade of the woman see that and grimace, even if only slightly. "Fact remains that it doesn't matter where she worked or the circumstances of the murder that those two youngsters walked in on. Your sister could have prevented a double murder, but she didn't, she was careless. That carelessness cost two people their lives. She may as well have killed them herself, it was good enough for me," Nathan took an extra step forward, the ghost taking another back.

"The Elite Commander," the ghost nodded, "still just a murderer." She slipped away, fading into atoms, dust caught on a breeze.

"Enough distractions," Nathan grunted, picking up the items he needed for the transfusion, and making for the back office, not feeling the need to explain himself.

"Packs of zombies walk the street and ghosts come out of thin air, accusing people of killing their siblings, gotta love this city," Miles shook his head, checking the sturdiness of a nearby coffin before hopping onto it, using it as a sofa.

Nathan reached the back office and set up the plastic tubing, the needles he needed for the transfusion, laying them out on the desk beside where Lena was just starting to wake up, still not entirely lucid. Cait entered behind him, kicking the chair out from propping the door open, letting it shut behind her.

"What's happening? Where are we?" Lena asked, looking about, looking to Cait.

"We're safe, Nate's just going to give you some blood, you lost some in the last attack," Cait replied to her, going over to the side table opposite where Nathan had taken up the other chair in the room, at Lena's side.

"Guess you have some emotions you wish to spew all over me," Nathan remarked as he used the screen mounted on his right arm to unlock the plates along that same arm so that he could remove them, revealing the black sleeve underneath.

"The way Xin talked about you when I first heard about you, he made you sound like some sort of legend, like you were some real big deal before the

Collapse. Or maybe you were always just a cold-blooded killer, huh, Nate?" Cait crossed her arms, leaning back on the table, rocking slowly to herself.

"You want to know why I killed that receptionist," Nathan nodded, placing his removed armour on the floor by his feet, rolling up his sleeve before placing a needle in Lena's arm, hooking up the tubing and connecting them to a needle in his own, waiting for the blood to start going then meeting Cait's gaze. "I did it because the whole city was corrupt, their vision of life was flawed from its very foundations, they simply didn't value life."

"And you did? Killing a young woman, that's valuing life is it?"

"Yes, and I won't apologise for that. The city was a breeding ground for indifference, the only thing they cared about? Getting the praise for whatever could stamp their name onto involving the contribution to the Board. That was the only important thing, recognition. This drive they all had, to live better than the ones at their side. It was a sickness. A person wouldn't bat an eye if their neighbour was murdered if they had something better than them, a better job, a better house, a prettier wife or a more handsome husband. The city was infected long before whatever caused the Collapse, infected with an intolerance for life. That young woman—the receptionist? You really think I just killed her on the spot, on a whim? I did my research. She wore those earpods every night she was on shift. And where do you think the patient's help button sent the signal through to? And who do you think couldn't hear it? Or should I say, didn't care to hear it?"

"That doesn't mean to say that she deserved to die, Nate? I used to listen to music while working," Cait offered, her eyes flicking over to the steady flow of blood seeping out of Nathan's arm, following the path of the tube and into Lena.

"Neither did the eight patients who died there, each of them having pressed their assistance alarm before they died of treatable illnesses or wounds," Nathan shrugged, checking the tubing.

"Oh, well maybe the alarm was faulty?"

"Look, Cait. You want to believe in people? That's fine. That's great, admirable even. But on the whole? I don't. Most of them deserve to die and I seem to lack the usual hang-ups that stop what needs to be done. If I hadn't killed that receptionist, other people may have paid the price for what would just be a self-serving conscience. Believe me, the Capital City was not the paradise that the Coalition paints it to be."

"Suppose," Cait looked down at her feet, not knowing what to say next or even think. "When did this happen, anyway?"

"Right after I became Elite Commander, a few years before the Collapse."

"You must have been young, it must have been hard to have such a dark view of things," Cait offered, trying to look beyond the killer to the man behind those choices.

"I was young," Nathan nodded. "It's a strange thing to think it was Elias's father that gave me the position, along with his entourage of supporters."

"Who were they? This entourage?"

"My parents, still loyal to Roderic, they serve at his side on Carmine. And a man named Ardamus, General Lux Ardamus, Commander of the Obsidian ground forces before the Collapse."

"You mentioned him before, you said he was locked inside this place when it sealed itself off."

"Yeah in fact he was the one to really make the case for me to hear Roderic tell it when he gave me the position. The General was always good to me, he taught me about the workings of the conglomerates, the Board, the Chairman. He tried to teach me his ideals too."

"And what were they?"

"The General held sway only because Roderic liked his determination. If something needed doing, no matter how difficult, this was the man to find a way to make it work, he was incredibly determined. Think of him as Roderic Thorne's man in Obsidian, the same way Elias figured for Captain Willis. But outside of Roderic's protection, the General wasn't well liked. He openly spoke out against the Coalition, he didn't hold with their ideas and methods. Mostly, he would speak about how the conglomerates were needed at first, that when the Old World fell, humanity needed strong leadership to escape extinction and it is true that the companies did that. But he would say that the need for the methods those early versions of the conglomerates used, such as binding their workers at birth to contracts, assigning their lives to determined purposes, limiting their capacity to experience life, as he put it, he hated them. He'd call the contracts archaic, an antique procedure."

"Really? I actually strongly agree with that," Cait nodded.

"Reckon that you do," Nathan removed his helmet and revealed the smile he bore. "Anyway, he said that the children of the tri-systems had to be given the chance to forge their own paths, to not be claimed by one company or another, or doomed to follow the beaten tracks of those that came before. He'd admit that they would make mistakes and that some would stumble on their way to discovering their purposes for themselves, but that it was necessary for future generations to be born free."

"And is that what you believe as well?"

"I used to, I used to be really swayed by what he had to say, he was a formidable man but a good one at heart, the type you listen to and really take onboard what they say, he genuinely cared for everyone under his charge. He was kind of a teacher, and I his student," Nathan replied.

"It sounds like he was trying to teach you about hope, hope for a brighter future, the same hope I have."

"Maybe, but if I did have that hope, it died with the man I used to be the day this city fell and I lost everything," Nathan averted his eyes, tending to Lena's shoulder, making sure there was nothing healed beneath the new layer of skin that had been grown, checking for infections.

"Maybe he's not as gone as you think," Cait proposed, standing up and walking over to Nathan, placing a gentle hand on his shoulder. "Don't be so hard on yourself. It sounds like you've had a lifetime's worth of tough choices and I'm sorry but there's still more to be made, just remember, you're not alone anymore. I'm going to go check on the others, can see you've got everything in hand here."

Nathan glanced up to watch Cait go before he removed the tubing linking his arm to Lena's and starting to put his armour back on his right arm.

"What, that's it?" Lena asked, even though she felt far stronger already.

"Too much is a risk, a small amount of mine will do you," Nathan replied, glancing up at her, watching her assess her shoulder though she stayed lying down.

"Why?"

"Obsidian wants its soldiers to be the best military product on the market, and the Elites are the pinnacle of that product line. We were all injected with compounds and the like, all to improve our concentration, our strength and stamina, our ability to heal," he said, raising an eyebrow to her.

"They did this when you were young?"

"And all the way up to the Collapse, my last compound was just two days before it."

"Wow, they really didn't view you as a person, did they?"

"No, just another product, I guess," Nathan scoffed.

"What were you like before the Collapse? Really," Lena asked, leaning on her right side, proving her shoulder was healed to be able to hold her up.

"I kept to myself. I did my job, went back home again, there's not much to tell. Never had a particular interest in people so never had the knack for friends. I had some, maybe enough to count on a full hand, and I was perfectly friendly when I was expected to be. Otherwise, I preferred my own company. Probably a strange thing to admit but Moni wasn't just my wife, she was my best friend, too, my only real friend probably, the only one I really let myself be my real self around, who I could be completely honest with," Nathan shrugged, putting his attention into reattaching his armour.

"So you lost your wife, your best friend and your son all at once, that's a lot to take, Winter," Lena offered. "Thing is, there's someone else you didn't grieve for."

"Who?"

"Yourself. You say it all the time yet you never allowed yourself to grieve for the person you were, the one who lost those who were closest to him, it's not healthy."

"What?" Nathan grunted, disinterested.

"Look at me when I'm talking to you all polite like, boy," Lena snapped and Nathan's gaze immediately shot up from where he was magnetically sealing the armour pieces into place, raising his head to show he was listening. "I saw plenty of death in the Stardust establishments I was sold around to, girls and guys who couldn't deal with what they had anymore and decided on the one thing that was in their control to do. They would kill themselves. All my friends would die, every single one, and the majority, that would be by suicide. Until I met Cait and she introduced me to her weird, little family you see here. But what I'm saying is, grieve for those who are gone, yes, absolutely, but you also have to accept that you are gone too, the person that they knew 'cause how can you possibly be the same person without them? Fact is that you're not. Seems to me that you haven't grieved for that version of yourself, more like piled a load of blame on them, like its rope and you've tied it into a noose and hung it round their necks, taking out the floor from under 'em. That person, that you, deserves to be recognised and grieved for, too."

"I won't pretend to understand," Nathan shook his hand, not impolitely, closer to confusion.

"Brass tacks are give yourself a break, honey," Lena said, giving him a wink that Nathan knew was condescending.

"Add that to my growing list of flaws," Nathan dismissed, finishing putting his armour back and checked his work before looking over at the X-Human staring at him. "Your coat's ruined."

"Shame, I like this," Lena put her hand through the hole at the shoulder where the creature's own, far larger and more gruesome hand had reached through.

"Tell you what, when we get back to the ship. Take mine. The one I used to wear before," Nathan didn't bother finishing the sentence, just widened his eyes and put on a disgusted face which he knew Lena would understand.

"Hey, the original inspiration coat? Sweet, I will take you up on that, thank you," Lena sat up, then looked around the room. "Where'd my rifle go?"

"Had to leave it, I had no way of carrying it," Nathan confessed, "take this instead," he said, giving her the pistol out of the holster at his left hip.

"Thanks, shame though, I had seven good shots left with that thing," she moaned, taking the pistol and examining it in her hands.

"Six," Nathan instinctively corrected.

"No, seven. Six in the fresh magazine I clipped in, after I'd loaded one in the chamber making seven," Lena dashed up a disapproving look.

"Really? But—"

"Gotta trust it with my life right? So I got to learning my weapon 'til I knew it like I know my own body, shouldn't that be the way?" Lena mocked him, but held firm.

"Of course. Right," Nathan said with a sigh, standing up. "Doors to the Leisure district are out, we're going to have to take the Metro to go under them."

"Couldn't you just fly over?"

"I can, but that leaves you lot on the wrong side. I've tried thinking out of the box on this one but metro's the only path open to us," Nathan grunted, not liking the idea any more than the others did.

"Yeah, you're right, you're no good at out the box thinking, are ya? Maybe stick to concerning yourself with my box, huh?" Lena replied back with a wink, and teased pulling apart her grey leotard between her legs but laughed when Nathan said nothing to stop her. "Come on, let's join the others, eh?" She stood up and hopped away from the desk, finding her legs surprisingly strong under her. "Fuck me, your blood's made me all giddy and strong. Let's fucking do this, huh?" Nathan turned to leave, rolling his eyes as he placed his helmet back on, stifling his long hair underneath. "Nathan," Lena called to him and she adjusted her coat, "it's good, you opening up like that, and just so you know, I consider you a friend."

Nathan, not knowing what he ought to come back with, decided to not say anything, instead turning and stepping out of the office.

Cait threw over his rifle as Nathan entered the room with all the others, Lena not long behind him, and he caught it, slung it on his back and looked around the room, "everyone ready?" He said, eyeing each of the group in turn, stopping at Sam, "this is going to be the hardest part yet."

Chapter 16

Dust and decay left a murky stain on the air inside the tunnels buried deep beneath the city, it took a long stairway to plunge into the depths of the platform where bodies were cast about, discarded, forsaken as refuse and litter. The platform ground, simple concrete, was nearly slippery with the thick layer of dust settled on it, stuck in place as if held by some aged adhesive, only giving way by the impact of the unwelcome boots pounding against it. Nathan led the way in, having taken a torch out of his belt, he scanned these new surroundings, with every surface touched by its light seemingly radiating with rage having been awoken from its near decade long slumber.

Twin tracks separated the two platforms, with the way to the other achieved by a small bridge spanning over the gap, with no decoration more than the natural stonework used to form this underground space. "Think you can do anything about the lights?" Miles pointed up to where the torch light found a series of lights spanning on a metal beam running parallel to the tracks attached to the ceiling, following the path into the mouth of the tunnel.

"Possibly," Nathan grunted, tapping the buttons of his screen, accessing the city's systems and directing the flow of power into the metro, causing the lights to flicker on, pushing back the shadows.

Revealed by the light were the makeshift barriers erected on either platform, made from anything from bags to bins and anything that could have been found nearby, with one larger than the rest protecting the bridge over to the far platform. But all had been smashed through, beaten down, the bodies of the ones who had cowered behind them were caved in, obliterated by some colossal force. The dust of the floor was mixed with a dark crimson as dried blood clung to the surface, vast pools mixed with the sickening blend of intestinal fluids, which the team had to be careful to step around. "Least we can see down here," Sam remarked, stepping around a headless skeleton, the head having been crushed, turned into paste on the floor.

"Maybe we ought to just travel the whole way down 'ere, huh?" Lena put forward as she hopped down onto the train lines, looking to either directions of the tunnel.

"No." Nathan joined her on the tracks and checked the compass on the inside of his left wrist, pulling out the gun at the holster on his chest with his right hand, "too easy to be ambushed down here."

"So then we move quickly," Tomen led the others down off the platform and onto the tracks just as the Elite found his way.

"The Leisure district is this way. The trains are all automated and I couldn't power up the lights without supplying power to them as well, keep your eyes and ears keen," Nathan led the way, passing beneath the mouth of the tunnel at its northern end.

"This wasn't a good idea, was it?" Cait asked him, jogging up to walk at his side.

"No, but what choice did we have?" Nathan grunted, he put his torch away, not needing it with the lights overhead but winced behind his mask when the odd one began to flicker and fade as he watched them. If they were to go out, they would be closed in under complete darkness, which the Elite knew, with his jetpack useless and losing a hand to keeping up his torch, he would lose some measure of attack.

"Can you imagine what it must've been like? Coming down here?" She asked him as they passed more bones, some too small to have known adult lives, next to the stuffed toys that could have provided them comfort in their final despairing moments. Even here, further as they went into the tunnels, they found more dead, lying on the blood soaked ground or up against the dirty walls, where history had all and forgotten them. Decomposed arms hugged loved ones who shared the same fate, left to wither, left to die, left to the fate of those responsible for the Capital Collapse, and to be dismissed by them.

"How could you imagine it? You weren't there," a ghostly shape of a man joined them at their side, the same shade of grey as the other one they had encountered, this one with his head crumbled inward. His voice was raspy but given strength from his anger, his hate, and the ruin he had witnessed. He calmly walked beside them, not registering how Cait was staring at his misshapen head, or how Lena, Sam, Miles and Tomen walked in behind, talking among themselves about whether it was possible to kill a ghost, weighing up if he was a threat.

"I was there until the gates closed, I got out of the city, but what happened to those who didn't?" Nathan asked the spectre across Cait as they continued down the tunnel.

"We died, you idiot," was all the ghost said.

"What caused the city to close?" Cait looked closely at what he was wearing. The colours had faded such as his life had, but he was almost certainly wearing an Obsidian technician's suit, the diagonal zip of the suit once bearing the colour of the conglomerate.

"After all this time, does it really matter?"

"Course, it does, look around here," Cait waved a hand over to where an improvised shelter had been built into the side of the tunnel, a basic sheet pulled across from the wall, held up by two stakes of metal, where three bodies lay beneath. "So much death."

"You really think it could all be worth something? Some greater plan at work? The old stories of Gods and their plans and grand spectacles? It's just what people do to each other, young miss, they find new and incredible ways to slaughter each other in pursuit of selfish ideas," the ghost spat, looking at Cait as he replied to her. His eyes were clouded, the pupils gone, and his face was destroyed under the pressure of whatever had come clamping down on his skull, where several punctures scattered across his head.

"Any selfish idea in particular?" Nathan put in.

"No, I don't know," the ghost admitted. "Is that why you've come? Why you stalk the echoes of the footsteps of the dead? Have you come to give us meaning? To grant us peace by telling us why we died? Was it for some purpose better than ourselves, more valuable?"

"We did come here for why the Capital Collapse happened, we came for evidence," Cait explained.

"Capital Collapse? An event so tragic they coined a name for it, how quaint," the man sneered. "You were talking about imagining what it was like, to live through this Collapse of yours, well, would you like to know?"

"Tell me," Cait replied.

"I was in the crowds with my husband. We were running for the docks, to get on a ship, any ship, but we were too slow and there were too many people ahead of us so the gates slammed shut and we were never even close. We could just about see them close over the heads of the people in front of us. And then the cover over the city finished meeting above our heads, pretty much at the same time and we left in the dark. It was the middle of the day but then suddenly it was night. The street lights were on sensors that were too slow to realise that the light from the sun was gone, we were left completely in the dark, just standing there holding each other's hands, just left behind."

"Must have been awful, I'm sorry," Cait glanced back at the others, not knowing what else she could say to this ghost but they had nothing to offer him, instead they had stepped off, leaving some small distance between them.

"No, that was just the beginning," the ghost sighed. "So we were standing there, in a throng of people, all of us trapped, we were forgotten about, sealed away. Then, well, what came next," the man made to breathe out to gather his thoughts but his lungs were empty, they were not even there. "For a moment, I could have sworn it was raining hard, there were these loud thudding sounds. And then the screaming started but there was nothing we could do, we couldn't see anything and they were coming from all around us. You have to understand, this was thicker than night, it was like being blindfolded, a drumbeat going on all around us 'til it dawned on us what was going on. People were dying, literally dropping dead."

"But why?"

"I've no idea but they were. Except for the X-Humans, they just started babbling nonsense or shoving people out of the way, trying to pretend like nothing was happening, like it was some normal day or some shit. But it was completely dark but I remember the hairs on the back of my neck stuck up, I could feel things I couldn't see watching me, unfriendly things. So we ran. We had no idea where we were heading, we couldn't see but we kept running because the screams were getting louder, getting closer, they surrounded us. We tripped over bodies, he, my husband, he helped me up several times and I had to pick him up, too, and we held hands running away together. You could feel the air change, like wind blowing all around us, it felt like you could be snatched away and attacked at any second but what could we do? We had to run, no use standing still."

"Where did you go?" Cait asked, even though she knew full well there couldn't be a happy ending to the tale.

"We ran down the boulevard across from the fountain and just kept running, and we weren't the only ones, you could just about make out other people sprinting the same way, could hear 'em too. We ran over the water, just to get away from the screaming but as we were going over the bridge I noticed my hand was empty, and he was gone, he was just gone, and I heard a splash, something took him over the side. It was so quick that I missed it, and it was too dark that I couldn't see it. But I recognised the scream. I knew his voice but I'd never heard fear like that before, it sounded almost like an animal, until it didn't sound like anything at all. When he went quiet, I knew I had to keep running. I loved him, I really did but there was nothing I could do and I could feel something in the dark, things coming to get me and I know I should have tried, tried to do something, to get him back but I knew he was dead and I knew I would be too if I stuck around so I ran."

"You were scared, that's nothing to be ashamed of," Cait consoled.

"I hope so. Eventually me and a few others got to the metro station, made our way down here, thinking we could make it safe, fortify ourselves here, catch our breath and think a little. And those things left us alone or couldn't find us, and we had at least a day's worth of time. We built walls, used the train to move about and try make something for ourselves, people were even talking about breaking through the lockdown to get out." They came across a train having barrelled into the side of the tunnel, coming off from the tracks having run over one of the beasts made from mashed up corpses. It was an enormous snake, trailing off down the length of the tunnel as far as they could make out, with its huge shape it worked with the deteriorating wall on the other side to make the way ahead a narrow corridor. This far in, the lights were beginning to shimmer and fail, casting a thicker gloom than that of the surface of the city above their heads.

"Then what happened?" Cait asked as she examined the train, wiping off the grime from one of the windows so she could peer inside but leapt backwards at the sight she revealed, where a man's head was being crushed under the power of the jaws of a gargantuan beast. The head was rotting, its flesh peeling away, its skull caving in, the teeth of the monster embedded deep within it, creating wounds just like the ghost had.

"What'd you think?" The ghost mocked with a chuckle, "Say hi to my body, having skin is so old-fashioned anyway."

"This is far worse than anything I pictured," Cait reeled away, Lena coming over to meet her, to hold her steady as she noticed what her friend had seen.

"That's because you don't know fear, not really. Not until you're trapped in the dark, your whole life stripped away in an instant, your loved ones torn out of your hand, surrounded by people as they descended into madness, losing their humanity, and you can't even put them to rest because their bodies come back with a vengeance. Half of our number died within a day and they killed the rest."

"You must have some idea what caused all this!" Sam yelled at the ghost, too loud for the others' liking.

"I've no clue," the ghost growled back at him, circling round until he was blocking the way forward, as the group had come to a stop with Cait hurling onto the train tracks. "The city died, that's all I know. The whole city. And now you will, too," he said in a strange tone, somewhat melancholy.

He evaporated, a puff of dust trailing on the stale air just as a rampaging beast burst through where he was standing, heading straight for Lena and Cait, but Nathan caught it at its throat with his left hand, wiping out the momentum of its strike, throwing it down on the tracks before stamping down on it. He fired his pistol into its twin skulls, killing the beast before turning his weapon on the second one that came hurtling towards him, putting a few rounds into it before Tomen barged into it before it could tackle Nathan. He rammed it into the side of the train, falling to one side so that Miles could fire a stream of lasers into its body, putting the beast down without giving it the chance to get up.

Without the snarling and crashing of teeth from the beasts, a quiet came over the tunnel, allowing the team to hear the vague veil of whispers rolling up to meet them as the flickering lights revealed a mass of undead stumbling towards them. With the rocky outcropping of debris on the right, and the train on the left, the tracks offered only a thin way forward, now blocked by the teeming corpses staggering up, with no end to their number in sight. Miles and Tomen began firing immediately, their streaks of green energised rounds smashing into them, holding the front of the line back but there some who came crawling up as well, the horde carried on to meet them.

Nathan glanced around and his eyes settled on the bullets holstered across Lena's chest, his head crooking as an idea came to his mind.

"Now really the time, sweetie?" Lena smirked, noticing the man's gaze but he paid her no mind, Nathan reloaded then holstered his pistol, took out his rifle and stepped over to her. "What'cha doing there, fella?"

"You never used these?" Nathan grunted, taking one of the red-tipped bullets out from Lena's chest holster, slotting into his weapon as he switched it over to the sniper configuration.

"Wasn't really thinkin' straight, gotta say, was more focused on fighting for my life," the green-eyed X-Human shrugged with a smile at Nathan's comfort in taking the bullet off from in front of her breasts.

"These are incendiaries," Nathan explained, having finished configuring his rifle for the new ammo type and aimed it down the length of the track towards their oncoming attackers. Then he fired, the bullet spiralling through the air, passing by the slower rounds of burning verdant, and hit a degraded corpse directly between where its eyes once were. From that impact point, an inferno erupted, engulfing the dead in a blaze of fire so fierce it washed up to the meet the team, Sam leaping to the side, Tomen tackling Miles up against the train, Nathan using his jetpack to reach Cait and Lena, pulling them to behind the debris, to escape the force of the blast. The heat was near unbearable as the tunnel gave no way for the flames to escape but they endured it until they could rise up again to see the thinned out herd crawling over what remained of the ones in front, still coming for them. "We need to get out," the Elite announced.

"No shit, but they're blocking the way and the only other way is back," Miles replied, using his rifle, firing down the range of the tracks.

"We passed under the wall already so the next station won't be far ahead," Nathan explained, switching his own weapon back to automatic fire, picking off the corpses before they could get near as he looked around. "All of you, get on the train, use it to bypass those things, I'll keep them occupied."

"What? Get on the fucking train, too, you lunatic!" Miles shouted back at him while Tomen got to work prying the doors open to the metal snake, waving Sam over to give him a hand.

"No, I'm going to thin them out, now, get moving," he said with a nod to the two struggling with the doors and starting to walk down the tracks, firing his rifle into the horde.

"You heard him! Get on! The doors are fucked and they're fucking heavy, so move!" Tomen barked and the others obeyed, scrambling in climbing onto the train, feeling the slime of the strewn bodily fluids underhand as they sought any grip to get onboard.

"Shouldn't we be helping him?" Lena asked them as Tomen and Miles pushed the doors back shut after everyone had got on the train, seeing the Elite press on through the dirty stains on the windows.

"He gave us our direction and we follow it to keep ourselves safe, that's why he's here, right?" Sam shrugged, they were all crouching down low, avoiding the sight of the crowd of dead things coming for them, and the thief crawled up to the window to peer out. "To die in our place," he said with a conceited tone.

"Shut the fuck up, Sam and come on, the lot of you, we're pressing on, now move!" Tomen gripped Sam and chucked him onto the floor of the train before leading the way through the lines of seats, up in the direction they were heading.

Outside of the train, Nathan kept the attention of the shambling corpses, slotting each in the head with a precise shot, but as he reached them, he strapped the rifle back onto his back and took out his pistol again. He kept using the gun so the loud bangs of his shots kept their attention firmly on him, rather than the steps ringing out from the train at the side. With his right, he wielded his pistol, using it to plant a bullet into the skull of the nearest carcass before moving onto the next, while with his left, if he wasn't steadying his weapon, he was wrestling them down or pulling their limbs as they went to grab him. But there were a lot of them and now he was surrounded on all sides, so he unsheathed the blade stowed on his left forearm and placed it in his left hand, simultaneously stabbing with his left and he shot them with his right.

Nathan held his knife with the blade pointing down, firmly stabbing the one come biting for his neck on his left, lowering himself down, shooting the two to his right as he spun, using his own body to throw the weight of the stabbed corpse into the ones eagerly approaching from the front. Then he fired off a barrage of missiles, blasting the roof of the tunnel down on top of the never-ending march of dead creatures coming towards him but the explosion was larger than he intended, Nathan using his quick-thinking to jetpack through the window of the train, joining the others. "Move!" He bellowed, still with knife and gun in hands, getting back on his feet, finding himself behind the team and waving them forward. The ceiling of the tunnel was disintegrating all around them, the outside of the train completely submerged in dirt and stone, while it rocked the train, burrowing under the wheels, hailing against its roof, pushing it against the side of the tunnel as the metal frame ached and creaked.

"Zombies! They're up ahead!" Miles called out, seeing more of the dead in the train carriage ahead of where the team were running up to. And there were a lot of them, they blocked the entire height of the train like a swarm, like a wave, crawling on top of one another, completely stopping the way ahead. There was a horrible scratching sound as they washed over one another, over the floor of the train, over the seats, breaking the poles in the centre, crushing them under the immense weight.

"Down!" Nathan shouted and once everyone was on the floor of the train, he grabbed Lena's ankle, yanking her back to him more roughly than he intended, but he needed another bullet, he reached for her chest and took out another incendiary round, loading it into his rifle. He fired the incendiary round, straight into the dead centre of the wave of dead things washing up the train before forward rolling to the front of the team and bringing both fists up in front of him, activating his shields just in time as the inferno from his shot reached them. The purple hue of energy he cast in front of him allowed Nathan to dissipate the flames, blocking them from burning the team that were safely down behind him.

"There's more!" Sam yelled, scraping the barrel of his shotgun against the train floor as he brought up to defend himself.

"Wait for me to thin them out," Nathan called back calmly, flinging his rifle over his shoulder and unsheathing his sword hilt, flicking out the length before igniting it. With the tunnel collapsing, the only light they could see by had been the flame of Nathan's fiery bullet then his energised shield, and now it was just his blade. The white of its flames running up the edge, the golden bolts of lightning striking out to the metal of the train framing, calm now, but then the Elite brought it up, ready to strike, grasping it with both hands, standing steady. Then he half turned around, peering over his shoulder, and something told each member of the team that their protector was smiling under his dark helmet, brimming with confidence, an unspoken 'watch this'. Fully composed, at ease with his situation, Nathan placed his hand at the base of the blade, withstanding the heat only by concentrating and being fast, as he ran his hand up, sliding it against the full length until the weapon came even more alive. He advanced forward and with each strike he landed on a shuddering carcass, his sword released an enormous explosion of lightning that struck out at the nearest ones, each kill wiping out a dozen more. Nathan pressed on, carving the way, but the train was starting to buckle under the weight of the ground above pressing down upon it.

"Can't stay here," Tomen shook his head and stood up, "come on." He led the others, keeping a safe distance back, not from the undead however, but from the lightning storm emanating from the Elite wielding his deific weapon, striking down the vicious things with unmatched ferocity. "Don't get too close," he warned, fanning a hand behind him, telling his team to remain low, all of them having to shield their gaze as the sword being used to its utmost destructive capabilities by the expertise of its bearer cast a scintillating, dazzling light, too bright to look at.

"Tomen, look!" Lena called over, pointing back to where they had come from to where the ground had claimed the train, breaking it down, the dirt smashing through.

"Nate! We need to get out, now!" Cait called up to the Elite but she wasn't sure that he had heard him, the crashing of his lightning strikes echoing like screams down the length of the train, so fierce that they shook it, vibrating it violently.

But he turned, Nathan looking back with his sword in hand, and stepped away from the next wave of undead, looking all around him, peering through the window, before meeting Cait's gaze. He strode back to the team, as calm as though he were walking through a park on a summer day, and looked past them to where the metal had given in to the onslaught of muck. "Only one thing for it," he announced, nodding over his left shoulder, gesturing to his rocket pack.

"No, no, that's not a good idea, Nate," Cait waved her hands in front of her, frantically.

"Least we're already buried," Miles pointed out solemnly yet sarcastically, nodding to himself.

"That's the spirit," Nathan said back to him with a cocky attitude. "Take no risks, never suffer defeat, but if you don't take any," he placed a hand on Cait's shoulder, mockingly consoling her, "and you'll never achieve a true victory." He then half turned away from her, and fired another salvo into the roof of the train above where the dead were making their next advance.

The blast was deafening and what was more horrifying for the team was the ocean of dirt that swallowed them, mixed with brick and stone, it was unbelievably heavy, and suffocating, but they clawed through, blind in the dark, in the earth. Miles came out first, not into the not-so-open air, but into a dimly lit room, finding himself fighting for breath as he was on all fours on a tiled floor in an ambient blue haze from a dangling bulb. His rifle was strapped against his torso so he didn't lose it in the muck and mire he had dragged himself free of, and it hung loose as he panted, exhausted by the ordeal. He collapsed, rolling onto his back, Miles was hungry, thirsty and in need of a pee, on top of his muscles aching in having to haul his full weight free of the collapsed tunnel, and now he had no idea where he or the others were.

"What are you doing out of bed?" A caring voice asked him, and an X-Human in a white leather Doctor's coat stood over Miles, staring down at him with his piercing green, bejewelled eyes above a surgical mask that covered the rest of his face.

"The fuck?" Was all Miles could say and we went to get up.

"Wait, you're not one of mine, you're not ready for bed, look at you!" The doctor hooked an arm under each of Miles' armpits, hoisting him up and dragging him. "Let's get you all set, shall we?"

"What?" Miles was too exhausted to fling his arms up in protest and he could only watch his feet drag against the tiled floor, he was powerless to resist.

"Now, now, you poor little thing, you must be so tired, so allow me just a moment and we'll have you in bed in now time," the X-Human carried Miles through a corridor of blinking lights into another room before he lifted him up and placed him down on a table in the middle.

"Am I dead? This isn't what I had in mind for what comes after, I was hoping more for naked women in droves and some place more shiny," Miles winced as he was placed down then he looked all around. There were tools on a tray atop a table at his side, of the surgical variety, and other such instruments that Miles didn't recognise but then his eyes locked onto the sign above the doors he was dragged through, reading 'Rose City Morgue'. "Ah, I mean not like it's not nice and shiny here, it's a very nice place you have here, sir," he rambled as he took in the sight of the dust and the filth of neglect on all the surfaces all around him. He went for his rifle but it was empty.

"No, no, no, no toys before bed," the doctor used a scalpel from the tray to slice through the strap of the rifle, and he delicately slid it out from under Miles, taking away the rifle, and returning with a needle.

"No thanks, doc, I'm feeling right and healthy, I don't need any shots or nothing," Miles protested, his hand going for the pistol strapped to his right thigh but the other man was quick, he injected whatever was in the needle straight into Miles's neck before the gun was halfway out.

"A little something to soothe you and guarantee sweet dreams, isn't that nice, dear?" The doctor ran a hand down Miles's chest, knocking on the armour plating, shaking his head. "These are not suitable pyjamas, friend, tut tut."

"What did you—" Miles could feel his body losing his fight, he was tired before but now his limbs felt as though they were crafted out of lead, he could hardly move.

"Well," the doctor gave him a bemused small recoil, then waved a hand over at the doors arranged on one wall, and Miles instantly recognised what they were, "I need to prepare you for your final rest. Wait! What are you do—" The doctor wriggled and writhed about as he was picked up at the throat, feet dangling above the floor, Nathan gripping him in a vice-like hold with his left hand before slicing across the man's stomach his blade, allowing for the contents of his innards to spill out.

"Been meaning to look into the good doctor, myself," Nathan shrugged before tossing the quivering body aside effortlessly, looking at the gap where the X-Human's intestines used to be.

"There's my favourite little psychopath! Here, hey buddy! Help us up, would ya? Doc gave me the sleepy stuff I think," Miles called over to Nathan, struggling to sit up, waving the other man over.

"Yeah looks like," Tomen added, appearing in the doorway. "So take it we're in the hospital now, then, huh?" He was caked in mud and mire, his jacket that had once marked him as a Stalwart man, was ripped and knackered.

"The blast opened the wall, fortunately the morgue was adjacent," Nathan remarked, picking Miles up and pulling one of his arms around his shoulders so he could walk with him.

"Yeah fucking fortunately! You nearly got us all killed with that stupid stunt!" Sam yelled from behind Tomen, with Cait and Lena next to him, getting the crud out of their hair as they tidied themselves up.

"I heard no better suggestions," Tomen growled over his shoulder at Sam. "Besides, we all made it in one piece."

"Let's get moving," Nathan looked to the ceiling, seemingly listening for something the others couldn't hear. "In the days before the Collapse, admittance numbers were through the roof with some kind of mysterious illness, we shouldn't linger here."

"You're saying those dead things have a home, and we just announced ourselves by blowing open their basement," Miles grumbled, addled by the drug in his system.

"Possible," Nathan grunted, adjusting his grip on the other man. "Right, I've got Miles that means, Tomen, you're providing our security and leading the way. Sam, grab Miles' rifle over there, then you, Cait, Lena, all of you hold your fire unless I call it, or Tomen identifies a clear and present threat. Let's move," he gestured with a nod towards the door as he made his way to follow.

They found themselves in a corridor with gurneys left adrift, with blood stained cushioning and abandoned torn gowns, the floor slick with dried blood and hardened sick. The lights flickered and blinked and rather predictably, the lift had no power when Tomen went to use it. "Hang on," Nathan said, giving Miles over to Sam to carry. He accessed his screen mounted to his right arm and sent more power from the grid to the hospital, and the lift came to life. "The power flow isn't steady but it should hold," he said, "go on, give him here," he took Miles back, noticing the other man struggling to take hold of the X-Human.

They entered the lift, the light inside solid as they crowded in, a gentle melody playing in the background that Miles began to whistle along to, "no," Nathan grunted and let the other man drop, giving him a gentle kick to rock him out of the lift just as it was about to depart.

"What are you doing?" Tomen half shouted, half laughed, hauling his friend back inside as Cait held the doors open wide eyed and aghast, "though I get the temptation."

As they rose through the floors to reach the surface level, there was a low level murmuring of sound to be heard as there were some kinds of things moving around there, which the team were grateful to avoid. The nearer they got to their destination, the louder the random crashing and snarling got behind those lift doors and there was more than one nervous glance exchanged. But when they did open, the way was clear. It was a wide open reception area, with only a brown, timber desk below a sign stating 'Rose City General Hospital, Brought to You by RCS', with various hallways spanning off from it, but the team's interest lay in the double glass doors across the way. Tomen led out while the rest remained inside the lift, checking everywhere before feeling safe enough to usher them out but he didn't lower his rifle, he kept checking the corridors attached to this main lobby.

"How many people came here on the day of the Collapse? After the city fell. Seeking help, seeking refuge, and how many died because of that?" Lena asked no one in particular as they travelled across the breadth of the reception, noticing the bodies scattered here as they were everywhere.

"Try to not think about it," Tomen advised her, and just as he was about to turn to head towards the doors himself, he saw a ghost of an old woman, walking along with an IV feed, push open the door to one of the hallways, revealing the mass of undead beyond it. They didn't notice, didn't pay any attention but the sight of even more of those things was even to steal the air out of even this seasoned fighter's lungs.

Once outside again a surreal feeling consumed Cait, stalling her mind, making her fingers lose all feeling. "We're halfway there," she whispered to herself but loud enough that Lena beside her could hear. "We're only halfway there."

"Halfway's pretty good, eh?" The red-haired X-Human offered, recognising the look of terror on her friend's face, dread filling those rich purple eyes. "We know what we're up against now, the next steps will be easier for it."

"But that's just it, Lena. We only just survived back there, I honestly thought, back in the train, that we were dead, I thought we were trapped," Cait admitted. "I've never felt afraid like that. I think I even peed a little, I was so scared," she let out a short chuckle.

"Doesn't matter, honey, 'cause we made it, and we will all make it," Lena pulled her friend in close, wrapping an arm around her as they carried on down the next dark street where a dog's bark snapped them away from their line of thoughts. "Is that a dog?"

"It is!" Miles shrugged off Nathan's hold and staggered over to where a dog had emerged from a bush, its fur a mess from its hiding spot but it otherwise appeared perfectly healthy. "That's a German Shepherd! I've read about these, one of the rare few pure breeds left from humankind's old world! So cool!"

"Keep your distance, mate, could be dangerous," Tomen warned his friend who crouched down to pet the dog who gingerly approached, not knowing whether to trust or not.

"Tomen," Miles swung his head around, clearly still under the influence of whatever narcotic he had been dosed with. "We may die here, we may not succeed. But if there is one thing in my power to do right, it's looking after this good boy, right here, you get me? I'm bringing him with us," Miles said as he gave the dog a scratch behind his ear.

"Bring the dog, don't bring the dog, I don't care, but we have to move on from here, we need to find a safe shelter to rest," Nathan put in, "there's an apartment complex I know, this way."

Chapter 17

"Who used to live here?" Lena asked, picking up a picture frame from the side table next to the red sofa. This apartment was styled in the colours of RCS, a dominant black but red here and there owing to the colour scheme of the region, the team dropped where they found themselves comfortable, either on the sofa in this living area, or in the bedroom attached. This main room sported an open kitchen, bearing red cupboards just as the earlier apartment they had visited bore orange for the Stardust ownership of the home. "Someone you knew?"

"This was my wife's, before we met. We kept it as a means of having a little base in the city," Nathan explained, taking off his helmet and smoothing out his hair back, placing it down on the short table between the sofa and holographic imager. He unslung his rifle and lent it against the wall, before sitting down with a sigh.

"And this is her? She was pretty," Lena pointed at the picture with a smile which disarmed Nathan, usually having to be reminded of Monique Monroe provoked his ever-present rage to rise out of the abyss in his chest, and he would react angrily, often violently. But the smile on the X-Human's face spoke only of innocence, and it was a compliment to the woman in the image.

"She was," Nathan stared at the picture of his wife then turned his gaze forward to the helmet in front of him. Monique was a human, with brunette hair draped across her shoulders and prominent cheeks surrounding an intelligent yet caring smile, in the picture she was in a simple yet sleek blue dress, her arms around a younger looking Nathan.

"And you look so different!" Cait exclaimed louder than she meant to, pointing at how the man sitting before her had once held a much shorter hair look, narrow at the sides with some length at the top, gelled to strike up at the fore, and he bore a charming smile. She had placed her shotgun down on the kitchen side then moved across the room to join her friend. She gazed at the picture as she sorted out her cloak that had become ruffled in removing the strap of her weapon from around her neck.

"Different man back then," the Elite Commander grunted, watching Tomen and Miles remove their weapons and their own helmets, taking a breath before easing down, finally able to properly relax. The dog that Miles had decided to take along with them sat on his haunches and simply watched the former Stalwart man disarm, big brown eyes excitedly watching every move of his new friend.

"Fancy something to eat, Impala?" Miles gave the dog a scratch behind the ear, shrugging off what remained of his backpack, heavily beaten up by the ordeals he had faced travelling through the city, layered in dirt, flattened by his time lying on the morgue slab. He found some snack foods though, more or less unaffected by the state of the bag, and split some, giving it over to Impala that lapped it up with glee.

"So the dog's sticking around, huh?" Sam asked, emerging from the bathroom, sorting out his jumpsuit after having used the toilet after such a long time of keeping the feeling at bay.

"Yes he is staying with us, to the end of the line, right, bud?" Miles backed into the wall and slid down it, slumping in a heap on the floor as he carried on tearing up his pieces of processed meat, more feeding the dog than himself.

"Everyone, find a spot to settle," Tomen instructed, taking a seat next to Nathan on the sofa. "We could all use a small measure of rest, take it now or lose it, we press on in a few hours."

The team knew the value of Tomen's words and heeded his advice without question, making themselves comfortable around the apartment, grateful for the moment to not have to fret for their safety, to doubt the peace of a still shadow. Nathan and Tomen remained where they were with Cait on the floor opposite, between the imager and the Elite's rifle, while Miles slept behind the sofa, his new friend tucked up to his chest, keeping him warm. Lena took the bedroom to sleep so Sam found a blanket and took the utility room, a small storage area with a washer dryer and various boxes, enough room for a man his size to easily lie down in. It was a spacious place, larger than the previous home they had seen which spoke volumes of the importance of those it was lent to. While it was always seemingly night under the shell of the lockdown, the team kept the main room dim so as to give Miles an easier time for sleep, and it gave a cosier outlook of a night away from the cold outside.

"So if Monique worked for RCS full time and you were off being the big boss Elite, who took care of your little one?" Tomen asked Nathan, taking sips from his canteen, only water, but he was careful to spread it out as much as he could, with the other man telling them to not refill from the city's supply.

"After Harkness was born, our careers took off really, the Board always does stress the need to raise families and the Coalition rewarded us with breathing room, special allowances to head out of the city more often, head to our home in Dunnfink to spend time with our boy." Nathan crossed his arms, lent back and flicked his feet up to cross them, propping them up on the small table in front of him. "But we also hired a stay-in nanny from Stardust, she took care of him while we were away."

"And that worked for you? You led a dangerous life, even back then—I just don't get how someone can reconcile leading a life like that and raising a kid at the same time," Tomen looked over to Cait. "There's something I want to share with you," he said, then flashed his gaze back to Nathan, "with both of you. Azuri and me, we're having a kid, she's pregnant."

"No fucking way," Cait blurted out, grinning but the reaction of the Elite on the sofa was far different.

"You're going to be a father?" He said, sounding absent minded, like a thousand miles away.

"Yeah, we found out some weeks back but wanted to wait to tell people, case something happened but given where we are and what we're doing here, what's the point in keeping such news under wraps, huh?"

"That's seriously good news," Nathan's eyes were wide with shock, his expression told of seeing the man next to him as a living, thinking, breathing man for the first time, witnessing his value.

"It is," Tomen nodded, looking over to Cait. "And it's what we want, we're happy," he continued, turning back, "but that's just it, how do I carry on doing what I do as a father? How can I justify the same risks when I have so much to lose?"

"You don't," Nathan put bluntly. "The same rules don't apply when you've been given this tremendous chance for something better."

"But I'm a fighter, it's all I've ever been, from tracking and dealing with outlaws as an enforcer for Stalwart to taking on the Coalition itself with our small sabotages of their operations, it's my purpose, Nathan. I wouldn't know how to live without the fight, I wouldn't be me."

"I know, I can see that," Nathan nudged his helmet with the toe of his boot so the dark grey eyes of it faced away from him, looking towards Tomen before unfolding his arms, resting his elbow on the arm of the sofa, stroking his beard. "You remind me of myself."

"I'm picking up that's no compliment," Cait put in.

Nathan just flicked his eyes up to her and shook his head, "Tomen, do you honestly believe that I didn't think much the same thing way back when? That I didn't possess the same arrogance, that I could just ignore the risk and endure the danger, sure to survive, guaranteed to win any challenge? It's hubris, Tomen, life doesn't work that way, it's not as fair as that. The second you have something in this vast network of starways, is the second they work to take it away from you."

"So what do I do? I didn't just bring this up for chit chat, I want your advice on this, friend."

"What you do is don't make the same mistakes I did. I wasn't there for my wife and son, and they paid the price for it. I was too forgiving to the nature of things, I figured them safe even though I'd no way of knowing that for sure. So what you do is lock away that part of yourself, the fighter as you put it, and you stuff it in a box in your mind and you bury it. After this job, you're done. No more risks, no more chances where you could lose everything you hold dear, because believe me, the purpose you've set yourself to will surely have made a long queue of those ready to take them away from you."

"I'm sorry for springing this on you, I just knew given your experiences that you'd be the one to ask," Tomen looked away from Nathan, he felt guilty. All this time, the former Stalwart man had seen this one as simply a weapon, something to be used, to put between life-threatening menace and those he actually cared about. But now, there was a glimpse of humanity returning to Nathan's eyes, the slightest glints of light, enough for Tomen to realise the pain he was inflicting by reminding this man of things he would much rather never consider.

"No, I'm glad you did," Nathan sighed. "The purpose we both set ourselves to, the fight, it's a drug. It's an addiction I know all too well. And I know that it feels so much like the right thing, but wait until the moment you hold your child for the first time. That feeling you'll get, nothing will ever come close to comparing to it. Being a parent, bringing a life in to mingle among the stars, being the focal point of another's life, there's nothing like it, and nothing beats it."

"OK, I guess I'll have to change my ways some, huh? But I think you're right, I think this will be the last job I pull personally. Thank you, friend, I knew coming to you I'd hear whatever it was that I needed to hear," Tomen looked back to Nathan and offered out a hand.

"Just don't make the same mistake I did, don't let yourself lose what I lost," Nathan replied, shaking the hand extended to him.

"I will do my best," Tomen then winced, a curiosity springing to the front of his mind. "Mind if I ask a personal question?"

"Sure," Nathan pulled out a cigar and prepared to smoke it, watching Cait process what he had said, he could practically see the workings of his mind ticking over, then he took out of his flask of whiskey.

"Talking to you just now, you seem perfectly normal yet Cait here has said that you're a serial killer, and having seen you fight now, I can tell for myself that there's something strong and aggressive inside you. So how'd you get from family man with a fucking nanny to a hardened killer that collects eye balls as trophies from the people he's killed?"

"You know the scary thing is how easy it was," Nathan said with a smirk having taken a swig of his drink. "I always was the violent type but maybe I was more restrained, the community none too keen to have a figure of authority lopping heads off for fun, and I had more of a sense for people, I used to value them to some degree. But when I lost Monique and Harkness. It was like my connection to people in the general sense was just lost, it was gone. I started to see them just as enemies or something so insignificant that killing them was less than dealing with a pest problem. I lost all sight of what it was to be a part of a society wider than the scene of my own mind. I lost my sense for living entirely, actually. My feeling of aggression was the fuel I lived by. I'll put it this way, have you ever been so angry with someone that you've eaten parts of them to feel like you've completely conquered them?"

Both Tomen and Cait's eyes shot wide open in expressions of terror and bewilderment, not expecting such a question in their wildest predictions to Nathan's answer to Tomen's question.

"I expect not," the Elite Commander resumed, taking a long draw of his cigar to intentionally leave the room in an uncomfortable silence for the two in his company. "I went far further off the reservation in the time immediately after the Collapse, I was still figuring out how I wanted to continue. How I like to kill now is to hang my victim upside down, talk to them for a short while, then extract an eye before putting a bullet in their skull, but I didn't start out that way. No, at first, I was consumed by rage, I'd hang them upside down still but I'd use this," he said, patting the sword hilt at his right thigh, "to remove a limb or two. I'd then cook it in front of them and eat while I talk to them about who they were and why I was doing this to them. Done that half a dozen times before I decided I was taking things too far."

"It took you that long to realise eating folk was wrong?" Cait asked, running her fingers through her dead straight brown hair tied back neatly before clinging onto it in front of her chest.

"I never said wrong, I said far. It took too long to cook and there was a risk in that, so it was cleaner just to kill them," Nathan replied in a deadpan tone.

"So what are your thoughts surrounding eating people these days?" Tomen queried, trying with all he had to sound calm and casual, and not freaking out on the inside.

"It varies from time to time," Nathan joked. "No, I don't do that anymore, the thought of it doesn't come up anymore, and it doesn't interest me now. No, now, it's all about the collection."

"The eyeballs?" Tomen asked, not relieved.

"Each one is unique," Nathan pointed out proudly, "so they remind of their former owners. And there's something to be said about preparing for another fight with a congregation of witnesses from conquered foes, they're powerless, left to watch as I venture out to add to their swelling number. It's an empowering feeling," he said, enjoying his cigar.

"So what must you think of us? Gotta wonder," Cait pressed, curious.

"Before coming here, I'd have killed the lot of you without a second thought," Nathan replied honestly.

"Good to know," Tomen nodded to himself.

"But having spent time with you," Nathan continued, with the other man looking back at him. "I'm not entirely sure, but I think what I'm feeling is attachment, I'm not really on familiar terms with the feeling but it's not exactly a bad one."

"Well, isn't that something?" Cait said back to him with a warm smile, "might be there's hope for you yet."

"Don't be so sure," Nathan huffed, flicking away the ash of his cigar onto an ashtray on the table with the picture Lena had been admiring. "You know, there's something I'm curious about you as well."

"Me?" Cait smiled, not expecting the effort from the man.

"Your kind, really. I've heard so many rumours, I'd just like to hear it straight. X-Humans—can your kind really read minds? Or is it a myth?" The sharp, brown eyes of the human Elite showed no signs of being unsympathetic, however there was a dark slant to his tone, almost a mocking dare.

"No, at least not anymore anyways," the purple-eyed girl replied, leaning her head back against the wall, remembering things she hadn't flickered her mind to in so long. "Older members of our community say they can pull it off here and there but truth is that trait was devolved generations ago, too much mingling with your kind, I'd bet," she said with a particular smile, eyeing the man.

"And then there's the other thing," Nathan pondered, taking a draw from his cigar so that the embers at its end flashed in his eyes, making them seem red. "This one has got to be a myth. It's said your kind can retain their consciousness after death, stay on with a loved one just like the ghosts we've encountered across this city."

"Sounds a bit too good to be true don't it?" Cait smiled sadly, "if it is real, then people don't talk about it, but I'll give you this, I've never heard it straight whether it is a thing or not. Maybe it's something widows keep private. But yeah, idea is that if a husband or wife or whatever dies, then they get to stay with their partner until the end of their days. It's a nice sentiment but I don't know. Can imagine why you'd be curious about that."

"Hmm," Nathan agreed briskly. "Too good to be true," he repeated Cait's words as he went quiet, seemingly lulled into a deeper thought.

"Well, boys," Cait announced, standing up awkwardly, "I'm gonna see if I can't get some small amount o' kip before we set out again." The X-Human received only slow nods in return from the two men as she set off in the direction of the doorway to the bedroom, opening it gently to not wake her friend already asleep inside.

Lena was completely submerged in the red duvet, hoarding it all around her, so Cait looked about the floor space after shutting the door but a near silent grumbling gave her pause. "Get your arse in here, girl, no comfort or warmth to be found on the floor," Lena mumbled, half awake, but scooted herself back some small amount to allow for Cait to join her in the bed. And with no better option available to her, Cait obliged, taking up the space vacated in front of friend before finding herself completely enwrapped under the blanket as an arm rose over her to reel her in tight. "Never do like sleeping alone," her friend whispered, tightening the grip around Cait's front, locking her in.

"Nah, really? Coming off so subtle and shy," Cait muttered to herself sarcastically but inwardly admitting that she was indeed extremely comfortable. The duvet was big and cosy, completely covering her from the toes of the boots implemented into her RCS jumpsuit up to her nose, and with Lena holding her closely, she felt incredibly warm and snug. But the most satisfying feeling was that of being safe. Lena had left Nathan's pistol on the bedside table so as to keep it in reach so the availability of a weapon along with her friend's presence was enough for Cait to recover her sense of wellbeing, to settle her mind. Even with what she had just learned about their travelling companion in navigating the fallen Capital where the threats they faced were vast and without end, here, in her friend's arms, she couldn't dream of a place she'd rather be.

"Hey, Caity," Lena murmured.

"Yeah?"

"Whatever happens, just don't let anything or anyone come between us? I think I'd die without my best friend in my life."

"I promise, Lena," Cait replied, glancing over her shoulder where she could just about make out Lena prop herself up, flick her stray red hair away from her face and plant a kiss on her cheek, then on her neck, just behind and under her ear. In this room, in the haze of having the lights off and the door closed, completely private and alone, Cait knew that she could easily get the wrong message from her friend and see the embrace and kisses as something more, but she knew Lena well. Her best friend had been forced to embrace her sexuality early in her life and more often than not against her will, so when she finally seized freedom and choice for herself, she had fully taken ownership of her body again. And in Lena's own unique fashion, she did so with enormous confidence. Hugging someone she considered herself close to, kissing them intimately, could be seen as signs of greater feelings, but Cait knew it was just Lena's over-the-top way of displaying her affection. And she was grateful for that. It was a feeling she knew she must never take for granted or let go of, that it was something to cherish and keep close, something special to preserve.

"They've sent another team into the city, Tomen," Azuri said, looking into the camera of the imager so that her full figure was illuminated from Tomen's device. "I've figured out some of these toys so I can track them, five of them, heading at speed through the Common district."

" S'pose it was to be expected," Tomen nodded, whispering to not wake the sleeping Elite at his side, or his friend behind him. "How long do you think we have?"

"Not even an hour maybe before they catch up." The pilot was wearing her RCS jumpsuit with a silver wing at either shoulder that reflected the light of the imager, lighting up her face, creating a frame for her radiant blue eyes to shine. "Maybe it's time to see what Cait's Elite can do."

"I've already seen what he can do, my love, he's incredible, a one man army," Tomen leaned forward on the sofa and looked at the man sagged next to him. "I'll let him know in a minute, but first. How're you feeling?"

"Well, I've got nought but time on my hands so I messed around with the medico-table downstairs," Azuri replied, sitting in the pilot's chair sipping on a cup of tea. "Got it to tell me that we're having a boy," she said with a grin she could never have contained had she tried.

"A boy?" Tomen shuddered, holding back the tears that came so suddenly to his eyes, "a boy of our own."

"Sorry, yeah, I'm fine yeah, I mean I feel a little on the queasy side, but who cares right? We're having a boy, isn't that just insane?"

"It is," Tomen bit his lower lip, nodding to himself with this ecstatic news. "I mean, wow, what are we going to call him?"

"I have no idea," Azuri chuckled, making herself cough as she awkwardly swallowed her last sip of her drink.

"Just not Impala, that's Miles' new dog's name," Tomen grinned.

"Miles got a dog?" Her tone was both shocked and amused.

"Yeah," Tomen flicked his eyebrows up with a smile. "What about Sterling? I mean if you're OK with that," he said with a humble smile.

"After your dad? Yeah, I'd like that, he was a good man," Azuri agreed, "he really meant a lot to you, I think he'd be honoured if we named our first after him."

"Yeah, he taught me everything I knew about the starways and the sure and narrow path of the good man to walk among them," he sat back, caught in a reminiscent thought before being snapped back, "wait, 'our first'?"

"Obviously," Azuri dismissed, "Sterling Malshux has a nice ring to it."

"He'll be Sterling Prime, we're not yet married, honey," Tomen corrected with a cheeky grin.

"Then best be proposing, huh?" She fired back with a serious hint to her otherwise mocking tone.

"All in good time, you know that, it's just got to feel like the good and proper time, like the only possible time, the right one," Tomen shrugged shyly.

"I know, was only teasing. You do what you feel like, when you feel like, I only want you to be happy," Azuri paused for a moment, "you are happy with this, right? Like, it's feeling like the right time for me to be pregnant? For us to bring a son into the worlds?"

"Azuri, my love, I couldn't be happier, and yes, this is the perfect time for our boy Sterling Prime to come into our lives and change them forever," Tomen smiled, taking a glance over at Nathan. "Speaking of which, I've made a little decision, honey."

"What's that?"

"After this job, no more. At least, no more where I'm directly in the line of fire, head in the crosshairs, not after this one, I'm done. Nathan gave me some real talk and I think I'm seeing what he was saying, no more risks, I won't let our kid grow up without a father like I did when my old man passed," Tomen replied, utterly sure of himself.

"No way! Really? Tomen! That's amazing, that's fucking outrageously amazing! I'm so happy, there's nothing I want more than for you to be happy and safe with me and our son!" Azuri shrieked, giddy as a child, almost spilling the mug clasped in her hands but not giving the slightest care to it at all. "Thank you!"

"Don't thank me, you idiot, this ain't that kind of thing. It's just the right thing going forward, to keep our family safe and intact," Tomen laughed.

"Well, if I were the happiest woman in the galaxy before, now I'm the safest," Azuri replied, taking a moment to just look at the man who emboldened her heart, who made her feel joy like nothing in all the starways could compare.

"And you promise they'll be safe? That we'll all be rewarded for our loyalty?" Sam grovelled to the man displayed on his tablet, of a figure sitting behind a grand desk.

"Deliver the data and any materials you can get your hands on relating to it, bring me Winter's head, and then, yes, you and your little family will be given the executive positions agreed, they will be safe and richly provided for in return for this act of service," Elias Thorne replied, his tone commanding and authoritative.

"Thank you, sir."

"Though I must admit my curiosity, you must know that by doing so will reveal your intentions, you're essentially betraying your family to protect them, an interesting decision," the man on the imager probed, wishing to study the other man's motives.

"I am doing this to protect them," Sam insisted from where he was squatting down beside the washer unit in the storage cupboard. "Winter is a psychopath, he holds distinction between the freakish monsters we've faced to get this far and us, it's only a matter of time before he dispenses with us. I'm thinking he's using us to help him get to this vault of yours then he'll probably open the city up to make good his escape, letting those things out in the process, not that he'll care about them rampaging through the streets of Dunnfink and other places. I don't really much mind all that but it's my lot that I'm worried about. See, we could've done this on our own and you'd've none the wiser."

"Is that so?" Thorne grunted.

"Speaking hypothetically, o' course. But my point is, we didn't need him, the team insisted, the idiots doubted their own skill and now 'ere we are in the darkest cesspit of nightmares, and we could've been done by now if we hadn't beennythingn' a guide who ain't got no clue about nothing," Sam ranted. "He's holding us back and he's dangerous. This here, what we're agreeing to, this is the only and right thing to be doing."

"Yes it is, so do your job and perform your purpose with excellence as agreed. I am keen to analyse your performance and results, Mr Cal," Thorne by way of signing off and then Sam was completely alone in the room once again.

A storm brewed in his chest. Tidal waves of emotions came crashing together, the seas of his mind were enraptured, he felt no solid ground under him as Sam delved deep into his thoughts, looking for anything secure to hold onto to help find some sense of stability. Only one thought revolved around enough for him to grasp it with all that he had and use it to tether his will onto. By doing this, by betraying not only the ones he held most dear, but also the most ruthless killer he had ever seen, he would guarantee them safety. He knew that they would hate him for it, most likely go so far as to leave him, abandon him. But they would be safe. He had to remove the temptation of the goal they had set before themselves, the data he was sent to retrieve, and he had to remove the one who would stand in the way of that. Only then would they be safe. Better safe and far away than dead, murdered at the hand of a serial killer whose only care was the destruction he wished to bring down on the people he imagined were responsible for the accidental deaths of his family, Sam reflected. No, he settled, he would rather sacrifice losing his family to betrayal than death, he would do what he felt was right. He saw only war and death by standing at Nathan's side, and the image of the bloodied bodies of his family stuck in his mind was too much for him to take.

Chapter 18

The idea of lowering himself, degrading himself to negotiate with a pathetic lowlife for what he deemed the most important thing in his life, his life's work, the sum of his purpose, his own property, left a putrid taste in Elias's mouth. He stood at the window of his office, casting his gaze upon the planet below, Ruby, the once thriving Capital of this region, with the city of Rose at its heart, the centre of everything. The memories of what he had done, what he had chosen to do, time and time again committing to that path, did not so much as haunt Elias but taunt him. The work was unfinished and ripe with opportunities, and the personal significance of it for him was too much to let it sit abandoned, incomplete. If this thief, this degenerate scum could deliver to him what he prized, Elias would stop at nothing to see it through to its absolutely essential conclusion. He had the full might of a conglomerate-owned region of space after all, he had the means, and he had the will.

"Sir? Is everything alright?" Vice-Admiral Reiku asked his Section Chief who had gone quiet, from his holographic projection cast from an imager set into the floor.

"Hmm, forgot you were there, Reiku, I was lost in thought," Elias admitted coldly yet not turning away from the window.

"I said I have my report from the Forerunner, sir, and that I've dispatched the second team inside the Capital, as per your instruction."

"Very good, and you made the parameters of their assignment clear?"

"Yes, sir, they know not to engage the Commander, to let your operative do his work, and to only intervene should he fail, and until such a time, to maintain a close distance to the target. Once the operative has the required material and the Commander is dead, my team will assassinate the operative and retrieve everything possible, to bring it directly to you aboard the Arcadia."

"Excellent work, Vice-Admiral," Elias nodded. "And now, your report."

"The culprit for the broadcast originating from this station refused to step forward, therefore we exacted the proper procedure," Reiku could not contain the influence of sadistic excitement in his voice.

"A shame, workers are the key resource for our company, but the procedures are set for a reason, and there's always more," Elias allowed himself a small smirk, despite the setback.

"However, sir, a small craft escaped the hangar before it could be destroyed, but it is only sizable for two aboard."

"And do we have a notion about whom those two may have been, Vice-Admiral?"

"My troops have scoured this place and collated a list of the dead which we cross-referenced with the lousy logs maintained by this shipyard, and there are two missing: one Stalwart man, one Stardust X-Human."

"Rats fleeing the flame, they're likely of no importance," Elias scoffed.

"Nonetheless, I've dispatched an Elite to track their course, we'll find them and interrogate them should they be the one behind the broadcast," Reiku concluded.

"I expect nothing less, no loose ends, Vice-Admiral, you'll do well to remember that," the Section Chief turned his head slightly to fix his servant with a powerful glare. "Now bring the Obsidian fleet to Ruby."

"At once sir, but should we not be engaging these rumours of the Sapphire conglomerate attacking the border?"

"No, even if their intervention is true, it will bear no fruit for them, we will soon have my work, and then it will be too late for them," Elias rebuked, disinterested.

"As you say, sir. Will there be anything else?"

"No."

"I'll await your command above Ruby," Vice-Admiral Reiku signed off, his image blipping out of the room, leaving the Section Chief alone to his thoughts.

Elias measured the things to come. Vague reports of an Azurite fleet annihilating his assets protecting that edge of his region, rumours of the Admiral, his own uncle, being a part of that unprovoked attack, the re-emergence of the Elite Commander. Usually Elias kept a plan several steps in advance, to outmanoeuvre any and all that might move against him, and it was a practice that had always served him well. But how does one plan when such events are utterly unpredictable? He hated it. To be caught up in someone else's plan, finding himself being the one manoeuvred around to a design not his own, by a powerful presence that was skilfully remaining anonymous. Someone had joined his great game and was playing at his level, of an equal match or more, and Elias was reluctant to meet them at their rules. While he would never admit it, he did feel a moment's pause, the briefest feeling of fear and apprehension but he rose above it and challenged the very stars to defy him. Elias stared hard at the planet below, the world that had taken his most precious possession, swallowed it up under that infernal armoured shell, but he wouldn't let that stop him from achieving his goals. He couldn't let it. He had to see through the path he had set before himself a decade ago. There was no other purpose that he set for himself, only to succeed. And now he had a team of Elites on the inside, and not only that, he had a man inside a team of WIDOWs already deep into the city, an expendable force, of no consequence, no cost to him. Should they fail, his team would prevail. He couldn't lose. Elias felt a swell of confidence rise up from his chest and saw the energy propel throughout his body, giving strength to his arms, to his mind, and he was ready for whatever might come next.

Chapter 19

The ground below their feet began to dip as they approached the gates to the Residential district, the decline starting as they began their venture downhill into the next section of the Capital city. Standing high and mighty, the walls that divided the districts were of a hard, unyielding grey stone, not a stain from the near decade of neglect on this side, except for the slightest discolouring at the base of those gigantic metal doors. Nathan stood at the head of the pack, using the computer mounted on his arm to access the city systems and provide power to the doors while the others took measure of their surroundings. They had left the busier streets of the Leisure district behind when they had left Monique Winter's old home, leaving behind the ambient glow of the advertising hoardings decorating the tops and faces of the buildings, providing the much needed light. Here at the gateway through to the next district, the streetlamps fought the losing battle in repelling back the shroud of darkness that had claimed this city. "I'm almost set," the Elite announced, transferring power from other systems to give life to the gates too heavy to move with muscle alone.

"Hurry up, I think we have incoming," Miles called over to him, standing next to his friend, the dog that was snarling into the perpetual night, standing its ground against the shifting shadows off in the distance. While Nathan worked, the others had formed a semi-circle behind him, aiming their weapons out but it was too dark to find anything to fire at, while the dog's eyes darted in all directions.

"It takes as long as it takes," Nathan answered coolly, looking up with the dark grey ovals of his black helmet at the doors that seemed to be petulantly set against him.

Then the fog of whispers washed up to meet them, the indistinguishable mutterings and groans and the team knew what was coming, what had been alerted to their presence in this border of the district. It was the sound of scratching that joined the oncoming murmurs that meant that they were out of time and Tomen strode up to the other man, hastily darting looks over his shoulder. "Don't tell me these don't work neither!" He growled frustrated, eager to get those huge doors between his team and whatever was closing in to meet them.

"Impala, stay with me," Miles kept his rifle butt shouldered, his eye never leaving the scope, but with his left hand, he removed it from where he grasped the base of the barrel to grip the dog's scruff and haul him back to his side. If it annoyed the dog, he showed no clear sign of it, maintaining his stance of a rigid back, tail down, legs apart and teeth showing in a display of standing his ground against whatever he could see through the veil of gloom.

"I see them, they're coming up the road," Lena pointed out, holding the pistol Nathan had given her firmly and Miles took a glance at her before seeing what she was talking about through the scope of his rifle.

"There's a lot of them," he agreed, resting the green cross that acted as the reticle for his scope on the one at the centre, a barely capable of walking, staggering shape. "How we doin' on them doors, guys?"

"The power grid sustained damage in this area, something else is taking up the bulk of what it has to give, it's fighting back against funnelling that energy to this system. It's like it's warning me not to," Nathan said in a calm yet inquisitive tone. He might have thought twice about what he was doing but he knew for a fact that a herd of the dead was coming up behind them, so he had to do something. Even if there were a greater threat on the other side, they would still be moving forward, so he ignored the system's warning and proceeded with unlocking and empowering the doors into the Residential district. "Got it."

"Good, just in time," Miles called back over his shoulder, seeing the faint glow of the streetlamps give form to the creatures approaching them.

The avenue that lent passage to the boundary gates was a steady descent as the lights and prestige of the Leisure district faded into plain walls, fewer decorative trees and flower beds, and more functional designs to the architecture. Buildings lined either side, restaurants, bars, and other things, encasing the road where the next horde of the dead came flowing down, crawling, floundering, stumbling towards them. In the blanket of darkness, the team could make out little else, and only the outline of these creatures were able to be seen. But the size of this grouping spanned from one side of the road to the other, and behind the front line, more and more of them followed in kind, snapping their jaws, their limbs barely hanging onto the sheer wreckage of their bodies. "Open fire," Nathan lazily ordered, without so much as peering over his shoulder to inspect the threat for himself, instead he carried on programming the redirect of power through to the doors, seeing them crack open at the centre.

"Miles, hit the flanks, I'll take centre—the rest of you, thin out the ones who get too close!" Tomen ordered, re-joining the line of his team just as they began to fire their guns into the crowd of undead making progress towards them.

"How much longer, Nate?" Cait shouted, firing her shotgun at a bundle of dead people that came crashing through a window off to her left, mindlessly pushing aside the tables and chairs of the once cafe out of their way in their rampage.

"Just about there, really," he replied coolly, inspecting the new landscape presenting itself in the slither ever widening as the heavy, clunky metal doors screeched open on rusted hinges, staring down as a wave of murky water washed up to just a few paces off the perimeter boundary. "Brilliant," Nathan grunted, sarcastically.

"What? What is it? Can we make our way through?" Tomen shouted, not daring to take his concentration away from stemming back the approaching the undead, raining down fiery, green energised rounds across the length of the road.

"Yeah come on, just watch where you step, could get your boots wet," Nathan nonchalantly answered as he stepped into the neighbouring district, peering left and right after seeing that the way ahead had been claimed by a great flood, having engulfed the entire lower portion of this new area.

"What?" Lena shot her head back and upon seeing what he had meant, she shook her head, "fuck sake, seriously?"

"Everyone! Move into the next district! Move, move, move!" Tomen ordered, knowing they had no other choice, aiming for the legs at the dead things in the centre mass of the horde, using their collapsed bodies to make small dams that tripped up the ones coming up behind.

"Alright, moving!" Miles shouted back, giving the dog at his side, barking and snarling at anything that came near, a light kick to tell it that it was time to go, and the dog understood, padding towards the Elite Commander who was staring off to the right, at something behind the wall.

The team made a hasty retreat into the Residential district, beating back the ceaseless dead as that got within clawing distance, reaching out with disfigured limbs and rotten fingers, seeking to grasp at anything to reel in their prey. Sam, Cait and Lena joined Nathan first, just before Miles herded Impala inside, with Tomen being the last and once he was through the Elite finally joined the fight, emanating an energy shield from a clenched right fist held before him. He returned to the screen at that same arm, powering up the doors to close while the others made sure nothing slipped in at the sides, frantically shooting at anything that moved. The dog meanwhile, softly and carefully crept up to the water's edge, sniffing at it before jumping back in a fright and baring its teeth at the slow lapping flood, going completely unnoticed by the preoccupied team at the gates. Once the gap in the wall had decreased to the point where Nathan shield was enough to cover it, he removed his pistol from the holster at his chest with his free left hand, awkwardly as the gun was positioned to be taken by his opposite side, then aimed it at the biting, snapping creatures. The shield being projected from his hand dropped a cropped out section to allow for his weapon and he calmly shot several of the things in what remained of their skulls, relieving the pressure of them pushing against his defence. Not that he had to keep it up for much longer as the doors finally sealed shut, halting the march of this most recent pack of undead former citizens of this once Capital City.

"Out of the frying pan and into the fire, I reckon," Sam sighed as he turned away from the shut doors and took in the scope of the next district. Most of it was submerged, lost to the flood that had claimed the rest of the road a short way from their feet as it lent downhill, with only the tops of buildings reaching up towards the ceiling of the shell still visible. Street lamps poked their way above the surface, the light sitting just above the edge, small globes of white, doing what little they could to shine upon the concrete surfaces just about above the utterly opaque sea. These were apartment buildings, clones of one another, striking up in an arranged pattern, bearing the neon sigil of Stardust at the fore of each one, giving testament to the fact that these homes were never really owned. Random other objects protruded up out of the flood but for the most part, the way ahead was completely swallowed by the water that shimmered in these dim lights, never quite sitting still.

"What happened here?" Lena asked, her bejewelled green eyes taking in the sight of one of the buildings having collapsed and leaning on the adjacent with furniture dangling between the rubble.

"We approached the city from the Dunnfink side," Nathan explained. "On the other side is a great lake which feeds the reservoir and pumps beneath the city, guessing with no one to attend to it, it failed and burst into this." He said, stepping forward then pointing with his pistol still in hand at the space between the first tower block and the boundary wall, a small alley, where some distance away, was a set of metal stairs leading into the building, off to their right. "This way."

"Just keep out of the water, guys," Miles announced, crouching beside Impala who was still baring his teeth at the filthy flood slowly coming up in shallow waves to brush against the hairs around the paws that he held wide apart to stand as firm as possible. "I don't quite think we've left the zombies behind somehow," the white eyes of his mask met the group as the former Stalwart man dared not move any closer to the water's edge.

"Smart pup," Nathan agreed, "steer clear of the flood," he said and made to lead the way, following the line of the boundary wall, glancing up as he could hear the scratching of the dead on the other side, desperately trying to claw through rock and stone to reach them. But another sound coming from further out in the district they now found themselves in captured his attention, yet he thought it best not to let his apprehension show. A different kind of murmur carried on the windless air, the stale, recycled, now stinking from the near decade long sitting water, a sound which gave him the slightest, albeit imperceptible pause. A thruster, kin to his own, but carrying something perhaps more deadly than himself. Nathan cast a glance as they passed by one half-lost building, to see out into the district, knowing one threat for sure that they would soon encounter.

As they moved along this alley between the buildings up against this side of the district and the boundary wall, various messages of hastily drawn, frenzied graffiti began to appear scrawled across the stonework. 'Death to the managers!', 'work together, survive together: what a load of shit!', 'you killed all of us!', 'we will rid the cosmos of our betters!' all slapped on in a suspiciously dark red paint. "I was going to ask," Miles started as he slowed down to take in all that was written here, but thinking better than to touch any of it. "If this is the Residential section of the city, how come your missus lived in the Leisure district?"

"It's just marketing, Miles," Nathan replied disinterested, carrying on towards the staircase. "The real citizens of the city were all managers, supervisors, officers and executives so naturally that meant they needed a large workforce to tend to them. Consider the one we just left as the real premium living in this region, and the district we find ourselves in now as nothing more than servants' quarters. The Residential district? A marketing pitch to cover up what it really was, a Stardust labour camp."

"When people talk of the Old City, they never mention that," Cait remarked. Her eyes were glued to the water not quite making its way up to meet them and was so full of dirt and muck that it was near impossible to see into, yet still she thought she could see even more skeletons under that layer of sludge.

"Well, they wouldn't, would they?" Sam scoffed, "better to make this place sound like a fallen paradise, better justifies the harsher, full of shit realities people have to suck up and deal with. It's clever."

"Clever? Really, Sam? They ruined people's lives here for their own gain," Lena spat.

"Never underestimate the value of comfort and cosy living until you've had the good fortune to experience it for yourself, my dear," the one in the Crimson Sun jumpsuit mocked back.

"And never underestimate the cost of quality life it takes for the vast amount of workers to provide that for you, dickhead," Cait said, agreeing with Lena.

"I don't know, I think I could easily forget that with no responsibility greater than numbers on a spreadsheet that I stare at all day long while one babe cooks me up a genuine cut o' steak, while another sucks me off," the man grinned through a black beard matted with sweat, with teeth yellow from the lack of care he gave them.

"If you're so self-absorbed, then why you here?" Miles asked Sam as he gave his dog a quick tug away from his curiosity at a bubbling near the water's edge.

"'Cause they couldn't've lied 'bout everythin' 'bout this city. I'm keen as anythin' to see what riches lay in this vault o' you's, and what the info you be seeking be worth to the right people, in the Sapphire or Emerald maybe," Sam smirked but hiding a smile to himself at a future he figured secure for himself by carrying out this venture.

"You're better than thoughts like that," Cait tried reminding her friend but not putting a whole lot of effort into her words, thinking that he wouldn't be listening to her properly in any case.

They reached the metal staircase, just like the one they had seen earlier in the city and began to make their way up, leaving the thicker stench of the water behind as they ascended through levels of corridors with apartments stemming off. At each of these doorways, spectres cast in an eternal haze of grey, stood at the entrances to where they once called home, unfazed by the scarring of different mortal wounds that they bore. These ghosts watched on silent yet unblinking as the team passed among them, ignoring them for the most part but Sam and Lena especially were slightly unnerved by their presence. Impala on the other hand didn't seem to notice their appearance at all. The German Shepherd with the rough coat sniffed the air in between every few paces but paid no attention to the shades of people that in return showed no interest towards him. "Where are we even going? With that flood, our path is fucked, surely," Sam moaned.

"You go ahead and try swimming," Miles laughed, "I'm with Winter in hoping for a different way."

"Swimming, yeah," Sam dismissed, following the others, itching for the tablet stowed inside his jacket, eager for the man at the other end of his transmissions to tell him that he had gone far enough, that his work was done and that he could claim his reward.

"Keep moving," Nathan shot over his shoulder back at the group as he led the way through the building, a relief in truth as the lights were still on so they could see where they were going, despite the grisly sight of the scattered bodies of those that had once lived here.

They passed through the complex until they reached the internal stairs, simple concrete leading the way up, and reached the top level where they were able to look across the plain of this district from the view of the end apartment. A tall section of the structure had long since given way forming a makeshift bridge across a wide gap to the next building, spanning over a pitch black section of the putrid sea below. Beyond this next building, they could not see, but on the wider angles, the landscape appeared the same as best they could tell. At least, eighty percent of the district was lost to the water that reflected the few sources of light there were, giving a bleak outlook for the way ahead. An object moved among the buildings, gliding over the surface of the flood but too far away to make it out but for the tiniest glow of a flame that seemed attached to it, but Nathan was the only one to notice this, he had been looking for it. "I'll go first," he said, holstering his pistol and taking out his rifle.

"You really think it's safe?" Cait asked him, planting a foot at the edge of the crumbled section of wall, testing it first before leaning over to peer down below them. "It's a long way down."

"You'd rather stay here?" Nathan asked, turning the faceless gaze of his helmet to her.

"Nope," Lena answered for her, looking around the apartment they found themselves in. It was similar to those they had already seen, plastered in the colours of the company, with basic furniture and furnishings, hardly any personal items. But the two rotting corpses lying on the floor gave Lena a powerful urge to carry on, no matter how unsturdy their bridge may be.

The Elite Commander didn't wait for any more input and he was acutely aware that the jetpack mounted to his back meant the flood was actually of no consequence for him but he knew abandoning these people now would not be his wisest choice, so he carefully took his first step. Dusty yet rugged, the concrete didn't so much as notice his added weight and he leapt on with an agile comfort seemingly without the weight of the armour he wore, or the weapon in his hands. He moved slowly, listening for any cracking or any other sign that the bridge might fail but with every passing step, he advanced closer to the other side. Nathan aimed his rifle all around, scanning the rooftops all around him, carefully turning as he carried on along the concrete beam, observing the other buildings in sight through his scope, checking the other end for threats. The section of wall had come crashing down into the next apartment building, the one he entered being identical to the one he had left behind as Nathan activated his comm piece. "Come on, one at a time," he said, aiming his rifle above their heads, checking the roof there for anything trying to follow.

Miles led the way with Impala in tow just behind staring at every step the man took, closely tucking in to him so that they crossed safely together and without issue. Lena followed Sam and the bridge held, with only shallow rains of dust and debris being the only signs of their passing, and they may be forgiven for thinking they had finally been handed some measure of luck.

Tomen secured their backs, nodding to Cait to begin making her way over as he intended to be the last to cross, better to make sure nothing caught them unawares. Cait stepped onto the concrete gingerly, half expecting it to pulverise into dust the moment she put some of her weight onto it but it didn't so much as groan, and she started her crossing. The water below her every step was completely opaque, with no smaller building or piece of road or anything able to be seen past its shadowy depths, and Cait mistrusted the way it never sat still. Small ripples broke out unevenly, there were waves emanating from nowhere, she could hear splashes without being able to see where they were coming from. She could see the others at the far end moving about the opposite apartment, safe and sound, and it gave air to her chest, emboldening her to finish her passage across the breadth of this road but that breath lost when the shadow struck seemingly from nowhere. A hunk of shiny black metal tackled her in her midriff, knocking the air straight out from her lungs, sweeping her off her feet, carrying her until they made their explosive contact with the water below.

"Cait!" Tomen called, alone on the original side of the bridge, aiming his rifle at anything that moved in the water below but he couldn't see much at all.

"Where'd she go?" Lena screamed, grasping the edge of the window that had been caved in by the concrete coming slamming down on top of it, but from her side she too couldn't make anything out. And then she had to duck as Nathan came hurtling over her at furious speed with his jetpack, not hesitating as he breached the surface of the water below near where the shadow had taken Cait.

The interruption of their attacker had broken the moderate silence of their surroundings but it had been restored as the team could do little other than gawk at the flood below them, anxiously waiting for any sign of their companions. They didn't have to wait long as Nathan came hurtling out of the water, rising at great speed, his sword ignited and impaling a dark, black object that he used to smash through the makeshift concrete bridge creating an explosion of rubble. Pieces of cement and dust came raining down as the Elite rose high into the air before hovering and casting his foe down at the feet of the group that had completed the crossing. It was a lump of black metal, a mockery of a humanoid shape cast in machinery with blaring red eyes and a deep slash at its chest plate revealing the inner workings of this technical marvel. "Grab the blue cylinder inside, quickly," Nathan said over his radio to the ones standing around the metal monster and Lena was the one to reach in and snatch the thing she hoped he had meant, breaking it away from its wiring with a forceful jerk. It was then that they saw the trail of undead dangling from Nathan's leg, a constant line of them reaching all the way down below the water's surface. They gripped onto him, crawling over each other in a mad struggle to sink their teeth into the one that had hoisted them up so high but they were sent flying when Nathan used his thrusters to spin violently, casting them away in all angles. One undead landed directly next to Miles but he easily shot in the head before it had the time to stand but one more came dragging itself across the stretch of open roof above their heads and dropped down on top of him but Impala was there. The dog pounced on Miles, knocking him and the undead creature over together, planted his jaws around the dead thing's neck and bit down hard, severing it before picking it up with his teeth and throwing it across the room.

Nathan, now clear of the things that had clung on so tight, burst downwards, back beneath the flood, having his sword lead the way, but even the light of this immense lightning inferno was lost once below the opaque blanket. As he had used his metal foe to smash through the bridge, the remnants and debris from it came hailing down on top of the water's edge but he paid it no mind, nor the innumerable dead that called the flood their home. Tomen, now stranded on the wrong side, found himself under siege from the creatures and the large merged beasts smashed their way through from the apartment above, rushing at him with ear-piercing roars. He fired his weapon steadily, doing all he could to not spray randomly and frantically, not letting panic take over, to not waste what ammunition remained to him. These monsters thundered towards him, swiping away any object that stood in their path but he was equal to them, dispatching them with the powerful green rounds of his rifle, seeing his energised beams meet their mark more often than not.

Then the water exploded again, this time the Elite carried Cait by grasping hold of her cloak with his left hand, his sword still firm in his right as he ascended through the air, touching down with the rest, dropping off the coughing and spluttering X-Human. Nathan wasted no time, powering across the gap with his jetpack, adjusting his body mid-flight to land with a powerful kick with both legs at the freakish beast that was so close to Tomen that it nearly locked its jaws completely around his head. The force of the kick cast the monster back, smashing into two of its kin that had joined the fray, and

Nathan used his sword to slash away the other that was close to them. Before the three that remained could muster themselves to attack again, Nathan took hold of Tomen by swiftly sheathing his blade and hooking his arms under the other man's, setting off with his jetpack as quick as it could carry them both. They shot over the gap in the blink of an eye and once the other man could be set down safely, Nathan turned back to the building they had left behind, firing a small volley of missiles from his launcher behind his left shoulder. Three rockets blasted the strong points of the apartment complex, caving in the structure, seeing it destroyed as the beasts inside screamed with sickening rage through morphed together skulls.

"That was too close," Tomen said through hurried breaths, his eyes darting all around under his grey helm with the white ovals, not trusting that the fight was done. But it was not a fight that was near that startled him. From where they were, through the breach of their building where their bridge had been made, they could see where the boundary wall encompassed the centre of the city, and from there a colossal storm of red energised rounds pierced the sky in the shell. The ceiling of the dome lit up as though it were aflame as these red lasers struck at it but most of them landed on the five small candle lights way off in the distance, the sound of which compared to a thunderstorm striking against a roof. These small shapes were cast out of the sky, rendered apart, trailing off and eventually coming down somewhere behind the enormous fortifications surrounding the city centre. The team initially said nothing, just gaping in wonder at the sheer firepower they had just witnessed, enough to light up the entire space above, and they had known what they had just destroyed. "Bye, bye, second Obsidian team," Tomen muttered in shock.

"The fuck was that?" Sam exclaimed, his face full of terror.

"That," Nathan sighed, "is justification for navigating around the Obsidian base at this city's heart. Some of the battalion trapped here still lives. We best hope the stars align in such a way as the General does not still lead them, or we will have a real skirmish on our hands."

"What in all the stars is this thing?" Lena asked Nathan, giving the piece of twisted metal cast on the floor a solid kick as she still held the blue cylinder in her hands, trying to job her mind away from the awesome force they had just witnessed.

"An RCS robo-sentry," Nathan explained, moving over to take the blue tube from the X-Human. "And this is what gives it the strength to repel any kind of gunfire. These are nanites," he said, taping the glass that contained the luminescent blue gel riddled with tiny black dots. "These are tiny machines that repair a robo-sentry of any damage during a fight. Only thing I've seen that kills them is an Elite's blade and removing the nanite chamber before it can restore itself."

"Fucking strong heap of cunt," Cait coughed, her chest pounding from the force of the blow where the robo-sentry had tackled her off the bridge. She dug her fingers in under the armoured corset she wore over her jet-black jumpsuit at the top hem to try to help her breathing after her time under the water after she had been smashed through it.

"You see one of these, don't daft, point it out and I'll deal with it with my blade, your weapons are useless against them," Nathan said, rocking the robo-sentry's head with the heel of his boot.

"If they're so tough, why have Obsidian in the first place if these machines can do the same job?" Lena watched the red eyes of the machine go out as it died, tossing the blue tube aside once she remembered she was holding it, she was surprised at the warmth of it.

"Because people are cheaper to make," was all the Elite said with a shrug as he pulled out his rifle again. "We're moving, can't stay here," he stated as he passed by a ruined coffee table and sofa to the entrance to the apartment but found it blocked by fallen debris on the other side. He then followed the wall to the window and looked down, seeing a building below, its roof above the surface of the water. "Down we go," he said, not waiting to explain what he meant, simply raising a clenched fist, energising a shield in the place of the window, smashing it out from the force of its emergence and looking out over the way ahead. A thought made him hesitate, however, what if General Ardamus had ordered that strike? But he shook off the thought as quick as it had come to the fore of his mind, focusing instead on the here and now.

"Winter, what'd you mean down?" Tomen asked but Nathan jumped halfway through the question, disappearing from view. When the team made their way over, they found their guide crouching down over a wreckage of another robo-sentry, the Elite's blade in its back, and him discarding the glowing blue tube aside carelessly.

"Keep up," was all the Elite Commander said over his radio comm as a way of getting the others to join him. It was nowhere near a fall far enough to break someone's legs on landing but it was high enough to give pause, yet it seemed the only way ahead as from this next rooftop the others could see the path that had been chosen for them. So they followed the instruction given to them, taking it in turns to leap down, Miles holding Impala on his turn, until they all stood on the flat stone roof of the neighbouring building. The next step was clear as the small orbs of light from the street lamps reaching just above the surface of the flood lit a pathway through the streets to where they could see the road again, where the dip in the land ended and rose up again to the boundary gates, the entrance to the next and final district on their venture. There was only the small haze of pure white from the lamps breaking up the fog of smoky green rising up from the dirty sea that had claimed this section of the city. And at the other end of their rooftop was a dome section of roof, basic composite plastic but perfect as an improvised boat to help them travel across the water.

Yet before anyone could make a move towards taking that next step, the flood all around their small square roof erupted in activity as undead sought to claw their way up on all sides. Bone with the barest amount of tissue and muscle left attached burst out from beneath the gruesome waves, latching onto any sure grip it could find before hoisting up the rest of the decrepit carcass. They were everywhere. The path ahead may have been lit but that was the only corner of this roof with any light, the rest was just a layer upon layer of shifting shadow, the threats behind them more heard than seen. As they had throughout the city, a fog of whispering voices preluded their attack as the undead rose, with the team finding themselves in three-hundred-and-sixty-degree fighting. Nathan fired first, taking out one of the beasts made from a collection of mashed corpses as it broke the water line, destroying its three skulls with his rifle. The team then fired against all sides, with Miles and Tomen lighting up this latest arena with their energised rounds casting an ambient, neon green glow to the firefight. "There's too many!" Tomen shouted, having to take on six in one go all on his own as the rest had their own battles to fight.

"Hold your ground, steady," Nathan ordered although he knew they couldn't for too much longer, there were far too many and there was no chance of falling back to anywhere, they were on an island essentially. But the idea in his head which was perfect for eliminating this sprawl that approached from all angles required them to come even closer, it had to be done right for it to work.

"Great idea, coming down here, now we're fucking fucked!" Sam cried, firing his shotgun with such a panic that his shells didn't strike one meaningful hit even though the shambling corpses were mere steps away.

"On my signal, everyone huddle in under me," Nathan instructed calmly, dispatching the larger undead with his rifle, leaving the nuisance crawlers to the others with their far less powerful guns.

"What?" Lena asked, reloading her pistol before immediately needing to fire it again, the corpses edging closer and closer to where the ones left with legs not strong enough to hold them up, slithering on the rooftop, scratched and slashed with violent arcs of their dislocated arms at the team's legs.

"Fuck!" Miles screamed as one caught at his ankle, hooking its fingertips in past his armour to cut at his skin, but Impala snatched at the one responsible, breaking its arm in two, biting away the end in Miles' leg. "Whatever you goin' do, mate, do it now!"

"To me!" Nathan shouted at the top of his voice and the team, even though they had no idea what the plan was, obeyed, and hustled in under the Elite Commander's body, huddling in close. He let off one last salvo with his rifle before flinging it over his shoulder, firing two rockets into the air from his pack, aiming directly up, and emitting both his shields to cover the team ducking down at his feet. The dead kept coming and went to claw at them under the purple energised boundaries as Nathan glanced up, waiting for the small bombardment to come raining back down, grimacing as he realised he couldn't completely cover himself in using the shields to protect the team, leaving his head and back exposed. So when the two rockets came crashing down, they annihilated the wave of the dead, and gave him a hard hit too, but Nathan maintained the shields, keeping his arms raised, successful in protecting the others from the blasts.

Shrapnel tore apart the dead, ripping them to shreds, and the force of the explosions blew a great amount of them back into the water from where they had risen. The light was comparable to a supernova given the armoured shell of the city looming high overhead stifling in all the elements, and it also made them far louder. Those not wearing protective headgear had their ears ringing, near to bleeding from the devastation Nathan had brought down but they didn't care, it had worked to push the dead back, even if only for now. "I think we got some breathing room, people," Tomen announced, seeing this, relieved that this latest attack was another victory for his team. They had all survived, with only Miles' minor injury being the only cause for concern.

"Then let's use it," Nathan announced, moving over to the decorative dome barely scratched by the explosions, the thing he had been looking at when the creatures had attacked.

"You're thinking we can use this, ain't ya?" Lena asked, kicking it and nodded when it didn't buckle, then turned her gaze to Nathan. "But how you reckon we remove it without damaging it?"

"With ease," he said, taking out his blade, igniting the edge, and slicing carefully around the half-circle of clear plastic, golden lightning bolts dancing against the material but not to damage it. It worked perfectly, the sword removing the shape away from where it was mounted onto the rooftop, revealing the hollowed out inside, ideal for the team to get inside. It was then nothing to Nathan for him to stow his weapon and pick up their boat, taking it over to the edge where he placed it on the water carefully, testing the buoyancy of it and gesturing for the others to get in with a sharp nod.

"You want us to get in that?" Sam crossed his arms and relaxed his stance, doubtfully eyeing the hunk of metal that he felt pressured into believing was a real boat.

"Plan B is to throw you in on the other side and I ferry the others across one at a time while the dead are busy tearing apart your screaming corpse, if you'd prefer that," Nathan said with a shrug, not letting go of the upside down dome in the water.

"The yacht will do fine," Sam nodded and was the first to board, in case the other man changed his mind and suddenly preferred the sound of his other idea.

"We're all going to die," Lena sighed, sharing a sceptical glance with Cait before they stepped inside too. Impala seemed the happiest to clamber in, scruffing over to the other side and mounting his paws on the edge pretending to be this boat's figurehead.

"Why's the dog the smartest of you lot?" Nathan grunted, glad at least one of his party didn't hesitate at his idea.

Once everyone was inside, Nathan drew out his sword again but this time didn't ignite it, instead this was what he used as a paddle, starting off by pushing away from the rooftop they'd taken their boat from. The composite bobbed uneasily against the water with all the weight inside it but it held afloat, the idea pulling off. He tentatively tested the idea of using the flat edge of his sword but was satisfied when they successfully moved forward and at little cost of sound. "Well, what'd y'know? Good one, Winter," Lena rolled up the sleeves of her tattered crimson coloured trench coat and rolled her head over to look at the man. "But what's to stop the zombies rocking our boat and we tip?" She asked, pursing her juicy red lips in a playful way, using her sexuality to soften the idea of a gruesome death but mainly intended to add an extra level to her mocking tone.

"Nothing at all, but I couldn't be confident of anything else," Nathan admitted, himself at peace knowing that should the boat be attacked, all he needed to do is take flight.

"So this was just a bored whim, huh? A way to speed things up? Fair enough," Lena nodded, teasing the man.

"Why can't all you be like the dog?" Nathan grunted, noticing how Miles' new friend was grinning, enjoying the ride and above all, was absolutely quiet.

"Pretty mean," Cait joked but gave the dog a stroke between his ears which he responded well to with greater swaying of his tail. "How'd you think Impala survived all these years?"

"He killed a zombie fairly confidently," Miles replied, "I doubt it was the first time he'd done it. Maybe he just had to fight to survive and whatever affected the people of the city didn't affect him as a dog."

"Good pooch," Cait smiled, scratching Impala behind his ears.

All around them, emerging from the buildings, passing through the stone and brick and mortar, were the shades of those who had once called these streets home, walking on the flood as if nothing were different from the city's hay day. Figures in grey, observing silently, not approaching or making any attempt to make some kind of contact, instead they just stood where they were and watched as this improvised boat passed between the orbs of light lining the road to the perimeter of the district. "We're being watched," Tomen pointed out as the team shifted carefully to look at these ghosts, not wanting to rock the boat.

"Pay them no mind, they'll do us no harm and they're not stopping our way," Nathan said to the team to ease their minds so that they wouldn't wobble the boat in wanting to get a clearer view of their spectators.

"Why though? Why do you think they're just watchin' us?" Lena asked him, seeing him so calm allowed her to lower her pistol, not seeing the need for it, despite that she could see the decomposed faces of the undead not so much as a metre below the water's surface as they glided over.

"They're probably expecting us to join them," he said, too calmly for her liking.

Chapter 20

As they stepped through into the final section of Rose city, the air hit them as strong as the threats they had faced so far had, there was a staleness to it, leaving a metallic tang in the mouth, which fit the sight of the ruin of the once Directorate district. This was by far the most well-lit, which was a certain relief as street lamps dotted the beige path that ran either side of the shiny charcoal road, but it was also the most empty. There were no bodies scattered about, not so much as one, nor any signs of a struggle or the sheer panic and terror, the chaos of the evacuation of the city. Everything was still and, if not for the layers of dust upon every surface, everything was absolutely pristine. In fact, if the clear signs of nearly a decade of neglect were not apparent in the way of the dust and the overgrown plant life sustained by the oxygen recyclers working tirelessly throughout the city, then this scene could be mistaken for a calm night in the district.

Nathan led the way through after he had opened the gates using the screen mounted to his right forearm, with Cait and Tomen coming in behind, the other three and their dog arriving just after them, each one of them in near shock at the utter stillness of the place. The reception they had leaving the shipyards, entering that first district, where enormous hordes of undead creatures attacked so viciously was a stark contrast to this final step of the journey. After the Common district had been the Leisure, where they had had to venture underground, becoming buried alive in the effort to keep back the ceaseless waves of an enemy without rage or motive. This foe was nowhere to be seen now, where there were no signs of any movement of the slightest kind from any of the surrounding buildings that were all made of a tinted glass mounted in metal beams, appearing as giant towering mirrors. If entering the Leisure district had been a trial worthy of all their skills and experience, then leaving it was a test of their endurance, to keep pushing forward. They had rested, having taken stock of what they had seen, and gained a new ally along the way, they had taken the chance to better prepare themselves mentally for what may lie ahead. Not that any of them had predicted the flood. None of the team could have guessed that the Residential district could possibly pose even more threats, in the form of a need to improvise a path forward, defeating even the machinations of destruction on the way. Not to mention the undead, unrelenting in their hunt for the living that had dared to disturb their home, rising beyond number from the flood that had claimed that portion of the city. But all that lay behind them.

"Finally," Cait breathed a sigh of relief, her whole body ached, not just from the near constant need to protect herself, but also because she could feel every step she had needed to take to cross the breadth of the once Capital City. She was exhausted. Her hood, made from the kind of fibres used to reinforce the clothing of people looking for a battle, had torn slightly at its hem, while her black jumpsuit was riddled with muck and dried blood. The corset, crafted to perfectly frame her body and from the same material as an Elite's armour, had performed its job excellently, but was now heavy as her tiredness grew. If she could have used her enthusiasm to succeed as a fuel, that deep desire to liberate the region with whatever truth they came here to find, then she would have long since run empty. Her intentions were still intact but her curiosity and excitement had waned with every step with weariness and a desperation to survive replacing them. Yet having now arrived in the final leg of their journey, or so she thought, she felt a surge of importance take over her, the accountability of what they had set out to do, a feeling of rejuvenation as their purpose was too important for her to let being tired stand in her way.

"We still have no idea where we're heading, or do we?" Miles asked, giving Impala a stroke as he sat beside his leg, nuzzling the barrel of the rifle that dangled from tired arms.

"This way," Nathan said, turning back to face the others, taking note of their knackered state through the dark grey ovals on his otherwise entirely black helm that consumed the whole of his head. "There's a few places this vault of yours could be, but most likely is a bunker I was told was a power station, an installation under the Consolidated Systems banner, one of the only a handful of places I never figured to see inside."

"Then lead the way," Tomen announced, shouldering the butt of his rifle once more, identical to Miles in the form of a Stalwart Ironworks enforcer, with the battered dark green jacket hanging over armour of a light grey, with the opaque mask of the same colour with white eyes through which he gauged the way ahead.

The Directorate district opened up on a street lined with glass buildings, only just shy of the height of the shell that engulfed the entire Capital City, with trees and street lamps in a uniform pattern before them, decorating the pavements that ran parallel to the road. It was here where the gulf in class, the difference between the grafters and the ones who dictated their purpose in life, was most evident. Gone were the simple aesthetics of a city road, a strip of concrete leading from point A to point B. Gone as well were the quaint shops and market stalls, advertisements promoting better living by varying career paths, the smaller touches of independent creation, albeit under the COC brand. In their stead were banks, offices of those who held the power of directing the flow of the Coalition's resources, the better to facilitate their all-important contribution to the Board, and other buildings bearing no markings or billing. The very surface of the road was more prestigious, a shiny, smooth surface of hardened porcelain, cast in a dark grey, surrounded by ornamental rivers of golden shingle. With great plumes of green leavery, the trees that lined the sides of the roads stood tall and proud, no matter that their roots were manufactured, a forced means of having nature adorn this most esteemed district.

"Where're all the zombies? Shouldn't they 've jumped us by now?" Sam asked, never resting his eyes on one spot for too long before darting them in another direction, quick to shift his gaze at the slightest imagination of movement. It was the experiences of the earlier sections of the city that made the complete silence of this one far too tempting to trust, but too comfortable to believe in.

"Just keep your eyes open and your weapons ready," Nathan instructed, assuring the others, his own nerves steady and unwavering. "This section of the city was the first to be evacuated and is the furthest from the shipyards, it also has no gate out of the city to a highway."

"So you're saying it's no surprise it's empty, right?" Lena asked their protector, the silver sheen of the skin on her hands glistening with sweat as she gripped the pistol in her grasp tightly, anxious that it would be needed sooner rather than later.

"I'm saying appearances can be deceiving," the Elite Commander replied. "Don't trust the emptiness, they could just be held up in the buildings, but also, yes, there could be an explanation why there could be fewer of them this far into the city."

The band carried on along this street until it met a crossroads where they bore a right turn, heading down an identical road which took them in a bend heading left where they ventured further until they met a small open square. This square had four roads meeting it, one at each side, and bore a small dome at its centre. A perimeter of lights allowed for a glow that revealed small stone walls erected in a decorative fashion that lined the walkways leading up to this dome from all of these connected roads. Reaching up to the top of the shell were towers of glass and metal overlooking this square, seeming as if the very city itself were watching the team now, patient for them to unlock the secret it had kept for eight long years. The bunker was a basic design, a heavy looking bulkhead with a console at its side acting as its lock, with all of it cast in the same black metal that the Coalition used for all of its structures. Were they without the employee passcode retrieved from the Obsidian Captain Tobias Willis, the bulkhead appeared impossible to break down or otherwise bypass.

"This is the most secure power station I've ever seen," Tomen remarked, looking past the entrance to the bunker to see the small stretch of dark stone walls continue until they met the next street.

"This has to be it!" Lena looked over the door with her bright green eyes that were enriched with a feeling of getting closer to their goal.

"So shall we take a peek before we get our panties all wet over nothing?" Sam mocked, impatient, eager to know his prize was found.

"S'pose you're not wrong," Cait shrugged, "Nate, care to do the honours? We'll be needing your code too to get this thing open."

At the sound of his name, the Elite Commander slowly turned his gaze away from a point in the distance, looking at Cait then nodding before making his way over to the console. The ground was all too familiar to him, and he hadn't been expecting to tread on it again after that traumatic day when the city sealed itself. His boots made a droning thud with every step that he took, the weight of his armour lending to it so his movements sounded more powerful, his presence more intimidating than the skill he had displayed already cast in aura about him. His mind wandered, he continued towards the console without any sign that he was not in the present moment, instead casting himself back, reliving a memory he had long since locked away. Nathan had been there, been here, in the Directorate district at the moment the deafening general evacuation alarm sounded. It rang out from speakers so forlorn in their purpose that he could remember rumours that there were ideas to remove them, so long ago their meaning was forgotten. He reached the screen mounted into the framing of the dome, and swiped away the dust that layered across the keyboard under it with his gloved right hand. The console came alive as he pressed the keys, coding in his own passcode first before adding the Police Captain's to satisfy the standard two-colleague protocol the Coalition used. In bright red lettering on the screen, Nathan found that his access was successful, with the huff of air coming from the bulkhead adding to that fact.

"This better not be some elaborate box you hide your porn stash in, pal," Miles quipped, smiling to himself behind his mask as the other man turned to face him with a sharp step back, knowing full well he annoyed him.

"Cut it out, Miles, and be ready people, this could be it," Tomen ordered, training the sight of his rifle on the right hand edge of the doorway that started to open slowly.

Nathan strolled around the group, circling them before he too readied his weapon, taking his rifle off from behind his right shoulder where he had tucked it against his jetpack and held it steady, aiming at the growing gap between door and frame. The air that had blown out when the bulkhead had activated finished, leaving the only sound to be the creaking scream of metal on metal where the door came away at a crawl. While their exploring and navigating a path through the city that kept them alive had been fast, rarely a moment's peace, the thick, unyielding door moved at such an incredibly slow speed that it beggared belief.

"Sam, hey, go on, give it a pull, mate," Miles said, barely containing his laugh, trying to sound serious to not give away his sarcasm. "Help it along."

"Shut up, you dick," Sam laughed, his hands holding the grip and underbarrel of his shotgun, anxiously waiting for something, anything to come out and attack them.

But when the bulkhead opened fully, stretching out to nearly touching the other side of the framing, with the mouth of the bunker gaping wide, a deep shadow clouding any view of what lay within, nothing did come leaping out. The team looked to each other nervously, not knowing whether to wait and see if anything did show its face or to delve in, to see if they had surely discovered their quarry.

"I'll go first," Nathan announced a moment later, "Tomen, you're rear guard, we don't want more of those things to come and clog our exit."

"Yeah, gotcha, go ahead," the other man agreed, turning around, putting his back to the bunker as the others followed the one who stepped first into the shadowy abyss.

"We got stairs, mind your footing," Nathan warned the others, not distracting himself by taking his eyes away from looking forward, activating the torch he had at the side of his rifle's barrel.

It was a long way down. The steps spread out after the narrowing of the doorway, with stone white steps stretching out and leading down as far as they could see with no end in sight. Their footsteps echoed off the surface of the stairs just as stones would ripple the water when thrown into it, a fact they could do nothing about but something Nathan cursed silently to himself, not wishing to announce their presence any more than they had to. With every passing moment, every beat of his heart keeping a steady rhythm in his chest, the Elite Commander expected to see something, to have something spring out and attack him, such was the journey they had undertaken. Yet they travelled the length of the stairs in peace until finally they came down upon a floor of ceramic tiles, pure white and leading out into a corridor, but first, on the wall to the right of the steps was a control panel. Nathan held his rifle aimed down the length of the way ahead but knew they would benefit from some light so he threw on the safety catch and stowed his weapon. "Miles, keep your rifle handy," he said, turning away from the way forward.

"What you doin'?" The X-Human replied, with impala padding softly at his side, silently staring into the dark void that lay at their feet, the rest of the bunker shrouded to them.

"We need light," Nathan answered with a glance back at him as he opened up the catch in his right arm, taking out and unspooling a length of wire that he connected into the panel. The screen on his armour was the brightest thing down in the depths of the bunker as he programmed the interface to wake up the systems he found, giving power and life to the facility.

"Here we go," Cait murmured as the lights that ran along beams of metal above their heads flickered into letting out such intense brightness that it was blinding after the blanket of darkness they had become so used to.

"This is no power station," Sam stated, looking down the length of the corridor that began at their feet.

The floor was of white tiles that led along a straight path to an end some distance away where there appeared to be another set of stairs going down, while either side of this channel were rooms separated by frosted glass and rudimentary metal framing. Even the smell was different down here compared to the rest of the city. It was a clean scent, born from chemicals aloft air that tasted pure, not the vile atmosphere they had needed to choke down on the city surface. But the silence was still there. Not so much an alarm was to be heard, no computer sounds or anything, it was utterly silent to the point of deafening.

"This has to be it," Cait nodded, more to herself, "we actually made it, this is the vault, this is it!"

"Now we just gotta look through any crap we find, something's gotta be here to explain all that insanity topside," Miles agreed, patting Impala's head as the dog started to pant and wag his tail, far happier to find himself in some light.

"Whatever happens now cannot be undone," Nathan said, solemnly. "Cait, I need to go to my old office now. I need to get what I came to this city to retrieve, but I need someone to watch my back, that was our bargain."

"I remember," the purple-eyed X-Human muttered and for all her longing to help the man that had helped her so much by safely getting her to this place, she couldn't bear to pull herself away from the secret she was so close to holding in her grasp.

"I'll go," Lena put in as she recognised the conflict brewing behind her friend's eyes and decided for herself to remove the tough choice from her friend's mind.

"No, it could be dangerous, I'll go," Tomen shook his head and shifted his gaze to Nathan who was clearly fixing the other man with a solid stare from behind the plate of his helmet.

"Can't have that, Tomen," the Elite Commander laid down. "This is where the danger will be, the knowledge that's residing here, waiting to be unearthed. You saw that team of Elites get shot down over the old Obsidian base, you've been expecting the same thing I have, for a legion of whoever was firing those weapons to find us and give us a serious fight. They won't come after me and Lena as we won't be gone long enough to distract them from this place opening up. And trust me when I say this, Elias Thorne never did anything without a reason. If he caused the Capital Collapse, then the Obsidian battalion locked inside the city was no mistake, they were left here to guard whatever triggered it. Keep your wits about you and your weapon at the ready, the real fight is yet to come," and with that, Nathan beckoned Lena along with a nod and he turned and made for the stairs.

"You both come back," Cait called up to them, making the two stop only a couple of steps up the way. "Whatever happens up there, you both come back here safe and sound, got that?"

"Yes ma'am," Lena winked at her before following Nathan whose only reply was to give a slow upwards nod.

"I'll join them for a moment," Sam put in when he figured Nathan and Lena were out of earshot. "I'll contact Azuri, let her know we've found the vault," he offered, giving his all to sound as though he had no other intention.

"Alright, not a bad idea, mate, to be fair," Tomen nodded, "but we're going to press on, so don't take long," he said and watched the man in the red jumpsuit ascend the stairs in some haste, assuming he was trying to catch up with the other two.

"So how we getting to your office, Crimson?" Lena asked with a wink and a smirk, "is it far?"

"Not like this," Nathan grunted as he shrugged off the light teasing before wrapping his right arm around Lena's waist and taking off with his jetpack, soaring powerfully into the enclosed sky.

Sam reached the top just in time to see the other two leave, crouching down slightly so they wouldn't hear him come up and would miss him if they took a glance behind them. It was at this moment that a realisation hit him. He had just left the security of his family to step out into the Capital City all alone. He knew what he had come up here to do, and he told himself that it was for the good of his family, even though he was betraying their trust to do it. But he saw a bigger picture than that, by aligning with the Section Chief, he saw an opportunity to take leaps and bounds in a single step towards a life without worry or restraints. Growing up on the fields of artificial crops in the muck of Scarlet, Sam had fought with everything he had for every scrap of possession that he could call his own. Every comfort he had known had come after he had left that life behind, and he had to watch out for Obsidian police and Stalwart inquisitors ever since to keep what little he could glean from any job he took as a part of Tomen's team of WIDOWs. And in the deal struck, his family would be kept safe and provided for. The same family that had kept him safe to get to the finishing point in the city riddled with the kinds of monstrous beasts that he could never have imagined, that he had now stepped away from in order to finalise his betrayal. The question that knocked around his head as he drew out his tablet from inside his jacket was a simple one, 'are you sure you are doing the right thing?' And as he started up the imager to broadcast to the Section Chief, he had made his choice.

"Mr Cal, I'm assuming you're contacting me as you are indeed onsite?" The voice on the other end of the holographic imager was stern, powerful and strong, asserting dominance straight away as the illumination of him sitting behind his desk appeared from the tablet bar.

"Yes, Chief Thorne, I'm here at the bunker, we've only just got inside," Sam mumbled, stepping away from the way back down inside in case his voice carried.

"Good, very good, and where is Winter?"

"He's just left for the moment, he's gone to get some holo-diary or something from his old office but he'll be back quick—so how do I take care of him?"

"You are holding a shotgun, hmm?" Elias Thorne sat up slightly in his chair then produced a strange smile, half curling his upper lip in anger and half showing his teeth in a wicked grin. "You won't even scratch his armour with that pathetic thing."

"Exactly! I can't waste him with this, so how can I do it?"

"That's your side of our deal, Mr Cal. The way I see it, that's your problem to facilitate a solution to."

"Faci-what? Speak plai-please, sir!" Sam shook his head, he was getting frustrated but it was terror that was making him panic. If he couldn't kill Nathan, then he couldn't fulfil his side of the arrangement that he had made with the most powerful man in the region. He had to kill Winter and obtain the data in order to guarantee his and his family's safety. Anything short and he would dooming them to the wrath of the man whose image occupied the screen that lay in his quivering hands.

"It means figure it out," Elias sneered. "Or I will."

"What'd y'mean?"

"I mean, kill that fucking traitor and bring me my data plus any physical assets relating to the project and I will provide my end of the deal. Or I can easily send in a team of Elites to dispatch the lot of you and seize the project contents that way."

"Your Elites are dead, they were shot down over the Obsidian base at the city centre, Chief Thorne," Sam grumbled, taking a nervous glance over his shoulder at the stairs leading down then shifting his gaze about the rooftops.

"Really?" Elias asked, leaning back in his chair and taking his gaze away from the imager for a moment. "So he still lives, that's very interesting."

"What?"

"Never you mind," Thorne snapped his attention back to the man he saw as grovelling as his feet. "See through our arrangement, Mr Cal, or I can just as easily instruct my Obsidian fleet to bombard the city from orbit. Sure, it will decimate the facility and everyone in it, but there is always something that can be recovered."

"I'll get it done, sir," Sam's bottom lip quivered, he was realising that he was out of his depth, dealing with someone he had no idea about, and was playing him like an instrument.

"Do not disappoint me, Sam," Elias picked his tone perfectly, expressing his threat in slow, cold words that struck at the other man's spine, breaking any will that might be rallied against his wishes. "Would you like to know what happens should your team succeed and I fail to stop them?"

"I guess," Sam lost his thoughts, not expecting this.

"You may not be aware of this but there is a fracture in Obsidian. My Chief Admiral is running amuck with his fleet and has taken up arms against his colleagues and myself along with a fraction of the strength of the Sapphire conglomerate that has invaded our borders."

"Oh."

"Oh indeed, this is not pleasant news at all. You see, the data your team intends to leverage against me is very valuable to me and is also very dangerous. If released, it could spark a panic among the workers. Should they down tools for any particular amount of time, our contribution to the Board is affected. Do you know what will happen then?"

"No, sir."

"Well, then we're deemed to be unprofitable. It won't factor into the Chairman's thoughts that we were dealing with an incursion from a rival, nor will he consider that we had to quell an uprising which he would absolutely agree would need to be done. He would, however, convene a meeting in the Board controlled region of space at the heart of the tri-systems, bringing together the might of the Sapphire and Emerald companies, and I would not be invited to represent our fair Crimson. They will then arrive with all their strength to seize our assets, to give them to the Chairman so that he might decide their fate. And do you know what our key asset is, Mr Cal?"

"The crops, sir?"

"That's our product, little farmer boy, yes, but you are the asset that tends to it. Without people like you, there can be no contribution. People are our key asset, and that's what these other companies will swoop in to steal. The people. And do you know what happens then?"

"I don't know, sir."

"People will die. So you see, even if my hands are not the most ideal, or the most morally right, or whatever you may think of me—at least, I am keeping that contribution flowing, staving off something far worse that seems to be ebbing ever closer on the horizon. But now at least, I do expect you to understand the grand importance in your role in keeping your region safe, yes? People's lives rely on your success, and I do trust that you will not fail them? That you will not fail me?"

"I won't, I promise, Chief Thorne," Sam bowed his head to hide the tears welling in his eyes.

"You love your family," the other man teased.

"That's why I'm doing this, sir."

"In my own way, as am I," and with that, the broadcast ended and Sam was alone again.

"You can do this," Sam muttered to himself. The jumpsuit he wore that was once red because of the colour of the company it meant he served, now was mainly because of all the dried blood that had spattered against it as he battled the undead through the city. He used his sleeve to wipe away the wetness in his eyes and took a moment to steady himself. "Get a fucking grip," he growled at himself through gritted teeth. "Think of the life you'll have once you see this through. Think of the money, the women, the position. All of it. All of it, yours. Now fucking reach out and grab the cunt, will you?" He then dashed back inside, knowing he had been gone longer than he ought to have been.

Nathan hovered just outside the window to the level of the building he knew his office was on, with Lena gripping on tightly to him, standing on his right foot for balance. He took a moment, just to see if anything was moving behind that near impossible to see through glass but upon being satisfied, he moved them in closer. "Use the gun, break the window," he said to Lena, not needing to raise his voice, her head was right next to his.

"Ok," the X-Human replied, flicking her red hair out from her face before slamming the base of the handle on the pistol in her hand down hard on the glass, seeing it only splinter.

"It shoots bullets, too," Nathan grunted, impatient.

"Shut up, I know, this is quieter," Lena scowled, trying again then one more time and the glass gave in, shattering and allowing them entry into the building.

"I'm heading to my office, keep a keen eye," Nathan instructed as he hovered them in through the gap in the windows that were taller than they were, making it easy for them to glide in and for him to set her down before stepping onto the ground himself.

"Sure," she said, taking a moment to accept where she was. A decal was stuck on the far wall, past the many black desks where red chairs sat abandoned, and that emblem was of the Obsidian Elite Division, a fiery sword in front with those words embossed on top. She had spent recent years running and hiding from the kinds of people that once called this office their home, and now here she stood, waiting on the one who had turned his back on them, and now hunted them for sport.

Nathan remembered his way through the corridors as if it were only yesterday that he had done the same journey, reaching the double doors that opened up into the large corner office, the view out of the windows that were the walls gave him pause as he stepped inside. This used to be a second home. He had been a different man then, one who would be abruptly angered by the state of the thick layer of dust that covered every surface, as he once held a personal ideal that he ought to keep his own space clean before seeking to clean his city. The office was a good space, stretching far to his left and right, with wooden panelling adorning the concrete internal walls, and a large L-shape desk sitting directly opposite the doors, with a large, leather red chair sitting behind it. Even though it was through the material of his glove, his fingers remembered the surface of this desk as he ran them along it, feeling the roughness of it that was bent to the will of its maker to be impossibly smooth. The desk was carved out of pure obsidian rock, exported from Carmine, the home planet of the company that took the volcanic glass as its name. It was blacker than black, fuelled by the primordial components of that world. And it was beautiful and utterly unique for its natural colours and textures, making it the perfect companion for the Obsidian Elite Commander at the heart of the Capital City of the Crimson region.

The melancholy of the moment was interrupted when Nathan saw the golden card that was the object he had come here for. He picked it up, inspecting it in his hands, savouring having it back as he ran his fingers across the grooves cast into this small metal rectangular shape. It was gold but for a small black sphere at its centre, and as he leant back against his desk, Nathan gently pressed the two sides of sphere in to flatten out the card, and begin the holographic display being illuminated out from the top.

It was the laughter that struck cold at his heart as Nathan watched as the image of Monique was cast in its purple glow, holding the small Harkness in her arms, both of them so full of joy and full of life, smiles ornamenting their innocent faces. She had her hair over one shoulder while letting it flow over the other which was the focus of the young boy's excitement as he ran his fledgling fingers through the river of brunette hair. Together they were laughing, caught in a moment of bliss like nothing Nathan could remember nowadays as he stared through the visor of his helmet at the days long since lost to him. "Put that thing away, Nate, we're almost at the lake," Monique was saying, "I need you to take him or I'll drop him!"

"Alright, let's swap," an all too familiar voice replied, and the image being projected swung round at the same time as the small child was awkwardly handed over and now a man was holding him, young and handsome, a certain confidence behind that grin. "Well done, Harkness, long hair's no good in a fight, gives you something to cling onto," the man said to the child in his arms with a wink.

"Don't encourage him," the mother laughed, holding the imager to film the father and son.

"What? You afraid he'll turn out more like his dear old dad than his polite and perfect mum?" The younger Nathan joked behind a smooth smile, the sort of smile a person frames when they are truly alive in that particular moment, no distractions or worries, purely present and with no other place clutching at them to be.

"Shut up, Nate," Monique laughed, "no, I don't think he will, I think he'll grow up to be a fine man, show you how it's done," she said, the imager thrown forward as she firmly poked the end of Nathan's nose.

"No fun being good and kind, son, these systems will take you for all you got if you stand idle and do nothing, better to be like me, strong and capable of anything," a tiny hand reached up and stroked against the skin on the father's clean shaven cheek.

"You know, one of these days, you're gonna give more people than me a chance, Nate."

"Who needs them? I've got the most beautiful woman in the tri-systems at my side and this rather dashing young man in my arms, I have everything I need right here."

The recording ended as Nathan watched the younger version of himself reel in his wife so that all three were fitted into the image, all of them smiling, all of them so full of an optimistic view of what the future held for them. Never once considering that there could be those seeking to deprive them of that bright fate. Back in the silence, back in the lonely dark of this alien room to the Nathan of the present day, the Elite Commander shut off the holo-diary after blinking his gaze away from the image it projected, hastily stashing it away in a pouch at his belt. He barely recognised himself. The one in the diary had been him, still violent, still of a bloody history predating the loss of his family, and yet it felt like a completely different person entirely. It was the similarities that brought out the stark differences. The confidence of being willing to fight and yet have people in his life that he was not willing to live without, having something so meaningful to lose, it was a contradiction that confused this present day Nathan. He stood up, pacing away from the desk and looking back on it, but not finding any sentiment in looking at the place he had spent so much of his time nearly a decade ago. This Nathan didn't understand the attachment, the willingness to accept being vulnerable, to accept the feeling of it, it left a pit in his stomach. But then the cause of the feeling flipped. He used to not be alone. He used to have people that he loved, that he trusted, he was capable of that. The question rattling around in his mind now was if he still was. Cait, Tomen, Lena, Miles, Sam and Azuri, even Xin, possibly Siobhan, all people he had come into contact with and not killed, was there a motive in that that he didn't realise, he couldn't say. Thinking on the X-Human with the beaming purple eyes, brown hair and the fire inside to say things to him that he would never expect anyone else to have the gall to say, Nathan had to admit, maybe there was something of the younger him still left. Maybe there was a chance that he could grow attachments again.

The sound of a gunshot echoing down the hallways to him shook him violently out of his passage of thought, slamming him into a memory he scarcely wished to register as his own. Gunfire all around him, plumes of smoke as tall as the sky, the heat of the fires cooking him inside his armour, and the bodies of the dead outnumbering the living that paraded through the streets of Dunnfink eight years ago. Nathan remembered the feeling that consumed him that day. It was the mistrust that caused his mind to burn. Kept away from the hushed and secretive conversations of those with power, his own people given their instructions at the same time as he learned of them, and then it was the sight of the Police Captain pointing, standing on the overpass coming from the Capital, and he was directing them towards Nathan's old home. There were many houses between the entrances to the small town as it had been in those days and Nathan's own home but he somehow knew what might happen next. His own people turned against him, blocking his path, trying to stop him, throwing themselves at him but none could withstand his strength and he powered through them, taking to the sky in his jetpack. But when he burst through the door to his home and saw what the people he had trusted had done to his wife and son, something inside him shattered.

Two sides of himself went to war, the one capable of letting people in, and the one who saw nothing but pain from doing so, and Nathan stood absolutely still as stone, with the hardest battle he had fought in days taking place inside his head. Letting people in again, after what it had cost him, seemed a bad idea, it seemed like something that he despised yet craved at the same time. Now the question in his mind was this, were people worth trusting? And without answering, he left, a slight guilt at the way he had turned away from the image of the holo-diary but it was too painful to realise just now. He didn't glance back at his desk either, knowing those days were done.

"Nothing I couldn't handle," Lena said with a smirk, her pistol in hand, bodies of the undead scattered about her feet on the floor. "Guess you got what you came for?"

"I did," Nathan grunted, still wrapped in his own thoughts, contemplating whether attachment was worth the price of the sickening feeling in his stomach when he considered being vulnerable again. But at the sight of one of the most beautiful women he had ever seen, silver skin bringing out the colour in that luscious red hair that was tied up at the back, framing those bejewelled, shining green eyes, Nathan felt the pull of going in a certain direction. He recognised this one as a friend, volunteering for the risk of staving off the undead so that he could know a moment's peace. If he were capable of recognising what he was feeling now as he passed next to the X-Human, looking at her all the while, then he would know it was gratitude. A feeling that acted as a doorway to greater meaning. Yet he shrugged off such thoughts, honing his mind to the idea that he still needed to be aggressive and protective, something he couldn't be while distracted by such things. So he brushed them aside, taking Lena back in his arms as they hopped out of the gap in the glass they had made to enter, before taking off with a rampant uplift from Nathan's jetpack.

Chapter 21

Not all of the rooms were lit, some were left to wither in shadows with only the barest red ambience from the emergency power, but for the most part the vault seemed fully powered up. Cait, Tomen and Miles stepped carefully down the centre avenue that ran down the spine of the bunker, with the rooms coming off to their left and right. Other than the thudding of their hearts, the only other sound to be heard were the soft padding of Impala's paws against the tiling on the floor, no one wishing to break that silence for the grim things they witnessed, starting from the first room. Here, the lights worked, this lab as it appeared to be was all in a bright white setting, except for the heap of intestines laying rotten and stinking on the surface of the large table that sat at the room's centre. Workstations surrounded it, all abuzz with data and graphs detailing the work being carried out to study the body that was suspended with chains above this table, with no way of telling when the innards had come spooling out. The once golden skin of this X-Human male had turned to a retching blend of green and brown, disformed from its exposure in being allowed to decompose fully open as it was. Its eyes were removed, once of a gleaming amber yellow, they lay on a silver tray beside a monitor that kept a live recording of the state of these decayed orbs. "What were they doing here?" Cait murmured, looking to the others for any kind of explanation but they were aghast, too.

"Something unnatural," Miles eventually answered, stepping up to the table and placing both hands on the surface, caught in a trance as he stared up at the body hung with no regard to respecting the person this once was. Impala let out a moaning sound before huddling down at the room's entrance, the smell of the corpse being too much for the dog, but the sight of the decomposing exhibition was too distracting to notice that he needed some comforting.

"Says here they were inspecting something called the 'X-Human phenomenon'," Tomen read out from one of the monitors, his voice hoarse with disgust. "They were studying this body and cataloguing the changes the body went through after death, but whatever for?"

"If there's a reason for doing something as barbaric as this, I'm not sure I want to know that could be." Miles turned away, closing his eyes for some time, desperately trying to conjure ideas on the level of anguish his fellow X-Human might have gone through before being suspended in a lab for study. When he opened them, he saw Sam standing at the entrance to this room, eyes wide and mouth open, Miles could even see him shaking.

"What is this?" The newcomer mumbled, looking at Cait.

"Whatever they did to force the Old City to close, they did it right here," she replied, "and this has to have something to do with it."

"Yeah but what? When you said vault, I figured it for some luxury safe room of the Section Chief's, where he kept his private data and trinkets of worldly value, not this freakshow," Sam shrieked, pointing at the body as if he were needed to point it out.

"Yeah, well, nothing to be learned here," Tomen stated, running his eyes over the poor suspended soul one last time before turning away, "we need to check the other rooms."

Cait was the last to leave the first room they had seen. The sight of the man hung by chains bound so tight at his wrists that the skin had ruptured so the metal was half underneath the flesh was sickening. Yet it was exactly what she had come here to find. The secret behind the Capital Collapse was here. No matter how grisly it was, no matter what horrible things she would need to witness to discover it, she was willing to find it. She had to, she had dragged her family this far.

The next room was not so well lit, only for the red light in the corner acting as a sign that this section was running on the low drip-feed of the emergency systems were the team able to see the peculiar sight that awaited them. Up against the far wall, constructed from the same metal used to house the frosted glass that separated the rooms, was a fountain, kin to the one they set eyes on back at the entrance to the city in the Common district. Water was cast into the air from a central spout and frolicked into the pool below, all while a monitor next to it measured the balance of chemicals supposedly residing in the water. "What do you think this was for? Doesn't really fit," Miles said, stroking the smoothness of the material used to create the attractive piece of blackened metal.

"Won't claim to understand the things on that screen, but even I can tell that ain't your average water, something's been done to it," Tomen winced under his helmet, remembering how that colossal beast had tackled him into the river earlier in the city. "They've tainted it somehow."

Impala trotted up to it but bared his teeth once he had taken a whiff of the water, not trusting it to even take in the smallest drink, and he barked angrily, making the others jump slightly. His tail went still, his claws gripped the tiles laid into the floor and his eyes locked onto the fountain, it looked as though he was prepared for a fight.

"Easy, lad," Miles comforted his friend by approaching him steadily before brushing his hand along his side then going to rub him between the ears. "Any ideas what they did?"

"None," Cait went to run her fingers through the water but shied away, "but whatever they did, if they somehow poisoned the water supply..."

"Then the evacuation alarm would sound, clearing the city before they all drink it and feel the effects of whatever it was, at least as early as it could," Tomen agreed, nodding. "Maybe it went off just in time to stop the rest of the population from drinking it, they were too busy running for their lives."

"OK, but what'd they add to it? I can't understand any of this crap," Sam remarked, trying to unpuzzle the chemical makeup that was displayed on the monitor screen.

"What were they doing here that could poison an entire city?" Miles wondered aloud before he pressed on, back in the centre channel, onward to the next room.

Here there was another body, this time laid on a table identical to the one before, a female X-Human, with the chest and stomach peeled back so that it was entirely open, with the organs and muscles all labelled with different colour flags stuck into the flesh. Paperwork attached to clipboards were littered about the table, with notes left where they had fallen on the floor, and monitors still bearing the last piece of data input into them, all to do with the study of this body. "Any guesses what any of this shite means?" Sam asked, mindlessly tossing a clipboard bearing a page from a researcher's notebook, not understanding the anatomical graph sketched on it.

"They're all X-Human," Cait stared into the eyes still inside the woman's skull but the light from those blue jewels had gone out so many years before, and she dared not imagine what they had seen before that.

"That has to have some significance," Miles said, standing beside his friend. "It's no secret Elias Thorne is no big supporter of the X-Human community, there's not a single one among his directorate."

"True, and then there's this," Tomen picked up a clipboard beside the woman's heavily decomposed feet. "These are notes left by someone who worked for RCS, they were studying the effects of the X-Human body from the terraforming procedure. Says here, that the X-Humans inhabited the tri-systems before the Board arrived, and had to adapt to the new climates being introduced, or become extinct." He flicked through the pages, not believing what he was reading, the heartlessness of it. "It goes on to say that they were curious about how the X-Humans evolved to withstand the changes to their atmosphere, how their bodies endured the shock, and they settled on something called the 'X-Human phenomenon thesis', but there's no explanation for what it means."

"X-Human phenomenon?" Miles took off his helmet, throwing it to one side, sending it skidding across the floor. "These scum were experimenting on X-Humans, and for what? Scientific curiosity?" The golden shine of his skin that marked him as a male of his race turned dull as his emotions took a sinister turn, "there's nothing that can justify this."

Tomen took his helmet off in kind, seeing the pain in his friend's eyes, "I know, and I agree. That's why we're here. To find out what happened to these souls and the countless others that died from the Capital Collapse."

"The big 'why' of it all," Cait murmured, "what could have possessed them to do these things?"

"You can't buy anything with reasons, guys," Sam shrugged, "better we just grab whatever we can, pry up some good equipment to sell, and make ourselves scarce, surely it's time we leave this city in the dust and get a move on."

"Not yet, Sam," Cait shook her head, "so far all we've seen is what was left behind by whatever they did, we still haven't found what actually done all this, or any evidence."

"Then let's move on," Tomen instructed and just as he was about to step out into the corridor, Nathan appeared, and would have knocked him over if Tomen hadn't sprung back in surprise. "Fuck me, where'd you come from?"

"Find anything out yet?" Nathan asked in his low pitched, authoritative tone, while Lena tucked in behind him.

"They were researching something they refer to as the 'X-Human phenomenon', heard of it?" Cait couldn't help a smile grow when she saw that the two had returned safe.

"Can't say I have," the Elite Commander replied, peering all around. "The architecture of this place lends to an RCS facility but this is like nothing I've ever seen."

"This place is a horror show," Lena blurted out in a tone which suggested she felt as though she were correcting him. "They were torturing X-Human people, what the fuck?"

"We haven't found any evidence yet," Miles added, "We should carry on."

Reunited as a full team, they passed through to the next room which was laid out not as a lab but rather as an office space, with a wooden desk sitting at its heart and filing cabinets lining up against the far wall. Red carpet took over where the white tiles ended and the walls were decorated with pictures of landscapes from all of the different planets that make up the Crimson region. A monitor was situated on top of this desk, facing the other wall but as Lena passed around to see what was on it, her eyes widened and she took a sharp intake of breath. "What is it?" Cait asked her as they all entered the room.

"This was Elias Thorne's office, back when he was Director of Ruby Consolidated Systems, before he was Section Chief," Lena replied and tentatively touched the keyboard placed in front of the monitor, seeing the screen come to life, removing the owner's name and replacing it with an array of folders. One was labelled the 'X-Human phenomenon thesis'. "Guys, we have it, it's here."

"What's here?" Sam asked, hiding the nervousness in his voice and channelling a great deal of energy into not taking a nervous glance at the heavily armed and armoured Elite Commander at his side.

"Thorne created the thesis and wow—"

"What?" Tomen was gazing at a picture from his home planet of Sanguine, of one of the thriving forests there but turned his head when Lena stopped.

"We have his holo-diaries, all of them, from back in the days just before the Collapse," Lena explained.

"Let's have a look," Cait couldn't help the excitement in her voice, she knew she was so close to realising their success in this city.

"Where do we start?" Lena shrugged, taking up the large red leather chair and scanning through the different files.

"Look for the more recent files, Lena," Nathan suggested, stepping up to the desk and removing his helmet, placing it down there. "See if there's anything marked as ongoing as well."

"Here's one," she replied, looking past the monitor for a moment, up at the ceiling, "and looks like we're linked up to an imager, hang on," she tapped some more keys and an image of Elias Thorne came raining down from above. He was far younger, as he would have been eight years ago when the diary was recorded but his visage, even in the purple hue of the holographic imager, was undeniable. Nathan stepped up to meet the image being projected from the ceiling, nose to nose with the man that ruined his life, but didn't let even one emotion flicker onto his face as he glanced back at Lena.

"Play it," he instructed, his tone strong and booming.

"Day 142 of the X-Human phenomenon research stage. The latest test subjects have all been processed and the autopsy outcomes are complete. While the X-Human subjects have all proven the already known differences to human physiology, no evidence has been found to suggest a source that generates the prolonged presence of the soul after death. We have had confirmed reports of this phenomenon having taken place that are all consistent in stating that a strong connection between the two individuals involved is essential for this event to occur. However, replicating this trait for humans to experience is proving troublesome. So far we have been unable to identify a means to harness this ability and produce a synthesised facsimile so that we can achieve our goal for prolonging and strengthening the physical state for all members of the highest hierarchy in the COC. If we are able to manufacture a means of extending life, then we can secure a far stronger position within the tri-systems. It's disappointing that the Board disapproved of these efforts, it adds to my already strong suspicions that the Chairman is in fact an X-Human—"

"Interesting," Nathan grumbled to himself.

"The Chairman could be X-Human?" Sam asked openly.

"Well, no one knows," Tomen shrugged, "we don't even know if it's a he or she, we know nothing about them."

"It's said during Board meetings he is never physically present, always represented by a solid silhouette on a screen with his voice dubbed," Nathan nodded. "I've always been curious who our mysterious overlord is, and it seems like Elias was, too."

"Well, he was definitely curious," Lena said, reading the screen and nodding. "The next entry is just text but it's a load of guesswork about the Chairman, and he's talking about needing to 'vivisect the spiritual nature of the X-Humans', whatever that means."

"What does vivi-whatever actually mean?" Sam shied away from looking at the now frozen image of the younger Elias Thorne, he couldn't stand having even a hologram of the man so close to him as to be in the same room.

"Kinda like an autopsy, yeah?" Lena explained, looking up at the man. "But the poor soul is alive durin' it."

"Fucking," Sam swore, expelling a deep breath and holding his sides, knowing that the man capable of desiring such a thing was holding his future in his hands should he succeed in his own private goals.

"Anything else?" Nathan wondered, not interested in the whims of someone he had long since deemed deranged.

"Yeah, hang on," Lena scrolled through the dates of the holo-diaries, looking for anything marked by a white star as her eyes strained from the old quality of the terminal monitor, not used to this older technology. Cait was beside her, kneeling down to be at her height and her hands were beginning to shake. "Here's something."

The hologram of Elias Thorne suddenly shifted position and stance, showing that a new recording was set to play, with Nathan still standing just before him, as though the two were about to have a heated discussion. "Day 168, with all the theories on the physical aspects returning nothing to work on, we have to explore the possibility that this could be a phenomenon that manifests from the spirit of an X-Human, not their physical being. I have tasked a team with investigating this avenue of research on two fronts. One is the route of invading an X-Human's mind using pharmaceuticals, while the other is far more complex. I've used all my resources with the RCS to uncover ancient X-Human sites where we have excavated herbs and objects, all used in a wide variety of rituals and potion craft. If we can harness those secrets, primeval rites that they are unwilling to share, a clear sign that there is something hidden in those indistinguishable babble that they come out with and those odd, rare products of the worlds before the terraformings, then that might be our route to success."

"What X-Human sites? I didn't understand any of that," Miles remarked, glancing down at his dog that left his side to sniff at the electronically produced image of the man, which seemed to baffle Impala to the point where he retreated back.

"Some kind of settlement before the humans arrived maybe?" Cait couldn't help sounding unimpressed, this wasn't what they were looking for and it didn't suggest a cause for the Collapse. "In any case, it's no use to us."

The image of Elias Thorne changed again, this time striking up as someone who seemed obviously stressed and dismayed, the uniform he was wearing of a suit was in some untidy state as the next holo-diary began to play. "Day 243 and the Section Chief, my ignorant loser of a father, Roderic Thorne, wants me to pull the plug. I am the Director of RCS, I say where I assign my assets and resources to. He wants us to abandon this project to shift our focus onto more 'lucrative undertakings' like upgrading the robo-sentries, expanding our range of security robotics. But the idea of leaving our X-Human thesis unfulfilled? Especially when we are so close. My vanguard researchers disagree, the incompetent scum, they request more time to run further tests but how? When we are out of time. And even if we weren't, there would be no guarantee on the results we would need to persuade my father of the need for this project to continue. How do I relinquish this grand opportunity to set my name into history? Should we succeed, not only will I beat the impossible and achieve my own personal needs, but we will produce a product that neither of the other conglomerates could possibly compete with. Our contribution would be so strong, to grant enhanced strength, robustness and a longer life, our product would have them on their knees begging for the most minute essence of it. We will establish the Crimson at the top of the hierarchy, not even the Chairman can deter the wave of demand there will be for our labours. Nor can my father, the failed Section Chief, stand in my way or his pet, Winter." Nathan's blank expression never changed, he didn't so much as blink. "No, not even that scum that father thinks should be Chief after him. Really, father? You choose a malignant psychopath over me! Yes, General Ardamus has taken a liking to him as well, and his parents are high up officers in Obsidian as well, but what about me? I am Director of the company who are recording the highest levels of quality contribution since recording began! And when I reveal this project's end fulfilled, there will be no stopping my campaign to greatness."

"This dude's got a serious ego problem," Miles sighed.

"Just a prick, they all die the same," Tomen shrugged in response.

"There's more," Lena pointed out.

"Day 245 and we have our method for testing the new prototype that has so far exceeded all expectations. We will use the city water network to disperse the product to all of the Capital citizens, they will be our test subjects, refer to Project V-1889 for details."

"So it was in the water, they poisoned everybody?" Cait mused aloud.

"Looks like it must have happened quickly because the evacuation alarm kicked in, or else everybody might've died," Tomen carried on the thought, "so what's this project he's meaning?"

"It's right here," Lena scrolled to the very bottom of the list of holo-diary entries to the one marked by the project number. "Oh my, that's no random number, it took them one-thousand-and-eighty-eight failures before they arrived at their prototype. So many people must've had to die for their tests, this is like, way, way, beyond fucked up."

"Lena, what's this project?" Nathan asked, cutting through the emotions in everyone's tones by using a calm, measured one of his own that made the others feel uneasy.

"It's a written report, hang on," the pupils within her emeralds for eyes flicked across the screen as she read but she shook her head, "I don't understand any of this."

"What does it say?" Nathan demanded, turning away from his staring into the projected face of Elias Thorne to lean over the desk, putting his weight onto its surface in two fists, the dark grey ovals marking his eyes pointing directly at the woman.

"It's an RCS project," Cait read, taking over from her friend who held her mouth in her hand as she continued to try to decipher some logic from what she was reading. "It was formed under Elias Thorne's direct authority and supervision. And he states it as a potion? Weird but that's what he refers to it as."

"Continue."

"Sure," she said, glancing up at him. "It's a liquid," Cait shrugged. "But it needs some kind of ancient X-Human ceremony to 'activate' it, whatever that means. And he says it's X-Human magic combined with scientific inquiry, which sounds perfectly sane and all. But, and here we go, it's a product designed to strengthen the human soul, as he puts it, it's meant to mean they can live longer, be stronger—but wait! He says it right here!"

"Says what, Cait? Cut it out with the suspense," Miles scoffed but was looking curiously at Impala to meet Cait's annoyed glance, as the dog was turned towards Sam and completely still.

"Thorne notes that the prototype could be toxic if it fails but the use of the water supply provided him with a test sample large enough to record clear results even if that should happen, which it fucking did. The mother-fucker knew even before he done it."

"What else?" Tomen asked, also picking up on the dog's awkward stance, casting a suspicious glance to Sam who seemed to be the only one in the room finding it a single degree above too warm for comfort.

"He notes that should the product be overwhelmingly toxic and produce a large enough fatality rate then the general evacuation alarm could be triggered as it would think it would be detecting a terraforming failure. Thorne even describes the lockdown, seeing it as a viable option as the purpose of it is to seal up the assets and resources stored here so they can be recovered. I mean, this clearly shows he meant to continue the work even if it failed, this has to be the proof we need. We need to copy all of this!"

"I've got a data card," Sam shrugged but he let slip his nervousness, his voice sounding just ever so slightly higher pitch than normal, and on realising this, he scrambled for more to say. "Nabbed it off some cunt back on the Forerunner, looks like it could come in handy right about now, huh?" He smirked in a cocky fashion, removing the smooth silver card from a pocket inside his jacket.

"No need," Nathan dismissed, turning away from the frozen image of his enemy. "I can plug straight in and download it to my armour's computer, much safer that way, too."

"Yeah but," Sam stammered as he watched the other man circle around to the main console of the terminal, plugging into using a cable he revealed from his right forearm. "Shouldn't we have a backup, just in case, say?"

Nathan fixed the other man with a stare that gave nothing away to what he was thinking or intending, it was an entirely blank look, but after a moment's pause he flicked his eyebrows, "couldn't hurt, I suppose."

"Yeah, I mean, why not, eh? 'Ere, should be a slot there," Sam passed the card to Cait who input the data card into the terminal, albeit while fixing him with a bemused look.

"There's one more entry, a last one by the looks of it," Lena stated, "as it's dated the day of the Collapse."

"No need to play it right now, just transfer it across," Nathan said calmly, looking over at Tomen who was giving Miles an upwards nod that the Elite Commander understood, a signal to be ready. He unplugged as soon as his screen told him the data was secure and he stepped away from the desk, all the while Sam's attention was fixed on Cait moving the files over to the data card, not seeing Nathan approach Tomen and whisper something in his ear.

"How we doing?" Sam asked Cait, leaning over the desk so much he was practically lying on top of it trying to see the progress of the transfer on the monitor more clearly.

"This takes time, Sam," Cait answered him but not taking her eyes away from the screen.

"You can't make it go any faster?" He pressed, his voice more intense, his breaths sharper and the desk creaked as he tightened his grip on its edge.

"No, not really, Nate's armour was already linked to the system, the data card is being swept for malware before I can raise it to transfer the files," Cait looked past Sam to Tomen who was nodding to Miles to stand in the doorway, while he took out his imager from inside his tattered green jacket.

"Cait, give me the data card," Sam stood back from the desk with a deep breath and stretched out his left hand.

"What'd you mean bunker?" A different voice asked, causing everyone not affiliated with the plan to dart their attention to Tomen who stood with his right hand ready on the trigger of his rifle that hung loose from a strap around his shoulders, and in his left was his imager, projecting an image of Azuri.

"No!" Sam gasped, and produced a pistol as quick as the eye could see from having it tucked inside his jacket, aiming it directly at Nathan's head. "You just stay back!"

"So I take it Sam didn't let you know we arrived at the vault?" Tomen asked the woman whose image he held in his hand, where she was sitting in the pilot's chair, staring directly down the lens.

"No? Baby, what's all this about? You're scaring me," Azuri replied as her eyes zipped around the room, hastily trying to catch up with what was transpiring.

"Yeah I'm scared myself right now, but all will become clear," Tomen answered coolly, striding between Sam and Nathan, the gun poised across that space aimed at his head for a single, tantalising moment as he crossed the room to place the imager down on the desk so that Azuri could see what was happening. "Sam," he said, slowly turning back to him, ignoring the presence of the gun, "is there something you wish to say?"

"Not exactly, mate," Sam shook his head then banged his free left hand down hard on the desk, "Cait," he said, glancing down at her, "give me the fucking card."

"Can't do that, Sam," she retrieved the data card, the download complete, and held it in her right hand, clasping Lena's hand with her left.

"What did he offer you?" Tomen asked Sam, giving a slight nod in the direction of the illuminated younger image of the Section Chief.

"A future," the man in the red jumpsuit of Crimson Sun replied, "which is more than what you're in for with him." Sam kept the gun trained on Nathan who didn't seem at all fazed by it. "Death follows you, Winter, and I ain't about to let me and mine dawdle down that little road along with ya."

"What'd you do, Sam?" Miles brought his rifle up, fighting the compelling feeling in his muscles to raise it further and blast the head off his friend that betrayed him. "How'd you fuck up?"

"I made a deal, mate. I made a deal with the Chief, a deal that protects all of us, and gives us a far brighter future than whatever this shitfuck has in store for us," Sam's hand that gripped his gun was beginning to shake, he hadn't expected to need to hold it up for so long.

"What you talking 'bout?" Lena scorned, "the fuck you mean deal? With the same fucker you just saw talking about murdering thousands, millions maybe and calling it just fine and fucking dandy?"

"He said he'd protect us," Sam spat back. "He promised us executive positions, all of us! That's luxury and security like nought we've ever known.

And all we gotta do is waste this piece of crap and give Chief Thorne what he wants, which is that little data card right there."

"And what? Forget what we just saw? Are you fucking for real here, Sam?" Cait shouted, "Thorne murdered more than half the population of this city! And you've seen what happened to some of the survivors! You really think any kind of pampered shite will help you sleep at night, knowing you let the guy who's responsible for it all go free? We have what we need to do something about it, right here! Let's just do what we set out to do! Use this evidence," Cait brandished the card, standing up, waving it violently. "And show the people of this region why the Collapse really happened! And with the sure fire motivation they'll get, we can start a real revolution, we can burn out the sickness that's been plaguing our home for years! The corruption can end with this, don't you see? We can set people free!"

"Your head's full o' bollocks if you think that can ever happen, love," Sam dismissed, shaking his head but not blinking away from staring down the barrel of his gun at Nathan that, to his complete confusion, still wasn't making a move to avoid the sights of his weapon.

"Gotta dream, Sam!" Cait pleaded, "What else can we do? I dream of the tri-systems ending the boot-on-neck of the work contracts we're all tethered to. And I reckon here's the thing that gets me one step closer to seeing that dream a reality, and I want you there with us, every step of the way. You're like an older brother to me, you're a part of this family!"

"It's for this family that I made the deal!" The corners of Sam's eyes began to moisten with tears as his frustration grew.

"No, mate, you sold us out," Miles corrected him.

"Miles is right on this one," Tomen agreed, "put down the gun, Sam."

"Yeah sure, then this one kills me," meaning Nathan who still stood absolutely calm and disinterested, "that's why I've gotta kill him."

"You ain't done nothing yet," Lena reminded him. "There's still time to make this right, drop the gun, Sammy."

"If you ain't taking a cock in it, keep your fucking mouth shut, whore," Sam swore, banging the desk again with his left fist. "Enough of this shit, I am doing this for all of you, why can't you see that? This fucker is a fucking monster! And to go up against the bloody Section Chief? Are you all completely mad? Cait! Give the fucking data card, now!"

"No, Sam," Cait muttered.

"Fine," Sam sighed, "but I'll do what I must." His finger was sweaty but his grip on the trigger of his weapon was firm, and he was ready. But what the man at the end of his sights chose to do, froze him, forced him to hesitate, he didn't understand.

Nathan blinked slowly and approached calmly. The steps from the burden of his armour rang against the floor as he crossed the gap to near place his forehead against the barrel of the weapon raised against him. He shifted his head to one side so it was of a clearer view to the other man, sighed and then with a flick up of his eyebrows, he simply said, "weak." And with that, the Elite turned his back, stepping away, seemingly signing off on the tedious affair.

"Well, I'm sure I speak for all of us when I say I'm glad we finally hear your detailed thoughts on this matter, Nate," Lena groaned, fixing Nathan with a disapproving glare as she huffed.

"You brought me along to deal with external threats," Nathan dismissed, "this one I leave to your discretion, Tomen, as leader of this group, unless you would rather I settle this matter in your stead?" He asked, knowing full well the other man knew what outcome that would be, but the former Stalwart man stood confident.

"No thank you, Mr Winter, but you are quite right, this is indeed an internal matter," Tomen agreed, stepping away from where he had placed down his imager on the desk and placing himself between Nathan and Sam's gun, accepting those sights aiming delicately between his eyes.

"Tomen, get outta the way," Sam pleaded, the tears in his eyes more evident now.

"Sam, you betrayed all our trust," Tomen began, removing his hand from the trigger guard of his rifle, using the sling to throw the weapon across his back so that he appeared unarmed to the man before him.

"No, no, I did more than you even, I protected this family," Sam wept.

"No, Sam, you've put us more in harm's way than ever before, or were you real naive to believe that a man capable of justifying mass murder would know honour enough to uphold a deal that he doesn't see an inkling of benefit to?"

"I don't know mate, he wants Winter dead, his research back. I actually think he'd reward the fella brave enough to hand those things to him on a silver platter."

"All you'd be handing him is your life and ours, exposed from the shadows that we call our home."

"And all this isn't that? You're standing in the fucking Capital, Tomen, on the brink of a war! We live in a fucking corporate society, we shouldn't even have the concept of a war! We live in a system that rewards individuals, the brave, the bold, the unapologetic few that reach out and seize an opportunity, not pander to psychopaths and be a means to an end for them, am I right, Winter? Got what you came for, buddy? Ready to off us all now?"

"Actually that's what I like most about my new friend here, come to think of it," Tomen smiled, looking back at Nathan who only shrugged and stepped towards the two X=Humans cowering behind the desk. "If he wanted us dead, he'd just do it," Tomen turned back to Sam with an honest smile, "it's as straightforward as that really, so us being alive, means he wants us that way, and there's a comfort to be had in that."

"Doesn't mean he won't change his mind," Sam's grip on his weapon was beginning to make the trembling in his arm more noticeable, as unpractised as he was in holding up a weapon for a prolonged amount of time, just as Tomen had planned.

"What, like you did? To turn against your own family?"

"It wasn't like that! I secured a future for us! We could have everything, real food, real homes, women beyond counting, we could all grow fat, old and rich together! The worlds be damned, this would be us set for life!"

"That's just your dream," Tomen strode forward a pace and growled through his teeth. "By handing over that data card, you'd rob us all of a chance at freedom like none we've ever known, ever dreamed of. We'd all be dead in a heartbeat once Elias Thorne has what he deems to be his. But this truth belongs not to him, or to us. It belongs to everyone, to the folks we drank with on the Forerunner, to the people still living the trauma of what happened in this city, to the poor souls tending the farmlands where you came from. The truth will set them all free, it is not yours to bargain with, and nor are our lives. Sam, this family, you've just lost the most valuable thing you could've known in your life, and it was all your choice."

"No!" Sam screamed, not able to hear those words. Words that cemented that he had lost the very thing he gave up everything to preserve, and he went to fire his weapon, Tomen being so close, he could see the disdain in the other man's eyes. But he didn't see Impala approach, blinded by his focus being fixed on the man standing right in front of him, and by Nathan covering the dog's movement as it slipped around the desk to gain a better position in which to strike. And the timing was perfect. The gun did go off, a shot was fired, but the bullet harmlessly splintered into the glass of the wall behind Tomen creating a radiant, rippling pattern as if a stone landed in water. Sam's right arm, the gun still in the grasp of that hand, was locked in the jaws of the dog, wrenched down, bathed in blood as the man writhed in agony, until the hunk of metal finally dropped to the floor.

"Impala, that'll do boy, there's a good lad," Tomen gave the dog a scratch between the ears as he passed, returning to Miles' side.

"You're choosing Winter over me?" Sam bellowed, cradling his ruined arm, pain infecting his voice so it sounded almost inhuman.

"No, Sam, enough. You're a grown man, you made your own choices, no one else is to blame for them," Tomen stepped up to the other man. "And no one else is to bear consequences for them on your behalf."

"I made that deal for you, for all of us, we could've stepped up out of the dung heap and stood among the betters!"

"There are no betters, Sam," Tomen knelt down to look the other man directly in the eye, "just people. You made that deal for yourself, putting our family, my family at great risk, and that is something I cannot abide."

"What we doing with him, then?" Miles asked, giving an upwards nod to his former friend now in a pitiful heap on the floor.

"I will not suffer someone to live that is a threat to this family," Tomen said, shaking his head, "even one who was once in it," his eyes fixed in staring into Sam's.

"I should've slit your throat in your sleep, Tomen, I should've done you all, you hopeless sacks of shit, you'll all die! Thorne's going to wipe the face of the starways clean of your filth!" Sam just about finished yelling as Tomen landed a firm punch into his head, then wrestled control of him so his head was completely in the power of the former Stalwart man, and then his neck broken, and his lifeless body slumped in a sickening thud.

"Was that the right call, Tomen?" Miles asked, his shoulders dropping as he watched his friend's body contort under itself from not steadying its fall.

"He betrayed our trust and put us all more in the crosshairs of the Section Chief than we already were," Tomen explained, "and who knows what he might've done to go through with that deal he made. You saw the desperation in his eyes, same as me."

"I really hope you didn't call me just to make me watch that," Azuri wept, the imager laid on the desk in such a way as she had full view of Sam's execution.

"I am sorry, Azuri, but I needed to be sure," Tomen stroked his beard, covering his mouth as his bottom lip began to tremble. "What have I done?"

"What needed to be done," Nathan knelt down, ruffling Impala's fur across his side before wiping away the blood at his snout, which the dog seemed to appreciate. "There was no bloodlust in killing him, he was a desperate man doing what he felt was right," he went on, "but he couldn't see that his actions would have got you all killed."

"He made a deal for us," Cait murmured, tightening her hand in Lena's, fending back the tears. "He tried to protect us."

"Elias Thorne doesn't make deals with WIDOWs," Nathan stated firmly, standing back up and placing a hand on his helmet where it lay on the desk next to the imager projecting Azuri. "He would've taken what he wanted and slaughtered you all for good measure."

"You know that for a fact?" Miles asked, oblivious to the challenging tone in his voice, the fiery eyes of his X-Human likeness never leaving Sam's face, locked in a state of unimaginable pain.

"You doubt the conviction of a man who you just saw defy a Section Chief himself to synthesise a product that brought down the Capital City?" Nathan bounced back, looking over at the other man. "And you think a man capable of a feat like that lets those who stand against him live and bask in luxury, the rewards he himself would need to bestow? Miles, It be naive."

"I'm just saying, Sam did what he felt was right."

"It would have got you all killed," Nathan corrected.

"I agree," Cait announced, nodding, "someone who can rationalise poisoning an entire city wouldn't blink at killing the people who recovered his work so he could carry it on, plus it would keep us from sharing it with anyone."

"I think you're right, Cait," Azuri put in. "Thorne sent his attack dog to the Forerunner, that Vice Admiral of his."

"Reiku?" Nathan shifted his gaze to Azuri, his eyes fixed on hers, "the man's a devout follow of Thorne's and his hands are stained with blood, probably more than mine."

"You could be right," the pilot continued, "I didn't know when we last saw each other, but a broadcast was sent out all across the region. It was found to 've come from the Forerunner station. It was a recording of your voice, Cait."

"Me? What?"

"'United we stand, divided we fall', isn't that your new motto?"

"But I—"

"Didn't record nothing? Doesn't matter, honey, it was definitely your voice, a recording from some time when you did say that new catchphrase o' yours. But no one stepped up to claim responsibility for it."

"Hmm," Nathan grunted, knowing the consequences of that.

"So Reiku wiped out everyone onboard the Forerunner," Azuri choked out.

"Xin's dead? They're all gone?" Miles' eyes widened, he couldn't take much more of this.

"No, no, Xin got out, thanks to Nathan's buddy. They're headed for Sanguine but they've been talking to the Chief Admiral, to Thorne's uncle, and apparently a rift has already opened in Obsidian. Rumour is there's gonna be a battle over our heads real soon, to determine who picks us up I guess. And there's something else, too."

"Really? There's more?" Lena chuckled in disbelief.

"To add fuel to a wildfire, the Sapphire conglomerate is here, and they're here in force. The border guard were annihilated, their fleet could be anywhere in the region by now," Azuri explained.

"I thought your idea was to ask *one* friend for help, mate," Tomen raised an eyebrow to Nathan.

"I did," he replied, "I didn't think she'd bring her Azurite with her."

"Shit, so what are the skies like? Are we good for getting out?" Tomen asked his trusted pilot.

"Fuck knows, Tomen, the shell is making it difficult to get anything through, I'm just about making do here. But I do know that once we're done here, we're heading into a right shitshow."

"Super," Lena crooked her head.

"Fuck," Miles swore, looking down at Impala that was nuzzling against his leg.

"So what's next?" Azuri asked the group.

"Cait, this is your gig," Tomen smiled at the girl who reluctantly let go of Lena's hand as she took a deep breath, taking a moment to gaze down at where Sam's head had rolled to.

"We stick to the plan," she eventually said, "even if we don't make it out, the people have a right to know what happened here. So we need to find a way of broadcasting this stuff to them, maybe this final entry will do the trick."

"I can see the transcript for it," Lena sighed, "it's a confession."

"That'll do," Tomen nodded, looking to his side at Miles. "So we see this through."

"Come this far," Miles bravely smiled back.

"Once we get a signal out, we'll need Xin's Stardust connections to use their network to bring the message to everyone," Tomen posed, "Azuri, contact him, set that up."

"I'll do that and prep the ship for take-off while you guys figure out how you're doing that," Azuri put in, "keep safe, y' lun's."

"Keep safe yourself, my love," Tomen replied to her, "and if the skies open, take flight, don't get pinned down."

"I'll be fine, Tomen, you just make sure you get your arse on this ship ASA-fucking-P, be seeing you soon," she said with a wink as a way of signing off and the imager went dead.

"So what we doing?" Lena asked confused.

"A facility like this would have the means to broadcast data in case of a biohazard emergency and the data needed to be protected," Nathan explained as he put his helmet back on. "The problem now is powering something like that up."

Chapter 22

Descending by the stairs at the end of the long channel that acted as the spine for the facility, the group came across the vast power plant that provided the colossal amount of electricity needed to fuel the bunker. Or rather, the machinery that would, if it were connected to the power grid for the rest of the city, whereas in the state they found it in, the enormous generators here were running on their own, supplying only a small stipend of what they could produce for themselves. The white tiles that made the floor carried on, leading into the wide open space lit by the dangling beams suspended from chains from the chamber's ceiling, with metal catwalks stretching out from a higher level from the left and right. Below these, were the generators, giant works of metal gnashing together like a drumbeat and hissing out smoke as they worked. They were set behind a fence line that marked out the floor space, bordering off the towering machines to their own near bottomless peripheries of the end of the vault. The generators were each set into two halves, smashing together and in taking a sharp inhale of air before separating and bellowing out a cloud of black smoke, the sounds they made when colliding were near deafening. And opposite the stairs down to this level, across the length of clear space, was a platform set against the far wall, reached by a rickety set of steps, with a lever stapled into the white brickwork there.

"It's still alive," Cait nodded, allowing herself to feel hopeful, seeing the generators creating enough power to engage the systems she had seen working meant to her that the facility was still hooked up to the power grid, it just needed to be engaged and then the whole bunker could come online.

"Don't get ahead of yourself," Tomen warned, "this city's been asleep for a decade, there's no telling the condition of the power grid."

"Well, there's one way," Miles grinned as he watched Impala rush ahead of them, his claws scratching against the tiling as he bounded over to the platform steps, ran up them and stood up against the far wall, sniffing the lever.

He and Tomen had abandoned their helmets where they had left them, his golden skin had lost its shine in the dullness of his surroundings, and also from the dust clinging to the air.

"The system seems to be connected," Nathan added, tapping the keys on his screen mounted to his right forearm as he crossed the open space with the rest of the team. "Looks like this lever will open the connection, start the power flowing in from the city."

"And that will power up the signal array? If this place even has one," Lena continued the thought process, doubting its success.

"All RCS facilities had to have them," Cait pointed out. "They were standard issue, like Nate said. If the factory or plant or whatever were to go up in flames or something, it needed someone to broadcast out its data or it was lost. You know how it is, the upper managers don't give two shits about the lives of their workers, it's their involvement in the contribution that matters to them, and they'd hate to lose their precious data, fuck the ones who actually manufacture things."

"Doesn't mean it'll work though, sugar," Lena replied, "it's been a long time since it had any juice flowing through it."

"Then let's boot it up," Cait said as they reached the other side, ascending the metal steps, with each step ringing out from the basic metal framing below her boot encased within her black jumpsuit. She had kept her hood down for the most part of her journey through the Old City and she did so here, not wanting to make history with her face hidden. Even with the entourage of ghostly spectres watching their move from the catwalks at either side, clinging to the shadowy recesses of the chamber, vacant eyes staring with a lack of curiosity.

It was Tomen who stepped up to the lever set onto the face of the wall, with Impala beaming up at him, excitedly anticipating something, but when he pulled the thing down, it immediately sprang back up again. "We may have a problem here," he grumbled, trying it again, holding it down more firmly this time. And as Nathan watched with his screen, power did begin to flow into the bunker's own power system, intertwining with the energy being created from the booming generators at either side, but as soon as Tomen let go, the lever returned upright, and the flow stopped.

"Shit," Miles cursed.

"Does it need locking in place or something?" Lena asked, joining Tomen, inspecting every detail of the lever and the plate where it was welded onto the wall but not finding anything in the way of a latch or locking pin.

"I mean, we can always just not broadcast, and take the data away with us and do something later, right?" Cait asked but she even disagreed with her own suggestion.

"Not worth the risk," Tomen said, giving voice to Cait's own thoughts. "If we're in store for a hostile reception as soon as we head to leave and end up getting blown out of the sky, dead, then all of this would've been for nothing."

"Yeah I know," Cait mumbled.

"So what do we do?" Miles asked, crouching down to give Impala some stroking as the dog began to whimper, sensing the frustration in the group.

"Well, this lever just powers up the facility, the means of actually sending out the holo-diary will be by using Elias's old terminal. So I'll hold this down while you all wait in his old office, sending out the broadcast," Nathan planned before looking back at the way they had come, "and you'll be safer up there."

"What you mean?" Lena asked him, stepping away from the lever over to where Cait was standing.

"When we redirected the power to the district gates, we didn't ask the nuclear reactor that supplies the grid to give any more output than it already was, all we did was send the flow of energy where we wanted it to go."

"Meaning?" Tomen stepped away from the busted mechanism too, deeming it too worn down, figuring it for not having been used for eight years.

"In pulling that lever and holding it in place," Nathan went on, "we will be demanding the reactor to produce more energy, more than the evacuation protocols need. It will bring the rest of the city back to life along with this bunker."

"You mean the shell will open?" Tomen put in.

"And the gates," Nathan nodded. "Essentially pulling that lever is reviving the system. We need a lot of power to bring this facility back to life but it's too specific to create the exact output we need and to have it only run here. No, the only way we get what we need is to bring it all back online, breaking the lockdown."

"And letting loose the dead on every town nearby, it'll be a massacre," Cait couldn't believe it, another stumbling block so close to the end.

"Not if the person who stays here also closes off the connection once the facility is powered up and the broadcast is complete," Nathan turned back to the rest of the group, placing his hands on his hips. "And that person has to be me."

"Guessing this is where you explain the safer up there part?" Lena put in.

"The inner gates will be the first to open, before the shell or the outer gates even begin to rumble," Nathan brought up his right arm, tilting it slightly so the others could see the map of the city he had pulled up. "The flow of power will come from here," he said, pointing with his left hand at the Commerce district. "From the RCS Central Office, it's showing a leak but we'll just have to trust it to produce what we need. But the flow of power won't simply cut across the length of the city to us, here, that level of power will be too big to just redirect how and where we need. So it will do as it was designed to, start at the centre, and make its way out."

"But the Obsidian base, where all that firepower had come from that knocked that Elite team out of the sky, that's in the centre of the city," Miles reminded him.

"Exactly my point," Nathan traced his finger to the centre of the city then to the Directorate district where they were. "The inner gates will open and it won't take them long to figure out where we are," he said, "so we're in for a fight, likely the hardest one yet."

"So we get attacked on ground level by however many still live in the old Obsidian base," Lena sighed, "and then we get attacked from above, soon as the shell opens. Not to mention the zombies who will be attracted by all the fighting, or they might leave the city and tear apart anyone and anything in their path. Wow," she said, wiping a hand across her brow, "we sure do know ourselves a plan, don't we?"

"I can stop the power flow between the finished upload of the holo-diary being broadcasted and before it has the chance to re-open the exterior gates, as the shell will open first," Nathan pointed out.

"But then they'll all converge on you, and you'll be stuck down here," Tomen squinted, "so why would we all be up there? No way, I'll stay with you, Miles, Cait, Lena, you secure the broadcast."

"Not going to happen," Nathan lowered his arm and stepped up to the other man. "Too risky for you to be here, it'll be safer for you to be up there with the others, securing the upload and keeping absolutely silent so they have no reason to suspect you are here with me."

"That's not your call, Winter," Tomen refused.

"No, I guess not, but if you want to live to hold your child in your arms, you'll do I say."

"Is that a threat?"

"No," Nathan shook his head, stifling a laugh, amused how bad he was at being genuine with someone to the point where he had to admit he did sound threatening. "I mean, I can survive whatever's thrown at me, I don't see the point in risking your life too, especially when you have so much to lose now. Don't go throwing that away, Tomen."

"I've no intention, but I don't have any inclination to leave you alone down here neither. You'll be trapped with them down here."

"Surely seen enough of me by now," Nathan chuckled, "no I won't be trapped down here with them, they'll be trapped down here with me."

"You'll be overrun and overwhelmed on your own," Miles added, "you won't stand a chance. They took out an Elite squad with a volley like it was nothing."

"Those Elites weren't me, I can handle it," Nathan rebuked.

"Guys, we can't stand around all day, we need to be doin' something, come on, what's the play?" Lena asked, getting sick of the back and forth.

"Go," Nathan boomed, barely a metre in front of Tomen, "I'm good, here."

"I don't like it," Tomen shook his head, "but OK. The rest of you, get to Thorne's office, get everything set, I want a word alone with Winter before I come up and join you."

While Miles and Lena gave Nathan only polite nods before leaving him, Cait stepped up to him and kissed him on his helmet, at the point where his mouth would be encased behind it. "I know what you're doing," was all she said, with more than a hint of affection in those richly purple eyes.

"What did you want?" Nathan asked Tomen once they were alone, watching the others take the steps back up to the central channel, heading to the room they had just left.

"To say thank you," Tomen said, pulling his jacket aside so he could stand with his hands resting on either hip. "You know, I didn't believe in this venture at first, you believe that?"

"Hmm," Nathan grunted, turning away from the other man to inspect the lever but glancing over his shoulder to show he was still listening.

"I didn't think it was worth it. I lost the sense for helping people, you could say, something I guess I'm more than a bit ashamed of," he stroked his sweat stained face. "And even when you stepped aboard my ship, after I had agreed to humour the idea, I had no faith in what we were setting out to do. At that moment, all I saw was someone who was a threat to my family."

"I'm no threat to you or your people, killing you doesn't interest me."

"I know. Funny thing is, it took not seeing you kneel down and take one of Sam's eyes for me to see it. You've changed."

"I doubt that."

"You didn't take a trophy from him as you aren't proud of that kill. You care about this family—"

"I didn't take an eye as I didn't kill him," Nathan growled over his shoulder, still taking a closer look at the mechanism.

"…and that means you are a part of it."

"Part of what?"

"Our family, well, your family, now," Tomen crossed his arms in front of him.

"What?" Nathan sounded more exasperated than anything else, turning around.

"You heard me," Tomen chuckled. "Day one, you didn't care, I had you pegged for having a thing for Cait, that being the only reason you chose to come aboard my ship and hear more of what she had to say. But since then? You've talked to my family, heard their stories and shared bits of your own. Our lives are short and dangerous, my friend, so we need to make bonds together quick and strong. And you've done that. I can honestly say that we trust you with our lives."

"You're saying you trust a man you know to be a serial killer? And I will kill more, I have no reason to stop," Nathan said, stepping up close to the other man, not understanding him.

"Our family's not exactly the conventional kind, now is it? I myself killed a lot of people the very day before I'd called friends and co-workers. That's the reality we live in, it's a shit, harsh one."

"So what made you believe in this venture? What changed you?" Nathan asked, changing the subject.

"I just told you, you did. Seeing you protect the things most precious to me, well it got me thinking, and then I found my own reasons to see this thing through." Tomen stroked his beard and gave an exaggerated smile, "how well do you know your Old World history?"

"A fair deal."

"Then you'll know people my skin colour were treated far different than yours. We were seen as less than human, kinda like those X-Human experiments upstairs, we were used and abused, sold as slaves, bent to serve."

"I'm aware."

"Well, the Board did well to stamp out racism, I'll give 'em that much, I've never heard of it outside the history books but that's likely 'cause they simply rebranded and re-merchandised it. Or am I the only one to draw similarities with those days and the ones we live in now? With work contracts drawn up in infancy replacing shackle and chain? I don't see the difference. And the genius of it? The Board don't discriminate by skin colour or sex, nah, they enslaved everybody."

"Slaves didn't get paid," Nathan suggested.

"True, but what these poor souls get is arguably worse, no? Given currency that they can only give back to their masters, to buy the fake food they are broken to farm? I get it that there aren't enough natural resources to go round, that's why they invented the artificial crop in the first place, folks gotta eat, yeah, but they could just as easily make it taste better, be more nutritious, no?"

"Suppose so."

"But they don't, because they eat real, natural food, cut from live animals, sewn from genuine seed, not the composite things manufactured."

"Your point being?"

"I got onboard when I realised the fight against slavery, against the idea that one can stand on the shoulders of another is still raging across the stars, and I want my piece of that fight. I don't want my kid to grow up in such a reality as having people assume they're better than them."

"As good a reason as any."

"So thank you, for helping me realise that reason," Tomen placed a firm hand on Nathan's shoulder, looking him straight in the dark grey oval where his eye was protected behind.

"Sure," the Elite Commander replied, reciprocating the act but not understanding its significance, yet satisfied that meant the other man was going away now. But while watching Tomen leave the platform, Nathan found himself thinking back to the conflicting feelings he had encountered earlier while watching his holo-diary, of whether the attachments he was forming were worth the price of being vulnerable to feeling loss again. He considered it for a moment before calling over, "keep your head down, Tomen. Don't give them any reason to come anywhere but here."

"Sure thing, Winter," the other man replied before crossing over to the stairs, leaving the Elite Commander alone with his chosen task.

"How're we looking, Lena?" Nathan asked over his radio piece.

"It took some doing but I got it all set to upload the holo-diary entry and broadcast with the bunker's array."

"Any word from Azuri? Is the Stardust network ready to receive and transmit?"

"She's just sent word," Miles replied, "I pinched Sam's tablet, she'll redirect the broadcast with a subroutine using your ship to bounce it over to Xin where he'll patch it through to the Stardust network. Every screen and imager will light up with our message."

"Good, so we're all ready to go?" Nathan nodded, taking his hand away from the small button at the centre of his chest, just below the holster for his pistol, the microphone for his communication piece.

"On you, Winter, just wait for Lena's go," Tomen announced as he rejoined the others in the former office of Elias Thorne, settling down behind the desk with Miles, Cait and Lena so as not to be seen from the doorway. Miles had even pulled some filing cabinets over to block off one side, and moved a side table to run at an angle with it making it more of an effort to see what could be behind the desk. But he was tired for it. Tomen's long lasting friend, bearing the same knackered, well-worn jacket of their former company on top of the light grey armour they both bore, was sitting cross-legged with his rifle across his lap, his head tilted back against the side table, and his eyes were shut. "Miles, wake up."

"I'm not asleep, just resting," the embers of his eyes flickered into life as he opened them, blinking and watching the other man sit beside him. "Though when I close my eyes I do picture a warm and snug bed." Impala must have had the same thought, tucking in as best he could into Miles' lap, sitting in the hole between his legs.

"And are you alone in this picture?" Tomen teased with a cheeky grin, taking out a snack bar from his backpack that had clung so tightly to his back, he'd all but forgotten it was there before casting it aside as the others had with theirs.

"I wasn't here, that's all that matters," Miles said, taking a deep breath. He slid back the cocking mechanism on his rifle, briefly seeing the glow of the green energy that was stored at the tip of the bullet being loaded into the chamber.

"Guess so," Tomen shrugged. "Right now, closing my eyes, all I see is Azuri, the oceans to bask in those eyes of hers. I can't wait to get back to her, y'know?"

"You will, we're near the end of the line now, pal," Miles gestured out a fist which Tomen bumped with his own.

"Can you believe we're really here? At the finishing line?" Cait tucked in close to Lena who had abandoned the red leather chair, favouring to prop herself up on her knees to finish using the terminal to distribute their evidence. She was admiring the shine on the data card that she clutched between her fingers before handing it over to Tomen who returned a nod to her, before he stashed it inside his jacket.

"Actually I can," the emerald-eyed X-Human answered, "'cause we earned this shit."

"Fuck yeah, we did," Cait agreed, stroking the barrel of her shotgun, allowing herself time to come to terms with the idea that she would be needing it again soon.

"When the shit hits the fan, Cait, just do one thing for me."

"Anything, Lena."

Lena stopped for a moment, peered down from her propped up position at Cait sat down next to her with eyes beaming back up at her and she took a breath. "Caity, when you got me out of Stardust, I didn't just get my body back, I got my life back. But life, it ain't worth living if you got no one to share it with. Just do me this one thing, please keep that promise you made. I want my best friend in my life forever."

"Never in any doubt," Cait replied, "I'm never leaving you."

"Good, now I can do this," and Lena got back to finishing what she was doing, setting the final holo-diary to the uplink array but resetting the parameters of the broadcast so that anyone could receive it, not just someone using RCS technology. Just as she was nearing the confirmation stage, an animated cat strolled across the screen, blocking her view of what she was doing, causing her to scrunch her nose in bewilderment. "The fuck," she murmured.

"Director, I'm Crimson the Crime-Fighting Cat," the ginger cat announced himself, wearing a red trench coat and bearing a lit cigar in his paw. "And I see you've lowered the security settings, mind telling me why y'all did such a clumsy thing?"

"Because fuck you and all you stand for," Lena whispered and brushed the cat away with a few strokes of the keys, clearing the terminal of the feline mascot of the Crimson conglomerate.

"Did you just say that to a cat?" Cait laughed, looking up at her friend.

"Yes, I did, 'cause now we're set," Lena grinned with her bright red lips that matched the radiant colour of her hair, and the shredded coat that barely clasped onto her body. "Let's do this, oi Crimson," Lena said, activating her own comm piece attached to her grey leotard beneath her coat. "Pull the lever, sweetie pie."

"Don't call me that, pulling the lever now," Nathan replied into the piece set into Lena's right ear, his tone clearly suggesting he was not impressed. "Power should be coming online now," Nathan announced over the comm pieces and the team watched as the room lacking in light came alive, their systems booting up as the whole bunker seemed to hum and vibrate with the introduction of the enhanced power flow.

"Do I want to upload holo-diary?" Lena read out from the monitor after clambering up to see it again. "Y-E-S spells yes," she said as she keyed it in, and the upload commenced, followed swiftly by the broadcast. "OK, here we go!"

Chapter 23

Alex Grey found himself visiting the sole survivor of the mission to infiltrate Rose City after most of his shifts ended, it became a regular occurrence for him to wrap up his assignments in time to give a brief handover then exit the Command Centre with a feeling of haste to get to the medical wing as brisk as he could manage. It was something he could never have predicted for himself and he didn't care if it was for love or friendship, he was just content that he had found someone he could really talk to, who valued him for exactly who he presented himself to be, his honest self. His co-workers had noticed the change, too. It had been a running joke among the junior technicians that their supervisor longed for more hours, that he would rather be slaving away at work, then enjoying some rest or form of fun. Yet none saw fit to tease him about his new hobby, no one except Elle Black, the one he spent so much time with. She had a wit and a cynical sarcasm that he felt as though he was growing addicted to. In fact, if he could barely stomach idle conversation with his peers before, now he would hardly entertain the idea, knowing it wouldn't compare to the conversations he shared with her. It had been some time since she had been rushed into the emergency division of the medical wing, aboard the Listening Post space station, but Alex never forgot that day. Not for the horror of her arrival, but because it landed him with a friend, no matter how much he wished for them to meet under better circumstances. He simply put down to the stars aligning in such a way as he had to accept.

"You gonna stare at that meal all night or you gon' eat it, Grey?" Elle teased him as they sat down together for a meal as they had done for the past couple of nights. She was feeling stronger, and more at ease with her replaced limb, able to use her chrome left hand without a second's thought that it was synthetic nerves that allowed her to feel what she was touching.

Alex blinked and rocked his glasses up his nose with the knuckle on his right thumb before looking down at the plastic tray filled with food that lay across his lap as he sat in the same chair he always did, at his friend's bedside. He rolled the sausage over his fork, recovering the train of thought he'd been aboard before he had been cast from it. "Yeah, sod off, my pork," he joked, eventually cutting into it, bringing a piece up to his mouth.

"Arm wrestle you for it," the woman replied with a wink, tearing a piece of bacon away from her fork with her teeth, her large brown eyes brimming with an innocent nature.

"Not a chance, not doing that again, my elbow still hurts from last time, you little shit," Alex laughed, striking up a middle finger in the same hand he used to raise another bit of meat.

Elle mockingly gasped then scooped up a heap of her mashed potato with her spoon, bent it back with her finger then pinged across to fly just over Alex's right ear, causing him to flinch away, hunkering down his shoulders which only made her laugh more. "Not exactly a brave one, are you?" She giggled, but not in a mocking way, she liked the man sitting beside her, having grown to look forward to his company.

"Not all Obsidian have to be, some folk like me are needed, to fit all the pieces together, to give you hard, hotshot types some direction," Alex shrugged with a cocky grin.

"Yeah, yeah, you're the brains, we're the brawn, I get it, I get it," Elle revolved her head around before shooting her attention back to Alex, "but end of the day, I can kick your butt. I can kick your butt easily, and that makes you my little bitch."

"Is that so? Appearances can be deceiving y'know? I could be stronger than I look," he played back.

"Oh I think you are," she gave him a warm smile, "after all, there's more than one way to be strong."

"Grey!" A shout came from over his shoulder, so urgent that Alex nearly spilled the tray of food all over himself as he spun round to see who it was. It was a junior technician that he only vaguely recognised, but the panic and terror in his eyes was something he definitely was familiar with. "Sorry sir, I mean Senior Technician Grey, you're needed in the Command Centre, sir!"

"What's happened?" Alex set the tray aside on a side table as he rose to his feet, taking a moment's glance at Elle who was just as surprised as he was.

"Plenty, sir. The Forerunner's been set to the ultimate dismissal proceeding! Vice-Admiral Reiku's already performed it, but now there's another broadcast incoming, all of our systems have been taken out again! We need you to come back," the young man squealed, clearly out of breath as well as he must have run from the Command Centre to reach Grey.

"An ultimate dismissal was enacted?" Elle gasped, knowing exactly what that entailed for all the souls present on the other space station.

"There's other Senior Techs," Alex accidentally mumbled, his mind speaking for him, he didn't want his time with Elle interrupted.

"I know but MacArthur instructed me to get you, said you were the only one he trusted to bring us back online!"

"Then I'll go, Mack's never been one to give pointless orders," Alex smoothed out his black Obsidian officer's suit and glanced over his shoulder back at Elle, "I'll be back as soon as I can."

"Yeah, man, go be amazing, be a fucking star," Elle put up a curious thumbs up but her smile told him to simply go, so Alex did, waving the junior technician to lead on, towards the lifts to the upper levels.

"Alex!" MacArthur bellowed from the management platform as soon as he saw the Senior Technician arrive in tow of the younger man sent to gather him. "Forget your station, come up here! It's a complete blackout, we're locked out of everything—it's the Stardust communications network, it's barring us from doing anything."

"On my way, Mack," Alex replied coolly, weaving a path through the many workstations abuzz with activity, all with technicians desperately trying to gain any response from their dead terminals. The red star of the region blazed a sea of crimson across the Command Centre as Alex made his way to join his manager overlooking the scene. "How did this start?"

"All systems running normal then suddenly it all went black, every single network has been stolen, torn from our grasp," MacArthur was looking out over his workers, his hands leaving sweat marks against the railing that bordered his higher position.

"I heard about the Forerunner, so I'm guessing whoever sent the revolution message got out?" Alex asked, taking up his manager's own terminal without asking. "But what's their play this time?"

"Fuck knows, Grey, that's why I summoned you," the older man stroked his baldness before turning around, folding his arms and leaning up against the barrier. "But it's not the only reason," he said, sounding a million miles away.

"Now isn't the time for distractions, Mack, the whole of Obsidian is blind and deaf, we gotta get things up and running aga—" A loud buzzing that turned more into a shriek with every passing moment interrupted Alex and sent the whole room into a silence, that proceeded all of the lights going out at once. The only way they could see, was by the red ambient light cast from the star through the window that served as the opposite wall to the manager's platform, with the enormous holographic imager at the centre of the room powering up. The screeching sound was deafening but stopped as soon as the image of Elias Thorne became illuminated out from the square table below, but not as anyone present knew him, as this image was far younger.

"Is this a holo-diary? The fuck is this?" MacArthur spun on the spot to have the shine from the hologram reflect off his face as it did everyone else in the room, capturing all of their attention, from the technicians scurrying below to the guards around the perimeter.

"This is Director Elias Thorne of Ruby Consolidated Systems, recording this for the benefit of the Board so that when this project comes into the light of day, that it will be understood and respected. The costs shall be struck off as acceptable losses in the pursuit of a product that is far beyond anything ever created by the combined conglomerates. The city of Rose will fall today, that much is already determined." The hologram said, towering over everyone in the room, loud and booming so everyone could hear it.

"Shut that off!" One guard shouted from the entrance to the room, one of the troops that arrived at the Listening Post at the same time as Vice-Admiral Reiku, assigned to guard the interior of the Command Centre.

"He knew?" Alex muttered to himself, only loud enough for MacArthur to hear as he turned to face his long-time friend, a strange look was caught in his eye and Alex could have sworn that the other man didn't seem as surprised.

"The general evacuation alarm has sounded as our boldest experiment has failed, but this product is something we cannot afford to let slip through our fingers. We have extrapolated the means to replicate the X-Human phenomenon of prolonging their metaphysical essence after death, from the study of the physical form and the paranormal of this species. This endeavour that I devoted all my company's greatest resources to must come to its desired result. To be able to extend the lives of all the members of the Board, strengthening their physical states as well as their spiritual entities, could prolong the terms in our positions enabling successes the like of which could be greater than anything we could have ever imagined. The achievements we could discover are beyond possible prediction and surpass human evolution. Let the record show that I formulated this theory, invested in its investigation and formed the resulting product on my direct authority alone." The recording continued to say, as the technicians below could do nothing but stand and watch, but some were being wrestled to the ground by the guards not wishing them to see anymore.

"Turn it off MacArthur! Or we will!" One guard shouted over the frantic chaos of the room, firing a single energised blast into the ceiling as a warning.

"I can't, we're locked out!" The manager shouted back, retreating from the railing so as to be out of view.

"Locked out? We don't even have power?" Alex asked him as he came up by his side at the workstation, and he fixed his friend with a suspicious look. "Mack, what's going on?"

"Just listen," was all the other man said, pointing to the hologram but he himself was looking everywhere else.

"The countless X-Humans put through substantial suffering and with their lives extinguished in the pursuit of this goal are meaningless compared to the potential gains this Coalition will create with this product, not to mention my own personal obsessions fulfilled. Now, Rose City will fall, yes, that is inevitable at this juncture, but we must continue this project through to its conclusion. For now, the data on this product will remain saved on this terminal, but after I become Section Chief for the Crimson, I will recover the components and this facility, and see this venture finished."

"Thorne caused the Capital Collapse?" Alex was stunned, he looked over at his friend with wide eyes and was even more taken aback when he saw someone he thought he knew simply nodding.

"What's he talking about? What did he do to X-Humans?" A technician called out, a woman with silver skin and bright shining yellow eyes.

"My idea for utilising the water supply for the city as a dispersal method is an admitted mistake, but we will finish what we started in this very institution. I take full responsibility for this error in judgement, but in doing so I take all the credit due for this landmark achievement for the Board." The holographic imager paused and went silent on the image of the young Elias Thorne, standing proud, standing tall, a certain sadistic intelligence behind the grin that showed his parted teeth while his mouth was open. Silence invaded the Command Centre and settled, with every person present reduced to it, fearful of being the first to speak after the revelation they had just witnessed.

"Thorne did it! He caused the Collapse! They're all dead because of hi—" A male X-Human technician shouted from among the workstations but was cut short as a powerful red beam of energy blasted a hole in his golden head. And then the only sound in the room was the nauseating thud when his body hit the floor. But the quiet was brief, as screams and shouts erupted from all over the Command Centre.

"By order of the Vice-Admiral Reiku, all those personnel found to have viewed this holo-diary will be subject to the ultimate disciplinary action!" An older guard yelled across the room before he and his men opened fire on the technicians on the Command Centre floor, with a volley of lasers striking against anyone and anything they found in their way, with people ducking down left, right and centre.

"We've gotta go!" MacArthur whispered, grabbing Alex's arm and hauling him out of the chair just as a laser struck against it. "We're leaving this station, right now."

"Mack, this is madness! That recording was broadcast over the entire Stardust network, everyone saw it!"

"I know! They don't care!" The older man barked in Alex's face so to be heard above the screaming and shooting but just as he finished, silence reclaimed the entire room accompanied by a long, cold shadow. The red star's blood soaked light was blotted out steadily by a vessel passing by the station just beyond the window wall, its shine reflecting off the smooth dark panelling of the ship until the sun was completely blocked away. It took up the entire stretch of glass and beyond it, stretching out further afield that the window granted a view of. And at the top of the cruiser, was its command bridge, notable for its broad red view, as it came up so close it seemed to nearly crash into the orbiting outpost.

"What's happening, Mack?" Alex murmured, deathly afraid for anyone but his friend to hear him. "That is a Marauder cruiser, the second largest in the fleet, but what's it doing here?"

"I know that ship," MacArthur sounded a curious blend of anxious and relieved but the urgency with which he gripped Alex's collar so tight lent to the fact that he was still very afraid. "We're leaving now, down the back way, quick," he snapped through gritted teeth, practically shoving Alex in the direction of the ladder down to the floor near the rear of the platform.

"Ah, from the mouth of the man himself," a hoarse voice spoke, coming in over the intercom system that ran through the entire Listening Post. All while technician and guard alike stood mouth and eyes gaping at the formidable vessel coming up not even a mile away from the other side of the window.

"Who is that?" Alex asked MacArthur as they reached the bottom, crouching down quickly to hide behind the wall of a workstation cubicle as a guard absent mindedly passed them by.

"Chief Admiral Thorne, Section Chief's uncle," his manager replied, not leaving anytime to discuss his comment, hauling Alex up to his feet, and near enough dragging him to the doors out of the Command Centre. "He's as much a psychopath as the rest of his family, but a supporter of Winter like me."

"What'd you say?" Alex muttered but was spoken over by the deafening speakers situated around the entire room.

"My nephew was always an ego-eccentric, narcissist. Credit for what achievement? I ask. For bringing a once proud city to its knees? For the murder of millions affected by the Capital Collapse? Or for the torture and mutilation of a species that has been nothing but brotherly and sisterly since our kind first sought refuge in their homeland?" The voice raged, his anger flooding the station's speakers, washing over all of the stunned colleagues who stood frozen mid-fight, not daring to move for the massive threat that lingered just beyond the hull of the station.

"MacArthur, get us back online," a guard hissed through his helmet as he rose the steps up to the platform, shifting his gaze from the manager standing up, to Alex who was seated at the terminal. "We need our defences back up, right now."

"I'm already on it," Alex said back but not sounding the slightest bit reassuring. The blackout of their systems meant rebooting the core which could only be done from this workstation but it was a painstakingly long process, with each system needing to be fully engaged before the next one could begin returning online.

"My name is Titus Thorne, Chief Admiral for Obsidian, loyal to the protection of these proud and decent colleagues of the Crimson Overseer Coalition, and it is to those who are loyal to the same cause that I say this: get out. Make for your hangar, get to the emergency rafts at the top of your station and we will bring you aboard this command vessel," the intercom said, causing the technicians and guards to look at one another, gauging their choices. "Or perish, as we take apart this station the same way we will take apart any person who stands in the way of that most essential goal. Did you really believe you could massacre all aboard the Forerunner and no one would notice? That no one would stand up and seek retribution for what you've done? For in the fight for people's liberty, no means are too sinister to reach a true victory we will achieve together, united we stand, divided we will fall!"

"Senior Tech Grey, please tell me those defences are coming online!" The guard shouted, leaning over Alex with one hand on the back of his chair, the other grasping the top of the monitor with the red visor of his helmet glued in staring at the systems flowing through a list as they rebooted.

"I'm going as fast as I can!" Alex answered, working away at the keyboard as fast and nimble as they would allow but then his eyes were drawn to the shop beyond the window opposite. Two colossal bursts of brilliant purple light erupted from the side of the ship, bearing down the tiny distance between vessel and station at a hurtling speed, heading straight for the Command Centre. "Shit," he swore, finding some extra speed as a dose of adrenaline hit his chest and he had to fight against the shaking of his hands to finish his work. The blindingly bright energy of the strikes coming for them was steadily blocking the view of the window beyond the room as they edged ever closer, the raw power of them rolling over as waves on a sea.

"Alex, come on, buddy," MacArthur muttered, a bead of sweat starting in his blad brow and rolling down his cheek until it was lost among the barely kept beard that encompassed his face. The streak of it moving in tandem with the epic energy tearing through the void to reach them, the light blotting out the view of the ship now they were so close to impact. "Alex!"

"They've crippled the system, Mack! Whatever caused the blackout introduced a virus! The whole network is failing!" Alex screamed, not taking the time to adjust his glasses slowly slipping down his nose as he relentlessly beat back attempts at something within the computer trying to shut down his attempts to reactivate the defences for the station.

"Stars, have mercy," MacArthur whispered to himself as he helplessly watched the guards leave his team alone, with such devastating firepower coming their way, they had forgotten the importance of their orders, waiting on certain death beside their colleagues. Out of nowhere, the manager flung a powerful punch at the guard still looming over Alex, knocking the man down, before he wrenched the rifle out of his grasp, using it hard against his head to render him unconscious.

"Mack, what the fuck?" Alex blurted out, having to lean quickly away as the guard flung out a hand in his struggle against the force of the fist that came at him so strongly.

"Alex, get up," MacArthur dragged the other man out of the chair with his left as he took hold of the weapon in his right, then shoving Alex in the direction of the ladder at the rear of the platform, a quicker way to get to the entrance. "Stop and we're dead," he barked as the other man went to stop and say something, thinking better of it once he had glanced back at MacArthur, seeing the seriousness of his expression, backed up by the blasts nearly meeting their mark.

"Mack, the doors can't withstand a blast like that!" Alex shouted back, having to shove a guard aside with all of his strength as the other man tried to bar his way to the entrance to the room.

"Just fucking move, Alex!" His manager boomed, firing the rifle he had taken into the chests of the next two guards that came worming through the workstations to meet them, before they reached the doors out. Others had had the same notion, brawling to try to escape against the guards still willing to obey their orders, blocking the way. But they didn't have weapons and most were shot as they tried to wrestle with their former protectors, whereas MacArthur did, and he made good use of it. While he gripped Alex's collar with his left hand, pushing him ahead through the crowd, he used his right to aim and fire his weapon, clearing the path until they hit the doors, having to pull against the weight of the guards backed into them.

"Mack! Grey! Get back here, traitors and help us!" One of the guards called after them through the closing gap as the two made good their escape, MacArthur firing his weapon to clear the hands stopping the door from closing.

"Grey, hit the panel! Now!" He yelled, giving Alex a hard shove towards a silver metal panel on the wall at the side of the doors into the Command Centre, a large black button standing out which he thumped with a fist.

"Got it!"

"Shit!" MacArthur grimaced as the energy blasts pulverised the window to the Command Centre and came straight for them on the other side, scorching everything in their path in purple lightning and flame until the security bulkheads dropped violently from the ceiling, blocking off the doors. A severed arm from where someone had tried to get through the other set of doors, only to be stopped by the thick metal panels descending, writhed and spurted blood all over the once pristine, white floor of the lobby area. The floor under their feet shook forcefully, nearly throwing them to the hard, unforgiving ground as the Command Centre was torn open by the outrageous arsenal deployed against it, and the vacuum of space it was left vulnerable to.

"Mack, we left those people to die in there, didn't we?" Alex instinctively put out a hand to steady himself against the wall, his jacket had come open where someone in the throng of people making for the exit had tried to cling onto him, desperate to follow. He took it off, tossing it mindlessly to the floor and smoothing out the red long sleeved shirt he wore beneath it as the other man threw off his jacket as well, it being torn at the hem.

"No, Alex, we survived," MacArthur sighed, pulling up the sleeves of his black cotton jumper then inspecting the weapon in his hands, eyeing the red energy coursing through the tip of the bullet he chambered.

"Yeah, but—" Alex needed to catch his breath, his mind was going a mile a minute, he needed to reel it in but there were so many branches to his thoughts that he felt his head burning up trying to contain them all. "Did Thorne really do all that? He did the Capital Collapse?"

"'Fraid so, mate."

Alex fixed the man he thought he had known so well with a curious, untrusting stare, measuring the calmness of someone who had just barely survived a slaughter after hearing a history defining confession, "you already knew."

"The Chief Admiral and I go back," MacArthur explained, stepping over to the lifts, pressing the button to activate it and breathing a sigh of relief when he heard the thing move inside the shaft. "He was there, mate, on the day," he said, half-turning back to Alex. "He saw how Elias behaved, how strangely. Then he saw how he instructed Elites, Winter's own people, to go murdering in Dunnfink, conjuring threats of WIDOWs waiting to ambush the Capital citizens."

"OK but—"

"To hear the Admiral tell it, Elias made those men and women so afraid of Winter, that to disobey him in that moment, that he would disembowel them on the spot for refusing the order. And keen to avoid that, they did it, wiping out most of the town in a matter of minutes, including one Monique Winter and her son, Harkness."

"Couldn't he have lied?" Alex asked, his whole life dedicated to his company, his purpose being to aid in protecting people, not to cover up a madman's lies, his Section Chief's unapologetic genocide, his mind turned upside down.

"No, Alex, I don't believe he did, and after what we both heard in there, neither should you," Mack glanced back to his front where a lift arrived to his relief. "Now, come on, you're a good man, Alex, I'm not leaving you to die here with the ones still loyal to Elias's lies."

Alex moved to step inside the lift but stopped just short when his mind hit him with a sudden memory and he backed away, "no," he said, looking the other man dead in the eye. "Elle, she'll be trapped down there in the hospital ring, I've gotta get her out!"

"Elle? The survivor?" Mack stood in the frame of the doors that were trying to close, with the lift in high demand given the urgency of all aboard the Listening Post to make their escape. "Alex, there are screens all over this station, she's probably been killed by now."

"No, Mack, I can't just assume that! I got her out of that hellscape just to abandon her here when she needs help again? Not a chance, I have to try," he spat back, finding a courage he wasn't aware he had.

MacArthur measured the look of the other man, but knowing refusing him was an argument he couldn't win, he nodded and hauled the other man inside the lift, "fine," he said, "but you're not going alone."

"Thanks, Mack," Alex stammered, correcting his glasses up his nose and steadying himself as the lift began to descend the levels, "this is insane," he made out just as another blast rocked the station, shaking their lift violently.

"You realise when we get down there, the guards will have got the same order, and there'll be chaos, we might not get this lift back, mate," MacArthur brought the stock of the rifle up to his shoulder and checked the sight. "This is gonna be ugly, pal."

"Yeah I figured," Alex steadied himself as the lift carried on downwards, past a level and onto the hospital deck with its outer ring housing the recovering patients. The doors slid open and MacArthur's prediction ran true as bodies with fresh gunshot wounds and scorch marks lay about the floor. Guards in the black armour of Obsidian were beating the medical staff in their white, leather jackets to the floor, pressing their weapons against their foreheads and opening their skulls with a single, executing shot. They didn't notice the lift's arrival with the screaming numbing out the sound, and the echoes of explosions rising up from below, so two men within were able to hunker down low, jogging over to the cover of an overturned gurney.

"Keep quiet," MacArthur whispered as they kept their heads below the bed rolled onto its side, out of sight of anyone curious about the sudden arrival of the lift to this level. It had opened up at the end of one of the crossroads that was the layout for the hospital ring, with the centre housing the most recent and less serious patients as white plastic curtains hung from basic metal poles, dividing up the section. They were erected to grant patients lying on the beds inside some measure of privacy but they were perfect now for hiding from the mass of guards going around the level laying waste to anyone they came across. Screams and shouts bounced off the walls and floor as the medical staff were killed where they were discovered, the Obsidian troops showing no mercy as they carried out their instructions. Some however must have resisted, as more than one body of a soldier lay on the ground, hands bound behind their back, helmet removed, an energy blast blown through the centre of their foreheads.

"Come on, we move from cover to cover, we need to get to the rehab area," MacArthur laid a hand on Alex's shoulder to hone his attention so that he could nod in the direction that he knew the other man was aware of, but was too panicked to recall.

"Ok," Alex replied as a large blast struck somewhere above their heads, seeing dust and debris from the ceiling rain down on them as they darted across a measure of open space to pass through an archway into the outer ring. Most of the guards were at the centre, close to the desk that acted as a reception and office space for the hospital, but some still patrolled this outlying area.

"We'll have to cut through the OR, no way around it," MacArthur pointed as the two men used the framing of the walls to hide, one either side of the curvature of the ring until they met their path blocked by a set of white wooden double doors.

"Yeah," was all Alex said to let his manager know he had heard him before they gingerly moved across, through the middle of the now vacant beds to reach the doors, ever so quietly pushing them open. They entered into the operating room and Alex did his best not to form images in his mind of the kind of trauma Elle must have experienced under the knife here to survive the ordeals she had been dealt by whatever lurked in the Capital City. Three tables were arranged at the centre of the room with a vast array of medical equipment accompanying them, as a litter of bodies adorned the smooth, dark floor, with pools of blood sitting stagnant. A single guard was posted here, checking inside the various lockers and cupboards up against the inner wall, presumably checking for anyone hiding away in them. They didn't turn around on Alex and MacArthur's arrival into the room. Being preoccupied opening a door, hastily raising their rifle to meet anything that might pop out, before scouring through what they found, the medicine and other medical aids.

Silently, MacArthur put a finger to his lips and led the way across, lightly jogging over to the cover of one table before moving onto the next, waving Alex up to the cover he would have just left, all the while keeping his eyes on the one guard far too close for his liking. More explosions and the sounds of destruction came from above and below them. Both men thought silent prayers to the stars that their way off the station was not the last thing they had heard just get blown up. As the entire space station shook from the incessant bombardment, a tray of surgical equipment slipped off from a mobile table, crashing to the floor, causing the guard spin on their heels, frantically raising their weapon in the direction of sound. Alex shut his eyes to the noise of the clattering pieces of metal that landed just shy of him but as he shot a glance over to MacArthur, he quickly realised he had to move. "Anyone there?" The guard called over, a female voice. "Someone skulking around? Come on out, I promise I won't hurt you," she said, moving with one light step at a time until she had a better angle on where the sound had come from, seeing the instruments strewn across the floor. She sprayed a few rounds of fiery red bullets, burning the surfaces they struck as she continued her passage around to see what might lurk on the other side of the tables. But as the guard was so focused on where the sound had come from, she neglected to see that away from that spot, the doors at the far end of the room had opened slightly, allowing for two shapes to slip through unnoticed.

Leaving the operating room, they arrived in the rehabilitation area, where they would leave the patients after their surgeries to recover, whether in the long or short term, never lacking for beds as this was simply an outpost, not advertising as a stop-by hospital. It took some travelling, moving from behind cupboards, from behind gurneys up the way around the curve in the outer ring to where Alex would usually come after his shifts, to visit the only other person than MacArthur he could stomach speaking to. But the bed was empty, the sheets thrown about, as three guards stood around, armed with their rifles, sifting through the personal belongings that, in her long-term stay, Elle had about her temporary home. These brutes in their bulky, dark armour cast the items not of any interest to them on the floor until one of them pulled open a drawer on the right side of the bed, on the other side of the cupboards to MacArthur. Whatever he picked out, it caused some alarm and urgency as he took a step towards his two colleagues. At the same time, while crouched behind a collapsed gurney riddled with burn marks from being laced with energised rounds, the body that was the target of them having rolled out onto the floor, Alex spotted where Elle was hiding. MacArthur couldn't see, being on the opposite side, standing behind the cupboards that the hospital level used to divide the patient beds, acting as walls, but Alex could just about make out the woman hunkered down under her bed. "This is definitely her bed," one of the guards announced, the one so fascinated by the object in their grasp.

"Ah, the Elite's weapon, she won't get far without it," one of the other guards replied, his voice muffled by his helmet but the distaste in his tone was obvious. "Come on, the bitch ain't 'ere no more, let's move on."

Just as the one in charge finished his instruction, Elle reached out from under the bed, using her new chrome hand to crush the nearest guard's ankle, making him collapse in an instant, howling with pain. He dropped what he had held so carefully and Elle snatched it up with her replacement hand, extending the elegant, thin blade before igniting its energetic core, slicing the man's neck open with golden lightning lashing out at his armour, and the metal cupboards next to the bed. The other guard that had remained silent up to this point jumped with surprise, "fuck!" He screamed, swiftly crouching down and emptying his rifle under the bed blindly but only having his shots strike against the tilework of the wall behind the bed as Elle sprang out of the left side. With a swift slash, she took off the head of the commanding guard, it flying up into the air as she leapt, spinning, catching it perfectly with her foot to slam it into the face of the remaining guard, blinding him for a moment so he could only spray in hope at where she had been. Yet she was too quick, Elle was already sliding under the bed, the floor slick with blood that made it easier, and she brought her blade down hard on the back of the guard's knee, causing him to collapse before she punched her blade through the man's helmet. The golden streaks of energy sparked off the edge of the blade wreathed in a bright, white flame as she lingered it in place for a moment, the only thing holding the body in her grasp upright as she caught her breath. Then Elle withdrew the length, allowing the blade to compartmentalise back into its hilt. She grasped it as though her life depended on it, her only remaining fleshy hand sweating against the black grip with the silver pommel, guardless in its straight design. It was an honest weapon, crafted for a single purpose which its design signified. Blood stained her hands, her patient gown, her legs and arms as she recovered herself, looking down on the bodies she'd left at her bare feet. "You can come out now," Elle said, smirking to herself, aware of the two men's presence.

"That was impressive, Elle, fuck," Alex stood up and stepped out from behind the gurney, glancing forward and behind them at the same time, wary of the guards still at the centre of the hospital.

"Don't worry about the others, they just took the lift out, I assume on account o' that," she said, pointing her left, shiny metal thumb over her shoulder at the enormous ship outside of the window firing sporadic energy blasts at the space station.

"Safe assumption, Miss Black," MacArthur emerged from behind the cupboards, watching the floor to not slip on the blood of the nearest guard. Just as he locked eyes with Elle to say a greeting, the doors to the operating room burst open with the guard they'd snuck past kicking them wide apart, raising her weapon to fire. She fired first and Alex was quick enough to use his body to shove Elle out of the way of the barrage, and MacArthur fired back, hitting her enough times in the chest to breach the armour, making the guard fall back against the doors.

"Thanks, buddy, but you can get off me now," Elle smiled, grateful for the save but her grin faded as Alex could only just about manage to pull himself up from where he had her pinned against the bed in flinging himself at her to push her out of the way of the gunfire. At his stomach, Alex had a hideous scorching burn, his shirt with a hole in it encompassed with small flames as within was a sizzling, disgusting wound. "Shit," the Elite murmured, her eyes wide with surprise, powerless just to watch as the man stumbled back against the wall, his hands hesitating to cradle the source of his unspeakable pain.

"Mack," Alex's voice was as weak as his legs as he slid down the wall, slumping on the floor as the other man spun just in time to see his friend drop.

"No! Alex, stay with us! Fuck, that's bad, fuck! Black, we gotta move him, we gotta get to the hangar!" MacArthur instinctively went to touch the blackened wound but refrained at the last moment, instead dragging the other man up, pulling one of his arms around his own shoulders.

"Every other fucker in this place will've had the same bright idea, it's gonna be awful crowded," Elle replied in shock, her mouth stuck open, gripping her weapon in her right hand for comfort.

"Does it fucking matter?" MacArthur shouted back at her before taking a breath to steady himself, knowing she didn't mean anything by it. "Look, the guards are housed at the base of this installation which means the longer we wait, the more they'll be on us. We gotta move, now!" He didn't wait for Elle to agree, MacArthur simply started towards the lifts, struggling with the dead weight of the friend he had hoisted across his shoulders.

"Mack, wait—" Alex started to murmur but a stab of pain stopped him, and a great explosion from under their feet distracted the others from pressing him to finish as they stumbled, MacArthur dropping him as he lost balance.

"I can take him!" Elle offered but MacArthur shook his head, preferring to grip Alex's right hand in his own, holding his arm across his shoulders, with the rifle in his left.

"I'm good, you're the better fighter, we need your hands free," he grunted as they crossed the centre of the hospital ring, stepping around the many bodies dropped there. MacArthur was by no means a small man, he was physically well built, and was able to lift his left hand, despite Alex's weight and the rifle in that hand, to call the lift back down to them. But nothing happened.

"Hang on," Elle said, trying the other one but again, nothing happened. "Shit."

"Fuck, stairs it is," MacArthur wasted no time, gesturing with an upwards nod to the door to the side of the lifts that he needed the woman's help to open.

"Is it a long way?" Elle asked, peering beyond the door as she held it open where it led into a space where a set of stairs led up and down, closely enclosed by plain, pale walls.

"It goes up the centre spire of the station," MacArthur awkwardly hoisted Alex inside, leading the way as Elle joined them in behind. "But after this level it opens up as we reach the mess hall level, from there we have to cross the way to the evac lifts at the far end."

"Opens up huh?" Elle sighed. "Then give me the gun, it's not like you can use it right now."

"True," he had to admit, handing the rifle over to the woman. MacArthur took a moment to look at her, she only had a patient's gown on that in its blood-stained, worn state hardly covered her tanned skin but it wasn't for admiring that his stare lingered. There was something about her that took him by surprise, a strength of character, to join a fight she had no knowledge of, to protect two people she hardly knew. "So this is what an Elite is like, huh?"

"Most would've killed you for your weapon and been at the hangar by now," Elle chuckled, "I guess I'm more sentimental than all that."

A terrible sound halted the conversation as from beyond the walls, they could hear the two lifts plummet from the top level down the shafts down to the base for the guards at the bottom of the Listening Post. They screeched as metal ground against metal as screams from those trapped inside followed all the way down until the loud crashes as they twisted and deformed from the whirlwind drop. There were more shouts as those on that level were impacted from the debris from the explosions of clashed metal, forming shrapnel sprayed in all directions.

"Well, that explains the lifts," Alex managed a smile as they arrived at the next level where the noise of people scrambling over one another to survive was everywhere. Immediately as they arrived, coming out next to the lift bank there was a mass of people, all in the different variations of Obsidian uniform, banging on the powerless doors, begging for the lifts to somehow come back. But there were also those with the same idea as them, making up the ramp that surrounded the eating area at the centre of this level, in front of the ring where the dormitories for the management colleagues were.

"Fucking cunts," Elle led the way, barging a path through the crowd, muscling a way through, leading with the rifle but grasping the hilt of her sword up against the underbarrel in case she needed it.

"They're just people, Black," MacArthur grunted, struggling with Alex's weight and keeping up with the Elite carving a path ahead through the panic stricken crowd. These were people he had known, people he had spoken to more or less every day, he knew their names, knew where they came from, what drew them to work for the company founded for protecting ones like them, providing security. It broke his heart to see them like this. Not just fighting but having to kill each other to gain any kind of advantage in the suffocating crowd where it was so difficult to even plant a foot to make the next step. It wasn't as though the man he held was heavy, it was the manoeuvring through the mass of people, taking the strain of the never-ending bumps and knocks, kicks and stamps that made MacArthur's journey difficult. Once or twice his grip was knocked, losing his friend to the crowd and he would either drag him back into sight or need to use his superior size to get to where Alex would be huddled on the floor being trampled on by the terrified horde of people.

"Move!" Elle was shouting, not afraid to use the heavy weapon in her hands to smash people out of their path and eventually they made it across the eating area where they had to awkwardly shift around the screwed in furniture, reaching the base of the ramp. At the heights of this level, below its ceiling, were windows showing the cause for so much chaotic distress as the immense vessel focused its fire at the base of the station, with unbelievably bright and powerful energy blasts. They could feel it beneath their feet, the levels below them were gone, laid to waste, as the floor shook unforgivingly violently, the closeness of the crowd becoming convenient to bounce against to keep upright. The screaming and shouting never stopped and with nowhere to go it ricocheted off the walls, echoing all around. It stank as well, so many people forced so close together, sweating from fear, no room to breathe as they shambled with no room to move up the length of the ramp.

"We're passing the Command Centre now," MacArthur pointed out as the enormous crowd ascended past the ceiling of the mess hall level to move past a solid wall. "So many lives lost," he stuttered, biting his bottom lip, blocking out the images poisoning his mind of having had to witness real, vivid desperation on the faces of those he wasn't just responsible for, but for the most part he considered his friends. But they were dead now. And if he didn't do all he could, then the friend remaining to him in his arms would fall too, so he pressed on, endeavouring beyond all he had to make it to the ship that destroyed all the lives he held dear.

"He called you, Mack, right?" Elle was forced in too, trapped in the tightness of the pack of people slowly progressing up to an escape they hoped was there.

"George MacArthur, but everyone calls me Mack," MacArthur replied.

"Mack, we should push past the hangar and make for the emergency rafts, reckon we'll have more luck that way."

"The rafts? But we'd need to cross the hangar to reach 'em, how're they a better option?"

"Elle's right, Mack," Alex breathed weakly, "all these people will be hoping to get on a cruiser, but the guards will be waiting."

"Yeah, they'll be waiting in the hangar, the same hangar you want us to cross? Surely we should just muscle our way onto the nearest, convenient craft?"

"I don't think it'll be that simple," Elle grimaced. "I mean look at these people, look at their faces. They're dead scared, they ain't no way they're thinking straight. Most will make for the nearest, biggest ship they lock eyes on, leaving the rafts free for smarter folk like us."

"We can only guess, we've no idea what we're about to walk into," MacArthur remarked as they reached the top of the ramp and suddenly had to find the nimbleness in his feet again. The ramp opened up into the hangar but directly across, the guards had formed a makeshift barrier that they used to fire their weapons from behind as a measure of protection, firing at anyone that dared to raise their head above the sea of bodies they had left. From there, there was no fighting back against them, as the countless bodies that blocked all view of the floor proved, so all Elle, MacArthur and Alex could do was to drop, with the bullets meant for them hitting those behind to crumble down on top of them. If it was stifling and suffocating in the crowd shuffling up the ramp, then buried under the warm, blood-soaked bodies of those who had arrived here earlier than them was near deadly to experience. The weight of the next ones to fall blew the air out of their lungs as the three tried to crawl forward, gripping the arms and legs of the corpses in front of them to get themselves up and over, to make some kind of progress. For their luck, the guards didn't notice the living riling about among the dead, but they still slaughtered the ones pushed to the front of the mass of people arriving at the top of the ramp, adding to the dense pressure raining down.

"I can't breathe," Elle coughed, her legs completely crushed by the bodies of the people unwittingly walking into the guards' trap.

"Disloyal bastards! That's what you get!" One guard cheered from behind his wall of crates and other containers that he fired his weapon from behind.

"Guys," Alex spat out a thick lump of blood, leaving his teeth stained a crimson colour as he rested his head on the leg of someone's body.

"Over there! There's some alive in there!" Another of the guards called out, firing rounds into the bodies all around where the three lay, forcing them into a stop where they had to shift corpses to get in the way of the gunfire.

"I don't have a shot, I can't get at the cunts!" Elle swore, not able to wiggle the barrel of the rifle between the misshapen limbs of the bodies laid out about the floor to get a clear look at the guards to fire anything worthwhile back at them.

"Guys, I can't," Alex huffed, "I can't keep going, I'm barely holding here."

"Shut it, Grey," MacArthur spat at him through gritted teeth as yet another body landed on top of him, blood warming against the small of his back, drenching his clothes.

"No, fuck off Mack, just fucking listen, y'prick," Alex closed his eyes, clenching his jaw against the throbbing pain at his stomach. "I—" a far more fierce stabbing sensation lit up his insides and he had to swallow it before he could continue, "really believed in what we did here, in Obsidian. I liked that we made this region a better place. But did we just send out a blanket coverage for keeping Thorne's secret safe? Is that all our work really comes down to? Is that the only difference we made on the starways? Not actually making anything safer for people?"

"It's not as simple as all that," MacArthur shook his head before having to quickly duck out of the way of a shot that would have just struck him.

"I think it is," Alex laughed. "We were used, all of us, and now we're a risk, we're being chucked aside, murdered. That's our reward for a job well done. What kinda bullshit is that?"

"Yeah I know, mate," the other man wanted to reach out to console his friend but he knew if he did it would reveal where they were, killing both him and Alex.

"I just," Elle said, more to herself than to the others, "need a distraction, or something, I can't get at 'em like this."

"Y'know I never really liked people, either, you believe that? Only really got on with the two of you, my whole sad, pathetic life. I chose work over all the rest, I chose protecting a lie that killed countless people, a genocide, over actually living a life I could be proud of."

"You can be proud, Alex, your work has helped keep the people safe, believe me," MacArthur insisted.

"But I'm not Mack, not at all. That recording killed my entire life," tears were in his eyes as he glanced over his shoulder, through the gap in the bodies, back at his friend. "That was my purpose, to protect people, to do some good in the worlds, but he took that from me! He defiled with his lie, it taints everything I ever did, every choice I ever made. But not this. From this moment on, I am my own man. I am making my own choices, with nothing out there in the shadows no more to betray me. I made two friends, that's what I am proud of. And I am proud to say that I can serve my purpose, at least to them."

"What're you saying, Alex?" Elle peered sideways out of her scope at the man.

"Remember when you said I wasn't really the brave type? And I said I was stronger than I look? Well, I stand up for my friends," he said, deploying all of his strength, fuelled by his hate for the crime done to him and the love he bore for his friends. He stood. The bodies that were on top of him falling aside as Alex stumbled up to his feet awkwardly, the wound at his stomach screaming at him to stop but he ignored it, staring down the three guards that raised their heads in confusion. "United we stand!" He yelled through blood-stained teeth, he didn't know why the revolutionaries had chosen the saying, he didn't understand why he chose it for his last words, but he just wanted to insult them, to get one over on them before the inevitable. He didn't have to wait long as all three focused their fire on him, tearing apart Alex's chest, a swarm of laser fire burning away at him. But it stopped once Elle saw the opportunity presented to her, rising out of the corpses, slotting a single shot precisely into the heads of each one in turn as quickly as they could have blinked.

Yet while the guards have been eliminated, clearing the way for them to reach the hangar and the emergency rafts after it, MacArthur took no notice, instead he knelt down beside his friend's body, cradling his hand within his own. "You stupid bastard," he swore, squeezing it with all his strength, "you damn, stupid, fucking bastard!" MacArthur's howling scream made the next wave of people arriving at the top of the ramp hesitate slightly, wary of coming near the big man, but eventually scrambling over the bodies to whatever ship they could find.

"He gave me an opening," Elle placed a hand on MacArthur's shoulder, "without that, we'd be dead."

"I know," he hissed back, "just give me a moment here, for pity's sake."

"You know I can't," she reminded him, flinging the rifle aside and offering the man up with her right hand as she clutched the hilt of her blade in her left. "This station's got a strong foundation, only reason we're alive. But it won't hold forever."

"Fine," MacArthur admitted, accepting the hand up and meeting Elle's gaze with the corners of his eyes welling, "but he comes, too." He didn't wait for a reply, stooping down and taking Alex's body up in his arms before nodding to the Elite to lead the way.

"So what's the plan?" Elle asked, the blood on her gown was getting sticky and dry, and she brushed a hand through her short hair, finding more blood there too, none of it her own. Her feet were stained with it too, as were legs and indeed most of her body now that she had a moment to peer under her gown at the hem to see it. She did feel vulnerable for nearly completely lacking in clothes but she didn't mind, she had just seen how much someone can do no matter how vulnerable they may be.

"We go over to the ship," the man replied, "I want a word with Chief Admiral Thorne," he said as he adjusted his hold on the body he was cradling. "And then it's onto Ruby. Commander Winter needs our help."

"Winter?" Elle gave the man a curious look but given that it was the only plan they collectively had, she kept silent, as they crossed past the vacant bays where ships had already taken off with their lot, leaving the emergency rafts as their only option.

"He's our best hope now," George MacArthur sighed, knowing the weight of his words but meaning them all the same as he led the way into the oval craft, laying Alex down on the floor behind the two seats, shattered glasses tucked away in his pocket.

Chapter 24

It all came alive as he held that lever down, Nathan could feel the ground and walls all around him rumble with the energy surging into the bunker as well as the city coming back to life beyond the stonework. The first sign he saw of the city becoming restored was the light of the sun, almost blindingly bright after the unchallenged reign of night, as it washed through a hole in the ceiling at the centre of this end of the bunker. He almost instinctively went to raise a hand to shield his eyes but stopped once he lowered his gaze to the sight atop the flight of stairs descending to meet him. Soldiers bearing the black armour of Obsidian had appeared, brandishing rifles, silently marching down the steps while others appeared at the catwalks high at either side. The booming and hissing of the colossal generators packed into the sides of this area covered whatever sound these people had made upon entering the bunker, but Nathan was certain that he would have heard any gunfire, and he hadn't. They marched in perfect formation, spreading out to encompass the far end opposite the platform Nathan was standing on and almost as soon as they had covered the sight of the wall behind them in their vast numbers, did they open fire. He had to be quick but one shot did land a glancing blow on his left shoulder before Nathan could raise his free left hand as he held the lever down with his right, casting his shield. Despite the enormity of the red fiery bullets raining down on him, his shield held, but the force of such a storm pushed him back, the purple energy of his protection striking against the tiles on the floor as it ground steadily back towards the wall. "Lena! How much longer?" Nathan grunted into his radio as his arm ached with agony from having to withstand such a force, just as the stone and tiles all around him were blown apart in micro explosions.

"It's at 70%," Lena whispered as she took a dangerous glance up at the terminal screen, begging not to be spotted by the bodies belonging to the footsteps they had all heard pounding their way down the hall to the end. They had needed to be low and silent, more than one of these soldiers took a curious step inside their room but were quick to move on to not fall too far from the formation. Miles had needed to firmly grasp Impala's snout, just in case the quivering dog let out some fearful sound.

"Fine," was all Nathan responded with as he devoted his effort to keeping his shield up. It completely covered his body so he was impervious to the rupturing wall and floor all around him but it came at the cost of the strength of his arm. The sheer force of the gunfire smashed against his shield as waves on a rock, with the inevitability of eroding it the more it applied the pressure. His arm was close to shaking with the effort needed to bear it up at the height of his chest, his boots were needing to hold firm or skid back as his shield cast up the tiles on the floor as it scraped against them, Nathan not able to push back. They fired from on high from the catwalks above his head, they fired from the right and the left on the floor below, they fired an incredible barrage from the centre, but they held off where one figure among them stepped forward. This one was different. The most obvious difference was the red cloak streaming from his broad shoulders, and while he bore the same armour as his troopers, his helmet was ordained with golden veins like stripes, symbolising his superiority. He was a large man as well, taller than Nathan and bulkier, muscular. And the detail that caught Nathan's eye as he just about found a clear hole in the glistening red energy being painted on his shield, was that of the blade in an identical sheath to his own, on the man's right thigh. This man stepped out of the crowd of soldiers and calmly strode the gap over to the platform, seemingly comfortable with the volley of laser fire cast all around his figure. Nathan knew this man instantly, not forgetting the unique armour and cape, and the slightest twitch of fear stole at his heart, a twinge of doubt.

"90%," came Lena's voice over the radio, "the upload's slowing down as power's being diverted to other areas but I can see the outer doors are still closed, we're ok."

"Let me know the moment it's done," Nathan grumbled, the effort obvious in his tone as he was powerless to fight back, one hand on the lever as it was and his other needed to keep up his defence or see him riddled with holes, blasted against the wall into oblivion. All the while, this figure approached eerily calmly, reaching the steps and making his way up, with the fire from his soldiers expertly shaping around the frame of the man. Not a single shot accidently caught him as he confidently walked over to being within only a mere couple of metres from Nathan before coming to a stop, silently staring at him. The barrage of fire was so loud against his shield it was an intense screaming match as energy dissipated upon energy with the casings for those bullets scattering across the floor. It was as though a thunderstorm had erupted within the confines of the bunker, the gunfire for the rain, the clapping of bullet on shield as thunder with the powerful focused infernos of the laser rounds making for the lightning in this cloudburst of carnage. All the while, this figure stood with arms crossed, simply observing the other man under his power, wordlessly watching as he was made to cower behind a shield to survive the onslaught. But with a firm raising of his right palm, the fire ceased immediately.

"It's done! Let go! The outer doors are startin' to open! Stop!" Lena's voice half whispered, half screamed into his ears and Nathan immediately let go of the lever yet it remained down, stealing a brief moment's glance from him before it did finally spring back up. The generators either side of the room blasted out a raucous boom as they were deprived of the connection to the power grid that was so starkly robbed of its life, just before it could be fully resurrected. And without the deafening waves of firepower, the bunker descended into a low quiet, a silence broken only by the tired thumping and hissing of the generators powering down, and the hum from the energy of Nathan's shield. He stayed hunkered down, protecting himself for a moment longer, not trusting the halt of the onslaught arrayed against him.

"So are you alive," the figure that loomed over him said in a disinterested, calm tone, "I was beginning to wonder." And he unfurled his arms from his chest and stepped away, moving across the platform again over to where a railing bordered it, looking out over the men and women under his command.

Nathan didn't respond, but did lower his shield, dropping his left hand steadily, his instincts forcing him to slow, they screamed at him to be ready for another attack at any moment, but it never came. The other man was bold, standing with his back to Nathan, and he knew of only one person willing to do such a thing, confident they could repel any attack he might spring. He stood up, stepping away slightly from the wall which showed an obvious shape from where his shield had protected it, all around this flawless outline was dust and debris, it had rained down on his armour. Nathan brushed off the crumbs of concrete before taking another step forward, all while the other man simply waited. A thought urged him to take out his blade, to fight as an Elite is trained to do, to not allow for another attack that might leave him dead with no weapon in hand, no chance to fight back, but he resisted. Instead, against his baser instincts, Nathan elected to join the man at the railing, gazing out at the mass of soldiers still aiming their weapons directly at him. "More of a surprise that you are still breathing."

"Is it?" The one in the black armour of Obsidian with the red cape, flying from his shoulders as a patriotic soldier of the Old World bore the flag of their nation, removed his helmet and placed it on the floor, revealing the grim effects of his near decade in a sealed away city. His long black hair was streaked with grey yet his face didn't match the sign of age as he seemed far beyond those years, nearer death and plagued with a strange discolouration to his skin, pockmarked with fissures of a dry maroon blood. These gashes appeared deep and unnaturally decomposed on a living face that held an expression of absolute focus, a serious intention to manage the moment. While it was the man's eyes that caught Nathan's attention the most, once being of a kind yet firm human brown, they were now of a dirty, shady yellow caught in a prism in the likeness of an X-Human. There was memory of the man in those eyes, fighting to endure but it was shrouded in an aged look of weariness. "Yet you avoided the path through the Obsidian base at the city centre yourself, and you must have witnessed when we tore yet another group of your Elite's from the sky above."

"The Elites are no longer mine, as I am no longer the company's," Nathan understood that he was expected to remove his helmet as well, so the two old friends could finally see one another again, but this time he listened to his instincts, refraining from doing so.

"Interesting," the man said through decaying lips in a tone of voice burdened with the fatigue of trauma while his expression never changed, though Nathan couldn't tell if it was because he physically couldn't, with the dry, muddy brown taint to his skin. "I expected you to be Section Chief by now."

"Chief? You lose your mind along with your eyes, General?" Nathan scoffed, grasping the rail with his left hand and he rested his right on the hilt of the sword sheathed at the front of his thigh.

"Roderic did say before the city fell that he had decided on you as his successor," General Lux Ardamus went on, "so what happened?"

"Elias is Chief now."

"Is that so?" The look that now occupied the General's face was a definite change in expression, one that spoke loudly of anger and disapproval. "The retch that cursed me here."

"So you're aware of what caused the Collapse?" Nathan felt an instinct tug at him, a feeling to keep his companions hidden, and he felt a weight at his right arm, as though the data stored there became a physical burden to carry.

"Collapse? Is that what they said of this city?" The other man spat, insulted, "this was no collapse, old friend. This was a murder, pure and simple, an entire city butchered by the arrogance of a single man. But to answer your question, yes, I am aware. I was suspicious of the Director of RCS for some time in the days leading up to the event, I discovered this place just the day before it all happened."

"Hmm, sure seems he is single-handedly to blame."

"Be assured that he is," those yellow eyes that were stricken with a sickly look to not appear anything like the natural bejewelled ones that X-Humans possess. "His compound or product, whatever he fashioned it, caused this," the General explained, raising a gloved hand to mean the ill changes to his face, "and this is what good fortune looks like. So many died, they are beyond counting."

"They didn't just die, Lux, whatever substance he created, it defiled people's bodies, turned them into abominations, and for what? He's Chief now, sure, but he hides in a fortress he's made that orbits Carmine. He's afraid, even with the power of an entire region in his grasp and the destruction of a city behind him."

"He's afraid of you."

"Hmm," Nathan grunted, dismissing the idea. He knew full well that someone like Elias Thorne was never likely to meet him in an open fight, but he settled for the idea that he never feared Nathan, not really, not when he had so much security, the robo-sentries and the power of Obsidian at his call. The question in the once Elite Commander's head was that how could someone feel fear when they are untouchable, immune to threat?

"You say he's built a fortress in space? What other clear sign do you need that he's scared of you and your inevitable assault? I do assume that you will try to kill him at some point? For the piles of corpses of the people you considered under your protection here in Rose?"

"I will, but the bodies here don't bother me, Lux, they were under my protection once, sure, but I don't really see it like that anymore. The connection's gone, the man that felt it is dead."

"What do you mean?" The General asked in an accusing tone. "The purpose we both serve remains the same, even if not everyone is alive to be protected anymore. We still serve, we still avenge, we still give the people a chance at a better life, or have you forgotten the principles I taught you?" A soft rattling sound shook from the sudden vibrating of the railing where the General grasped it, not that he showed any sign of noticing it, yet Nathan took note.

"What purpose? What's the idea of protecting people in the face of such wanton mass murder?"

"It's everything, Winter, you used to believe that, too, or have you really abandoned it all? Roderic made you his successor because your parents and I agreed with him that you had the strength of will to overpower any corrupt son of a bitch seeking to turn the system against those it is designed to sustain, just like Elias did here. And not just that, you had the aggression to kill anyone who stood in your way but with the sense of mind to make the right choices for who died and who was in need of protection, you were a good man. Don't tell me you threw all that away, don't tell me you forsook the survivors of this slaughter, don't tell me you turned your back on what it meant to be Elite Commander!"

It was no common frustration that Nathan sensed in the other man's voice, a tone he was most familiar with hearing, from the vast array of victims he had amassed since the day of the Capital Collapse, the once owners of the eyes now adorning his trophy collection. He deduced it was more of an obsession, a near addiction fuelling those words and that made Nathan wonder, as the Lux Ardam us he knew had no such affliction. An obsession with an idea, it made this man far more dangerous than first anticipated. "I told you, I'm not with the company anymore," Nathan dismissed as his eyes analysed the armour these soldiers wore. It was clear to see that they had spent considerable time and effort to keep it in good shape, you could see the pride they took in it, respecting the purpose the General was speaking of. But Nathan couldn't find that same purpose in himself anymore.

"They would've needed you after what happened here, the survivors. They would've needed your leadership, your heart—that strength you have, to care and yet be absolutely savage in keeping them safe. I would never call you perfect, but you were exactly what this region needed, a strong, emotionally dynamic leader. And you were a man I could call friend," the General sighed in a nostalgic sigh.

"That was you, old friend, that was always you," Nathan disagreed, shaking his head. "You just reflected off me, I was always more concerned with who I could hurt, who I could kill. I was your blunt instrument, don't overstate things in your high of sentiment."

"Is it easier for you to think of it like that?" General Ardamus fixed Nathan with a supportive stare, "these years haven't been kind to you, have they? To make the past seem so brutal that you had to leave it all behind."

"It was brutal, or are you the one with holes in your memory? I was just a child when, at your recommendation let's remember, I was thrown into the Elite Academy, forced to kill or die, moulded into Obsidian's deadly product, a fine contribution to the Board in the way of an undefeatable weapon."

"Don't play weak with me, Winter, you chose the life, and if you're looking for blame for how you turned out, look no further than yourself."

"It's not just me to blame," Nathan admitted, knowing he had chosen for himself to wallow in his grief, to use it to justify the things he did, but that wasn't to say he wasn't proud of the things he had done, or that he wouldn't do the them again presented with the choice a second time.

"If you're at a crossroads in the stars, then just pick a constellation and travel down it, looking back suits for lesser people, lacking the strength to determine their path for themselves. And that is why you are here isn't it? In this place of all the worlds you could lay at your feet. You came here, to the forlorn Capital."

"I vowed to never return here, albeit a private promise. But somehow, I knew I'd come back here one day, that fate wouldn't leave me be, that I had to return here to know the why of it all."

"The experimentation on the X-Human species," Lux Ardamus scoffed, "more like torture and mutilation. All for a product to hoard the Chairman's attention or overthrow him, whatever it might be, the costs were too great for any of it. To bring down a city," he waved a casual hand at the soldiers still maintaining their ready to fire stance, "and to betray its people, how in all the starways could Elias justify this?"

"No reason would satisfy what he's done," Nathan shut down, his tone hardening by being forced to recollect the days of the Collapse, the build-up to it flowing in his mind, leading to its inevitable, chilling conclusion.

"Why do I sense there's something you're not saying, old friend? As though there is something more that Elias Thorne has done to you? For you to turn your back on your purpose and hide from who you are." The General put a comforting right hand on Nathan's shoulder, which was odd to the other man seeing as he still had a vast amount of guns still trained on his head.

"Monique and Harkness are dead, they died that day," Nathan was surprised by the sound of his own voice, he sounded hurt, he sounded haunted, it was a tone to his own words that he never heard before, he thought himself weak and twitched his head violently.

"Oh no," Ardamus bowed his head and closed his eyes, "I'm so sorry, Nathan, I should've asked first, but I—" he raised his head and took a deep breath to steady himself, using his left hand to wipe his brow. "I thought you were my enemy, I thought you were coming to take the information stored in this facility away to bring it back to Elias, to carry on his work."

"Hmm," Nathan grunted again upon knowing his instincts were right.

"Fuck," the General let out a similar, throaty, dismissal, "your family was the bedrock of it all."

"What?"

"Your family kept you balanced, we needed your aggression but they were essential for keeping you on track. With them at your side, you were the leader we needed you to be, so without them—" those swampy, yellow eyes shifting slower over to Nathan, those dark pupils honing in on the dark grey ovals masking his own eyes. "Well, I guess I'm just now meeting you, aren't I? So who's this? Who is this new Nathan Winter?"

"I'm a hunter," Nathan felt the cold retreat of that supportive arm on his shoulder, feeling a tension rise between them. "I track down and kill the members of the hierarchy, I take an eye from each of them to add to my collection, I make them all pay for what they did, supporting Thorne."

"You're a serial killer? You?"

"A very basic way to label a highly successful vendetta but it's accurate," Nathan could feel the General's mind ticking over, he could practically hear the inner workings of the other man's brain changing to the idea that he might be under threat, even with his army standing ready. The soft rattling of the railing intensified, not loud enough to break the conversation but now a nervous eye from the General peered down to see his trembling hands.

"You abandoned your career where you devoted yourself to the purpose of protecting people, for a purpose bent on murdering them instead? You possess the strength of will to show them a better way, only killing those who refuse to follow, yet you don't even give them the chance? You just butcher them? Robbing them of an eye? That's—" The General hesitated as he saw where his sentence was leading him to, "not the man I knew."

"Judge me if you will, but the opinion of a man who's been dead for near a decade doesn't bother me in the slightest. Fate has turned cruel in your absence, Lux, and the starways lead to bitter ends, but I am proud of what I have done, and the choices I've made. I am the man this region needs me to be, I'm sure of that."

"A murderer?"

"Yes," Nathan was so sure, his tone was frightening, his unwavering certainty intimidating.

"So why are you here? Really? You know why the city fell now, why your wife and son died, so now what?" It was now that the General looked back over his shoulder at the power lever, considering the meaning of where he had found this stranger to him. "What were you doing?"

"Powering up the bunker, to broadcast Elias's confession," Nathan had no reason to fear that element of truth being given.

"To what end?" The General took a step away from the railing to stand side on to Nathan, his right hand resting on the hilt of his own blade, stashed at the front of his right leg the exact same as the man across from him.

"You know, I never held much stock in people after the Capital Collapse," Nathan nodded to himself, grinning under his helmet. "But I met some people, Lux, and these people showed me a way forward, a new purpose to devote myself to and that's why I'm here. Because it's perfect. This new idea, this brilliant new idea, it doesn't just act as a smokescreen for all the bloodletting I still have to do, but it gives me a chance to connect with people again, something I didn't even know I was capable of doing anymore, let alone wanting to."

"And what is this idea?"

"Revolution."

"Revolution's a bloody notion, old friend. If you topple the system, bring it to its knees, you'll just be removing the very thing that provides for the people, even if it is a drip-feed rather than a bottle. Something is better than nothing," the General warned, as he placed his helmet back on from where he had set it down on the platform floor, sensing a need for it.

"It won't have nothing, it'll have me," Nathan stepped away from the railing, feeling his killer confidence bloom inside him like the first embers to start a wildfire.

"An unforgiving killer? You've not just shunned the purpose you used to serve, you've stained and covered it in blood!"

"I'll come for the data, too, Ardamus. I'm going to need it in order to prove what Elias did, I can't just have it as our word against his, and I don't see you stepping up as a witness somehow." Nathan paced steadily across from the other man, stopped, and turned slightly so that his left foot was forward and his right hand was gripping the hilt of his weapon, the perfect stance to launch from with his jetpack.

"Our?" The General asked, seizing on the word.

"Pardon?"

"If those Elites weren't with you, then who are you with? You didn't come to this city alone, even you can be overwhelmed."

"No, a pilot is waiting aboard my ship," Nathan replied, thinking quickly to answer honestly while not giving more away.

"Hmm, but I sense there's more," the General flicked back his red cape that flapped lazily to the platform floor, dirtied by the dust it found there, its red turning to a different shade. "One that accompanies you that inspired this idea in your head?" Ardamus probed as he tightened his grip on the hilt of his sword but he held his nerve to not draw too soon as to welcome a strike against him.

"Hmm," Nathan huffed, not rising to the challenge.

"It's a woman, isn't it? Eight long years and yet now you are ready to move on, the great Nathan Winter, smitten and driven to genocidingly compete with Elias Thorne for who's the bigger mass murderer? I think you're confusing love and rage, my old friend. I think you're afraid of that attachment, especially the meaning of it, and the potential for losing it, feeling that pain again, the grief."

"Quiet," Nathan growled, deep and low.

"Why? Am I wrong? Not that it matters though."

"And why's that?"

"The region knowing Elias's guilt? That's bad, that's something I didn't want at this moment but it's not insurmountable. But letting that information, those details that are kindling for a great fire that would see everything burned, and I can't allow that. My purpose cannot allow that."

"Your purpose? You have been sealed away and forgotten, Ardamus, expertly discarded by Elias, what care should I take in dismissing your imagined purpose?"

"Imagined purpose? My purpose is the same as the one we served together! To protect the people! I was sealed away, yes, I was played, fair enough, but I'm not weak like you to abandon my purpose. If anything, Elias did me a favour locking me up in this city when he ordered me to secure the Directorate district, knowing full well my battalion and I would run out of time to evacuate ourselves. It allowed me to serve my purpose like never before, to safeguard knowledge and secrets that could see the greater picture of this region's future crumble. And I know those secrets are on that terminal mounted to your arm," the General pointed at Nathan with his free trembling left hand. "You! I wanted to see you again, I really did. I dreamed of this moment but you've let me down. You betrayed me! You were the one I'd hoped to come here, to liberate me and my troop, to set us free, to stand by my side again or even be the one to obliterate us. Even if you came as servant of Obsidian and slew us all with that sword of yours in service to your company, that would've been better than this, better than more and more years of the kind of misery you could never imagine! At least then it would've been you. Not this monster I see in my friend's armour."

"He killed Monique, killed Harkness, you really think—"

"You really think I don't want him dead for that, too?" The General shouted as best his voice allowed, hoarse and tired, lacking the strength to sound more authoritative, interrupting Nathan. "That is no excuse for bringing that data into the light of day, because it's murdered thousands, maybe millions, and you want to quench its thirst even more? You're either ignorant to its silcance, or naive to its importance, its power you can't handle that's for sure."

"I think you're putting way too much value in a few lines of text and a mixture of herbs and chemicals," Nathan dismissed.

"You fool! You're talking about interfering with the genetic makeup of a people, not to mention the inter-species rift, or even war, it could start! Do you understand why this work is so awful to let it be seen through to its end? Can you imagine how powerful someone would be if that compound were successful? What they would be capable of?"

"Never considered it," Nathan's patience had run out, he had no idea if Cait and the others had left the bunker or were choosing to remain hidden but he could feel the soldiers on the floor, on the catwalks above his head beginning to stir.

"Well, you wouldn't, would you? Not you, not this new you, I mean. The old you, he would delete those files and put a bullet in his own brain, but this one, you're a different breed of dangerous, aren't you?"

"Enough, Ardamus, I'm leaving, with the data," Nathan shook his head and made a move to go towards the steps down from the platform. It didn't matter that he was fully aware that Cait had a copy of the files, too, so he could make a show of deleting them and maybe then there would be no cause for violence. His senses were far more attune now that he was embracing his aggressive energies, allowing them to fuel him as he felt the electricity flowing through his blood. Nathan knew somehow that even if he did choose the potentially peaceful option, Cait was still in danger. For all his show, for all his effort to put on the image of a stable man, even after his years of unspeakable trauma, Nathan could see through the other man, see at his true self. Because he had known Lux Ardamus, been close to him and even idolised him growing up. So he could notice the shaking of the other man's hands, he could see how he was quicker to stand ready for a fight than even he who wanted it, and he remembered how Ardamus had stood over him while the full firepower of his soldiers clashed against his shield, the indifference in his stance. Nathan saw through the posing, the need to cling onto a past self, to tell oneself that they are sane, that they are exactly who they think themselves to be, and not to have lost that fight before they even realised it was happening. He knew, he was certain. If he made a show of relenting, of deleting the files he downloaded from Elias's terminal, it wouldn't matter in the end. Because in his obsession to fulfil his purpose, Nathan knew that General Lux Ardamus would find Cait and kill her, for inciting the idea of revolution, an idea that poisoned his mind, that he felt was the ultimate threat to the people he still held onto protecting.

"I can't let you," the General drew out his sword, extending the shaft of the blade. It was as long as Nathan's but a different shape, the blade curved, stemming from a handle with a single guard protruding forward. It was crafted in a wood encased in a dark grey metal and when its bearer ignited its heart by flicking down the guard, it became awash in flame, more yellow than white however, as the blade was older than Nathan's, not as well maintained. But the golden shoots of lightning originating from it and sharply slashing against the ruined tiled floor were still of immense power, showing no sign of having lost their destructive prowess.

"Your purpose is conflicting with mine and so here you are standing in my way," Nathan stopped and turned to the other man, "that is no safe place to stand." He was sure now. Nathan had known the risks from the moment Cait had taken that seat next to him in that bar back on Vermillion, when she pitched her grand idea for what the data he intended to take would unleash. The risk of revolution, the true nature of that idea that he was fairly certain Cait was underestimating, but Ardamus was obsessing over. That people would die. A lot of people would die. That interfering with the Coalition's contribution was the same as going near a predator's food, or going to steal a child from their mother, it was not a safe thing to endeavour and it put them at odds with powers equal to them or stronger, and that meant conflict. And the debate of freedom was a fuel like no other for a conflict the like of which could be on a scale like no one in the tri-systems could have possibly experienced, or known of since the Old World was abandoned in that same spirit. Revolution was a bloody ideal, Nathan knew, and that was partly why he agreed to it. It meant fighting, and fighting was what he was good at.

The first strike was a downwards one as the General took several paces towards Nathan before putting all his strength into a swing that the other man easily stepped aside from before bringing the blade about again, then again and again. Nathan dodged every attack, calmly taking one step to move out of the way from the force of the slash with the slightest of effort until the other man grew frustrated and charged. The General rushed forward, going to stab at the chest but Nathan lazily moved to one side which invited an upwards slash from hip to shoulder but it didn't land. Nathan easily swooped down low out of the way, connecting a powerful right handed punch to the other man's mid region as he passed him. Now he finally produced his own weapon, twirling the handle of his sword around in his right hand before extending its length and setting it aflame in the same motion, bringing about a hard, powerful backhanded strike that Ardamus needed two hands to repel.

Chapter 25

Once the upload was complete, Cait could feel the power leave the bunker, sinking back, as she knew that Nathan had let go of the lever, and she could see the relief on the faces of her friends. She was hunched down low, hiding behind the desk from the view of the soldiers that had streamed without end down the corridor, with Lena at her side, Tomen and Miles across from her, the dog, Impala, too, and Sam's body twisted in the corner. The fear that had clung at her heart was easing, where it had felt like it was dragging her to the grave before, when those heavy black boots were marching by, so many guns, so many bright red visors. But her hands were shaking, and Cait knew she was far from safe yet, so she gripped Lena's tight, so hard that she was afraid she was digging her nails into her friend's skin. But Lena showed no sign of being bothered if that were happening, instead she held a firm expression, a silent 'we will get through this' that made Cait feel bolder. "We gotta move, stay low, stay quiet," Tomen was the first to make the first iota of sound in the office since Lena gave Nathan the word that it was done.

"Ok," Cait replied, following Lena who gave her a strong nod upon letting go of her hand as they crawled into standing, making for the doorway, having to go around the desk and side table they had used to hide behind. She took one last glance over her shoulder at Sam's cold body dumped unceremoniously in the corner but there was no time or even a possibility for taking him with them, they had to move quickly. Besides, she wasn't sure the others would want to. Once in the hallway, she could hear it. It sounded like screaming. But it wasn't human, it couldn't be, it was so loud and ear-splitting, the echo of it was a roar rising from the end of the facility up to meet them. Bursts of light shone from there, bright and golden flashes in fight, a battle of light and sound, a storm of past and future endeavours coming to clash, over the idea that she held so close to her heart. It was in that moment, as she stood just beside Lena, gawking at this terrifying sight, wincing from the howls from the deific weaponry brought to bear against one another, that she decided this idea needed the man she had left there to fight her battle. Nathan had ensured their survival through the city, through ordeals and threats that the two men shouting at her to catch up could never have combated alone. Tomen and Miles were people she adored and greatly admired, but they were deeply outmatched by the things they had found along their way through the city. Cait was certain that without Nathan, they never would have left the square beyond the shipyard gates, they never would have known the secret to the cause of the Capital Collapse. Success would have been as sand falling through their fingers, unattainable and impossible to grasp.

"What are you waiting for? Move!" Miles yelled as he stopped, seeing Cait and Lena fall behind, grabbing at Tomen's jacket so he would notice, too. Impala heard the lack of footsteps treading in behind him and glanced back from the base of the steps up to the surface, barking at them madly, begging for them to join him.

"We don't have time," Tomen shook his head and without a word of prompt, he sprinted back, grabbed Lena around the waist and lifted her up. The X-Human wasn't caught in the same state of shock as her friend, standing idle just so Cait wasn't alone, and screamed in protest, stretching out a hand to grab Cait, to shake her out of whatever trance had captured her but her fingertips fell just shy, finding air instead of that battered, black cloak. "Get Cait!" Tomen boomed to Miles as he jogged by with Lena raining down hard fists against his back.

"Put me down, Tomen! You can't just leave her!" Lena landed a hard knee into the man's gut that saw her collapse from his arms and they landed in an awkward, twisted heap together as Miles ran towards Cait.

"Cait! Come on!" He shouted, a bead of sweat forming in his hairline and flowing down his brow to trickle in one amber bejewelled eye filled with anxiety.

But Cait had already made up her mind. She couldn't just leave the man who had got her here behind. Revolution was a vague, formless fantasy without Nathan, she decided, and she couldn't leave him to fight that small army alone, she couldn't turn her back on him, no matter that Tomen had the data-card, the prize they had set out for. And then an image popped into her head, one that sealed it for her. Back in the apartment they had found as the only safe spot in the city to lay their heads down for some sleep, she hinted at a possibility for

Nathan to have hope, but he quickly dismissed it, not believing her. He'd huffed, lost in his darkness, but Cait saw something when he mocked her, "don't be so sure," he had said, but there was something else being said by his eyes, and she was sure there was an element of gratitude there. She had shown some small level investment in him, some awareness of his better self that even he didn't possess, and it wasn't something she felt like she could just turn her back on, to flee and save herself. No, for Cait, the idea that she had seen something more in her protector's sombre eyes was enough to risk it all. Before Miles could reach her, she grasped the shotgun still draped across her shoulders and sprinted, making for the end of the bunker, ignoring the pleas behind her as best she could, tenacious in sticking to her decision.

Nathan's swings of his sword were powerful and the sound of their blades clashing was an attack to the senses. As golden lightning smashed together with metal it created an orchestra of torment, a skirmish of godlike power and the harrowing banshee screaming emanating from the collision of blade on blade. The energies empowering these weapons came together with immense booming thunderclaps, the sight of their smashing one another blinding, as white infernos clung to an unbreakable edge, encased in golden streaks of power, warring furiously. And while Nathan was strong, raining down blow after blow, the General was stalwart enough to break them, parrying and bringing his own swings and slashes to bear, stabbing at any opportunity. The two men circled one another on the platform as the eyes of the mass of soldiers watched on, not interfering for they had not been given the order, trusting in their leader to prevail. Nathan blocked a downwards strike from his adversary before using the other man's momentum to his advantage, allowing him to shrug away from him to deliver a hammer blow of a backhanded attack with only the slightest action to power up but it was blocked expertly. The General hadn't seen the shrug coming so he had carried on his stride, open to the attack but he raised his sword in time to stand a staunch defensive and use the opening to land a heavy boot in Nathan's gut. The force of the blow cast him back and Nathan found himself tumbling over the railing, landing with a crunch of metal, the air stolen from his lungs, his blade still ignited, burning and sizzling against the tile floor.

"We need to go back!" Lena screamed in Tomen's ear but they were already stepping over the threshold of the bunker and the sight they beheld upon doing so was enough to rob her attention, as well as that of the others. It was the first time they had seen the yellow sun of the Crimson region for days now, but it was blotted out. A colossal black vessel hovered in the way of its arm embrace, the cold shadow of the beast looming over their heads down the stretch of the boulevard that lay at their feet. The glowing red bridge of the ship felt as though it were glaring right at them, so they immediately leapt to the ground, scrambling across the loose surface to the cover of the low walls. Smaller crafts were whizzing and whirling across the sky above, tiny versions of the monstrous ship that brought them, securing the air space above the Capital City. Different shaped crafts emerged next, coming from the side of the one that kept at bay the sight of the sun, as they were more the shape and size of shipping containers. Simple in their design, basic black boxes that dropped, plummeting to the ground, only relenting in their fall when a short measure from the ground, using thrusters to stall their impact. The narrower edge of these containers opened and out spilled the colleagues of Obsidian, clad in their pristine jet black armour, brandishing weapons of all shapes and sizes, all of them sprinting towards the bunker.

Azuri kept the ship going at a fast pace, sporting a smile as she felt the controls scream at her for more, relishing the unstable, reactionary flying of combat as she weaved a path through the crowd of Obsidian craft barring her path. Her take off from the shipyard had caught them all unawares, as the last thing they had expected was the sight of the Elite Starfighter ascending among their ranks, blasting them into oblivion, its full arsenal catching them off guard. While it bore the style of the Obsidian fleet, the sleek, shiny black armour, the seemingly glowing red cockpit screen, it was the one of its kind in the skies above Ruby. It was to Tomen and Miles that Nathan had explained that he had made some modifications to this already incredibly impressive piece of technology, but it was Azuri feeling those benefits as she was able to out-manoeuvre, out-gun and fly far faster than the lesser Obsidian vehicles that were doomed as soon as she set her sights on them. Yet they were far greater in number. Once she had got word from the others of their plan, she raised the shutter on her hangar dock and prepared the ship for flight. And it was when the light invaded that she was witness to the strength of the force they had come to this place to overcome. Immediately an Obsidian fleet had arrived, passing through transit gates in the upper atmosphere, and she took to the skies to meet them. While she was able to strike off a half dozen of them in her sudden appearance, the Obsidian fighters soon wisened to her presence and began their pursuit. What took days for the team to navigate on the ground, by foot, she did in a matter of minutes, navigating a path across Rose City, keeping low, using the taller buildings for cover from the Marauder class vessel dominating the sky. Tomen had told her where the bunker was, she had plotted out a path using the console behind her right shoulder, and now she was coming up on the Directorate district, bearing witness to the army descending to take back what was theirs, and her family having to cower down low to avoid the barrage of fire meant to destroy them. She knew exactly what she wanted to do, banking to the right, passing behind tower blocks and skyscrapers to mask her approach as she thundered the craft a sharp left when the moment was perfect. The ship was in tune with her thoughts, agreeing with every burst of the throttle and turn of the controls, they were an elegant match, a skilled team. And when she found herself flying straight forward, looking directly down the length of the boulevard ahead, all those Obsidian soldiers right in front of her cannons, she didn't hesitate.

Cait stopped immediately at the base of the steps, the sight of her protector, the warrior she figured to be without match, on the ground, his enemy standing above him, was enough to freeze her in place. The soldiers were everywhere. Luckily for her, she had been quiet in taking the way down so their entire focus was on the battle playing out in front of them, giving her the moment to peer her eyes to the left and to the right, to the catwalks above, unbelieving the sheer number of them. She stood absolutely still, stunned anyway into silence as she watched Nathan pick himself up, while the taller man in the bulky armour, with the red cape flowing from his shoulders, steadily made his way down the steps of the platform. Then she heard it. The sound had rung up to the upper level of the bunker, but to stand before it was an entirely different experience as her ears shot with agony at the splintering sound of the lightning of those two blades vigorously clashing. Cait pulled her hood up which only mildly clouded the deafening screeching and watched helplessly as the two men fought, desperately scrounging for an answer to the question she begged of herself in her head: 'now what?'

While the General used both of his hands to add more power to his attacks, Nathan preferred to use only his right, comfortable in his strength and skill to repel and strike one-handed, using it as a psychological edge. The impact of the ground had done no damage to his body, but his mind had taken the hit, Nathan's aggressive energies still surging, still granting the violent high in his brain, but it was with a punch from reality. He found himself reminded, this man is strong, this enemy will give you a fight. He parried one blow to the side forehanded, casting the tip of the General's blade towards the ground, before rolling the hilt in his hand, delivering a powerful thrust at the other man's head. The General glanced his head out of the way just in time for the blade to only strike against the armour plating on his helmet but Nathan's strength kept it there, digging into the man's head, putting his weight behind the effort, using both hands. But the armour on the helmet held, and the General raised his own blade in a swipe which was erratic and aimless but worked in staving off his attacker. Nathan danced away, feeling the rhythm in his feet, his arms, his mind in tune to a macabre theme, as he found himself enjoying the challenge, grateful for the rare opportunity to test his skill. He spun his blade around his right hand, toying with the ideas in his head for his next move, as the two men circled one another, neither daring to take their eyes away from the fight.

"You've abandoned your training," the General spat at him, "you fight like a savage."

"Better than fighting like a dead man," Nathan mocked in return. They were caught in a moment's stalemate, neither wishing to be the first to move, leaving themselves open for a deadly counter.

"The man I knew would've respected the gravity of his actions," the General went on. "You would spark a flash-fire revolution, but to what end? Without the system, the people will suffer."

"How would you know? The people you so love and protect are starving, ending their days reeling from shifts where they grow a manufactured crop or sustain a cloned animal that they see only the slightest stipend of. Where is the care in that? The system has the means to look after its people, it simply refuses to. And that's where I come in."

"Because you care so much!"

"Not necessarily," Nathan chuckled, "but I can do a better job, I have no need for hiding behind entrenched space stations, I can build a better tri-systems for everyone, I'm simply the only one with the will strong enough to do so."

"You're only one with the insanity of thinking that's the only way, to burn the old tri-systems down first to make way for your vastly depleted new one, is that it?"

"Revolution is the way forward, the people must stand united, even I can see that now," Nathan's tone changed, his killing swagger shifting into a more serious, measured exposition. "But the powers of those rallied against that wave of change are far greater than I or any army of the common people can stand against with words alone. We cannot argue our case because our ideas and desires mean damage to their precious way of life, their obsession with standing above the rest of us. No, Lux, they must die. There is no other way of it."

"You are strong, Winter," The General stopped their slow moving circle, standing still, his army arrayed behind him. "But you don't know Hell. Hell is where I have been for the past eight years, wading through the destruction from an idea born from someone who thought they could change the big picture of people's lives quickly. I've witnessed the tortures and agonies that arrogance and a lust for power can conjure. I will not let you do the same on a vastly exponential scale, I cannot." The General glanced lazily over his shoulder and raised his empty left hand, "open fire!" He yelled, bringing that hand down swiftly, pointing his flat palm at Nathan.

This time however, the Elite Commander did not go on the defensive. He raised his left shield, blocking the immediate wave of red energised fire but floated swiftly up with his jetpack, before hurtling at great speed into the centre of the crowd of troops. His impact was explosive, using his shield to smash away the soldiers standing where he landed, and once he was among them, their weapons counted for naught. Nathan was too quick, using his sword in slashes and blows too fluid and fast for the soldiers to do anything to defend themselves. One approached him with his rifle, bearing down fire that struck harmless against the metal on Nathan's armour before a darting slash took off the barrel of his rifle, and in a blink of an eye, the blade came round again to slice at the back of his leg, breaking him down in a slump of the floor before being beheaded. Another tried charging Nathan, firing his shotgun manically but he was met with a left handed punch to the head, the shield engaging at the moment he was struck so his head popped and exploded as the purple energy took shape. Nathan used his shield to block the fire from a group to his left, spearheaded by one carrying a far larger weapon, a combination of twelve barrels spinning at great speed, spitting out a storm of tiny crimson energised rounds that battered against his defence. Yet he remained calm, steadily stowing his blade in favour of shrugging his rifle off his back, bringing it about his front as his shield lowered, detecting the barrel, and allowing him to fire off a single shot, blasting the skull of the soldier with the enormous gun. Nathan kept that stance, slotting a single ballistic round into the helmets of the soldiers that were too panic-stricken to fire back at him through the opening he was using, instead seeing their efforts wasted against the impenetrable shield.

"Nate!" Cait yelled from the side-lines, huddling down, cradling her shotgun, and getting knocked about by the bodies of the soldiers all trying to find a better position to fire at Nathan. She shot one who turned to face her, having backed into her and nearly lost their footing, but the fighting was too loud for even her cannon of a gun to be heard. She realised quickly that if the soldiers directly in front of her had not heard her killing one of their own, then Nathan had no chance of hearing her calling, so she used her surprise to her advantage, attacking them from behind.

Nathan's anger grew as his head was pelted with fire from above, so he unleashed his final two rockets, one for each catwalk, tearing them down with raging crashing and explosions, shouts of agony piercing through the mist of dust and debris from the metalworks' collapse. Then he eyed one of the soldiers firing at him, a launcher kin to his own behind that one's shoulders that was firing his rifle uselessly at him. He was among a grouping but it mattered little, Nathan flung his rifle back over his shoulder and unleashed his blade as used his jetpack to power across the gap in a heartbeat, plunging his sword into his target's chest. While he worked the empty cartridge behind his left shoulder, he held his right hand up, his shield casting from his sword grip, so he could more easily reload his launcher. And once done, he rose to his feet as the soldiers had closed in all around him. They fired their guns, the force from that barely stalling Nathan who hardly felt it, making a sharp slash at the one to his right's neck, then landing a devastating, crunching blow to the knee of one to his left, bringing his blade about to slash open the throat of the one behind him. Nathan's attacks were deft and swift, landing a single blow to each soldier in the group surrounding him until they all lay at his feet, allowing him to see the small group of their number making for the stairs, making to flee. A single rocket saw to blocking their way, erupting the archway at the top, bringing down the ceiling as chunks of concrete skipped down the steps, barrelling into the ones running from him.

"Stop this madness!" The General shouted, thrusting his sword into Nathan's midriff but finding his effort blocked by a left-handed shield. The two battled, neither gaining an upper hand as they were of an equal match, Nathan's efforts held back as he was forced to use his shield to repel the swarm of gunfire otherwise rattling against his armour. They stepped over the bodies of the ones cut into pieces, rendered apart until Nathan saw a swing blocked and he couldn't stop himself going forward in his momentum and he was struck with a forceful knee to his stomach. His sword battered out of his hand as he slumped by a quick flick of the General's blade. And that was when he saw Cait. She was desperately holding up a dead soldier close to her body as a shield while firing her gun with her free right hand but they were closing in. So he devoted his focus to launching a rocket barrage at the ceiling above her attackers, instead of avoiding the General's next attack.

Azuri's run couldn't have been more successful as she left a litter of bodies in the wake of her attack. She banked at the end of the long road, now beneath the belly of the beast, and made for a path to her right, but a swarm of fighter craft were heading straight at her, coming from that direction. They had the upper hand, having coordinated this attack, with their fireballs of red lasers, glancing off the Elite Starfighter, and while she took two down with her own cannons, she beat a retreat. There were too many. And they had caught her scent. Azuri glided over the perimeter wall with more of a dozen smaller ships in tow, using the full power of the engines, one attached under either wing, and used the towers coming out of the flooded surface for cover. The concrete, metal and glass of these structures saw sections of them pulverised as the attacks intended for her smashed against them, Azuri having to be as agile as possible to avoid having that fire, and to not crash into the buildings taking the hits for her. Smaller, quicker silhouettes that pulled at her attention in the wide view she had in the cockpit emerged but she kept her focus on her flying. That was until one such shape burst out of the surface of the water she was skimming against, a frightening monstrous merge of three or four people into a sharp-toothed abomination leapt right at her. Despite the thrum of her engines, Azuri could hear its roar as it soared through the air from its tremendous leap but she quickly edged to her right, dipped her left wing and used it to fling the shape into one of the pursuing ships coming up on her on that side. She was quick enough to catch a glimpse of the thing as he tore off the cockpit hood of the fighter craft and brought down its combination of jaws onto the screaming head of the pilot clutched in its horrifying grasp.

"The fuck was that?" Azuri murmured to herself but she had no time to dwell on what she had just seen as the swarm of fighters behind her, though fewer of them now, were still relentlessly firing against her. She dipped her right side wing to turn fully around and head back to the Directorate district and bring some of her own weapons to bare but there were so many, another squadron having joined her pursuers and they were all unleashing their payload of armaments at her. Red, fiery electricity scratched against the cockpit screens and Azuri could barely see a way ahead past the sprawl of crafts flying directly for her as the armour of her ship began to thud and wail for the pummelling it was taking. She fired back, using the cannons at the ship's fore but there were too many, and the force of the hits were making her wings unsteady and she was forced to take her fingers off from the triggers to better handle the control stalks. But they were coming. More and more firepower rained against the cockpit as they got closer and closer, the gap between them a mere few roads now, and they showed no signs of stopping, seemingly not caring to shoot her out of the sky or smash into her, bringing her down that way. Azuri's hands were shaking as fear gripped her, a hidden hand crushing her heart, another one teasing at her belly where her young one slept, her mind wondering whether she would get the chance to ever be awake. Her thoughts spiralled away from the controls begging her to change course as her mind was plagued with terror, she couldn't break free from the terrible realisation that she hadn't just put herself in the sights of all those guns, but her yet to be born child as well. She winced, she couldn't help it, flinching at the cockpit screen being engulfed in an energised inferno, waiting for the inevitable.

Nathan felt the heat of the blade even before it struck as the General landed a strong slash at his neck, but his armour held. The roof of the bunker caved, sections of concrete thundering down, squashing those underneath it, echoing loud explosions as Nathan, still on the ground, was able to turn and grasp the length of the other man's blade with his left hand, and despite that arm being invaded by flames, he was still able to push it off from his neck. Then with a roll, he was able to recover his own sword, blocking the next attack, a downwards strike, and then Nathan was back on the offensive. His left arm ablaze still, he slashed with more concentration and accuracy than anyone in his state ought to be capable of, his attacks calm and swift, forcing the General into a retreat. A group of soldiers then grasped at the other man as Nathan watched, forcing him out of the way so that they could get in between them, doing their best to provide their leader some time to recover. But they could not bear to stand against him. Nathan effortlessly stabbed and slashed them away, slicing away limbs, removing heads, disarming then disembowelling before they were out of his way and he could see the next soldier, giving the General a rocket launcher. Ardamus didn't aim for Nathan, figuring he would raise a shield or swiftly dodge it, instead he fired his tube's single missile at the ceiling above the other man's head, just as he had done, casting down huge chunks of the structure. Nathan sheathed his blade, looking up expectantly. The debris fell on him, he was lost in the veil of dust from the concrete breaking apart but he emerged powerfully, emitting both shields in clenched fists to cast the rubble off from him in a second explosion. Nathan lowered his shields, striding forward. The now unarmed soldier threw himself between Nathan and the General, but he was torn apart down his middle as Nathan clenched the man's chest plate with both hands and activated his shields at the same time as separating his grasp, coming away with a section in either hand that he mindlessly cast aside.

    The General lost his grip on his sword when he was thrown to the ground by the explosion of the ceiling having come down and now was scrambling back as Nathan stepped towards him, and he was terrified. The sight of this powerful warrior bearing down on him, especially when Nathan took out his blade, igniting its core, holding it out in his right hand, the General scuttled across the floor for where he had dropped his own weapon. "Nathan!" An unfamiliar voice shouted from the periphery of the bloody scene the General found himself in, and it captured his attention.

    Nathan stopped in his tracks, taking an extra moment to peer down at the pathetic sight of the man who had struck fast, now laying at his feet, but he turned instead to see Cait sprinting towards him, before she tripped over one of the pieces of an Obsidian soldier Nathan had strewn apart. "Cait? What are you doing here?" He asked her as she skid on her knees across the tiles slick with blood before finding her balance, standing up and pulling back her hood.

    "Getting you out of here," she replied in a frantic tone, unable to hide the adrenaline pumping through her body. Cait stepped up to him but stopped short of looking Nathan in the eye as the soldiers reforming their formation caught her eye instead.

    "So it's you," General Ardamus said as he picked up his still blazing sword. "The one who puts ideas of genocide into the heads of psychotic killers."

"Ideas of freedom," Cait corrected, firmly. "Although I do agree the line between them is blurred," she continued, fixing Nathan with a stare that silently told him that she had heard him talking to the General, "but that's why I'm here, to keep this one in check."

"And what a job you're doing, though you have arrived late to the massacre, you are obviously not so blind as to not see the blood staining that man's hands."

"Nate's hands were stained with blood long before he met me," Cait replied, shaking her head, "but at least with me, I can limit it to the ones more deserving of that level of aggression. And who knows? Maybe one day I'll be able to rekindle the man he used to be and bring an end to all this fighting."

"No, I don't think you will—Cait, was it? I knew this man in his prime, and while he was always capable of great and violent things, yet at his heart he was never cruel. The man stands between us however, cruelty seems to be something of an addiction for him." The General took a look over his shoulder, taking comfort in troops readying behind him, prepared to defend him.

"I disagree, as I expect I would on a multitude of things," Cait turned her attention back to Nathan who never took his eyes away from the fight he was eager to continue. "Nate, listen to me," she started, and finally those dark grey ovals found her. "We haven't got long until this whole place collapses and even then, the others won't survive long without you. We need to get back to them, right now."

"Others?" The General asked, listening intently. "How many?" His hand was shaking rapidly, the tip of his sword glancing off the tiles on the floor with a distracting high-pitch scratching. And when neither Nathan nor Cait answered him for a brief moment, he stepped forward, "how many of you fucks want everything we built to burn? How many of you crave the blood of infants and innocents, because that's what you'll get!" He raised his sword, pointing it first at Nathan, then Cait. "Revolution is a bloody game to play, Cait. If you don't have all your pieces set upon the chessboard quite right, you'll be outplayed and that means everyone you care about dying. Just ask the man at your side."

"It was you that first planted the seeds of standing up against the corporations in my head," Nathan spoke through gritted teeth, "you stood against corruption when no one else would, now you expect us to just roll over for them? People die every day anyway, may as well die for something more."

"The people don't care about grand revolutions or uprisings! They just want roofs of their heads, food on their tables, water in their cups! I will die to protect them, that is my purpose but I'm realistic about them—they're too expertly divided, drowning in apathy! They won't stand together for something, and they'll fall to their knees for anything. Take away the system that sustains them and you're robbing them of that safety, of the food they are employed to create so that all might have a chance at eating, the employment that gives them security. What makes you think your revolution will be anything more than an excuse for slaughter? Naivety is not an excuse for the mass graves you'll be forced to dig!"

"It won't be that," Cait replied calmly. "Because all we have to do is expose the corruption and the people will choose revolution for themselves, we won't force anything for them. And you're wrong, the people do want freedom, they've just been too scared up to now to reach out and take it."

"So what's changed?" The General lowered his blade from pointing it at Cait and took another look over his shoulder, nodding at the sight of his troops standing ready before looking back at the woman.

"He did," was all Cait said at first, nodding in Nathan's direction, causing him to look curiously at her. "With him back in the fold and by our side, we can't lose. That strength, we need that, and it's a long road ahead most likely, but I know, with Nathan, we can reach the end, and come out of this all the better for it, no matter the cost."

"That's unbearably optimistic," the General scoffed.

"Isn't that kind of the point?" Cait laughed, "what's the point in living if you're not looking for better?"

"The tri-systems were founded on the principle of survival, young miss," the General patronised. "They were mankind's voyagers, the ones to survive the breakdown of the Old World. Hence why we call what the regions produce: contribution, because we all must contribute a purpose in order to see our civilisation survive. But if your purpose is to bring that network down, to burn the thing that grants people a chance at surviving, then I've got to stop you. Kill them both!" His roar was hideous with a strange ailing to his voice, it hardly sounded human.

Chapter 26

Azuri raised a hand to keep out the sheer light of the firepower pushing against the cockpit screens that could only hold on for so long but the sudden influx of the light from the sun was what was truly blinding as well as startling. For right in front of the nose of the Elite Starfighter, the crafts of Obsidian were being destroyed, splintered into wrecks of twisted metal cascading in flames and smoke into the ruin of the former Capital below. The sight of what replaced them did nothing to brace her heart however as the ships she saw next were kin to the ones just ripped from the sky, but she recognised a familiar craft in among them, different to the rest. "Looked like you could've used some help," a familiar voice spoke over the communications equipment in the terminal directly behind her.

"Some fucking heads up, Xin!" Azuri screamed angrily back, "For fucking fucks sake!"

"Well, that would kinda be counter-productive in a surprise attack, no?" Xin chuckled down the radio, besides, "it's my new friend here, you need to thank, say hi to Siob-han."

"Hi shithead, next time to feel like dropping in, fucking say something first, huh?"

"Apologies Azuri, I'm not in command here, Admiral Titus Thorne runs a tight ship, we had our orders, and surprise was the best tactic we had," the former Stalwart man replied from behind the controls of his silver ship as he kept formation with his Obsidian counterparts.

"Well, thanks for the save, anyhow," Azuri said, letting out a deep breath, "so what's your plan? And why the fuck are Obsidian ships saving this most precious piece of ass?"

"Yeah, err…what? Ah, yeah, they're with us, or rather, we're with them, Azuri. We're here to help you and your team," Siobhan explained, taking down another Obsidian craft of the other side with his own green energised rockets.

"We're here to help extract Commander Winter, Azuri," Xin added, "the Admiral is extremely keen to speak with him and see what information he has found."

"This is an Admiral in Obsidian? One of the highest levels of executives within the company? Have I fucking missed something here, boys?"

"Elias's confession was a mere formality for some in Obsidian, as they already deeply suspected Elias Thorne, they formed a breakaway group," Xin answered.

"Of course, the vast majority of Obsidian is still loyal to Elias as their director is his dad, but we're hoping with Winter, we can gain the upper hand," Siobhan put in.

"And why's that?"

"Because he's probably the only one strong enough to not only go after Elias, but Roderic Thorne as well," Xin replied.

Nathan was swift, raising his left shield and reeling Cait in behind it as he took his rifle off from his back, maintaining his focus on not allowing any of the fire blasting against the shield to catch any part of her. "Take this, the shield will sense the presence of the barrel, it'll give you a window, just detach the sling so you can use it," he explained to Cait, nodding to the buckles that kept the weapon strapped across his torso. She clicked together the notches on the side of the buckle and it worked to let her take control of the rifle, the strap dangling down to her feet as she raised it up, the shield lowering as the barrel breached it. And she fired. Nathan meanwhile had his eyes on the weapon at his own feet, the minigun from the soldier he had killed earlier, and he got the toe of his boot underneath it, before flicking it up into his free right hand. While Cait did the best she could with the rifle, also needing to duck or swipe her head to the side to avoid the fiery bullets flowing in through the gap in the shield, Nathan moved to her right, obliterating the soldiers with the loud, heavy gun.

"I need more ammo!" Cait had to shout to be heard over the roar of Nathan's minigun despite the fact that she was in his arms, tight to his body, her head directly next to his. Nathan didn't reply, only nodded downwards, tilting his head down to his left, towards the magazines stored at his belt, where Cait also found some grenades. She ejected the rifle magazine and reloaded the gun first before carefully taking a grenade and tossing it through the gap in the shield, landing near the feet of the larger cluster of soldiers. The explosion wiped them out, the force of the blast stalling the fire from that section and the General had to leap out of the way to not be caught up in it. He landed ungracefully, clattering to the ground before standing back up and prowling over to where Nathan and Cait were standing, approaching on their left so as to avoid the arc of fire from the minigun. He raised his sword high and swiftly brought it down, smashing a furious strike against Nathan's shield, capturing his attention and he turned so he could use the gun against him but the General sliced off the spinning barrels, rendering it useless.

Nathan pushed Cait to his left before unleashing a rocket barrage and the few remaining soldiers so all he had to contend with was the General stepping up to meet him. With a quick step to his right, Nathan dodged a stab at his chest, and landed a sharp elbow to the General's head, knocking off his stride as he unsheathed his sword again. He attacked first, swinging strongly for the General's neck forehanded then back, spinning down into a crouch to avoid a slash at his own head, while landing a strong connection with the other man's left ankle. The successful blow had bypassed the General's armour and left him bleeding, reeling from the throbbing, burning agony rising from that side, struggling to gain his balance. But he did, seeking to strike back with a series of attacks of slashes and stabs but Nathan was equal to all of them, fending off the last one with quickly engaging his left shield to stop the blow and then using it to push the other man back, putting him off his footing.

Nathan tried seizing the initiative but the General kept his own defence, using both hands to block the incessant, powerful attacks raining down on him, forced to stumble backwards. Seeing that his attempts with the sword were failing, Nathan used his free left hand to awkwardly take out the pistol holstered on his chest, the grip meant for being removed with his favoured right. But he retrieved it and instantly fired a bullet into each of the General's eyes. The armour of the helmet held so that he was only blinded for a moment's flinching but that was all the time Nathan needed to take a longer step up to the General's right, and connect a short, sharp slice to the back of the other man's knee. The General, still haphazardly thumbling his way backwards, stepped on his cape and collapsed to the floor.

Cait raised the scope of the rifle she still grasped, landing a shot behind the man's other knee, rendering him unable to get up. Nathan stood over him, holstering his gun and looked over to where he had unceremoniously thrown

Cait out of harm's way, not that she seemed to mind as she made her way to stand.

Ardamus's blade clanged sharply when it fell to the floor, shaking as it steadied into a stop, its white flames burning the fragments of debris it lay in as golden lightning struck against anything metal nearby. Nathan stooped down and picked it up, admiring the handle for a moment, stroking the wood encased inside it, appreciating the craftsmanship before retracting its length and stowing it at his belt, before sheathing his own blade. "You said I don't know 'Hell', what is that?"

"Typical, that you've forgotten human history as well as your own," the General was sprawled on his back, but he managed to roll onto his side so he could take his helmet off and throw it aside. His skin was a clammy, sorry imitation of the golden sheen of an X-Human, and the yellow of his eyes was muddy and murky, his pupils wildly darting between Nathan and Cait as he ignored his pain to go onto his knees. "Hell is where the religions of the Old World believed that those who were evil in life were sent to live out eternity in torture and anguish when they died. That was the last eight years for me. I did everything I could to keep me and my own focused on surviving, I drilled our purpose into them and me until nothing was left. All memory of family was lost as this sickness has stolen us of our senses and our decency. Yet I cared for my people, right up until you massacred them, Winter."

"These fools of the Old World, did they believe there was a place where the good people went to when they died? What was in store for them?" Nathan went down on his hunches and removed his own helmet, cradling it in his lap, looking the other man in the eye.

"Heaven, it's a place called Heaven," Lux Ardamus bit back a sharp wave of pain, he was putting his weight down on his shattered kneecaps so that he could have some measure of pride, high enough to be able to look the man in the eye when he killed him.

"And?"

"It was meant to be good, peaceful," Ardamus sighed.

"Good, you've earned it," Nathan remarked as he took his handgun again, this time using his preferred right hand and put a single bullet into the other man's skull, coldly watching as the body reeled back, then slumped over to the side. Then he took a moment, while Cait walked over to join him, as he ran a gloved thumb over the initials engraved into the gun's casing: 'N.W', and if he felt something in doing so, he showed no sign of it in the vague expression on his face.

"That was," Cait had to pause to gather her thoughts on what she had just seen, "kinda kind, actually."

"He was a good man," Nathan stood up and put away his gun, holding his helmet under his left arm. "I don't know what Elias's compound did to him but that wasn't the Ardamus I knew, the man I knew you would've liked, you share similar views."

"Then it's a shame how things turned out," Cait peered down at the General's body, curious at how his eyes and skin were emerging in the shades of an X-Human but she knew Nathan didn't have any answers about that so she didn't ask.

"It is," Nathan nodded, placing his helmet back on, "still," he said, taking out a vial and a peculiar shape from his belt pouches and Cait immediately knew what was next.

"No, Nate, you don't have to do that," she said, placing a hand on his that held these items, and making him pause. "You respected him, leave it at that," Cait gave the slightest push so that Nathan retreated and she knelt down, closing the General's eyes carefully.

"That's not the way I do things," Nathan didn't put the vial and shape away, and his tone suggested he wasn't about to.

"Tough," Cait dismissed, and gave him a sharp look before standing up. "Come on, we need to leave," she held out Nathan's rifle, knowing he couldn't take it without putting back what was in his hands, and as she expected, he did, stowing the vial and container so that he could accept his gun. He strapped it back across his chest and took one last look at the General before stepping away, moving towards the centre of the space, into the light cast down from the circular grate at the ceiling. "So how are we getting out? You blew up the exit," Cait mused before following the line of sight of those dark grey ovals to the ceiling, "oh."

"Keep your head down!" Tomen shouted at the top of his lungs so that Lena could hear him on the other side of the path that led up to the bunker door. He was on his own, while Lena and Miles were on the other side, on their backs to avoid the never-ending gunfire hurtling over the top of the short wall that served as their only cover. Impala was with them, with Miles keeping a firm hand over his back in case he panicked and ran straight into the volley of Obsidian fiery bullets.

"Yeah, sure, great, and what? Live here now, is that it?" Miles sarcastically shouted back, "I think I could make a tiny mound of dirt and make a kitchen to add to my one bedroom, living room—oh! Impala, you need a room, well, there's plenty of dirt under this fucking wall where we are keeping our fucking heads down!"

"Just shut up, Miles!" Tomen poked the barrel of his weapon up before his head, and shot down three Obsidian troopers making their way up the road to get at them, landing his own fiery bullets, green energy cast into the tips of his rounds. The relief he had felt when Azuri lit up the boulevard with fire from the Elite Starfighter was gone, as Obsidian simply sent up their next wave of troops, paying no mind to the burning trees, scorched earth and the black haze of smoke in the air. For that was the only pass that she was able to make, Tomen was just able to see through the buildings that a pack of fighters had been chasing her away from the fight, but he had no idea if she was still alright. And that bothered him, it struck a cold shank at his chest but he knew he had to ignore that for now. He had to remember that Nathan's ship was still the safest place she could be, and that she was more than a match for any Obsidian pilot, especially in that craft. Then there was Miles and Lena that were in his immediate care that he felt he owed his attention to at this moment, as he risked another sight of what approached, but only hitting a glancing shot off one of many soldiers making progress towards them. One shot from one of these troops landed just shy of the hand he used at his rifle's trigger, casting up a gust of dust from the wall into Tomen's eyes and he slid down wiping it away.

"How 'bout you keep your fucking head down?" Lena screamed at him, clutching the pistol Nathan had given her but not daring to use it, the wash of gunfire over her head certain in her mind to find her should she try.

"Your side ain't too bad," Tomen called back, "Miles, I know what I just said, but you gotta fire back, mate!"

Miles didn't reply, he just gave Tomen a stern, disapproving look.

"Don't do that to me, man, get your weapon up! Look, Impala's ready to fight!" Tomen was right, the dog was baring his teeth, only held back because Miles had his arm on him.

"Ok!" Miles yelled and carefully got up, removing his arm from Impala's back at the same time as placing a leg over him in an awkward crouch that meant he could fire back and ensure the dog didn't run away at the same time. As he rested the barrel of his rifle on the brickwork, the fire coming his way seemed all the more intense, and his nerves made his hands quiver but he raised his scope all the same, doing his part. One, two, missed the third but he killed the fourth as Miles went for being sure about what he aimed for rather than spraying and hoping for a hit before he had to slide down low as red beads of bullets seemed destined for his head. "There's too many of them!"

"Cait should'a come up by now, I need to go get her!" Lena cried but Miles put a strong hand on her shoulder, too strong for her to resist and she couldn't get off her back to get up, "let me go!"

"The door's in the open, you'll be torn to shreds before you ever make it, dipshit," Miles said, and let go, knowing he could trust her to keep her head.

"Keep firing! It's all we can do, we have to hold out!" Tomen instructed, raising himself up again, firing at whatever he could but there were so many, each of them firing back at him and he could barely keep his head up. It was the same for Miles now as more Obsidian troops moved up and applied even more pressure, until the fire stopped. Both former Stalwart enforcers looked nervously at one another as the endless barrage of red hail scanned upwards, aiming at something else, high up in the sky. Way above their heads, further down the stretch of road they found themselves on was a small spec in the sky, two shapes, shrouded behind a purple haze, floating in mid-air.

"Yes!" Lena shrieked, her feet skidding up and down the dirt as she excitedly waved her hands, her whole body relieved and overjoyed.

"Is that—" Miles muttered but before he needed to finish his question did he get his answer, as the two shapes accelerated down towards them despite the enormous amount of gunfire greeting them, a purple shield leading the way, until they were overhead.

Nathan dropped Cait down on Tomen's side of the wall and fired a rocket barrage before landing with a drop of the shoulder and rolling forward, standing, sprinting into the explosions with sword in hand. The soldiers not killed in the missile attack were left dazed by it, disorientated, making for easier prey and were sliced apart in seconds. The ones at the flanks avoided the blasts but met the same fate when they drew in closer, their weapons not effective in breaching Nathan's armour as he severed limbs, sliced open throats, cut guns in two. A new troop container dropped from the monstrous ship high in the sky directly in front of where Nathan was finishing off the initial wave of troops and more soldiers came sprinting out the moment the doors opened. In light of the new threats being so closely packed together, he ran his hand up the length of the blade, unleashing its more hungry nature as the golden streaks of lightning cast from it ran alive with a greater lust for destruction and so he used his jetpack to charge at a greater speed. Nathan sliced the first soldier in half at the waist, his lightning flashing out to kill the three nearest to him as he propelled forward, rolling over the severed top half to land in the middle of the pack, slashing at the troops to his left and right, killing the ones all around them with the chains of bright light bound between them. To finish off the squad of troopers, he flew straight up into the air, then reversed the thrusters on his jetpack so he came down in a powerful drop, his left fist down below his body and emitted his shield on top of them, spraying fragments of bone, spatters of blood, burst intestines in all directions. While he was occupied, three more containers came hurtling down from the cruiser above, and though he was able to bring down one before it got to the ground with a single rocket, the other two were able to deploy their troops that scattered immediately. Nathan stood idle and ready, sword in hand, waiting for the next squad to engage him but instead, it was the cruiser that fired down its immense payload of a sphere of pure, raging red energy, with him raising a shield just in time to withstand it, though it knocked him down to the ground. He looked up, seeing another one coming, and sheathed his blade as quick as he could and raised both shields to better take the powerful hit that would otherwise see cast into dust.

"Get back!" Cait screamed up the way to Nathan, seeing the cruiser that commanded the sky opening fire but he couldn't, he was pinned by the constant fire raining down on him, unable to shift as the weight of the fire drove him down into a crouch to keep up his shields.

"Get down!" Tomen shouted at her and hauled her down just as Obsidian soldiers emerged at the side, having used the buildings for cover from Nathan's devastating rage.

"But he's going to get himself killed out there!" She protested, fighting back against the man's hold on her, pinning her to the ground with a knee, so she shoved him off. "We need to distract that ship!" She scrambled up to see over the wall again but Tomen just brought her back down, shoving her into the dirt.

"Stay down!" He screamed in her face, and Cait found herself too afraid to shout back at him, he was like a father figure to her, and felt like a scorned daughter now. "Azuri," Tomen said, backing off and using his comm to speak to the pilot, desperate for a reply. "Azuri, you there, babe?"

"I'm here, Tomen, I got some friends, too," the pilot's voice was a most welcome relief.

"Friends?"

"Xin's here with Siob-han, and they've brought Admiral Thorne with them, we're thinning out the smaller fighters before I can come collect you guys."

"Ok," Tomen murmured confused, "but listen, we need you to do something, and baby, it's dangerous but without this, we're fucked."

"What?"

"I need you to distract that Marauder, distract it or we lose our Elite," Tomen explained, daring a quick glance forward only for a wave of gunfire to shy back down into cover before he fired off a blind salvo in that direction.

"I'll do what I can, but that fucker is big, Tomen, he big," Azuri complained, her tone was obvious that she didn't like the idea, "but I'll try." She was following a pack of Admiral Thorne's crafts over the Obsidian base at the city centre and dipped her right wing to return to the Directorate district. "Hey, Xin," she said, talking now to the other communication line she had open.

"We heard it, Azuri, we're relaying the message to the Admiral but it could take some time for him to order a re-assignment of his forces," Xin replied.

"Then fuck him, I'm going," she powered the engines up to their maximum, bounding over the length of the structures stretching up the skies she soared through, tilting left and right to avoid the taller ones until she directly behind the enormous beast of metal. A twinge of uncertainty clouded her mind, to assault a cruiser of this size had to be suicide, even in a craft as impressive as this was, but she knew she couldn't risk any less than the father of her child had this whole time. So she powered through the sky until the bridge came into view below and behind her left wing and she banked, bringing the ship about in an attack run, honing her eyes on that bright red streak. The Marauder took notice of her appearance and began to fire, and Azuri had to be swift to dodge the colossal energy blasts it cast her way but she flowed through the air with unmatched nimbleness, hailing rockets of her own against the cruiser's bridge.

"It's working!" Cait exclaimed as she dug her elbows into the top of the wall to see the fire aiming for Nathan being turned against Azuri, the Elite shutting off his energy shields and turning back around to face them back at the bunker's entrance.

"Down!" Tomen shouted as a barrage of red bullets flooded in their direction and Cait found herself hurled down to the dirt once again, but this time something struck at her eyes, she had just about shut them in time for it not to sting too much. She felt the air go out of her lungs as she knew Tomen must have landed on her but she couldn't see, desperately wiping at her eyes, feeling something wet there, she thought she had cried. Then Lena screamed. Cait got the last of it out of her eyes just as she felt the first warm feeling on her shoulder and her hooded cloak felt damp, and when she looked over, she saw Tomen's headless body lying on top of her. She couldn't move. She couldn't speak. She had no idea she was still breathing. She could only stare. Blood was trickling out from the gap in Tomen's neck where his head should be, replaced by a scorched end of his spine where his skull had been completely pulverised by a well-placed shot.

"No," Miles mumbled as he collapsed, Impala nuzzling at him with his nose to try to rouse any kind of response out of him, but the amber-eyed X-Human lay perfectly still, his golden skin bereft of its shine.

Cait gingerly wiped her eyes one more time as tears welled, blending with the blood still there to blur her vision and she jumped when Nathan suddenly appeared, having flown over the wall with his jetpack, and was now scrambling across the dirt to her. "Nate?" She asked, not knowing what exactly she was asking as she just watched him carefully remove Tomen from being on top of her. "Nate?" She asked again.

"Are you hurt?" Nathan asked her, looking up at her and placing a hand on her shoulder. "Cait, were you hit?"

"No, I—"

Nathan nodded, carefully removing Tomen's blood-stained green jacket and gently resting it over the top of his neck, covering up the disgusting sight beneath so Cait could stop staring at it. He almost went to punch Lena, as was her arrival so quick and sudden, having leapt across the gap, miraculously avoiding the incessant gunfire to wrap her friend in a tight hug. Then Nathan's gaze met Miles who was like stone, staring off at a faraway place, his dog licking his cheek, whining at the petrified state of his friend. He looked at these people, and then he looked down at Tomen for himself. Grief was something he was used to, it clung to him, was a part of him, and it walked hand in hand with him and his aggression. Nathan pushed Lena's shoulder back, forcing them to break their embrace which caused a panic expression on both X-Humans' faces but he only meant to get at what still remained stowed in her bandoleer, pulling out three of the bullets with the red painted tips. Next, he brought his rifle to bear, reconfiguring the weapon to its sniper modification and inserting the first incendiary, and then he stood.

The shot that had taken down Tomen came from a charging group making their way up the right flank, passing through the pavement on that side of the road, between burning decorative shrubs on one side with their reflections cast in the glass panelling of the buildings behind them. Black armour against darkened glass but it was something beyond those panes that Nathan took note of, seeing the shapes obscured there thrashing against the windows, desperate to plough through. He fired his first shot. The firebolt round smashed into the helmet of one of the troopers near the back of the pack making their swift advance and his head erupted in an inferno that spattered the molten metal of the scorched helm in all directions. The two either side of him were cast in the volcanic slur while the hit soldier's body was cast by the force of the shot back into the side of the building, hurtling through the glass, releasing the wave of undead, keen and ravenous. The Obsidian troops were caught completely unawares. Half were set upon immediately, hardly given a breath before being tackled to the ground, forced to defend themselves in intimate struggles with unbelievably strong, frail attackers. The other half were either stricken by super-heated metal slurry or shards of helmet or were cemented in place with shock, their minds failing to process the sight of this new threat rallied against them.

Nathan let the undead enjoy their victims as he loaded in the second bullet without a moment's gratification at the accuracy of his first one, his aggression pushing him on, onto the next act, aiming his rifle with steady hands now at an Obsidian fighter jet, soaring through the sky above. He tracked the movement, anticipating the pilot's path, considering the image they had in their mind of where they were to go and when the craft lined up perfectly, Nathan didn't miss his opportunity. He had to aim further along than the craft was on its course, knowing if he aimed exactly where the ship was, then the bullet would be moments too late to strike, so he let his eye do the aiming, and trusting his finger to know when. And then he fired. Nathan had been still only for the briefest second from the loading of the bullet to the firing. The round flew as intended, high into the sky, meeting its mark, annihilating the cockpit of the fighter so that the pilot was unable to stop its trajectory as it powered through the clouds directly into the bridge of the Marauder class vessel. The collision made a mighty roar that bellowed throughout the sky as metal smashed against metal, twisted, contorting, burning, as the command bridge ceased to exist, its once beaming red presence now a smear of flame on its dark armoured shell.

Yet Nathan did not pause to relish in his success, loading the final round as a troop carrier container landed down the boulevard stretching out at his feet, its doors opening wide, the multitude of Obsidian inside coming streaming out. But their assault was short lived, Nathan aimed for the head of the spear, catching them in their centre, throwing them back, knocking over the rest in their path as the fire exploded, catching them all in the confines of the container, setting them all ablaze. The Obsidian troops howled and screamed but the one who sentenced them to such agonising pain had no sympathy, configuring his rifle back to its standard setting, he could have given them a quicker end, but his hand remained still. Nathan merely took a breath as a second Marauder emerged from a transit gate right above the group, the egg-shaped ignition cores nearly within arm's reach as they spanned the sky, allowing entrance to this colossus that blotted out the sun. But instead of giving the group something else to contend with, this new enormous ship targeted the cindered original, hanging in the sky as its command bridge burned and fired upon it with a grand arsenal, a spectacle of destruction raining down on its opposite number. "Azuri, now's the time, come pick us up," Nathan called over his radio, eager to make use of this new distraction to the Obsidian forces still descending from orbit as far as the horizon all around.

"OK, en route," Azuri replied as she weaved through larger craft waging fierce battle, her eyes flickering to the downpour of broken sections of these ships' hulls, coming crashing down into the city below. She had found herself an escort, having been identified as Commander Winter's own ship so she could see Obsidian crafts, the exact same as those trying to kill her, flying at her flanks, keeping her safe, even diving in the way of rockets, anything to protect her. Azuri brought the starfighter around and felt a tingle of hesitation creep up from her fingers as she witnessed herself fly towards a vessel so big it encompassed most of the sky, kin to the one straight opposite that she had needed to be so quick to avoid. But this newcomer was slaying the beast that had kept her under so much pressure to stay in the air, and breath returned to her chest as she flew towards the smoking Directorate district. The plumes of darkish grey competed with the shadows cast from the giant ships to make the space under those two great hulks seem as night in the middle of the day but Azuri steadied the ship in nonetheless.

The wind kicked up the embers of the smouldering fires all the way up the boulevard teaming with the updraft caused by the engines of the two competing massive vessels, as well as her own, to make a grey haze outside her cockpit. Through the glass she could make out Nathan, standing at the fore of her group, fending back any stragglers of the Obsidian landing parties, and once she brought the ship lower, Azuri could see Cait and Lena pop their heads up on one side of her view, Miles on the other. But she couldn't see Tomen. There was no time to dwell. Azuri spun the ship about so that the ramp at the rear would land just in front of her team so they could beat a quick exit from the albeit quieter conflict flooded in the city, but she dare not linger for longer than she needed to. Bits of the ship above came raining down in metal droplets as the recently arrived Marauder unleashed its full payload of weaponry against its counterpart above the far smaller Elite starfighter. "Get on!" She shouted down the open radio channel as she could see reinforcements for the battered Marauder in the way of a large contingent of fighters swing in at the end of the street, hurtling towards them. Azuri fired with the forward cannons, not aiming as such, just laying down enough pressure for them to think twice about taking on the little ship instead of the far more menacing target high in the sky. But her eyes were caught by movement on the ground. By now, she had touched the ship down, slamming a button down with a fist to descend the ramp at the back and she felt even greater urgency to get back up into the air again as a swarm of terrifying, walking corpses awkwardly scrambled over walls and obstacles, heading directly for her ship.

"Miles!" Nathan barked at the other man, trying to shake him out of the trance that had taken hold of him, "Miles!"

"What?" The X-Human man murmured, his amber eyes feeling like lead as he brought them up to meet the cold gaze of Nathan's dark grey ovals.

"On your feet, we're getting out of here! I've got Tomen, you get your rifle up, now!" Nathan ordered as he fired at the undead with his right hand pulling the trigger on his weapon, while he used his left to wrench Miles to his feet. "Open fire or we're dead!"

"I got it, I got it," Miles drowsily replied, lifting the barrel of his weapon, but it felt so heavy in his arms. His aim was as weak as his body, he fired wide and high of the sprawling carcasses taking over the street, as one shot at a time, his glowing green bullet failed to hit anything.

"Get up!" Nathan grunted, taking his attention away from Miles and to Cait and Lena who still cowered below the low wall despite the Obsidian fire having stopped when Nathan unleashed the flurry of undead. He gave a firm kick to Cait so to separate the hold the two shared so that they both finally recognised his standing there. "Get up," he growled again, and this time they listened, gingerly using the wall to prop themselves into a cowering stand.

"What about Tomen?" Cait asked in a voice that sounded a world away but Nathan ignored her, slinging his rifle over his shoulder as he peered past the two, measuring the distance between them and the wave of dead things coming to kill them. He then knelt down and scooped Tomen's body up in his arms with a great amount of care, hooking one under the knees and cradling the chest with the other. "Oh ok," Cait muttered, seeing her question answered, and she turned to see the Elite starfighter sitting in wait, its engines so loud she was astonished at herself for missing them. "Wait," she said, a thought suddenly catching her and she reached inside Tomen's jacket, blocking out the thought of Tomen's exposed spine under there as she retrieved the data card, the prize of their venture.

"Now, move you two!" Nathan ordered Cait and Lena before turning his head to Miles, "keep up, don't concern yourself with killshots, just slow them down!"

"Alright," Miles could feel himself say but his senses were shot, he had no idea where he was firing his gun at, his mind swallowed up his grief. It was Impala at his feet that gave him enough measure of mindfulness to stagger forward towards the ship, to step onto the ramp and make his way up, more following the dog than any thought to do anything else. He hadn't landed a single hit on the horde and it took Lena to turn around and close the ramp for him to not get snatched by one of a dozen arms reaching inside the ship, mere indistinguishable distance away from grasping at his jacket.

"Azuri, we're onboard!" Cait's voice rang over the radio and as soon as she heard it, Azuri took the ship off the ground, much to her relief. The putrid things heading for her scraped their bony fingers against the glass of the cockpit seeking any hold to get at her but in the lift from the take-off, they fell away, exploding as they hit the ground, their thin, rotten flesh giving way for their mortified organs and bones to lose their hold in the body.

"Tomen?" She asked, wrestling with the controls to get the ship to follow a path out from under the two warring cruisers and begin to rise away from the city, leaving it in its wake.

"Just get us into orbit, Azuri," Nathan answered.

"Where is he?"

Chapter 27

The first sign Azuri got of others aboard her ship was the resounding banging and shaking of the ladder aways behind her, at the other end of the passenger tunnel, on the other side of the cockpit doors. She did the best she could to keep her attention on the controls, to bring the ship up through the battlefield raging all around her, to fly as straight a path as possible up through the sky and into orbit but her mind tugged at her. She had heard the voices of everyone but Tomen. She loved them all, Cait, Lena, Miles—even Nathan who had kept her beloved safe, but where was his voice? That which she craved the most. Azuri begged, pleaded with the stars to hear his voice as the cockpit doors opened behind her, she wept with a sickening anxiety, not wanting to ever see again if the sight was anything but the man who fathered the child growing inside her. But it was Cait, and a single glance over her shoulder told Azuri what she already knew. Cait's face told it all, her eyes, those dazzling purple gems stolen of their beauty, a grim bearing taking its place as her misery told the pilot without so much as a whisper, that her husband was dead.

"Azuri…" Cait began but her words choked in her throat, she had started without any thought how to continue, how to tell someone that the one they held most valued in their heart was dead, decapitated and lost to them forever. "He's erm…" She tried again, failing again.

"Where is he, Cait?" Azuri asked, unaware how she was keeping her nerve to still fly the ship as Miles and Lena appeared behind Cait, entering the cockpit.

"He's downstairs, Azuri," Lena explained, her shock had slipped away, she felt an eerie calm ebb and flow in her body, and the X-Human frightened herself slightly at how she was able to keep composed. "Nathan's laying the body on his bed and then he'll be right up. I'm sorry, my love, I'm really sorry."

Azuri darted her eyes forward again, muttering a curse to herself as she narrowly avoided colliding their ship against an Obsidian craft chasing after one just like it as they slipped through the upper atmosphere. The controls in her grasp began to shake, her hands resisting carrying on when she wanted nothing more than to run away, to go see Tomen, or what was left of him. Yet the sight that awaited them upon entering space gave her pause, and hit her with enough sense to not let go of the steering, to not slip away from what she was needed to. The Marauder class vessels they had left behind were as children to these Cosmic cruisers that waged a battle so fierce, the lights from their lasers and rockets, the deployment of their vast arsenals raining down on one another seem to dwarf the light of the stars beyond. These flagships of either side of the Obsidian split were the size of small moons, deploying smaller ships from the fighters that whirled around the orbit of Ruby all the way up to more Marauders lowering themselves out of the bellies of these goliaths. All around the planet, blanketing its entire globe was this colossal warscape steadily morphing into a graveyard of ship carcasses and twisted, deformed metal the more the battle raged on.

"Did we cause all this?" Miles muttered in disbelief, such was the grand scale of the onslaught of Obsidian on Obsidian, with the odd Stalwart Ironworks starfighter added to the mix, such was the influx of WIDOWs brought on by this rebellion.

"No," Nathan appeared behind them, removing his helmet, brushing a hand through the long, sweaty strands of hair, combing it to the back, as he made for the co-pilot's seat, stowing his rifle in a compartment beneath the console. "This rift has been apparent for some time, think of a depot of fuel, we just threw in a match to light it up."

"Is anywhere safe to go? What do we do?" Lena asked, taking the seat next to the terminal that controlled the transit gate coordinates.

"I have to go see him," Azuri consoled herself, not speaking to anyone else, and as she stood up, releasing the controls to the ship without warning, Nathan had to be quick to leap over and wrestle the trajectory of the craft away from crashing into a Stalwart freighter joining the fray.

"Where y'going?" Lena pleaded but it was Cait who caught Azuri before she could make for the exit, grasping her arms, locking her down.

"Let me go, Cait, I need to see him," Azuri wept, her eyes feeling heavy, she stared at the floor, through the glass, to the area of the battle below.

"Look at me, Azuri, really look," Cait shook the other X-Human, forcing those rich, luminescent lagoon eyes to meet her own shining amethysts. "I loved him, too, he was like a dad to me, Azuri, but we can't mourn him yet, we're not safe. Look all around you, these are the bastards that killed him, that robbed him from us and want our necks firmly placed under their boots again or have us six feet deep in the dirt." Cait raised her hands from where they gripped the arms of the other woman to gently rock her head towards her own so that their foreheads touched, never breaking eye contact. "I hate doing this, I hate to tell you to stow your grief for now but we need you to pilot this ship, I need you to let yourself feel something else, something that will get you through this, feel your anger instead if you have to."

"But he's gone, Cait, I don't know who I am without him, I don't even know how to fly anymore!"

"Yes you do!" Cait took one hand and poked at Azuri's chest hard with a finger, "Tomen is here, and so are you. They can never take that away from you, but punish them for taking him away from ever embracing you again."

"You're right," Azuri's eyes glowed with a renewed feeling, moving away from the despair that sought to ruin her. "They need to die for what they've done," she growled, coldly.

"They do, but this is all bigger than any one of us," Cait reminded her, "the secrets we've uncovered, the core of what shaped this region? We need to get somewhere safe and think of our next move, the costs of what we've done are too big to ignore."

"Then let's go," Azuri broke the embrace not unkindly and tapped Nathan on the shoulder to non-verbally assume the controls again. The man understood, shifting back to the co-pilot's seat before he turned to face Cait and Miles still standing.

"Behind those doors you'll find a turret either side, get shooting at anything that comes too close," Nathan ordered them before the screen on his console lit up with a broadcast. "Go," he said, turning back around.

"Commander Winter," an older male voice announced as Cait and Miles departed the cockpit, the doors sliding closed behind them as they entered the transport tunnel. They never had the chance to explore the Elite starfighter properly so they were both steady in approaching the mechanisms mounted either side of the ship's hull but they were simple enough to figure out. Miles got it working first, taking command of the rig for the turret mounted to the outside of the ship with the display of beyond the armour of the vessel lighting up in a holographic image in front of him as a window. Cait copied him, spying over her shoulder but she hesitated firing once she got a view of what was transpiring all around them. There were ships everywhere, in every direction, as far as the eye could see. Some were shattered wrecks, torn apart with the bodies of their crew impaled in the sites of the destruction that killed the ships, or were lost to the vacuum of space. While others moved between blinks of an eye, flashing between the carnage to gain any upper hand, firing a wild blaze of laser rounds and rockets that added to the obstacles every ship had to dash to avoid. The Obsidian crafts were identical and Cait had no idea how to tell the two warring factions apart, or whether one side was truly an ally to her. Meanwhile, hulks of a lighter grey hunted their prey, Stalwart enforcers and inquisitors, their WIDOW targets out in the open like never before, letting loose a menagerie of emerald plasma weaponry on any Obsidian fighter they deemed not on their side.

"We don't know who's who, what are we firing at?" Miles asked, swinging the barrels of his gun left, right, up and down, not knowing where to look for all the ships whirling around them.

"They shoot at us, we shoot at 'em right back!" Cait called over her shoulder, yanking on the triggers for her gun, lighting up a sleek Stalwart ship that attempted firing a hailstorm of rockets at them.

"Chief Admiral Thorne, what a mess you've made," Nathan replied to the man occupying the screen in front of him.

"Like you're one to talk, it was your assault on the Capital that triggered all this," the Admiral remarked, he was in his full uniform, kin to the more decorative armour that General Ardamus bore, except for silver figurines of Cosmic cruisers, one adorning either shoulder signifying his role.

"So Obsidian was just ready to split in two? Was the security company really so fragile?" Nathan dismissed, his gaze flicking up to the view beyond the cockpit screen. Azuri was being more aggressive than the other pilots all around them, using the superior armour of the Elite starfighter to ram lesser crafts from her way, smashing them with the wings. Three Obsidian fighters launched from the side of a Marauder vessel and Azuri wiped them out with the forward cannons, lashing at the buttons at the top of her controls. Once those smaller ships were out of the way, she sped into the hangar they had departed from. It was brightly lit in an ambient red glow, people hurrying about the place in the black uniform of their company, rushing to join the battle scene as more and more fighters were loaded into the take-off space at the centre of the hangar on large conveyor belts. But they never stood a chance. Azuri opened the fore-facing cannons up, spraying out powerful bolts of energy in all directions at the same time as cutting power to the right side engine, plunging them in a hurtling spin so her firing was cast in all directions. Turrets were mounted on the walls inside the hangar but they couldn't penetrate the armour of the Elite ship and were blown to scrap by Cait and Miles unleashing their full firepower. Once Azuri fired a missile at the armaments cache loading up the fighters it set off a stupendous explosion, at which point she fired up the second engine again and blasted them out of the Marauder before it imploded, wrenching itself apart.

"Well—" The Admiral began before noticing what the ship he was talking to had just accomplished, with an opposing Marauder class vessel now suddenly dispatched in flames and shredded metal. "Bloody good pilot you got there, Commander. But yes, to answer your question, Obsidian was ready to fall before you had even stepped foot in Rose City. We knew Elias caused the Capital Collapse, his ascent to power was too clouded by a certain focus one only gets when the biggest mystery the tri-systems has ever known is not on his agenda to resolve. Any other Section Chief would have devoted resources to building proper infrastructure for the displaced workers, not manufacture themselves a floating fortress to live above them, thus his guilt was obvious. But what we didn't know was how, how he managed to bring down one of the finest installations ever constructed by the Crimson Coalition."

"So once we offered that explanation?"

"Then we were able to begin our resistance in earnest, beginning with making some new friends," Thorne went on.

"I'm not your friend," Nathan shook off.

"Forgive me but you weren't my meaning, Commander, yet you are at the forefront of my mind, hence this conversation."

"Yet you've not reached your point, hence my disinterest," Nathan looked over at Azuri, her determination was clear and struck across her face as she used the wreckage of the Marauder she had disposed of to block the sight of a pursuing fighter, to come about them and blast them to pieces from behind, inspiring a cold smirk on the pilot.

"By entering the Capital, you gave the people of this region hope, you've ignited a revolution, Commander. Your very return to the spotlight is an emboldening feeling to every man, woman and child to join us in taking down Elias's corrupt regime! How can we fail, when we have the legendary Elite Commander leading us to victory?"

"That wasn't my intention, Thorne," Nathan ignored.

"Then what was? Why did you go into the Capital?"

"I just kill one thing then another and somehow a plot threads itself together," Nathan answered truthfully. "I was asked to protect a team to extract the cause of the Collapse, job's done now."

"Then why don't I believe you? There's something you're not saying," Thorne announced doubtfully but his transmission was cut off before he could add anything more. "MacArthur! What happened?" He turned away from the imager to call across the bridge, over to the man leading a team manning numerous screens, all maintaining his vessel's stance in the fight.

"We lost 'em, sir! There's a second Cosmic out there, they just hit our comms!" George MacArthur was able to shout back just as their own Cosmic took another hit, followed by another and then the feeling of the artificial gravity keeping their feet on the ground being shaky became something they were finding themselves getting used to as the pounding they were taking never relented.

"If there's two, that's too much firepower for us, we'll be choking on the void in no time," the Chief Admiral grunted from his command seat on a platform raised above his officers, granting him a view over his entire operations at work. "Move us away from the thick of the fight, we have to get Ruby between us and them!"

"Yes, Chief Admiral!" MacArthur responded and dished out the instructions to his technicians to move the Cosmic behind the planet to stave off the bombardment, a thought in his mind appearing as he wished he had his trusted right hand man who could fulfil his instructions in half the time as the lot he had at his disposal now.

"I can't just watch, I need to do something," Elle shook her head, she was never one to stand idly by as others took up the risk for her, and she placed a hand on MacArthur's shoulder, "I'm grabbing a fighter and heading out there." She had taken up a set of Obsidian troop armour since their arrival on the ship but went without a helmet or anything to cover her replaced left arm that was composed of a far denser material.

"You just be careful and make it back here in one piece, yeah?" MacArthur replied, knowing better than to try to disagree with her.

"Oh yeah, back in one piece, because I have such a good track record at that," she laughed, giving him the middle finger with her chrome hand before leaving him and making for the hangar.

"What'd he mean?" Lena asked from behind the pilots' chairs but they all became too distracted to ponder the Admiral's words as one of the Cosmic ships dominating Ruby's orbit was joined by another, and together they combined their immense firepower on the lone cruiser of their class across from them, over the busy battle stretched out in between.

"Hmm," Nathan grunted, knowing the two were of the loyalist faction of Obsidian, a fact he was immediately proven right as another transmission filled his monitor.

"Winter, surrender the data you possess and we will treat your co-conspiring WIDOWs with a kinder disciplinary outcome than their inevitable obliteration at the hands of our far superior fleet," the familiar groan of Vice-Admiral Constantin Reiku boomed out of the microphone at the co-pilot's seat.

"Reiku, it's been a long time," Nathan grinned back at the man darkly, leaning forward, "you have such lovely eyes."

The other man, standing before his imager as intimidating as he could with a calm, aggressive posture, was taken completely aback, not knowing how to respond.

"Don't get me wrong, old friend, I'm not flattering you, I'm savouring the thought of slicing your throat and adding one of your eyes to my vast collection, you'll be reunited with a lot of your friends."

"Vile monster," Reiku spat, "agree to stop your activities and your crew will be spared. Fail to do so, and I will render your ship into a tomb, where I will idly stride over your breathless corpses to retrieve the data myself."

"Alas, I'll settle for killing you with my ship, a shame though, to lose such a valuable prize, but can't be getting attached to frivolous things, now, can we?" Nathan shut off the connection, turning halfway to face his pilot, "Azuri, engage the Cosmics, get us in close."

"Are you insane?" She shot an angered glance his way but her raging tempests inspiring the most violent of waves in the oceans of her eyes were calmed by the absolute confidence in the man's look.

"Don't stay still for a second," he assured her, "keep us buoyant, keep us moving," he then swivelled his chair further to look back at Lena. "Switch off the safety parameters for the transit gates, then hit that red button, it'll turn them all over to manual, to the pilot's control."

"What're you planning?" She wondered but did as she was instructed all the same, pressing the necessary controls to turn the green indicators on her console all over to red before lifting the clear plastic casing that housed the control button. Lena pressed it and saw the terminal for the console light up with a front facing image, projected from a point by the transit gate cannon attached to the ship's belly, signifying her part was done.

"We need to take them both out if we are ever going to make it out of this," Nathan spun back round to face forward and nodded in the direction of the two Cosmic vessels, a wide and powerful range of artillery was being spat out from them in all directions, wiping out anything close by.

"This is suicide," Azuri murmured to herself as she guided the Elite starfighter on, weaving a path through desolated ships, past fierce firefights, avoiding the barrage of missiles intended for them from the Cosmics at their front.

"Aboard one of those flagships is the Vice-Admiral Constantin Reiku," Nathan explained to her. "He is one of Elias's closest confidants. If you wanted to strike out the people responsible for Tomen's death, you'd do well starting with him," he said, egging her on.

"Then let's go kill him," she smirked back at Nathan before unleashing a staunch bead of laser fire into an Obsidian fighter that couldn't navigate a way out from her sights.

As the Elite Starfighter bore on towards the two looming vessels, Cait and Miles never let up in the fire as their unique ship attracted the attention of any loyalist that caught sight of them, departing their private duel with a resistance craft in favour of pursuing them. Their fire was a constant thread of blazing red light, lashing against ship after ship as they journeyed through the planet wide battlefield to engage the domineering command cruisers nearer the edge of the conflict. The armour of the Elite ship was far more rugged than that of an ordinary fighter and while they took a great deal of flak, the starfighter held itself together, protecting its crew as it sailed through the warring armadas.

"The transit gates have been switched over to manual control, they're line of sight now, aim for one," Nathan pointed forward, explaining the plan to Azuri, "and then you'll have to set where you want us to emerge, paint the target as the other Cosmic."

"And this'll work?" Azuri queried as she barely had the courage to fly directly towards these enormous hulks, let alone try to destroy them by not using a weapon, but by using a device meant to enable travel across the planetary map.

"Cosmic armour is nigh impenetrable, we need something that tears a hole in the fabric of space," Nathan grinned back at her, then glanced back at Lena, "better grip that chair tightly." And as he had said, coming up closer to them, they could see that the armour on the two vastly larger ships were unmarked for all the firepower they endured rallied against them from smaller crafts trying anything to damage them. The Cosmic class vessels were essentially larger versions of the Marauders, with the same shining black armoured hulls, beaming wide red command bridges and the hangars located at their base, in the shape of a diamond, they were steadily invading the landscape of the battle. The other Cosmic, the one being relentlessly attacked, was manoeuvring itself away from the wash of missile and laser fire, desperately trying to put the planet between them. It was this spray of firepower that Azuri had to avoid in order to get close enough to unleash their plan, zipping in between the debris of the battle to gain some cover from the ferocious payload of weaponry being unloaded by the twin ships. But finally they were within range and Azuri didn't hesitate, using the triggers behind the control stalks to blast out the transit gate housed below them, the egg-shaped ignition cores sent spiralling out into the void, colliding with the hull of the nearest Cosmic.

"Good aim," Lena announced, her console lit up with the point of view of the cannon, seeing the gate hit its mark.

"Good, but seeing as it's gotta power up first," Azuri reeled the ship up, having needed to fly full throttle to get anywhere near the Cosmic in order to launch the transit gate and she danced the Elite Starfighter up over the lip of the hull of the larger ship and across its surface. While she travelled over the face of the cruiser, battling with the turrets entrenched there, the cores for the gate began to cast their lightning web, spreading apart, rotating as they began to carve a hole to another point in space. The igniting energy was too much for the armour of the Cosmic and it was strewn apart, scorched as it was ripped asunder, the crew sucked out into oblivion as the transit gate spread itself wide, conquering the space it needed, tearing a hole with its unstoppable force. Azuri avoided the storm of incoming fire by flying directly over the breadth of the damaged cruiser, turning about above its engines before deciding she wanted to deal some damage more personally. She powered the engines at full thrust until she was over the centre of the Cosmic before killing the propulsion, reversing the engines with a button on her dashboard and bringing the ship around violently to avoid the rockets intended for them. Then she flung one engine around and slammed it into full power, making the starfighter spin as it rolled across the width of the cruiser, and she opened fire. The forward cannons found their mark at the command bridge, accurately smashing into the bright red visor there until it finally gave, spilling out its occupants in a blaze suffocated by the vacuum. Azuri wrestled with the controls again to bring the ship back to a more steady flight path as she looped back around, then through the now fully powered up gate, and out through where the other side was slashing open the armour of the second Cosmic. The oval ignition cores had split in half to trace an exit in the hull of the other cruiser, its web of unquenchable energy resurgent in forcing its opening despite the bulk of armour in its wake.

"Chief Thorne," Reiku begged of the hologram of Elias Thorne standing before him as his Cosmic flagship tore itself apart beneath his feet, yet he never let his expression waver from his determination for the fight. "Winter's crippled my Cosmic class ships and I'm losing this conflict, I need your support."

"It would seem I placed my backing in the wrong Admiral, Constantin, this is most disappointing. Your failure to subdue these WIDOWs will undoubtedly setback my plans," Elias scorned from the safety of his office on the Arcadia space station.

"But Elias, I can turn this around, deploy the garrisons at Carmine and I can beat back these degenerate scum!"

"You've already proven to me that you can't, you deployed two of our finest shipcraft against one and a handful of lesser fighters, and now you're reporting that you've lost both, if I understand correctly? So why would I devote more resources for you to simply squander? No, I think not."

"Then what happens now, Chief Thorne?"

"Well, you die, a bitter disappointment I must admit but not a complete burden to my mind and yet my plans to secede from the Board to create an independent region will be far more problematic for the loss of two Cosmic class. I'll have to step up the development, stop the contribution now, reroute the food and safe water only to those loyal to the Coalition. Sure, it'll be adding fuel to an already raging fire but here I stand with a hose and an extinguisher, ready to put it out. We could have avoided further loss of life, Reiku, that's on you, my friend."

"Thorne!" Reiku yelled into the imager as the floor under him cracked, the visor for his command bridge splintered and the hologram of his leader flickered as his ship's power began to fail.

"Goodbye, Reiku. Die now, an utter disappointment to me," Elias flicked off the holographic imager with a relaxed hand, plunging Reiku into the darkness of his falling ship, surrounded by terrified strangers all looking to him for leadership and answers, while all he could do was fall to his knees and scream.

"Oh yes!" Lena cheered as both Cosmics erupted, tearing themselves apart from the catastrophic damage they had suffered, their engines failing from the carnage and they drifted into one another in a blend of contorted metal as they tumbled together into the upper atmosphere of Ruby, to plummet to its surface in an enormous, fiery cataclysmic explosion.

"Hold your excitement, Lena, we ain't outta this one yet, babe," Azuri pointed out as there was still a fleet of Marauders on the battlefield and now they all knew what ship to target as they unleashed a tidal wave of laser fire, a tsunami of firepower as all the batteries mounted to all of those vessels aimed for the Elite starfighter that had wiped out their commanders. The wrecks and debris from the victims of the two Cosmics provided ample enough cover for Azuri to beat a path away from the swarm that had claimed the northern territory of the planet's orbit but rockets and lasers crashed into them, scorching as they struck against the armour. Instead of firing at ships, Cait and Miles on their turrets found themselves firing at the payloads of destructive power raining down on them, anything to lessen the battering they were taking. Hollowed out shells of broken ships were engulfed again in blazing fire as Azuri sought after any cover to put between them and the pursuing Marauders now ignoring every other fighter, focusing their ceaseless array of weaponry solely on them.

Smaller crafts, one-manned fighters, spilled out from the hangars of these moderately sized vessels, a hive going in only one direction as they fizzed in between the firepower amassed from behind them to give chase to the Elite ship. A group peeled off from the rest, banking to the side to avoid the field of debris Azuri used for cover while the others pursued directly in behind, some being shot down by the Marauders that refused to let up their fire. Azuri piloted expertly around the ruined hulls, jerking the controls one way then the next, never lulling herself into thinking she was just flying straight, she made full use of every direction. But there were so many fighters and while their numbers diminished as they crashed into the wrecks that their prey was able to manoeuvre around, they still maintained a deadly chase. Then the team of fighters that had split off appeared again, they had found a shortcut and were now in front, coming straight for the Elite starfighter, laser rounds pinging off the outer casing of the cockpit, until a fighter just like them wiped them out with a stream of concentrated fire. This fighter turned the hunters into the hunted as they were wiped out one after the other, the chasers caught out in their eagerness to prowl their target that they were caught completely unawares by this surprise attack. "Oh yeah, baby!" Elle shrieked over an open comms channel, not caring who could hear it, as she picked off fighters with ease, navigating the terrain far better than they could.

"Damn, that's a good pilot!" Azuri laughed, grateful for the save as she listened to the other pilot cheer from over at the co-pilot's console and she was able to make for a way clear of the debris of sunken ships, feeling a bout of relief flow into her chest. Until another transit gate opened, this one far larger than the one they had conjured.

"The fuck's that?" Lena swore, the green of her eyes reflecting the bright surge of energy being conducted from all across the circumference of this planet wide gate that bore the entry of an entirely different looking ship that was easily larger than the Cosmic class Obsidian vessel. This one wasn't just larger but its design was completely different, opposing the colours of black and red were white and blue, and the shape of this craft was more rounded. Even its arsenal was different, albeit all it fired was a singular glowing blue shell, a sphere of energy that never sat still, its waves of power overflowing and devouring itself over and over but never breaking the shape of a small ball.

It lazily tracked its way into the path of the Marauders, it was slow as it found its way.

"Move us away from that, Azuri, or we'll be caught in its blast radius," Nathan calmly yet firmly commanded the pilot who was caught up in the new weapon's dazzling appearance as well as that of the ship that had fired it.

"What in all the starways is that?" Azuri didn't wait for an answer but did as she was told, diving down to find a clearer route, snaking a path through the unbridled battle scene still developing with seemingly no end in sight until the weapon just introduced detonated. An unbreakable shockwave of surging glowing blue energy burst-forth from the ball that smashed through the armour of every vessel it found in its path, ceaselessly eradicating anything unfortunate enough to be in the vicinity of its eruption. The Marauders giving chase were ravaged by the wave of light, sliced in half, utterly annihilated by the devastating weapon introduced into the skirmish of fleets. Yet the energy wave didn't stop there, it carried on, flowing seamlessly through the orbiting cemetery, blasting fighters without an iota's chance of surviving the assault. It continued to swell, catching the edge of the tail of the Elite starfighter as Azuri frantically flew as fast as she could away from its destructive prowess, until eventually the energy dissipated, the light of the weapon faded into atoms.

"Commander Winter," a new face took up the monitor of the co-pilot's station, this time a human blonde haired woman with serious blue eyes lit up the screen, she was beautiful but for the expression she wore of a honed aggression. "Long time, no see. Come aboard if you will, we have much to discuss."

"Who's this now?" Lena half-laughed, half-cried, not knowing which of the two to do.

"That was Molly Monroe," Nathan pointed out as the transmission ended without him getting even a moment to reply, "She's Monique's sister, you could say she's my opposite number in the Sapphire version of Obsidian, Azurite. I got Xin to ask her for help but I never thought she'd bring her conglomerate with her."

"What do we do now?" Azuri asked, peering all around her with the vast view afforded her with the near hundred and eighty degree field of version the cockpit offered.

"We go aboard their ship, hear what they have to say," Nathan nodded, hiding his frustration at knowing full well that they had no other choice.

Chapter 28

Flying up towards the wide open hangar that struck out at the front of this Sapphire ship felt for Azuri as though she were bringing their ship right into the jaws of a gigantic beast, one that had devoured a greedy portion of the opposing Obsidian fleet, and now sought to claim them as well. Miles and Cait had returned to the cockpit just after the weapon had detonated, the immense shockwave that had effectively brought the chaos to a close, the remains of the armada Elias Thorne had dispatched to Ruby to deal with the revolutionaries' threat were fleeing. A multitude of transit gates opened spanning over the entire globe of the planet below to allow their escape to places unknown. All were all silent for a time, the wake of the devastation enough to enthral the senses, such was the epic power they had witnessed. Each of them, other than their protector, considered themselves a lowly rogue, a Worker in Deviation of Work-orders, a small disruption to a network of operations they deemed, without ever really considering it, to be too large and too efficient to ever properly dismantle. Yet here they found themselves. On the cusp of a resistance to that omnipotent authority, having dealt it a significant blow. The Capital Collapse, the cause for the turn of the fortunes of many a Crimson colleague, was uncovered, its origin known, the truth told. "You say that's the Sapphire conglomerate? Who knew they had such muscle?" Miles stared up at the vessel far larger than anything he had ever imagined, it was nearer the size of a station.

"The more curious question for me is why they used it, why help us, why interfere in a Crimson matter? Can't be for any reason we'll like," Lena remarked doubtfully, not trusting a convenient good thing.

"Xin contacted them, you said," Azuri recalled, nodding upwards at Nathan who had gone quiet since dictating they should go heed the call to board this mysterious ship. "If we asked them to come, then…"

"Yeah but what's some bartender to a power of this size? Why would they listen to him?" Miles pondered, taking the chair opposite Lena, glancing at the screens that showed the condition of the Elite starfighter, its armour and ammunition reserves severely depleted by their escape from Ruby.

"I agree, I don't get it either," Cait added, folding her arms in front of her chest as she stood before the console at the centre of the cockpit, glaring up at the Sapphire ship that was steadily swallowing them up inside. "Yet here we are, it's not like we can run for it."

"So what do we do?" Lena put out into the room, looking to each person in turn.

"We hear them out," Cait was the first to answer. "We see what they have to say as we haven't got any other moves to make, but we must be careful. I don't want to be provoking this lot, we've already started something with one conglomerate, I've no desire to go to war with another."

"Ok," Miles nodded, "we ought to leave our weapons on the ship in that case, not like they'll be any use to us anyway, they'll have an army in there."

"Good call," Cait nodded, "and I have another call I want to make, Nate," she said, looking to the Elite that was being suspiciously quiet, "I want you to follow my lead in there, that means not threatening anybody, not saying anything unless I say, you do what I say, when I say."

"What?" Nathan chuckled, "first you want me to go unarmed, now you want to gag me? What is this?"

"We can't be at war with these people as well as Thorne, we'll be dead before the day's out, and our best chance for negotiating some sort of support is if you stay quiet, stay out of the discussion. You're too…what I mean is…you're too threatening, even just being there, you're enough to have every soldier on that ship on edge. Say the wrong thing, even without meaning to and you could get us all killed." Cait did her best to keep the tone of her voice away from apologising, she knew she was putting him down for something he most likely had not thought to do but the risk was too great.

"What did the Chief Admiral mean?" Lena asked Nathan, out of the blue. "He said he didn't believe you when you basically said all we've been through together was just a job done to you, what'd he mean by that?"

"I don't know," Nathan dismissed, not meeting Lena's eyes.

"Nate, come on, what is it?" Cait persisted, seeing no need for shyness when they had just survived the torment of the Old City together.

Nathan took a deep breath then sighed as he stroked the hair around his mouth, giving a scratch to an itch that came up at his neck before finally looking up to Cait, "Thorne's always had a knack for seeing through people. When I said this was just a job done, most of me meant it, that was the intention I had entering into this team, just to see this through and no further." He considered his words for a moment, pausing to just stare at Cait, feeling a disarming twist at his gut as he realised he was deciding to be more honest than he had been for nearly a decade. "When the Collapse happened, I lost everything, I lost what it meant to be me, I saw a stranger every time I saw my reflection and over time I got used to seeing that person, I got comfortable being that man, being nothing more than a serial killer, there was a comfort in how simple things became. But it was a cold comfort, a lonely way to live, or just not to die you could say as it wasn't really living. Until I met all of you. The first people I tolerated for longer than a moment, without killing of course."

"It's obvious you've changed Nate," Cait offered, "a serial killer would never have carried Tomen's body aboard this ship, they would never have left Miles, who was out of his mind in grief, to provide the necessary cover for us all to get to safety. But you knew you were the strongest out of all of us, that you were best suited to respectfully carry Tomen's body so it wasn't lost, a man who lives only to kill would never've done that."

"I'll be honest, it felt good to be fulfilling my old purpose again, protecting people, being among those I can call friends, not being alone," Nathan almost choked on the words, remembering he had only just killed the man he once considered a mentor for pressuring him to return to that purpose.

"Thank you," Azuri put in, "for returning his body to me," she said, holding back the tears that tried to escape from her eyes.

"You did a good thing, doing that, mate," Miles agreed.

"Yet I still feel the same person," Nathan felt he had to admit, his gaze falling to the floor. "I still feel the need, the hunger, the energy inside from my aggression, it pounds and pounds inside my chest, bursting, bristling inside me, I can feel it flow in my veins to my hands and down to my feet. I am more now than I was before but I am a killer still, all the same. That same dark temptation, that same abyss inside, it's still there, and that's why I think I have to agree with you, Cait, I can't be trusted."

"The fact that you acknowledge that now, means you're not my enemy anymore," Cait smiled back at him, "so we can work together, what'd you say?"

Nathan stood up, half to escape the clutches of a feeling of being vulnerable, and stepped towards Cait, taking a deep breath and offering out a hand, "by your lead, Cait."

"Thank you," she replied, taking his hand in hers and giving it a firm shake, with no doubt in her mind that he would keep to his word.

"We're just about ready to land, people," Azuri announced as the Elite starfighter passed over the rim of the hanger doors and into the atmosphere generated inside, where a mass of soldiers clad in the armour of Azurite stood waiting for them. This armour was similar to that of the Obsidian variety but of a pure white colour as its main feature, and a streak of blue where the red visor would be on a soldier of the Crimson region. Their helmets were slightly differently shaped, where the Obsidian form would be a simple design, protection for the head and little else added to it, these bore more resemblance to the face beneath them with the panelling of the plates indenting and shaped around the natural features of the bearer. It gave the soldiers more of a robotic appearance, for a metal face with a single, beaming blue visor. Most grasped pale rifles, the rounds loaded into their magazines brimming with a brilliant blue energy encased in silver shells. While others held tall spears at their side. These weapons were far taller than their bearers that could only hold them at the third quarter of their height and were lean and impressive, a single length of shining silver coming to a spade at its head, with only a short patch of black attached acting as the grip. Those that were equipped with these elegant weapons stood sentinel around the exits of the hangar and a handful had their energy cores active, brilliant shoots of sharp blue lightning prancing along with the spear's length, not unlike an Obsidian Elite's blade.

"You're sure about leaving our weapons behind?" Lena chuckled after seeing these fearsome troops line up to welcome them, a figure among them stepping forward, presumably their leader.

"Sends the right message," Cait replied without looking at her, preferring to look around the hangar they were slowly descending into, measuring the strength of those ready to greet them.

"Cait's right," Nathan took out his own Elite blade handle first, before retrieving the one he had recovered from General Ardamus, where he had stowed it away at his belt, and placed them both beside the rest of his gear on the console where Lena sat. "The Crimson region contributes to the tri-systems with its artificial farming and superior soldiers that provide security for the settled worlds and lend the opportunity for adding more. While the Sapphire manufactures a wide range of pharmaceuticals and medical technology, they are at the forefront of creating the peak of physical strength, the leading light in having a healthy workforce, it's why so many people try to transfer to a position there. But that reflects on their security forces. While Obsidian are simplistic, stuck to a purpose, see a threat, kill the threat; Azurite are far more sinister, they take prisoners, using the chemicals synthesised in that region to do horrific things to people. So all the better to seem less of a threat to these people, unless you want your mind to turn against you and your nightmares manifest before your waking eyes."

"Ah, yeah, nah, not my kinda party, pass around the whiskey and I'm game," Miles nodded slightly panic-stricken, "but pass around the deadly toxins? Nah, think I'll woose outta that game, I don't wanna be seeing no more zombie, ghosty shit, I'm done with all that crazy stuff."

"I'm staying on the ship," Azuri announced, more as a murmur to herself finally deciding than for anyone in the room to hear, "I'm gonna go sit with Tomen for a while."

"Alright, honey," Lena half smiled to come across more comforting just as Miles placed a hand on the pilot's shoulder, where a silver wing on that black jumpsuit marked her as an RCS pilot so long ago.

"Come on then, I'll take you to see him," Miles said, ushering Azuri out of the cockpit and turning around just before leaving with her, "I'll catch up with you guys downstairs." He followed Azuri out into the passenger tunnel, walking by the walls lined with empty seats, trying to not smile to himself remembering how Azuri's flying had flung him and Cait about so frantically they had needed to hold onto the gun rigs for dear life, but he knew now wasn't the time for any joke. The air in the ship felt far colder now as he followed his friend down the ladder at the end, into the tiny lobby area before making for the bedroom, passing through the armoury. It felt all the more real to Miles that the man that was as close a person could be to him was now dead, as he led the man's wife to where his body lay. As the doors opened to the room, Impala grew restless on the bed beside Tomen, baring his teeth to Azuri who was a stranger to him until the dog recognised the fearful sorrow plastered on her face.

"It's OK, pup, I'm his wife," she said in a homely voice that instantly calmed the guarding dog who returned to laying down beside the body he felt compelled to stand vigil for. Azuri felt the breath leave her lungs as her eyes shifted from the dog to the sight of the body laying still atop the bed, the green jacket that once served as the man's uniform now covering the top of his corpse. She chose to sit beside Tomen, just in front of where Impala lay his snout against the bedsheets, and she placed a hand on her man's chest, holding back a horrified shiver that sought to quake her entire body as she felt no warmth or heartbeat beneath her palm. Azuri sat still and quiet for a moment, allowing herself to truly be present in her surroundings, to know her husband lay beside her, his spirit lost to her, and knowing that she would need to quickly come to terms with that if she were to survive. Impala let out a whimper and something told Azuri that this dog was aware of her loss, aware of her agony and so she kept her left hand on Tomen, but used her right to give the dog a stroke between the ears. "Thank you for being here for him," she told him, relishing the innocence in those big brown eyes staring up at her, feeling warmth find her again, coming off from him, from the life in him.

"He's a good lad, a solid companion, he'll keep you company I bet," Miles said from where he stood, leaning up against the inside of the doorframe leading into the bedroom.

Azuri didn't really listen to him though and she wasn't all that aware that her left hand had left Tomen's chest and was rising up his body to remove the jacket, some crazed thought possessing her to try to see his face once more.

"Don't do that," Miles spoke in such a firm way that he shocked Azuri out of her trance and she recoiled, yanking her hand back embarrassed, instead preferring to reel her hands into her lap. "I want you to remember him as he was, there's nothing for you under there."

"Weren't you able to bring back Sam's body?" Azuri asked, not wanting to picture what Miles was referring to.

"What for? The cunt sold us out," Miles dismissed, in a tone that heavily suggested he wasn't interested in humouring a conversation about another of his friends that died today.

"He has family on Scarlet, a mum and dad. I'm sure they'd wish to bury him, no matter what he'd done." Azuri went on, oblivious to Miles' uncomfortable stance on the topic, "he was sweet in his own way, always caring for us, acting tough to try feel like he belonged with you and Tomen as one of the harder men, kinda cute actually." She took hold of the hem of Tomen's jacket in her left hand as her right carried on stroking Impala and her mind wandered again. "When we're finished with this Sapphire lot, I want to take his body back to his home, on Sanguine, to where he grew up. There's a spot there he always like to take me on our downtime, deep in one of the forests there where the snow is like jackets on the tall trees and a beautiful lake stretches out as far as the horizon, it's so peaceful, I can't think of anywhere better where he'd like to stay."

"I remember, he told me about it. It was one of his favourite things. To spend a little time away from the family with just you, to be lost to all the chaos and confusion of the worlds, to just be alone with you there," Miles nodded, letting go of the resentment that was building in his chest.

"Can I be alone with him for a while? Sorry, I don't wanna be rude, I just want to sit here with him," Azuri cried, her left hand drifting to find Tomen's, finding it cold and hard, unable to squeeze hers to let her know he was there.

"You don't need to apologise," Miles replied, stepping forward and brushing a loose strand of Azuri's flowing black hair back over her shoulder, and seeing those bejewelled blue eyes look back up at his lit by fire. "The others are waiting for me by now, I'll try be back as soon as I can."

"It's OK, I'm not really alone here, I don't think this pup will leave his side," she said with a brave smile, clasping Miles' hand with her right hand as his met her shoulder and she nodded in Impala's direction.

"Good boy," Miles winked at the dog before taking his leave, heading back through the armoury. His own grief clouded his mind and for the briefest moment he considered sitting down in the armchair in the corner, to wait for Azuri to have some time with Tomen before he could return and be with his brother, but shook away the thought. He decided to join the others in meeting the Sapphire conglomerate, as it was better to do something, anything, than to sit silent and wallow in his grim thinking, he concluded. Miles opened the door from the armoury to the small lobby area and found the others there patiently waiting for him which fuelled his confidence that he was making the right decision to join them.

"How is she?" Cait asked as she hit the button to lower the ramp, flooding in the light from the hangar as the ship steadily opened up.

"About as you might expect, but she's content to stay aboard. Impala's keeping her company. Besides, I think we have plenty to distract us here," he replied, his gaze shifting over to the soldiers standing ready at the ramp's base slowly coming into view.

"Let's just get this done," Lena remarked with a sigh, adjusting her tattered red trench coat to sit on her shoulders slightly more comfortably as they prepared to disembark, out to meet their hosts.

The one they had seen standing in front of the others stepped forward further to greet them as they gingerly made their way down the ramp, flanked by the Azurite soldiers at either side, and once they stood facing him, he removed his helm to tuck it under one elbow. "Hmm, more X-Human than human, one might have guessed I suppose," the man began, shaking out his long blonde hair that had become stifled under the helmet. "I'm Kristoph Andreas, Section Chief's son and Director of Azurite, a pleasure to have you all aboard," he introduced himself and while his tone was friendly, his piercing blue eyes darted among the team with not a hint of welcome.

"Our thanks for allowing us to board, and for the rescue," Cait replied, taking a step beyond the rest of the team. "I'm Cait," she said with a hand towards her chest before she half turned on the spot to introduce the others. "And this is Lena, Miles, and Nathan," she went round in turn, "but Azuri, our pilot is remaining on the ship, we lost a member of our team in the bedlam of the Capital, she needs some time alone with him."

"Tell her to come out," Andreas snapped coldly, his eyes darting up to the top of the ramp, wincing slightly and the corner of his mouth contorted slightly as he glared.

"No, it was her husband we lost, she needs time to grieve to herself, she won't be joining us," Cait cut off, her tone exactly how she meant it to be, challenging and strong, knowing Nathan, standing silent behind her, true to his word, would be eager to break the other man for his tone alone.

"Fair enough, a pilot's not worth the time to argue, it's you she wishes to see," Kristoph Andreas returned his gaze to Cait before flicking it over to Nathan over her shoulder, "him, on the other hand, can count himself lucky he knows one of my most trusted underlings or I'd have had shot on sight. Anyhow," he sighed, looking back at Cait, "let us not keep her waiting," he said, turning to leave.

"Who?" Cait asked.

"My mother, Section Chief of the Sapphire Conglomerate And Region, she is most eager to meet you in particular, Cait Jxinn. The voice that roused a resistance to a tyrant that's long overstayed his welcome in the region—'united we stand, divided we fall', was it? Good words, dangerous words." Kristoph didn't wait to be stopped again by another comment, this time he turned and made for the bulkhead double doors, great panels of metal that parted as he approached, a blue cape flowing from his shoulders in a similar style to how General Ardamus wore his.

"Good start, first one we meet's a prick," Lena scoffed but shied down after Cait shot a scornful glance back at her and together as a group they made to follow Kristoph Andreas out of the hangar, the eyes of every Azurite soldier peering out from behind their gleaming blue visors never leaving their every step. The exit to the hangar led out into a long, wide corridor of absolute white, the floors, walls and ceiling all so bright the newcomers had to wince at first to be able to see the way ahead. For as they carried on behind their host, they met the corridor's end at a large elevator, a circular shape big enough for twice a dozen people to use to ascend or lower throughout the levels of this enormous ship. But once they had all stepped onto the platform, it was up that the lift went, rising through levels of the same intense brightness. It rose right to the top where, being a new experience for all involved, the walls were all clear, granting a spectacular view of the outside of the ship, the vacuum of space kept at bay by energised barriers that recycled with a blueish haze, only visible once or twice a minute.

"Don't honestly trust that," Miles let slip as they stepped off from the elevator, his eyes glued to a section of wall as if daring for it to fail.

"It's perfectly safe," Kristoph rolled his eyes as he led them onto the floor at the highest level of the ship. There were few furnishings here, the view beyond predictably intended to be too distracting for any guest to step foot here that they need not be pampered as they visited this office for the Section Chief. A large, fluffy blue rug blanketed the centre section of the floor over the same bright white floor that was of the same material that covered every inch of the ship's interior, while a sofa of the same white encompassed one side, opposite two armchairs, with a desk opposite the lift. This desk was immaculately hand carved from a tree none of the team had ever laid eyes on in the Crimson region. It was of a mineral shine of a dark blue shade but it was the texture of it that marked it as a section of timber rather than stone. And behind this desk was a woman whose beauty could not be outshone by the elegance of the design where she sat behind, only standing once her guests had arrived.

"Finally you've all arrived," she exclaimed, stepping out from the desk, revealing her long dress in the colour of her conglomerate. It hung off her body perfectly from a single strap at her left shoulder, the cloth racing down, splitting at the legs to leave her right side exposed, with leather boots of the same blue being revealed there. Her skin was pale as milk but it only added to the golden shine of her hair that ran down in front of her right breast in an especially long tail, tied with a band made of twinkling small sapphires at the top of her temple. Her exuberant blue eyes filled the room with a lively energy and her juicy pink lips formed a nigh perfect smile that greeted the exhausted team with a wave of warmth and a seemingly friendly welcome. She stepped forward onto the middle of the rug, in the centre between the sofa and the two chairs. So much was the appearance of her sincere greeting, the team would have been forgiven for dismissing the sight of the three guards standing beside her. She was distracting for them, none of them had expected someone as alluring as her to be the face of the force that had saved them, yet here she stood, proud and confident. Behind this leader was the battlefield in all its wanton destruction and wayward loyalties as ships beyond counting were discarded in the orbit above Ruby, their ruin strewn across the stars as this figure grinned a promise of safety away from that warscape.

"Mother, this is the team that infiltrated Rose City, exposing Elias Thorne's illicit activities," Kristoph Andreas introduced. He waved a lazy hand behind him as he didn't stop his pacing, heading straight for one of the chairs where he sat rather unceremoniously, not shy in showing his distaste for the setting he found himself in.

"Ah yes, most impressive," the Section Chief nodded, before ushering the team to take a seat on the sofa with a graceful hand before she herself took up the other armchair, "please sit," she said, flicking her right leg over he left, resting her hands on her lap.

"Thank you," Cait led her people as they crossed the level to sit on the sofa, only Nathan chose to stand, his eyes studying all he could see.

"No seat for you, Commander?" Their host asked in a half mocking tone, she eyed him from head to toe and back again, a smirk emerging from one corner of her mouth.

Nathan simply shook his head.

"Suit yourself. Everyone, I am Annika Andreas, Section Chief for the Sapphire region, and allow me this opportunity to welcome you. It is a true pleasure to have you all here, I've been so keen to meet you all." Annika allowed her gaze to waft from Nathan down to the X-Human man sitting on the sofa, with the red haired woman beside him and then to the subject of her curiosity. "You must of all, my sweet. To challenge an entire conglomerate, an empire really, you are bold, most bold indeed."

"Thank you, Chief Andreas, and we thank you for your timely rescue. And as for your compliment, I only meant to seek out the truth behind a disaster that affected all citizens of the Crimson region," Cait answered, being as polite and political as she could muster. She desperately clawed at her brain for any advice, anything she could use to keep her balance as this was a certain decorum she had never experienced before. In the darker pockets of memory in her mind, it was an image of Tomen that gave her hope. A memory from so long ago, back when they had only just met. She was so young, so brash, only recently fled the RCS factory her family had worked at for generations, not knowing what the future held, not knowing anything about the worlds beyond the machinery she had tinkered with night and day. And he had given her a piece of advice that she had forgotten she had taken to heart, 'always be yourself, as no one can be you for you, and there is only ever going to be one of you among the starways, after all'.

"Yeah, well," Annika chuckled, "because it's such a region worth saving, am I right? I mean look at you all, look how much you've had to give to be here, what you had to experience just because no one else wanted to take up the mantle of putting a wrong to right. The Crimson's always been a problem, even before its Capital fell. One such example, is look at your jacket, my dear," she said, raising a palm in Miles' direction, meaning the green jacket of his Stalwart days. "Do you know why that company identifies with a green shade despite being in the Crimson region?"

"Yeah," Miles shrugged, "Stalwart Ironworks was a company in the Emerald conglomerate, years and years ago. It was one of the companies that first built the infrastructure for the Crimson region, they played a large part in building Rose City, too. The first Section Chief of the Crimson bought the company for the good work they did, they just never changed the uniform."

"Exactly my meaning, and well put my dear, but that is entirely what I mean. The Crimson conglomerate has been a ramshackle mess for a decade or more now, it's made of ill-fitting pieces formed together, forced together, to make this thing that barely supports those that live and work within it. Or you would never have desired to stand against it and its interests by unlocking the mystery of the Capital Collapse, now, would we, dears? Elias Thorne inherited an awful congregation of corrupt and idealistic fools, but instead of trying to build something good out of it, he went the way of his forebears and desecrated it even more. You know, I met him once, before the Collapse, back when he was just Director of Ruby Consolidated Systems. You could tell there was something off about the man," Annika gave a disgusted expression, as if she were putting on a show. "It was clear something like the Collapse was going to happen. Too much pride, too much ambition, and no fear of any consequences. A formidable character, to be sure, not to be crossed lightly, but lacking everything it takes to be a successful Section Chief."

"That ambition brought a city to ruin," Cait put in, "he ruined so many lives I doubt anyone could ever list the thousands, millions affected."

"That's absolutely true."

"But I must ask," Cait hesitated, sensing what she intended to ask could change the tone of the conversation dramatically, "by consequences, do you mean you? Is that why you've come? Because of what he did."

"To an extent, yes," Anikka shrugged, nodding her head, her golden hair elegantly swaying against her chest. "The Chairman was actively investigating the source of the Collapse and he recently sent word for us to more directly intervene, to put an end to Elias' term as Section Chief by force. Now, no one as far as I'm aware has ever met our all-powerful overseer, but when the Chairman demands, we obey—something Elias should have learned from his father."

"You mean Roderic Thorne?"

"Yes, that man always was a scheming bastard but I have to admit he was clever. Always a favourite of the Chairman, that one, always having private meetings, maybe they even met in person." Annika held out an open hand in showing she had no idea about anything more, but it was Nathan's reaction that caught her eye. The Elite Commander had been silent up to now with a face of stone, giving nothing away to the thoughts behind his suspicious brown eyes, but at the mention of his former Chief, his eyes flickered over to Annika in avid curiosity. "You were a favourite of Roderic's, isn't that right, Mr Winter?"

"He granted my promotion to Elite Commander, nothing else," Nathan replied with a displeased, low voice.

"He wanted to grant you Section Chief, even we are aware of that. He must have seen something in you," the Sapphire Chief sat forward, wrapping her knee in her hands, "did he ever tell you that I once made an offer to him for you?"

"Hmm," was all Nathan grunted, not caring.

"I told Roderic I'd give him five hundred platinum credits right there and then if he could arrange a meeting between you and I where the guaranteed end would be you joining Azurite as its Commander of my Guardian Guild. He refused. And that was when he told me of his plans for you, a Chief with a heart to protect and a mind to kill, he favoured you over his own son, a fact I'll never understand." Anikka glanced over at her own son sitting still as a rock in the next chair. Kristoph, however, did not return the gaze, favouring to glare directly at Nathan, anticipating a need to command his troops to attack. "Of course that was before Miss Monroe over here ascended the ranks to be my most successful Commander, someone who has my absolute faith." One of the guards that stood by their Section Chief grasping a spear, face hidden by an armoured helm, approached the chair at their leader's mention, revealing themselves, placing the helmet under their free arm. It was the woman from the message inviting them to come aboard the Sapphire ship, Molly Monroe.

"Looks like things turned out well for you," Cait dismissed, sensing no need for this line of conversation to go any further, wishing to get back on track. "But it's how things will progress for the future that concerns me. Never before has another conglomerate taken such an interest as to invade another region, this kind of thing just doesn't happen."

"You're right," Annika smirked, "but your need for us is dire. I take it you're not aware of what has been transpiring in your region while you were navigating Rose City?"

"What'd you mean?"

"The Forerunner, a space station I believe you are all familiar with? It was deemed unprofitable and all those aboard at the time Vice Admiral Reiku arrived were killed."

"The fuck!" Lena blurted out, "did no one survive?"

"A small handful slipped through the Vice Admiral's clutches, yes, including a certain bartender I've heard your team liked to frequent."

"Xin's alive, thank the stars," Lena gasped, unable to control herself.

"All those people," Miles thought aloud, remembering all the faces they had brushed by on the busy promenade each time they docked at the station.

"That's not all," Annika continued, "while Elias's uncle, Titus Thorne was able to give us an entry point, directing us where the Obsidian border guard was at its most vulnerable. It seems our show of strength only pushed Elias to close ranks. He's stopped all shipments to the other regions, cut off the contribution to the Board and ceased all movement of food and drinking water around the Crimson. It's clear he wants to starve your people, a kind of ultimatum of eat and work for him, or die starving if you're not shot by an Obsidian gun still faithful to him. So if any of you had any doubts about why the battle outside took place, that's why, because people's lives are literally hanging in the balance. Make no mistake, my dears, this is a war."

"So what happens now?" Cait asked, failing to hide how the stakes of the game they were all powerless to stop playing were far higher than she realised.

"Well, that's just it, what does happen now?" The Sapphire Chief spread her hands apart and shrugged. "My son, the Director of my security company tells me this is a conflict he can resolve, that his Azurite can conquer Elias and his Obsidian, to seize control of the Crimson. While my loyal Commander of my most skilled warriors informs me that an all-out war is avoidable, if I just point this man in the right direction," she said, pointing directly at Nathan. "You know, when I did visit Rose City, and we're talking some time ago, I visited one of the schools—I wanted to see how the hearts and minds of the Crimson workforce were being moulded. And I watched, I sat in on a few of their lessons being taught, and you know what was funny? Your name was mentioned, Mr Winter. This mascot for your company, this dumb cat smoking a cigar in a coat, well, rather like your one, my dear," she gestured to Lena, "was talking about the history of the tri-systems, blah, blah, blah but then, he goes on about joining Obsidian. And then he refers to you, Commander Winter, the Crimson conglomerate's 'finest servant'." Annika scoffed and flicked her eyebrows up in a mocking glare, "and so when Miss Monroe came to me saying she got a message from you asking for her help, I just couldn't contain myself." She started to laugh, flicking a hand over to her son who began to chuckle alongside her. "I mean, really? Roderic's lakey, come out of the shadows after so long away, hiding from his purpose, I mean it was just too good to be true. And begging for help, now that just made it for me. The man

I had been willing to spend a large fortune on, one I had heard of his brutal means and savage style, the one who I had scarcely believed re-emerged from his self-imposed exile, and you ask for help? Just maybe you're not all you're cracked up to be, huh, Mr Winter?"

"Where are you going with this?" Cait asked, bored of the other woman's thinly veiled insults and tired of not getting to any form of point to this meeting.

"I'm saying while my son may be right, it's Miss Monroe who has captured my curiosity. It's intriguing isn't it? To wager one Crimsonite against an onslaught of Obsidian's finest and a host of robo-sentries in the most secure installation ever built? I'm leaning towards her suggestion of using this Winter to bring this conflict to a swift end, if he is truly as capable as she stacks him up to be. Especially if it means far less loss of Sapphirean lives."

"What'd you mean?" Lena put in but Cait waved her down.

"I mean now is the time for you and I to have a more private conversation, Miss Jxinn," Annika smirked, "your companions can go with Mr Winter who is needed to accompany Miss Monroe for she has something to show him, a key, she says, to victory over Elias Thorne." And as her name was mentioned, Molly Monroe stepped forward, clutching her spear in one hand and her helmet in her other, tipping the end towards the lift.

"Come with me," she said, and jerked her weapon forward ever so slightly, but enough to reaffirm her message.

"Don't worry, Caity, I'm not going anywhere," Lena placed a hand on Cait's leg beside her and glared up at Molly who returned a disapproving stare.

"Actually, Lena, I need you to go," Cait said, turning to face her friend, "I need to hear what she has to say. We need this, we don't have the means to feed people, but these people do. We need them, and if they won't talk with all of you here, then I need you to go."

"You promised you'd stick by me, and I promised I'd stay with you. I don't trust these people, Cait. You'll be stronger with me at your side," Lena replied, not understanding and biting back a teary reaction to her friend's words.

"But that's just it, Lena, we're not strong. We need these people and I need you not to talk like that if we're going to build any kind of relationship with them."

"What're you saying? We're stronger together, we're staying together!"

"No, Lena. I have to do this, and it looks like I have to do this alone. Now go, you're just delaying things, this has to go this way," Cait shuffled away, Lena's hand limply slipping off her leg.

"But I—" Lena could see the Sapphire Chief and the Director of Azurite across from her out of the corner of her eye, both of them looking away, and she realised they were embarrassed for her, as she felt the start of a warm trickle of her tears roll down her cheeks.

"Lena, go." Cait held firm, no matter how much it burned her insides to turn against her friend, to cast her aside. But in her heart she knew she had to. This was bigger than her and her feelings. For Cait, she focused only on the larger picture at work. She was heartbroken at the Forerunner's massacre and how the food was being deprived from the kinds of towns like the one they had passed through on Scarlet. She knew they would never have escaped the carnage that they could still see all around them, and they would never accomplish establishing a new and better order for the Crimson, without the Sapphire conglomerate's help. She believed that with everything she had. Cait devoted all her strength, all her will, to the idea of helping make better lives for the people of the Crimson, she knew she had to try. And if that meant discarding her friend for appeasing these potential allies, then she was firm in knowing that it had to be done.

"I guess I'll see you back at the ship?" Lena sobbed, standing up, with Miles and Nathan just behind her, both of them lost for what to say.

"I wouldn't wait around, my dear," Annika Andreas put in, "she has a great many things to attend to, maybe you should just be on your way."

"What?" Lena started, staring wide eyed at the Section Chief but Cait darted up, grabbing her arm tight, bringing her focus back to her.

"I'll be fine, just look after the others for me, I'll join you when I can," Cait reassured, giving the other woman a tender kiss on the cheek, making the effort as a way of apologising for her blunter first attempt at encouraging her to leave.

"You better," Lena insisted, finding some resolve, and nodding as she turned around to follow the others back to the lift.

"Where're we going?" Miles asked as they stepped onto the lift circle again, it immediately began to descend once they were all on.

"To my office, there's something I want your Commander to see," Molly explained, placing her helmet back on.

Chapter 29

They followed through twisting turns and many corridors but eventually they found themselves heading towards a set of doors similar to the ones that marked the exit of the hangar, with Miles and Lena in behind Nathan in keeping up with the Guardian Guild Commander leading the way. The walls here were the same as the rest of the ship, a bare white but it was the feeling coming from the Azurite guards posted at various junctions and points along the way that was different. It didn't sit right with Lena, especially after they had been so rudely dismissed before. She stared at each one as they passed and she could sense something was wrong, something had changed, something they were walking into that she knew she wouldn't like. "What's going on?" She finally asked, having had enough of seeing the soldiers get more and more tense as they went on, fully expecting them to open fire, they seemed so nervous.

"Would you be so calm with someone as dangerous as Winter strolling around your base, interacting with your boss, the one who ensures your pay and protection? No, I didn't think so," Molly explained without looking back or stopping.

"Hmm, they're scared of you," Lena whispered.

"They're armed, we're not," Nathan reminded her, "besides, SCARs breed good soldiers, these people are well capable of giving me a good fight."

"SCARs?"

"Sapphire Conglomerate and Region—SCAR, look closely at them the next time you see one without a helmet on. You'll see a small scar under their left ear that reaches down to their neck."

"Why'd they have that?"

"In the Crimson, our work contracts are signed with blood taken from a small prick of a finger when we're first born," Nathan explained. "Whereas if you're born in the Sapphire region, they take a lot more blood and leave a kind reminder that they did. I hear, they do that so whenever they move their neck, they feel that scar there and it reminds them of the company, it's something they can never quite get used to."

"That's fucking barbaric, they do that to infants?"

"Keep on your guard, we're in an extremely dangerous place." Nathan warned her as they reached the end of the corridor with the bulkhead doors opening at their arrival to reveal a large room, alcoves at every wall in this hexagonal shape, with blue drapes decorating the walls and lazily cast on the floor where they had not been picked up.

"You two wait outside," Molly commanded, her voice booming and menacing behind the armour of her helmet.

"Not again," Lena spat.

"No way, what're you thinking of doing in there?" Miles demanded, but was shut down when Nathan turned back to them, taking the time to fix each of them with a calming look.

"Just give me a minute, I'm sure this won't take long, see if you can contact Azuri on the ship, tell her to get the engine running if you can," Nathan told them and followed Molly Monroe inside. The doors slammed shut before the two X-Humans had the chance to reply.

"Azuri, you there?" Miles asked over the radio piece he was still wearing and gave a look to Lena that displayed his annoyance at being kicked out of yet another discussion.

"What a bitch," Lena swore, trying the button on the control panel to the left of the doors but it did nothing, the doors were locked.

"Hmm, the radio's dead, I can't get through," Miles announced, getting a concerned look in return.

"Yeah I didn't hear you over my earpiece, I hope bad reception is all that is," Lena sighed, giving the bulkhead doors a solid kick with her boot.

"I don't like this, we gotta get in there," he added, giving the bulkhead a hard whack with his fist before taking a closer look at the control pad Lena had tried.

Nathan glanced over his shoulder at the thud resounding off the bulkheads behind him but he paid it no mind, he just followed Molly over into the centre of the room where a holographic projector sat, looking identical to the one aboard his ship. "So what is it? What's this all about?" He asked, his patience run out.

"I just need you to look at this," Molly rounded the imager and stood at its far side, looming over it, her spear propping her upright.

"I'm growing weary of this, Molly, I—" Just as Nathan's rage was beginning to spark into life, he was disarmed by the image flickering into being between them, a hologram of Monique Winter, with the small Harkness in her arms. "Why're you showing me this?" His voice losing all of its aggressive potency as he couldn't take his eyes away from the image of his dead wife and son.

"To remind you," Molly growled, leaning in behind the image, her visor glaring at him. "They died because of Elias Thorne and yet he still lives. You've killed so many, slaughtered them in Monique and Harkness's names yet Elias you won't touch, why? Why let their murderer draw breath? Take a deep breath, Winter, let the air fill your lungs, breathe it in, really think about it."

"He-He's too well protected," Nathan felt his arms disappear and legs drop from beneath him, he fell through the floor and he drowned in the metal, swallowed by it, engulfed by the darkness he found there with the only light he could see being the illuminated image of his wife and son.

"Since when would that stop the likes of you? They died! They fucking died, Nathan! Because you weren't there to protect them! Now, what are you going to do about that?" Molly pressed and Nathan didn't recognise her voice anymore, it had turned cruel and sharp, it breached his mind and clawed at his brain. "They died, because you failed."

"No, they died because of Thorne," Nathan begged, his head splitting. He couldn't look away from them, some invisible force holding his head that way, keeping his eyes open and the only thing they could see was Monique and Harkness.

"Then why is he still alive?"

"I can't get to him, he's too well guarded, he's out of my reach," Nathan drooled, feeling more powerless now than he had ever thought possible as his whole body betrayed him, he was glued in place, forced against his will to keep staring at his family.

"No," Molly went on, "you didn't even try."

"But it's impossible!"

"So was entering the Capital, yet you did that, didn't you? So why, why then is Elias still alive? Breathe deep, really think about it."

The image of Monique and Harkness, illuminating out of the imager that stood between Molly and Nathan twisted and reshaped before his eyes as he watched, his wife clutching their son whose eyes began to fade until it was clear they were both crumpled down on the floor, dead. Some unfathomable strength returned to him and Nathan went for the holo-diary at his belt. His arm felt as though it were composed of lead but he persevered, bringing it out and clutching it in his right hand, and though it was painful, agonising, he raised it to be in front of his face. Nathan begged for more strength as he needed to see them as they were, happy and alive, anything but the dead state this image was forcing on him. Yet when he activated the card, pressing in the orb at its centre and projecting the image, he only saw them alive and happy but for a moment before that image became warped, too, displaying them dead on the floor. But this time his son, buried in his mother's decaying embrace, stared directly back at Nathan with hollow eye sockets and a blank expression. "It's because I was scared!" Nathan cried, pleaded to his son, crushing the holo-diary in his grasp, breaking it, losing the memory forever.

"Scared of what?" Molly insisted, leaning forward further so that her helmet nearly breached the holographic image from the imager housed on the floor between them.

"I was scared, I didn't want to die, I didn't try because I was too scared to, I—" Nathan lost himself in those hollowed out eyes of his son glaring down at him and he felt as though his spirit was plunged into darkness, lost to the shadows.

"Elias Thorne murdered your family, Winter! He took them from us, my sister and nephew, your wife and son, he murdered them! So what are you going to do !" Molly screamed in Nathan's face, and as she was so engaged in what she was doing, she missed seeing the doors to the room open, Miles and Lena rushing inside.

"The fuck you doin' to him!" Lena yelled as she saw Nathan sprawled on the imager, on his knees, staring into an image of who she recognised from a picture she had seen back in the Capital City, it was Monique Winter and their son, they looked happy but she had no idea why it was being projected. Then she saw what was being bellowed out from the base of the hologram, a grey smoke that Nathan was breathing in, and he seemed like he wasn't aware of it as he didn't move. "Nathan!"

"Get out, you two! Leave!" Molly stood upright and slammed the base of her spear onto the floor, letting the sound ring out.

"I was afraid?" Nathan murmured so softly that the others broke off from their own thoughts, straining to hear him.

"Get up Winter!" Miles encouraged and stepped forward to help him but Molly lifted her spear, pointing it firmly in his direction.

"Why was I afraid?" Nathan went on, sounding confused and half asleep, as if he were waking from a terrifying nightmare. "When it's them that should be afraid." Molly moved back to the imager, to get a better look at Nathan, to see if she was getting the reaction she had hoped for but when she peered down at him, what she saw made her jump back. "They should all be afraid, of me!" And then there was a sound no one knew how to describe, the closest it could be said to be was an animalistic roar as Nathan looked up, his eyes flooded with blood that crystallised, forming the eyes of an X-Human, dark and shining with red. At their centre, pitch black pupils, raw and brimming with rage struck out as he rose back to his feet.

"You will kill Elias Thorne," Molly commanded, not sounding anywhere near as authoritative as she had meant, her shock diluting her tone.

"I will kill Elias Thorne," Nathan repeated back to her with his gaze seemingly passing through her at first before focusing, the shadowy sheen to his red bejewelled eyes fixing on her before he turned to leave.

"Winter?" Miles took a step back, the eyes of the other man plunging him into a state of fear greater than when they navigated the Capital and he stood aside as Nathan passed between him and Lena, and out of the room.

"What just happened?" Lena begged, looking first at Miles then to Molly, "the fuck you do to him?"

"The compound in the gas attacks the limbic system of the brain, it attacks all of it really," Molly went to explain. She stood petrified, not knowing whether her plan had truly worked as she removed her helmet, placing it down as the gas dissipated. "It blocks emotional attachment, it makes the subject suggestible by making them forget their friends, even their family. It's horrific but it had to be done."

"So he's forgotten us? Is that what're you sayin'?" Lena screamed at Molly, not caring that the other woman was armed with a tall, menacing spear.

"I don't know. Maybe. The attack on the subject's attachments is only a by-product of the compound, it's just to make them more suggestible, get them to do things."

"Like go on a suicide mission to go kill Thorne alone?" Miles shouted, not sure if he should be challenging this woman to a fight or go chasing after his friend that was now suddenly even more terrifying than he already was.

"He can do it," Molly insisted, nodding, regaining her composure. "He can actually do it."

"How d'you know that for sure? Sounds like your SCAR cunts win either way," Lena swore.

"I know because he and I grew up in the Elite Academy together, I've seen what he's capable of. Listen, he lost his wife and son, I lost my sister and nephew, I need him to succeed as much as he needs to."

"And the eyes—how'd you manage that?" Lena asked, watching Molly switch off the hologram projector.

"That wasn't the compound, that was already done to him," Molly remarked, failing to hide her surprise.

"Yeah, but, I ain't ever seen a red eyed X-Human before," Lena replied.

"Nor have I," Miles agreed.

Cait felt the loneliness of her position. Sitting across from the Section Chief of the Sapphire region and the Director of the equivalent company to the forces that just sent a small army to wipe her and her family out of the sky, that the people sitting here slaughtered with a single weapon. She held onto her memory of Tomen, despite feeling like he would have heavily disapproved of sending Lena away from her side, but she knew it was the right choice, she had to make allies out of these two if she were to convince them to help her rebuild the Crimson.

"You know, we didn't just saunter into this region blindly, my dear, oh no, we've had our network of operatives deployed here for some time, studying all the major activities, the major players," Annika Andreas went on. "It's how we know about you and your little family, the places you went, the things you did. And might I say, darling, I am mighty impressed with you. That tagline, 'united we stand, divided we fall', that's inspiring, that's something the people of this region can really get behind, I love it!"

"Thanks?" Cait awkwardly replied, not knowing what the other woman was getting at.

"Because, look, here's the thing, sweetie," Annika sat back in her chair, fixing Cait with a serious look. "I'm going to make this explicitly clear right here, right now: the Sapphire conglomerate is not here to stay, we are not taking over your region."

"Ok," was all Cait could answer.

"Because that would be breaking procedure, little one. The Chairman and the rest of the Board, other than myself of course, wouldn't allow it. It's just not how things are done. They would say there always needs to be a conglomerate in the Crimson, and I would have to agree. Competition makes our species great, it brings innovation to new ideas, it provides the means to take leaps and bounds ahead in our technology, it allows us to keep on evolving, keep on getting better, you with me so far sweetie?"

"Yeah."

"Not to mention the contribution. You see, the Board and the tri-systems we govern were founded on the principle that all survivors of the Old World must contribute something for us all to survive and prosper. We must all offer something, and as companies that means we must be profitable, we have to be good for something. We in the Sapphire make the best medicine and provide the best care in all the tri-systems. Those louts in the Emerald have by far the largest standing workforce, they offer the best resource there is, people, for any need or task imaginable, that's their business, my dear. And the Crimson, it keeps us all fed. It really is as simple as that. So if we were to take over, who would know how to carry on the manufacturing of all that food? Well, sugar, that would be the ones we put deep in the dirt choking on the mud and grit they rightly deserve but then all the tri-systems suffers, don't it? Just like if you were to take our medicine out of the mix, or the Emerald's workers, the whole thing just stops, and that ain't good for nobody, sweet thing."

"No it wouldn't."

"So we need the people of the Crimson to take back their homes, to take back their work as their work is super special, important to us," Annika smiled, "their lives, too, of course."

"And why are you telling me all of this?"

"Because dumby, you're it."

"I'm what?" Cait shifted nervously on the sofa, suddenly finding it too big for just her to be comfortable on.

"Why, the Crimson's new Section Chief, honey," Annika Andreas winked as her son watched Cait silently with his strange scowl.

"Fuck off," Cait laughed, not believing it.

"I see you're not lacking a silver tongue, are you?" Annika laughed, shifting in her chair. "But you heard me. We can't install just anyone to take over after Elias, we need someone the people of this region will rally behind, really support in our transition from Thorne's corrupt regime to a better one where we all benefit."

"Why me? I have no idea how to be Chief."

"Well, sure you don't honey bun but that's where we come in. We'll guide you each step of the way. You'll be our ally and trading partner of course, so we're invested in seeing you succeed."

"That still doesn't answer why I'm the one. I don't really want to be and if this is some kind of joke—"

"Let me just stop you there, Miss Jxinn," Kristoph raised a hand, finally lending his voice to the conversation. "I fully understand your misgivings but I can assure you this is not a joking matter to anyone in this room. The future of too many lives depends on the actions we choose from here on in. And the action we consider to risk the least loss of life is to have the Crimson gain a leader with some traction with the workers. Someone they can trust, not Thorne, and not some outsider to them from our region. Now, they've already heard your voice, and I can tell you that pockets of resistance are already growing throughout the region with those words of yours as their rallying cry. But my question to you is not if you would like the role, it's how could you prove us right, that you would be better than Thorne?"

Cait was taken aback by the man's sudden involvement and to be asked such a heavy question, she hesitated to reply. She took a moment to herself to give him the respect of thoroughly thinking through her answer before lending it to them. She was more nervous than she realised, having been rubbing her hands together the entire time, toying with the cuffs of her jumpsuit, tracing the outline of the branding burned onto the inside of her wrist. A memory flashed to her, of the ghost they had met in the city. The one that recognised her brand and asked about her parents. And while Cait couldn't remember the whole conversation, she did remember telling the non-corporeal girl that she wasn't what was important. And that was where she found her answer.

"Because I'm not what's important, it's not about what I want or what I believe in. We all must stand together, we must strive for a common goal, we must all work together, believe in the same things. We must stand together, or fall apart alone."

"Hmm, a similar note but changing the words," Annika nodded, "a fair point though and well made, that was exactly what I was hoping to hear. But even standing together, they will need a leader they can trust, why would that be you?"

"Because I'm one of them," Cait said confidently, raising her hand to show the brand to her silver shined skin, and she instantly knew it was the right move as Annika smiled warmly back at her, leaning forward.

"Well done, sweet thing, well done. So onto the next point. Do you understand why we cannot simply name you Section Chief for the Crimson conglomerate, right here, right now?"

"Not really," Cait had to admit.

"Well, it's all to do with power. You see, my dear, stations such as Section Chief have their powers locked into the person's DNA that performs that role, linking to the sample taken from their birth added to their contracts. It means that only that person can enact those powers, granting pay, allocating food, assigning tasks, it's all encoded in the DNA of the person of that station having the authority to do as much. But the locking in process, it does have its flaws. Especially when it comes to elevated positions like a Section Chief, their DNA is needed to transfer their power, and it can't just be taken. Their life signs are checked by special terminals, it has to be a genuine transfer of power, not coerced. It's a means of security, actually against what we would be meaning to do, to force a new leader for the conglomerate."

"So you mean to take Thorne alive?"

"We have to, to get that transaction of power or else the powers of his position are lost into the ether of the Board and all the politics that entails. And the suffering of the Crimson people is drawn out from a matter of days to years of deliberating and debating."

"That's what your Monroe wants? For Nathan to go get Thorne for you?"

"Exactly that, exactly that, because should he succeed, little Caity, he will be severing the head of the snake, so to speak, rather than have us tangle with loyalist Obsidian forces for who knows how long until we finally breach Thorne's defences. We can end a long and bloody conflict in a single day, doesn't sound like the ideal solution to you?"

"If he can manage it," Kristoph put in, clearly in disagreement with the notion. He was older than Nathan, his age shown through a large golden beard that covered most of the lower half of his face that he played with now in his impatience.

"You know, he just might," Cait nodded, thinking it over, thinking back to how she saw him take on a mass of General Ardamus' forces, including the man himself, by himself, but for her minor help. "Then Thorne can answer for what he's done to this region and my people." Her exotic purple eyes gleamed as she imagined a future without that tyrant haunting her every thought, his Stalwart inquisitors stalking their every move as WIDOWS, hunting them.

"Yes, it was all rather tragic what he did to those poor X-Humans," Annika agreed with an exaggerated, sympathetic nod, "and speaking of that. We will be needing that data card you possess, my dear. The information stored on it is of a high interest to the Chairman, I simply must have it."

Cait had completely forgotten about that. She remembered now, taking it out of Tomen's jacket and needed a moment to think about where she kept it for herself, eventually finding it tucked into a shallow pocket in her jumpsuit at her hip. "What does he want with this? This is the evidence of what Thorne did."

"I honestly didn't ask," Annika answered her. "But as I said, the Chairman orders, and we obey. Now hand it over, sweetie," while she didn't stand up to take ownership of the data card, she did lazily stretch out a palm.

"And if I don't hand it over?"

"Then you wouldn't starting off this fresh, new relationship with another conglomerate on the best terms, now would you?" The Sapphire Chief grinned, "Consider it your means for barter, in return for our aid to your people. I can get thirty thousand units of processed meat to this region at a snap of my fingers, but I never do things out of the goodness of my little heart, pumpkin, that's just not good business. Not to mention, my Azurite troops will liberate the farms under Elias's control, giving the means of production back to you, and out of his grasp."

"And all that costs is one little data card?" Cait asked, thinking the deal too good to be true, especially when she considered that they made no mention of the copy of the data still stored on Nathan's armour.

"I think you know full well the value of what's stored on that little card, sweet thing."

"Alright," Cait stood up, her hooded cloak shifting about her shoulders and she had to adjust it to be more comfortable as she passed over to the other woman which allowed for a simple extra moment to occur for her. As she placed the data card down in Annika Andreas's hand, she looked at her, directly in the eyes. "Wait a minute, why would Nathan do anything for you?"

The Sapphirean Chief could not hide her displeasure at Cait's question, snatching the data card ungracefully and sharply nodding upwards for her guest to return to her seat, to back away from her. And while Cait obliged, shifting back to the sofa, she never blinked, her stare demanding a reply. Annika blew out a deep, exasperated breath before rolling her eyes and returning to Cait's gaze, "Because he'll be programmed to," she shrugged.

The walls were so bright it was a rude awakening when Nathan returned to remember that his feet were moving, that he had been walking, fast, somehow knowing the way back to his trusted ship, a new job to do, a new purpose to fulfil. What he couldn't tell himself was why he stopped, here at the circular lift, when the way to the hangar was straight on, what compelled him to realise his senses again. Strangers banked him at either side as his escort, two soldiers clad in white armour, each with a rifle they led him back to his ship and he could see the way, and he remembered that there were more soldiers there. But they didn't bother him, not in the slightest. Nathan had stopped in the middle of the hallway and peered down at his feet that seemed to have turned against him at some point, leading him down a path he never remembered choosing. His black armoured boots were dirty, he was tracked mud in spits and sputters on the floor behind him, yet he struggled to remember where he had been. And yet there was a familiarity to the dirt, a place he had been to recently, a place he had known, a place he had been to before this most recent visit. A place that held great meaning to him.

A nudge behind his arm came from one of those rifles the soldiers were carrying and Nathan could sense their anxiety, he knew they never intended for him to stop, they didn't want him to remember. "Keep going, Commander," the trooper instructed behind his mask, a voice that meant nothing to Nathan, he didn't recognise it or the need to follow what it said. Especially when a different pull was ushering him elsewhere, capturing his attention, he looked with new eyes towards the lift. While he couldn't see his new appearance, Nathan didn't feel anywhere close to being himself. His vision felt sharper, with every surface more defined than ever before, and there was a new red haze everywhere he looked that he couldn't explain. "You need to keep moving, Winter," the soldier pressed again, impatient at Nathan standing still, vacantly staring at the lift rather than the way ahead to the hangar.

"Aye, just not in the direction you intend," Nathan replied coolly and took a step towards the lift. There was something up there, at the highest level of where he found himself that he felt he needed to see.

"Not that way," the soldier raised the barrel of his rifle, aiming it directly for Nathan's head, "stop or I'll be forced to make you stop, murdering scum."

Nathan didn't say anything back, he just looked back over his shoulder at the two soldiers, wondering whether they really did wish to challenge him, and when the other joined in with raising his weapon, seemingly fully intending to use it, he was sure. In the blink of an eye, he snatched at the nearest rifle, seizing its barrel, forcing it away from him as he took a step to one side, placing that soldier under his control between him and the other one. With an easy movement, he then stamped down hard on the first soldier's knee, hearing it break as the man collapsed, held up only by Nathan's grip on his weapon. But before the second soldier could use the opening to open fire, Nathan shot across and elbowed him fiercely in the neck before sweeping a leg under him to knock him to the floor. The first soldier still held onto the grip of his rifle, his finger still on the trigger, not wishing to let go but it made no difference to Nathan who raised the gun despite the added weight, fired several energised rounds into the face of the other soldier, before turning the weapon on its owner who lay at his feet. A guard who heard the commotion from a room off the corridor rushed out, spear in hand, charging at a full tilt sprint but his attempt to thrust his weapon into Nathan's midriff was simple for him to dodge. The Azurite soldier's momentum carried him forward until Nathan grabbed him by the throat, lifting him up off the floor with his right hand, his legs swinging out in front of him. The shock from the grab made the soldier lose his grip on his weapon as it clanged noisily against the floor. With the soldier firmly under his power, Nathan stepped onto the lift, still holding the other man high with ease.

When he reached the highest level, all memory flooded back to him and Nathan felt alive again upon seeing Cait sitting across from him, yet her reaction was not of relief as his was. Panicked and stunned, she could only stare as Nathan returned to the top deck, a soldier struggling where he was held aloft by his neck. "Nate?" Cait gasped, wanting nothing more than to run over to him but the sight of his bright, blood-curdling red eyes froze her in place.

"There you are," Nathan replied, tightening his grip on the soldier until he heard the inevitable crack, at which point the body stopped writhing, and he allowed it to be dropped to the floor. "I've got to go, but I couldn't leave without saying goodbye. This one had a problem with that," he said, nonchalantly waving a hand at the body he had discarded onto the floor. And yet he had to be quick, as a spear was cast across the room faster than anyone but the thrower could have known, but Nathan reeled to the left, catching it with his right hand. It was then a simple thing for him to take it in both hands and smash it down onto his knee, breaking the weapon in half where he idly tossed the two pieces to the floor.

"Stand down!" Kristoph Andreas commanded the two guards behind his mother, who deemed Nathan a threat to their Section Chief.

"Nate?" Cait asked again, this time rising to her feet and steadily walking over to him, confused as to whether she wanted to slap him or hug him. "What's going on? They said—" She looked back at the Sapphire Chief, still not understanding what she had meant. "She said you'd be programmed?"

"They tried," Nathan smiled back at her, stroking a gloved hand through her brunette hair, pushing it back from where it had come loose, tucking it behind one ear. "It didn't take."

"Your eyes—"

"Are what? They do feel different," it was then that Nathan glanced over to the two in the armchairs over Cait's shoulder, once of a calm, powerful control, now frightened and uneasy, glaring at him.

"They're X-Human, they're red," Cait murmured, reaching up a hand and caressing the side of Nathan's face, taking in the sight of the new eyes staring back at her.

"It's still me, Cait," his voice was soft, warm even, yet also hoarse and rough sounding as his voice tended to be.

"Is it permanent?"

"No idea," Nathan shrugged.

"You're going to go deal with Thorne?" Cait asked, blinking, trying to not be wide-eyed and staring at him.

"His time has come," was all Nathan said in answer to that question. "I'll be back as soon as I can."

"You don't have to worry about me, I'm handling myself," Cait replied confidently.

"Good, don't give them an inch, this is our home, not theirs. If something doesn't feel right, don't do it, trust your instincts, Cait."

"I will," she said, giving him a short kiss on the lips before parting from his embrace with a small skip. "Now let's take our teamwork to the next level, you deal with Thorne, I'll ensure our future."

"Make it a good one," Nathan winked, and he turned around, and made for the lift again.

"Hey, Nate!" Cait called over to him, just before he made it there, causing him to turn around. "You've done it, you've impressed me! Now go cause some more damage!"

Nathan just smiled, remembering their first meeting and a small feeling in his gut told him that this would not be their last, so he confidently strode onto the lift, patiently allowing for it to start to lower him down so he could make for the ship's hangar. Cait, meanwhile, watched him leave with a wry smile before returning to her seat opposite the two most powerful people in the Sapphire region who had been stunned into silence. "Well, that was exciting," she chuckled, sitting down again. "So shall we move onto our next topic? Because if I'm going to be the new Chief, there're some changes I want to make. Starting with the nature of the work contracts."

"Hmm, a curious place to begin, my dear. The contracts ensure every colleague of a company is entitled to fair treatment, to food and safe water, to a place to live and a means to start a family—so what about them?" Annika asked, her tone not hiding her lack of interest in this particular conversation, especially after seeing the kind of support Cait has in her corner, the man with the bright, red eyes.

"That they do but they also tie a person to a certain fate, often a nasty one. I have a friend, a sister really, and her contract doomed her to people using her body in ways I'm sure I could never survive to experience. Now, she's strong. I reckon the strongest person I know. But she shouldn't need to be, and I don't want anyone else going through what she did."

"Just because the work contracts meant your friend had a rough go at things doesn't mean they are all together useless, or evil in any kind of way, dearie."

"Not really caring, Annika. 'Cause if it can happen to one, then it happens to all of us. We must stand together and protect one another or we're alone forever, a fractured region of folk drowning in the apathy that things will never get better. I intend to be the hand reaching through the muck to pull them out of that, but I guess I gotta ask you both, are you going to be there to help me? Do you really have the best interests of the people at heart?"

"Of course, we do, we're here aren't we?" Kristoph Andreas sighed, not feeling a great swell of need to respond to questions asked of him in the midst of his own fleet.

"We do, my love, absolutely," Annika replied with a warm smile.

"I really do hope you're being sincere," Cait said, leaning forward with a grin of her own, "because you have such lovely eyes."

Epilogue

"You surely had to be expecting this," Nathan strolled calmly around to Elias' front so that the man just waking up could see him, albeit only his boots from the height his head was at, from being suspended upside down from the ceiling.

"Help! Guards!" Elias screamed as soon as he had shaken off the last remnants of his sleep from where he had been caught unawares, rendered unconscious to wake up as he was, bound and hanging. His throat was dry and his head was pounding from the blood rushing to it. He tried to free his arms then his feet but he was too tightly restrained, he couldn't break free for all his efforts.

"Relax, Elias, it's just you and me now, everyone else on this station is dead." The porcelain tiles echoed Nathan's heavy boots with every step he took, and he took them slowly, relishing every moment of his success. There was little light to be found in Elias' office after Nathan had killed the power to the building. The only light there was to see by came from the red star just beyond the view from this side of the Arcadia space station, but it did enough from where it crept in through the glass wall on one side. Its glow radiated the room in a spectral ambient red flare that was at ease with the shadows, and the one that circled his prey among them was content that his setting was perfect.

"Winter? Winter, I—" Elias began but stopped when the other man knelt down in front of him, and now he could see his face. Two glowing red eyes, kin to the star that dared not invade this man's space any more than it did, glared right at him, and there was amusement in them. "What—"

"What was it that made me this way? Good question," Nathan chuckled, removing the knife he had stowed at left wrist, stroking the tip with his other gloved thumb, toying with his prey. With his left hand, he reached into his belt, taking out two items, a box that was flat until he intricately constructed it within his fingers, along with a vial of a thick liquid gel. "But I doubt you know anything about that."

"Please, Winter, you need me, you need me to be Chief, there's things you don't know—" Elias whimpered, pleading with sweat dripping from his brow onto the cold, tile floor. And he was unbearably uncomfortable. The suit he wore, the uniform of his office that kept pressed and ironed to perfection, the symbol of his power was forced tight to his body, it stifled his breath, held a grasp of his lungs.

"I really don't care, Elias," Nathan tapped the end of his knife that he gripped with his right, against the knuckle of his thumb on his left hand.

"But you should, you should! The Sapphireans! You can't trust them! They'll turn on you, they'll turn on everyone you hold dear, listen to me!" Elias wept, shouting at best he could, the confines of his head feeling like they might explode. "And the X-Humans, I've kept them at bay, but they'll rise up, I promise you, without me spearheading our response, they'll have their chance, they'll take back what they believe is theirs! And then-then there are things you don't know, things you haven't seen! From beyond tri-systems! Yes, even more threats from the outside that even the Chairman isn't aware of, but I know about them! We-we could work together, yes!"

"Die with some dignity, man," Nathan dismissed, utterly disinterested, studying the length of his knife, running his full, bold black pupils up and down its serrated edge.

"No, no! I can't let everything I've built be for nothing!" Elias wrestled with his bonds again but he wasn't strong enough to break free, and for all his squirming and thriving, he only mustered a quick flick of an eye from his captor.

"Look, you really are the prize, here, you're the end of this road, so I really want to savour this moment: you got any last words? And I mean, real words, meaningful ones, not these lies to save your skin," Nathan said, resting the tip of the knife in the corner of Elias' left eye, his hand careful and balanced. The sharp edge found the flesh there, bedding in just shallow enough to draw a small trickle of blood, to inspire fear rather than to cause any substantial amount of pain.

"No-no, but yes-yes! If I'm going to die, then so be it, OK, my work will outlive me but please grant me this one thing, and I promise it's in your favour, I beg you it's something you'll like as it will really ruffle them Sapphire shits!"

"Go on," Nathan lent in, the shadows retreating from his face more so that his beaming red eyes were not far from Elias' face.

"Let me make one last move in this great game of ours! I see the move they made, the move that brought you here, in this precise moment, at this time! I can see how they want matters to unfold, but what say we shake things up? Throw a wrench in their plan? Take their prize out of their reach?"

"Get to the point." Nathan brought his face in further; his red eyes were so luminescent and frightening that Elias felt a need to wince to look directly into them.

"OK, OK, but you're going to have let me down for a moment, we need to use that, the terminal over there," Elias pleaded, throwing his head behind Nathan, signalling to a console in the corner of the office.

"Very well, you have my curiosity," Nathan said and removed his knife from Elias' eye socket, even if only for the moment.

CPSIA information can be obtained
at www.ICGtesting.com
Printed in the USA
BVHW052133170323
660681BV00008B/112